P9-BYS-984

PETRICHOR

David Scott Ewers

Pelekinesis

ISBN: 978-1-938349-04-1

Library of Congress Control Number: 2012918764

"Weather" from *The Devil's Dictionary* by Ambrose Bierce (1911).

Copyright © 2013 David Scott Ewers

This work is licensed under the Creative Commons Attribution-Non-Commercial-NoDerivs 3.0 Unported License. To view a copy of this license, visit http://creativecommons.org/licenses/by-nc-nd/3.0/.

Book Design by Mark Givens

Cover Photograph by David Scott Ewers

Author Photograph by Violet Rose

Printed in the USA

First Pelekinesis Printing 2013

www.pelekinesis.com

For David Stanley Ewers

Petrichor

David Scott Ewers

1

"You guys ever been to Disneyland?"

There's no answer. Stevie's a spring, the headwaters of a wild and indivertible river of words. There are signs, however, that the river has crested. His pauses have been getting longer. "You know those little rides they got for the little kids, like Mister Toad's Wild Ride–"

"Dude, you are Mister Toad," Keith says. "You're fucking clucking like him."

Stevie ignores this, and continues:

"–how they got those black lights or whatever they are and they make like your white t-shirts glow?" He spins around and looks across the expanse of lakebed they've already crossed. The almost-full moon is starting to settle toward a long, steep bank of mountains to the west behind them.

"Disneyland," Lee grumbles.

"Look at how the lake is, the way the moon is hitting it makes it totally look, it totally looks like how it looks in– it's like the moon is a black light or some shit. See? Doesn't that look–"

"Fuck the lake. Fuck your fucking...wild ride, Stevie." Keith takes a swig from the bottle of Baileys they pooled their money for earlier that night. He laughs, sort of.

Keith's getting a little anxious. They're an hour's walk from Cartago. Up ahead is just big, dark and empty clear past the Talc City Hills; a hundred miles of nothing just to get to the Death Valley road. "I didn't know it was this far. Fucking Toad. This is all probably just some fucked up dream you had. Oh, wait. I forgot. Your lurpy ass don't sleep."

Keith and Stevie have known each other since grade school, and have spent a fair amount of time together, there being few companionship options to choose from for either of them. 'Lurpy' goes back to a time when Keith could only comfortably attack at Stevie's physical characteristics. Stevie for his part never made the counter-assault. Not directly. He didn't have to. But Keith never stopped waiting for it.

"I gotta say, just... just for the record... toads don't cluck. That's chickens. Hens." Stevie half-sings, half honks: "Clucking hens/cluck all day–"

Lately Stevie's lifestyle choices have led him to adopt a sort of 'reach into the grab bag' approach to thinking, and Keith relishes his new advantage.

"Man? You're shot out. When are you gonna shut the fuck up?"

Dena laughs.

It's past midnight.

"Toads... croak–"

"Shit. All right, croak then. That works."

"–and hens cluck. But roosters... they crow. That's trippy isn't it... seems like crows should crow, but what... what do crows do again?"

"They sit on telephone poles and watch your sorry ass, fucking wander around talking to yourself."

"Nah... that's not it..." Stevie says casually, dismissively.

"Caw?" Dena suggests.

"Caw." Like he's trying it on. "Caw... I think you're right. Caw..."

After a spell of silent trudging wherein the only sound is the low hiss of a breeze none of them can feel:

"...Crow, cluck, croak, caw..."

Silently, gradually they descend. Eventually they hit a sort of atmospheric boundary and the air around them abruptly drops in temperature. They step through it as if wading out beyond an invisible shoreline. They're in the ghost of deep water now.

"We're getting warmer. I swear."

"Bull shit we are," Lee says, rubbing his arms for emphasis.

"You ever wonder? How come if there's such a thing as warm, like between cold and hot–"

"Ahh shit. Here we go–"

"–and if you start with something cold and add heat you say you're making it warmer, like closer to quote unquote warm... but if you start with something hot and add cold to get it closer to quote unquote warm, you know? You can't say you're–"

"Hey quote unquote dingleberry! Who quote unquote fucking cares," Keith barks. Not yet finished savoring his wit, he adds: "quote unquote douchebag."

The grunts of general concurrence compel Stevie back to bargaining.

"I'm telling you, you're going to trip. All you guys. You'll see."

"Motherfucker you're already tripping. Serious, you probably just hallucinated this shit. Then I'm gonna have to fuck you up. Watch."

Stevie isn't listening. He's watching his feet as they crunch over the salty crust of the dry lakebed. They are making their way around a small promontory and into a large bay. Because of the way the peninsula curls around its mouth, the bay can't be seen from the 395, or from Cartago for that matter. Likewise, the lights from the road and town are completely hidden from their view. They're alone.

"Okay, turn on the flashlight now."

Dena hands the flashlight to Stevie, who starts sweeping the spot of light around chaotically. It darts around on the surface like a particle.

"Give me that fucking thing!" Keith says, getting loud. "What the fuck you doing?"

"Hold on. I'm looking for the end of it. I don't want us to step on it."

Dena, sensing that the scene could use a note of hysteria:

"Step on it?! Step on what?"

"Look." Stevie brings the light down to the area around their feet. The spot shakes in place, insect-like.

"See how the ground is so smooth here? No cracks or big pieces? See how it's like paper almost? Come on this way." He stomps over to where the shore once was, taking the light with him. The others follow. Dena takes a swig from the bottle.

"What were you doing here in the first place, Stevie?" she asks.

"You don't– I don't even want to go into that. Let me just find it first." They follow the old shoreline, keeping the volcanic, sage-covered hills a few feet to their right. Stevie sweeps the light back and forth—from just in front of them out toward the middle of the bay—with a sort of fly-fishing motion. The moon falls out of sight as they walk, and the flash-lit spot grows brighter in contrast. After ten more minutes of hypnotizing and thoroughly frustrating the party with his spastic illuminating (while half-singing snippets of 'The Seeker' and just starting on 'I Still Haven't Found What I'm Looking For') Stevie finally yells:

"There it is. I see it."

Keith exhales sharply.

"Uh… you better fucking see it," he says.

"Hey I told you. You guys are the ones who didn't believe me–"

"Chssshhh!" Lee puffs. "What am I looking at, dick-weed?"

"Well? Look at it! You tell me." Stevie twists the neck of the flashlight. The spot dims and spreads.

"I don't see... no, yeah, I do see it!" Keith shouts.

"What did I tell you?" Stevie shouts back.

Soon they all start discharging in audible sparks the nervous energy they'd gathered during the trek.

"No. Fucking way..." Dena shouts.

"Way! Fucking A, right?"

"Who the...? What the?" Dena stammers; speechless-on-purpose. "Man-o Jeez-o..."

"Did you do this?" Lee shouts as he walks into the dry bay toward the oval of light, "on one of your speed binges?"

"Not even! I told you– Dude, you're fucking stepping all over it! Look at your footprints!"

"So what? I don't give a shit." Lee keeps walking. But no one joins him, and Stevie takes the light away, so he gradually works his way back to the edge.

"All right, then. Well let's, fucking... see how far this goes. It's huge, huh? It looks like."

"I bet it goes all the way to the end," Stevie points the flashlight straight ahead of them, then attempts to focus on the spot in space where the beam gets digested by the darkness.

"I'll take that bottle now, Dena." Lee says. "All right

then!" he repeats, taking a hearty swig, "who's got the weed?"

"My guy's out."

Keith spits.

"Fuck your guy. He ain't ever out of crystal though, huh Stevie." Keith allows a few seconds to pass, then slowly sighs, playing up the reluctant hero routine. "All right. You fucking leeches. I got something. Good a time as any I guess." Keith unzips his jacket pocket and takes out a heavy-duty brass and steel pipe. "Flash that light over here, Mister fucking Toad." Keith's the man now. He unscrews the pipe, bisecting its abdomen, tears at something he finds inside, shoves that into the bowl, reassembles the pipe and hands it to Lee. "I've had this bud in my chamber for like, a month. It's gotta be sick by now. But we're walking and smoking, cause I got shit I got to do tomorrow. Shit. Today, I mean."

"Me too." Stevie adds.

"Shit... What are you worried about? Your ass don't sleep, remember?"

Lee takes a hit and, without exhaling, says: "What do you got to do tomorrow, Keith? Watch the Price is Right?"

"Bitch, shut the fuck up! I got your Price is Right right here." Keith grabs his crotch. "I'm talking about making some ducats."

"Yeah right."

"Yeah right." Keith studies Lee for a second. Stevie came

through after all; time to lay off him and back into his usual foil.

"Maybe I'm thinking about getting with Esther–"

"All right Keith. Now you're just being stupid."

"–she's got this fucking freeloader, living in her garage–"

"Shit."

"–that she's got to support. Buy him cereal, and fucking pop tarts–"

"Damn dude why do you got to get all personal. Shit's twisted–"

"Oh right! Woops. That's you, huh!"

"Man that's cold blooded. Even you saying that is–"

"What? I'm just saying your mom's fucking got it going on."

"Whatever, Dude."

Lee lives in his mother's garage and, to Lee at least, there has always been a mystery surrounding how her (and, by extension, his) bills get paid. There's the long sequence of 'relationships' she's had; the interchangeable succession of truckers; the 'visits' of a few days, every few weeks or so, for a few months or so. Thought-wise, Lee keeps his mom's situation in a perpetually unformed state. It's an approach he takes with most things. Two years older than the others, Lee boasts a premature potbelly that he leads with when he gets riled up, like a sea elephant. When they're together (which is most of the time), he generally prefers to let Keith do the thinking.

Stevie winces as he takes a hit. Crude shit talking makes him uncomfortable, especially with a girl around. Even Dena. He passes her the pipe and watches her say, pipe in mouth: "You guys are retards. You know that, right?" cough, then choke "–oh my god this shit is strong, huh…"

Stevie has settled the light; as they walk it floats along next to them like a spectral tour guide. As they talk, they stare; as line after line of print tumble from the diffused, parabolic frontier of the light field to clarify themselves— briefly, at just perpendicular, into a neat, regular script— before peeling away and dissolving again behind them.

Stevie shoots for changing the subject. "I know man; you got to clean your pipe. There's like a tar pit in there–"

"Dude. Let me clean it for you," Lee says.

"Why? For the resin? You probably would, too. Fucking sponge."

"What?" In the tone of someone defending a deeply held conviction, "Fuck yeah I would. I love resin. You know that."

"You, motherfucker– " Keith, exasperated, starts to say, before dismissing the subject, and Lee.

"Hey Stevie how'd you get that fucking gig washing cop cars or whatever the fuck you do over there? They got you mowing their lawn and shit?"

"I don't know, it kind of fell in my lap–"

"Shit. Fell in your lap… you mean you fucking fell in Sergeant fucking Slaughter's lap. Is that what I got to do, Stevie? Service Officer Dale's fucking unit?"

"You're such a fag, Keith. I swear to God," Dena says.

"Maybe. Shit, I fucked you didn't I?"

"Damn, dude." Lee says quietly, gazing at Dena and hoping Keith doesn't notice.

After an ugly little pause, Dena mumbles, "That what you call it?"

There's another, longer silence as the pot takes hold. The black-on-black silhouette of the ridge line more and more noticeably closes in, nudging them with something like a gentle gravity in a radial arc toward what now feels to all of them like the top; or the beginning. But the words are upside down, and the end is their destination.

The bay has narrowed into a broad box canyon. The lines of print have gotten shorter, the letters smaller. After a few more minutes the words stop coming. They've reached the end. They stand still there, rapt in the visual silence. The backstop of black hills looms directly in front of them. They're standing at what would be—if the bay were a giant printed page—its lower-right-hand corner. Stevie follows the last line with the flashlight. The print is only recognizable as such for a few feet before dissolving, but Stevie keeps following the line before settling the light on a dark form near what should be its middle.

"What the fuck is that?" Keith says, stressing 'that'.

"What the fuck is that?" Stevie replies, stressing 'is'.

"Is that a animal?" Dena asks.

"Maybe it's a cougar."

"Your mom—"

"Not that," Stevie pleads. "Please. Besides, looks like it's too dark to be a cougar."

They head towards the form while Stevie keeps the light on it. The last line of print drifts by on their left, too dark to read.

"I know what that is! Holy shit."

The form clarifies itself to them all, more or less simultaneously.

"What the heck, Stevie?" Dena says angrily.

"Is that a human?"

"Dude that's a fucking body," Keith says, stepping up a register. "Looks like it's burnt or some shit." Everyone looks at Stevie.

"Don't look at me. Swear to God I never seen that before right now."

"Let's bail," Keith says as he scans the huge, black piles of volcanic debris that box them in quickly, blindly, as if he's expecting an ambush at any second. He spins.

"Yeah, fuck this noise. I'm out of here." Lee chips in—

"You don't want to check it out? We're right here. We should—"

"Are you fucking crazy, Stevie?" Dena grabs the flashlight and points it at Stevie. Stevie tightens up like a worm that just got his rock pulled out from over him. He closes his eyes to slits. Dena shouts at him.

"We're out in the middle of nowhere... in the middle of the night... with a dead body–"

"How do you know–"

"–and no idea who else is out here, I might add. And how'd you find this again?"

"He hasn't said–"

"I know. He ain't said shit."

Stevie would like to tell them something; only he doesn't know what to say. He can't tell them how he just had a feeling. He would have to tell them how he spent all those hours—so many hours speeding while they slept. He'd have to admit to his thievery. Stolen time spent pacing around in that concrete bunker out where Lake Street dissolves into the trona, frantically staring through that blown-out window toward the lakebed, staring at that framed-like-a-projection-screen view that invariably conjured images of atomic test site buildings from the old military footage— of that split-second sucking pause, that freakish emptying between the brutal blur of the initial shock wave and the obliterating, transplanted-from-the-surface-of-the-sun tsunami, moving so insanely fast—of the blast... all the while scribbling his thoughts into a spiral notebook. He'd have to explain about how the parallel headlands that enclose or, maybe, embrace this bay are perfectly framed by that rectangular hole-in-the-wall, and how if you stare at it long enough (kind of like those posters he'd seen at the mall in Tehachapi that just look like a design until, right when he'd get ready to give up on it, another image would emerge) it sort of reveals the space it is harboring, and how from that space he could have sworn he heard people, and lots of them? Now, would he believe that if he heard it?

2

This is (I hope) a true story. The first draft was written over the course of several months—by me—at a desk in a corner office on the 17th floor of an outmoded skyscraper on the edge of San Francisco's financial district. It is a story pieced together from memories, recollected more or less at random, which I've used like crude blocks to rebuild the narrative. It is my sincere intention that this be a true story; and I have done everything in my power, diminished as it may be, to ensure that it is. However, as I have been watched and handsomely paid while writing the first draft—my de facto 'job description' at the Institute being merely to be physically present; to sit at my desk with no responsibilities, no directives other than to affix my signature to documents which come across my desk only occasionally... and which I do not read—it is impossible for me to know with any certainty whether this is ultimately a manifestation of defiance (as I hope) or (as I fear) compliance. Whatever the case may be; it is. Temporarily: and all the better perhaps. This is no more or less than an attempt—by me—to pull myself back into the world on things, through the world of things, before it is all lost completely.

As I say: I have done my best.

"What the hell."

"Listen Gary. That kid there, Steve...?"

"Ludich. Yeah. Say no more, Chief. First thing I thought, too. You know, apparently he's been writing all kinds of crazy stuff on the menus over at the Golden Empire. Ray say anything to you about that?"

"Noop... But I can't say I've been down there lately."

"Yeah? Why, something happen?"

"With what? Ray? Naw. No, no. I can't be drinking coffee no more is all. That's doctor's orders. She knows all about it."

"That's right. You told me that."

Chief Officer Hill chuckles wistfully.

"Yeaup. I had to tell her no more of them cinna-buns of hers neither. Think I heard her heart break when I give her that news." Chief Hill wipes his brow, dramatically. "I tell you, Gary, they say the Lord's got His reasons for old age and all. I won't doubt it but I'll tell you one thing–"

Chief Officer Hill gives another chuckle. I'm just chatting, it says. Shooting the shit, nothing to worry about. "–Lord He sure can keep a secret." Chief Hill raises an empty hand. "Dry toast this morning."

Damn. Is he making a toast or eating toast?

"You're being a little cryptic today, Chief." The chief is looking down at the note, transfixed. Officer Gary Tales squints and sucks on an eyetooth. "Well, she's not letting him in there any more is what she tells me. And... so you're thinking that logically speaking he likely was the one who did this. Am I right?"

"Oh, I don't know about that. That what you think, Gary?"

"Who else? You can't tell me he just strolled out here and what? Stumbled into this?"

"Who's to say? Would be a strange thing to do, give you that... but then he's a pretty peculiar kid, ain't he? He's not so bad. I feel sorry for him, if you want to know the truth about it."

"I don't buy it. Listen, whatever it is I still say we ought to have done a little interrogating before letting him off, you know... He's probably headed right now to go get his story straight with the rest of them... those–"

Chief Officer Hill jerks his chin up and nods into an imaginary rear-view mirror at the scarecrow-like figure he knows is a few hundred yards of lakebed behind him.

"Now come on Gary. You know well as me he ain't going nowhere. He come to us in the first place, remember? Besides, Steve Ludich is about the worst liar of any druggie I know. Hell, you seen him try to lie before. His whole dang face freezes." He chuckles again. "Don't it?"

"Yeah. Sorry Chief. I hear you, but I'm not buying it."

Chief Hill glances down—offering a hint to the younger officer—then stares off to the east. No deal. The chief sighs.

"Well why don't you explain me that there."

He points—while keeping his gaze fixed on the far end of the bay, the side with the body still on it—at the sheet of canvas that's nailed with a pair of rusty rail spikes to the ground at their feet. Upon the canvas is written, in magic marker, what is evidently a one-paragraph preface to the sea of words that surrounds them.

"That look like Stevie wrote that to you? That isn't his writing. I can see that from here."

"But Chief–"

"No; something tells me this is a whole different animal from what old Stevie's capable of." Chief Officer Hill looks back down. "Tell you what. Here's what I figure we do. He's just about done with them community service hours of his. Least he ought to be by now."

"Well," Gary pauses to straighten something out in his head, "…getting there, I guess…"

Chief Officer Hill sniffs at the air.

"What say we get that portable recorder cleaned up, and–"

"That old reel-to-reel?" Gary laughs. "Chief that's not what's considered portable these days. Don't know if you're aware–"

"It's as portable as it ever was, ain't it? And it's what we got, ain't it? Now you're ticking me off." The chief tosses a hot-potato smile at Officer Tales. Maybe he's kidding. "As I was saying, I happen to know that the kid's something of a reader. I see him he's always got some book with him. So we tell him the department'll pay—I'm talking officially pay, now—oh, let's say ten bucks an hour for him to come out here and dictate this all. I don't imagine it should come out to more than–"

"Whoa. Wait, what? Why?" Officer Tales begs. "What do we want to do that for? Putting Steve Ludich on the payroll sounds like the opposite of what we should be doing."

The chief's new half-smile suggests some mild moral irritation.

"Simmer down, Gary. Getting a little bowed up there, aren't you?" The chief pauses.

"Listen, Chief–" Gary's still defensive, but he's quieted down.

"Gary? We're going to try it this way. It'll be fine."

Chief Officer Hill runs the tanned fingers of his steering-wheel hand through his thinning but still dark hair. The son of Oklahoma dust-bowl refugees, Scots-Irish more or less and with a little Cherokee mixed in there somewhere, Chief Hill's been on the force, such as it is, for almost forty years. The old photos at the station show a well-built, handsome man with a laid-back manner and satisfied smile on his face. Someone who might enjoy giving the occasional lady speeder a warning in return for a little sweet-talk, from time to time. He still wears himself comfortably enough, all things considered. He turns his thick—but not blubbery—torso to face the town, aqueduct, and escarpment beyond it.

"Smell that? I seen they're gonna get some pretty good rain down in Bakersfield. We're gonna get some of that over here, I'll bet you." The chief pauses again; then he makes it conclusive. "Yep. On the books it is. Hell, offer twelve if you think it'll motivate him to work faster. Half a dozen of one..." He claps his hands. "Let's go. Let's get him back out here."

Officer Tales, sensing the thing slipping away from him, tries again.

"Wait one more second, Chief. Let me make sure I'm hearing you straight." With a tone of exaggerated reasonableness measured to convince the chief of the contrasting absurdity of his plan, Gary reiterates: "You want me to bring Stevie out here with that old reel-to-reel. And for him to read all of this. Stevie Ludich."

"Unless you're volunteering to do it. Anyways, I figure you'll be here to keep an eye on him. Look, Gary. I don't feel like advertising this here. Fewer people know about it the better, till we know what we got. And I'll say it again; I don't think the kid's so bad as you got in your head."

"What about the others? Shouldn't we bring them in?"

"Let's hold off on that for now. Those boys are easy enough to find if we need 'em."

"And the girl?"

"Dena Arroyo? She works over at the bottling plant, right? I'll make a call, make sure she stays put in case we need to talk to her. She's hardly a flight risk."

The chief turns to face the junior officer. Officer Tales starts rotating his head from side to side, quickly and precisely, as if to deflect something.

"If you got a better idea I'm all ears. Gary?"

Officer Tales stops shaking his head.

"This all–" the chief makes a sweeping motion with his arm, "–it could be anything. Who knows, could be one of them manifestos maybe, like what's his name, ... Kevorkian."

"You mean Kozinski. Ted Kozinski. The unibomber?"

"That's him. Kozintski. Of course logic tells us it's most likely a suicide note, something along those lines. It'd be about the damnedest suicide note I've ever laid eyes on…" Then quietly, as if he's thinking out loud: "Awful lot of work for someone fixing to chuck in the towel…" Chief Hill drifts then as if waking from a brief coma, or hypnosis, and reemerges almost cheerful, "–point is Gary, right now we don't know thing one. And we won't ever know if the rain beats us to it. Now that's a fact."

Chief Hill starts making his way back to the truck. Officer Gary Tales—as of today exactly nine months removed from his eighteen months in the Gulf—kicks up a cloud of trona dust as he turns to follow. He mumbles under his breath.

"That reminds me," Chief Hill says without turning, indicating with a jerk of his head the distant figure of Steve Ludich that oscillates, liquefies, now merges into mirage. "should find him one of them respirators to use. Won't have to worry about him snorting any of this here pixie dust, huh?" He lets out a monosyllabic guffaw. "Never know when temptation might hit. We'll just swing by Valleroy's place after talking to the kid. Be willing to bet that old frog's got a whole heap of them things lying around somewhere."

The chief leads them in a chuckle, thinking about the Valleroys. So true.

"So. Get him out here tomorrow morning to start? Hell, might as well get him out here today, if he's up to it."

The chief assumes that the conversation is over, but Officer Tales doesn't relent. At the risk of sounding insubordinate (or, even worse, like he's having a temper-tantrum), he adopts an even more protestant tone. He can't help himself.

"I don't know what to say. You really want me to spend the next who knows how long out here watching some tweaker." He snorts bitterly, incredulously. "Watching him read. You really think that's a good idea. He's a mess, Chief. He'll just be out here... well I shouldn't need to tell you. Or maybe I do. It's crazy."

"You made your point, Gary," the chief says with some genuine irritation now resident in his voice. "I heard you the first time. But we're done talking about it. This is my call to make. You know you ought to look at it this way: It'll give you a chance to do some detective work, right? Use that horn of yours to poke around some."

Chief Hill taps Officer Tales on his forehead, lightly. Officer Tales flinches. The chief continues.

"I know all them pothead snowboarders are gonna really miss your speed trap over on Ash Creek..." he says, "but

I'm sure they'll get over it. And I sure as hell can't be running around out here myself." He taps on his torso vaguely. They've reached the truck. Officer Tales puts the canvas note in the bed and weighs it down with the iron spikes.

"First things first, though. We got to do something with that mummy out there before them Rio Tinto boys get curious."

"Mummy?"

Chief Hill stops and quickly, efficiently studies the younger man's face.

"Actually, I'll tell you what. Why don't you go break the good news to Stevie there, get him back out here soon as you can."

"I thought you wanted to–"

"Don't worry about it. I'll care of that. I'll go ahead and visit Guy, pick up a couple of masks. I'll bring them out here to you."

Officer Tales sits quietly steaming for the short truck ride to his Crown Victoria. When Chief Hill pulls up next to it Officer Tales jumps out before the truck stops completely and slams the door behind him with an aggressiveness that the chief can't ignore. Chief Hill honks the horn and yells through the window:

"Tell him he gets paid at the end of the job. But let's get going on it, before it gets too hot out here." The chief smiles as if he's just heard a bad joke. "Hey Gary!" he shouts playfully, "Why don't you pick up some of them ham and cheese croissants for you guys's lunches? On me. Say hey to Raylene for me while you're at it."

Officer Tales glares through his windshield, a middle finger curled around the steering wheel.

"Hell! Get some lemonade!" the chief shouts as he drives off, pantomiming like he's swigging from one of the Golden Empire's big styrofoam cups. "Have yourselves a picnic."

3

Chief Hill rattles his B2200 to a stop at the top of Guy (rhymes with "Gee!") and Jeanne Valleroy's donut-shaped driveway. The gravel driveway—circumscribed by a ring of twisted and dying cottonwood trees whose shadows make capillary designs on a strange topping of black walnuts—crunches under the truck's tires. In the donut hole there crouches a large scrap metal-and-auto parts Tyrannosaurus Rex set in a habitat of torch-cut steel ferns. The chief gets out, bending his ankle on a walnut shell as he does, and looks around. The motel is vacant as usual. Its original hot-pink paint has faded to a dusty rose.

"Hehhhh... loo? Hehhhhlo!" He is answered only by the wind-stirred clanking of cable-and-crampon 'chimes' (which Guy had tuned to 'play' a convincing marina, or perhaps a fishing village), and the swooping, circling, omnipresent hum of electrical transmission. He walks, slowly and casually, around the back of the motel toward a sheet-metal and wood structure that Guy erected in the early eighties after convincing himself that a communal orgone accumulator would be just the ticket to get the 'peoples' (as he liked and still likes to call his theoretical clients) flooding in. At first, when zeal and self-awe were at their peaks, he even took to calling it an ark or, according to his own improbable pronunciation: arck. But that was a long time ago. Intervening years have forced Guy to temper his enthusiasm somewhat. There has been no sign of flood, human or otherwise.

"Y'all...looo? Geee? Bawn-Jrrrr?" Chief Hill looks back toward the court. Behind the only pre-Guy structure on the property (an old bungalow, pink shipboard around the front and sides, wavy-edged avocado asbestos shingles around back; a shack, really, that's appended to the bleak stucco strip of rooms that is the hotel) and beneath a lip-stick-red on lipstick-pink sign that reads, in a misshapen approximation of—as Guy specified to the consumptive drifter that painted the sign—"fancy writing": *Discretion is the "better" part of "Valleroys'"*—sit three four-wheeled all terrain vehicles. They are all painted using the classic amoeba-form camouflage design, but with each possessing its own eye-baffling color scheme. There's the relatively understated blue/green-on-green/blue Honda, the frustrat-ingly incomprehensible black-on-white-on-black-on-white Polaris, and Guy's 'everyday' ride, a fluorescent, amphib-ious orange-on-pink-on-yellow fiberglass tub outfitted with homemade shell-form roll-bars and powered by an antique Indian two-stroke that renders it no less confusing to the ear than it is to the rest of the senses. These account for the sum total of the Valleroys' motorized transportation options.

"Well where is that old frog?" Chief Hill murmurs, the words barely escaping the back of his throat.

"Coa coa!"

"Sakes alive," involuntarily; then, more on purpose, "–

where in the–"

"No. Here. Ribbit. Ribbit?"

Chief Hill traces the thin, watery sound to a flared plastic horn that's peeking out from a clump of creosote. The volcanic soil has blackened all ground-facing surfaces of the area's plant life, giving the landscape a cauliflower-roasted-on-a-cookie-sheet aspect. The long pipe that's attached to the horn is black as well, and is well camouflaged by the crispy scrub. Chief Hill follows the pipe for a few yards to where it dips into a sort of sinkhole. He peers down to find Guy smiling up at him from within the depression, his grey jumpsuit mottled with oil and sweat stains both old and new. Ribbons of sweaty comb-over are pasted across Guy's hot pink pate. Chief Hill thoughtfully puts himself between Guy and the sun.

"About gave me a heart attack," he says.

"Sheriff Heel." Guy greets the chief's silhouette; the angle—not to mention Chief Hill's body-type—recalling for him a still from an Orson Welles movie. Still speaking into his end of the tube: "Looking good."

Chief Hill smiles and cheerily salutes.

"You know it. Pretty as a seed bag full of rear ends. How goes, Valleroy? Good to see you got yourself a... ummuh... well... what do you got there?" The chief makes a stirring motion with his hand; encircling all the coils and corded lengths of copper pipe, piles of couplers and nested stacks of two and five-gallon buckets both sealed and open (is that full of metal shavings? are those... crystals?) that litter the large crater-like pit. In the center Guy squats like a gnomish toiler, torch in hand.

"I don't know should I tell you. Maybe I just invite a... hard time."

"Hohh hohh," the chief growls with some lecherous-French inflection. "You do know how to pique my curiosity there, Guy. Sure as eggs is eggs." Guy mentally rolls his eyes at the seed bag full of hayseed routine as the chief continues: "I was just making conversation; hell you could've told me anydamnthing. But now," squatting down himself, "I'd say I'm almost interested."

Guy, in reality not at all unpleased by the chief's attention, snaps into an eager homily of elucidation.

"Okay," he says, gathering in his callous-thickened fingers the ends of a half-dozen lengths of pipe "I join some pipes together in this way..." Guy looks around, grabs a disk from a pile then holds it up for the chief to see the hexagonal pattern of holes he'd cut out of it, "with these template here. I will make three, I think. It should improve maybe the probability from only one."

"Probability of what exactly?" Chief Hill asks.

Guy goes on, maybe or maybe not shifting his explanation toward answering the question: "I will set them in this buckets. I use a mixture of this" (pointing to the bucket of metal shavings) "and some this" (kicking a drum labeled 'resin'.)

Chief Hill massages his forehead in exaggerated confusion.

"And…"

"Oh! Oh yes. First. Most important–" Guy grabs a handful of quartz crystals, each one shaped like a double-ended obelisk, "for the end of each and every pipe it gets one of these, in…" he grabs a cap "…one" fitting the crystal into the cap "of" gesturing how it fits into the pipe "this".

"Lemme guess. This here's another one of your—what do you call 'em?—New-Agey devices. Let's see; you point it at the highway and zap whatever fry oil smelling hippy mobile like that bus I seen out here last week? Make 'em all of a sudden need a room, or itch for some of them vibrations you got stored in that magic silo of yours? Some kind of… flake magnet?"

"Snow flake magnet, maybe. Raindrop magnet, maybe. Cloud magnet… One bundle, by itself it's called a cloud-buster. One of my favorite doctor's under…underunderstood? One of his marvelous inventions. Same as like the accumulator. Only–" Guy tries to make a tee-pee, or three-legged stool shape with his fingers, but finds to his bemusement that he can't. He shakes the hand, as if erasing the attempt from time/space, "–I make three and focus them, maybe, to a point. Compound might be better design. Then maybe, voilà."

"Voilà what? A cloud? What do you want a cloud parked over your spread for?"

"You see my trees, Share-a-feel? They go downhill fast, I think, soon."

"And…"

"For the peoples. For their comfort."

"I was right. It is a flake magnet. I'll give that you're one screwy old Canuck, Guy, but you really believe…?" Guy makes a series of wet slap sounds with his tongue and the roof of his mouth.

"Tstststs! Believe, Cherief, I don't know about. Believe this, believe that, just a choice to me. That's all. It's okay. Faith, being faithful, maybe that is more important. I don't know; believe is maybe beside the point for me."

"Uh oh. You going Buddhist on me now?"

"Where…? Maybe I am faithful of what could be, and so then I know some what will be. I dream it, that I build this just how I think best; then it will be… built that way. All what could be to the best I can do. I assure that, yes? Then we see what else."

"You're scaring me now, Guy. That almost makes sense, when I don't think about it. But listen. I got a deal to make you. I got a sort of situation on my hands, and it's clear out the other side of the lake. I need a little assistance with it and, well, with the sort of thing it is Guy, you're the only person I can think of—well you just might be the best person to help out. It's pretty…far out, I should tell you right now." He smiles sheepishly. "Just up your alley, I'd imagine. And now that I know about your being so—faithful and all…"

"Crazy enough to trust, huh Sharif? Isn't that what I was just, maybe, saying?"

* * *

As they make their way out to where the body lay, Chief Officer Hill idly sweetens the deal, which initially was simply 'I won't give a good... build any damn thing you want out here', to include the possibility of a four-by-eight foot sign on the 395 heading into town from the south, advertising the compound cloudbuster and communal orgone accumulator. Guy reminds the chief that if the machine merits an advertisement then no advertisement will be necessary. The cloudbuster will supply its own signage, high over the desert and well beyond the competitive reach of any logoed crow's nest.

Guy is driving the neon Indian wide open while Chief Hill sits on a pile of tarps in a picket-fence-paneled trailer. They almost skate across the trona, the chief rolling on oversized, underinflated tires that make for a surprisingly comfortable ride. He has to yell to be heard over the engine noise and through the wind, but the sound of tires on lakebed is nothing but a gentle, sustained 'whoosh'. They arrive at the site and get to work like they've drilled in advance. Wordlessly they lay a tarp out next to the body; smoothly they pass the edge underneath. It's the tablecloth trick in reverse. Then, mindful to touch only the tarp, they slide the improbably light form to the middle, wrap it loosely, and lift it into the trailer. Guy takes it easy on the return trip, and the vehicle slides back to the Valleroy compound as if on rails. Chief Hill sits next to the body (according to Guy: "wrapped like a crêpe") and stares at it. He can't make out a human shape. It just looks like an empty tarp. He peeks once to make sure nothing's being pulverized to dust or... or some other thing that none of his previous experience, all of which having nothing to do with mummies, might help him foresee. Everything seems to be fine. The figure is the color of wet concrete in this light; its facial features eroded like desert arroyos toward an almost clownish mouth—shaped like a backgammon shaker and lined on the inside. The torso and arms are tightly bundled and striated; the ligaments and tendons are strained and taut, as if frozen in exertion.

4

"Okay." Stevie speaks into a baton-style directional microphone. "Okay." He checks the VU meter, adjusts the stiff vinyl straps and swings the apparatus onto his back. "So," holding the mike à la Bob Barker, "I'm starting now." Stevie starts reading; perpendicularly, heading into the words as he reads, and smearing them with the soles of his winos as he passes. This document is only getting read once, he notes to himself with pride. By me: Steven Avery Ludich. "As read by Steven Avery Ludich–"

"The morning of the day of my initial interview; more precisely upon my first arriving to the Paradigm 'campus'.

By the time I reached the top of the rise I was cupping my hands on my legs and shoving, while keeping my head down like a plow and my eyes rolled up, burrowing for shade, to make the last few steps. The last bit was the steepest. It was like climbing a volcano. The air was still, and the sun hung tiny and mean in the noon sky. Immediately after my impulse-response to the Craigslist ad, I was sent a map that directed me up there into the hills. According to Mapquest, the street didn't exist. But it was there. The curb was crisp and brand new; the asphalt still had some of its just-poured ooziness, and reflected a viscous obsidian gleam. The trees at my left—some massive, dusty eucalyptus and burly madrone—were motionless. They faced the road, glaring dryly, with bark peeling like sunburned skin. There were cameras tucked in the trees. I had counted eight of them without trying. A stone wall stretched out to my right. I guessed the stones to be some species of east coast blue granite, like something you might find buttressing an old Manhattan skyscraper. They were fitted together beautifully, even artistically, but only to convey heaviness and imperme-ability. The wall was bejeweled with sensors and semi-opaque, charcoal-colored plastic inlays enclosing various other elec-tronics. A light blinked through the plastic dimly; like a red giant in deep space.

A few steps beyond the crest the street curled tightly and ended at a burnished steel gate that telescoped neatly from a pocket in the wall. There was, to the left of the gate, a bank of exotic electronics, more sensors, a very sophisticated-looking lens, some sort of keyboard behind more grey smoky plastic, and an oversized steel button. On the right, inlaid into the stone, was a steel number five. The last addresses I'd seen were in the 3000's. I had begun questioning the sincerity of the request for an interview. The only address information I had been given was "the last gate you will reach will be number five. When you arrive at the gate, please press intercom for admittance." Though it was unmarked, the large steel button was the only choice available to me; so I pressed it. I was met by a strange sensation, as if the molecules of air around me had been briefly ionized. Nothing else happened for the next 30 seconds or so. Then I heard the high spinning frequencies of a small engine running at peak revolutions and coming from what felt like directly below me, then whirring to a stop on the other side of the gate. With no sound other than a faint 'click', the steel door began retracting into the wall. I could see, idling on what looked to be a platform, a sky-blue SmartCar. Brand new. Standing next to it was a man dressed head to toe to match the color of the car. His face, however, matched neither. It matched the wall, not in color so much—though it did some—as in spirit. It was the kind of face Ambrose Bierce might have described as "high-nosed, with a broad forehead and grey eyes." He was a ringer for General Sherman, only sporting a bleach-blond mustache and sky-blue linen suit. He was reaching out his hand. I stepped through the door (which had opened only wide enough to allow me to enter) and almost stumbled forward to meet him. He flashed a broad but not disarming smile in which his eye did not participate and directed my gaze to his hand. It held a pair of gloves. "I'd like to ask you to wear these while you are here. They have not been worn previously, and should fit comfortably." He watched my face as I went from 'oh, would you...' through 'he knows they'll fit?' to, as I considered the cameras: 'I don't think—'

"Nothing to be concerned about," he said, "we ask it of all our applicants." The explanation was a subtle form of coercion aimed at my curiosity. It said: "Why not?" As he spoke a fly landed on his eyelash, and he stared right through it at me. He didn't blink. I took the gloves while wondering if maybe I'd be interviewing for a job at some Heaven's Gate-type cult commune, or maybe a biological weapons facility. The gloves fit as promised, though there was clearly more to them than met the eye. The palms and fingertips were fitted with gelatinous pads. Gelatinous rings wrapped comfortably around my wrists. "If you will come with me we can get started," he smiled, opening the passenger-side door of the car. With another soft 'click' the steel door began protracting behind me. "Where?" I squeaked, trying unsuccessfully to sound willful while folding myself into the roll-cage. "It's not far. As we've a number of applicants, we have provided you with a waiting area. A 'green room', if you will." He got in himself, started the car, and launched us, in low gear, from the platform on to what amounted to an extremely steep, meticulously paved cart path. "You'll be free to relax there with your co-applicants, or to freshen up if you choose. The interview process itself should be brief, but as I've said we've a number of applicants, and it may be some time before you are directed to the interviewing room. Try to make yourself comfortable."

At that point I was hardly listening, stunned as I was by what I was seeing. We had just finished diving into a damp shaded creek valley and were wrapping our way around another small hill. Only it wasn't a hill. It was more like the conceptual extreme of a living roof, at least a hundred feet high (or tall, as it were.) It had been recently planted with chaparral, individually hydrated plots of Ceanothus and Manzanita, and live oaks that must've been dropped in by helicopter. It was dotted with precisely spaced clumps of sedge and seeded—complete with undesirables like foxtails and poison oak—to a sort of bit-mapped perfection that reminded me of a half-tone photograph. The 'hill' itself was vaguely cranial in shape, and very elegantly contoured. My suspicions of its artificiality were only fully confirmed when we reached the 'brow' of the hill. The brow was actually a wall of enormous windows sev-

eral hundred feet long that, though I couldn't tell for sure from where I was, must've overlooked the entire bay area. Each individual pane couldn't have been less than fifteen feet tall by maybe ten feet wide. The panes seemed to be suspended by a truss-work of thin cables strung from within the wall and attached to the glass by way of titanium disks. Judging by the complexity evidenced by the system of stays, every pane was individually articulable. The enormous structure gave the impression of a fantastical machine-organism, like something from a prog rock album cover. The hillside seemed to peel away from us as the road we were on sliced into it at a careful, spacecraft-entering-an-atmosphere angle. We carved our way around until the path opened onto a small courtyard. The courtyard contained two SmartCars identical to the one I was in. My driver, perhaps realizing the redundancy in pointing out such an obviously remarkable set of stimuli, kept silent. We parked next to the other cars. I opened the car door and stepped out.

We were not exactly outside. There was plant life surrounding us, and I could smell and hear that there was some sort of a stream very nearby. We were on what appeared to be another platform; as I started walking I could see that the stream wrapped around its entirety. There was a large wooden door at the other end of the platform, accessible to us by way of a small, arching footbridge. The proportions and spatial relationships within this courtyard environment suggested a refinement not usually reserved for carports; it suggested more a Japanese garden or some monastic sanctuary. There was only a moonlike sliver of blue sky above us. It was impossible to tell if we were deep within the interior of the hill or if the walls tapered as they rose above us. My driver motioned with his eyes for me to follow him to the door. The door opened as we crossed the footbridge. We entered what seemed to be a simple shed. There was a bench set along one side of the shed. Laid in front of the bench, and positioned as if already occupied by an invisible sitter, was a pair of slippers.

"You can take a seat there to remove your own shoes. Just leave them here. The slippers are for you to wear inside." The flash in his eyes seemed almost like a challenge.

"I can't wear my shoes inside?" There was something irritating about his change of tone, his assumption of my compliance, that compelled me to say something, and it was an observation of the obvious that came out. He didn't appear to notice. I stood there for a couple of seconds staring at the slippers.

"No, you cannot wear your shoes inside." I exhaled stiffly then slowly sat down to change shoes. In order to avert his gaze, I let my eyes wander around the room. The shed I was in was constructed entirely of a beautiful pinkish wood I'd never seen before. All the planks were hand-hewn; the joinery was masterfully done, without the slightest hint of metal. "Remember not to remove the gloves, Mister Edwards," my host said matter-of-factly, having established his authority. "Please follow me." I stood up and followed him through the inner door.

It takes a half hour for Stevie to read this much, and

he's barely made a dent. Having to bend over these ridiculously long, thin strings of words and pick each one from the furrow; like by hand. The recorder on his back (...just like a cotton sack, and just like you wouldn't think cotton would weigh that much...) seems to get heavier as he fills the tape, and his throat is drying to brittleness. He squints across the overexposed plain and sees a strangely articulated vehicle floating along the perimeter on a cushion of heat refraction, landspeeder-style. It stops briefly at Tales' Crown Vic, which is parked at the end of an old telephone company service road (really a raised jetty jutting far into the dry lake, planted with tar-covered telephone poles to the spot where the car is parked) and darts off, vanishing into mirage.

"Thirsty!" Stevie tries to yell across the expanse at Officer Tales, who sits inside the open door of his cruiser with his feet planted on the lakebed. Watching Stevie out there with the pack on his back, the cord wrapped around him and holding that chrome baton, Officer Tales is also being reminded of science fiction movies. No particular film, just a generic Saturday Afternoon Movies image, one that might reasonably include some bomb-shaped spacecraft, crashed or just broke down and maybe some clumsy aliens. Officer Tales shrugs his shoulders theatrically—in the Esperanto of body language even a lost astronaut can understand—saying (lying): "...can't hear you!" Of course he can hear him just fine. There's nothing else to hear out here.

"Thirs - Tee!" Stevie yells again; painfully this time, with his hand cupped over his nose and mouth. He gets the same shrug; only this time it's saying something more like "whatever you're doing is pointless. Don't bother me."

"Fucking power tripper," Stevie says into the mike before switching the teardrop-shaped knob to record, and—heading luckily in the general direction of the car—resumes:

I didn't feel uneasy, exactly. On the contrary, I was feeling rather exhilarated, enjoying the same combination of preemptive defiance and creepy feeling of smallness that I brought to my first job interviews. I had no idea what the job entailed. I had the sense that I had been prescreened to some degree and, somewhere, passed muster. Despite the fact that my driver wasn't exactly regarding me with esteem, I thought: whatever this was all about, these people obviously know what they're doing, and it doesn't seem like the kind of operation where they would go to a lot of trouble for just anyone. And it sure as hell beats staring at another stream of crappy job listings on the computer, wondering how long I would wait before getting started on the wine. So I was hopeful.

We stepped through the door and I froze. There was color and light coming from all directions; there was no dimensionality other than the space between my companion and me. We were in a sort of color field that soon clarified itself into a maze of semi-opaque, semitransparent panes, each tinted to a unique color value somewhere between blue and green. I assumed the panes to be glass, though it didn't occur to me to find out. On the contrary, touching anything was just what I was trying not to do. As we moved along, planes of color would pass in and out of one another continuously to create countless, briefly lived hues. It was like walking through what those computer models of hypercubes seem to be hinting at. After a minute or two I noticed that the colors were taking on a darker, greener quality. We were coming up to something; I felt for a second like I was drifting into the open mouth of a psychedelic whale.

"You done or what?" Officer Tales grunts with a mixture of mockery and malignant boredom. Stevie has peeled the sticky vinyl harness from his shoulders and is squatting at the other, shady side of the cruiser.

"That's some trippy shit out there. Wow. I need some water, man. My mouth feels like it's packed with toilet paper."

Officer Tales leans back slowly, growling. He stretches with exaggerated exertion while reaching over and grabbing a shrink-wrapped package of 12-ounce water bottles. He sets it in front of himself, in the sun.

"Water's over here. And watch who you're calling man."

Stevie walks around the car and disgorges two bottles from the casing. They've been sitting in the backseat long enough for the plastic to soften in the heat. The plastic imparts a subtle man-made quality to the taste of the warm water.

"Oh man!" Stevie gasps. Just so Fairytales knows who's being called 'man', he addresses the empty bottle: "I needed that." He sees two respirators sitting on the hood of the car. Must be what got dropped off, Stevie thinks. "One of those for me? I probably should be using one of those, huh."

Officer Tales gets up and stands next to the masks.

"You should. Only how do you plan to do the recording with a mask on? We need sound clarity, don't we? That's what we're paying you for." Officer Tales pauses as if something has just occurred to him then tosses a respirator at Stevie. "Go ahead. Figure it out yourself," he says. "Get busy, though. Break time's over." He goes back to his seat and picks up an empty clipboard. After looking around for something to occupy it with, he finds the Jumble puzzle, clips it in and gets back to ignoring Stevie.

Stevie puts the pack back on; then he tries on the mask.

"You don't want to know–"

"You still here?"

Stevie heads back out. The sound of his breathing lets him imagine himself first as a scuba diver (he is searching a lake bed, after all), then as back on Tatooine (only this time as Darth Vader), and finally as a data scavenger sent out after that blast he always 'sees' from the bunker; a sort of human sensor. He pulls off the mask and looks at it. Fairytales is probably right, he tells himself. I'll have to yell… Then he gets an idea. The mask has jowl-like filters on both cheeks, coincidentally manufactured in a color that perfectly matches the trona, and a rubber exhaust valve, like a pair of puckered lips, right where lips would be. Stevie tears away the valve (clammy; mollusk-y... hey, bivalve!) with his teeth, then takes the mike and twists it into the opening. It bores into the hard–yet-pliant rubber with a squeak. Perfect. No hands! He puts the mask back on, adjusts the microphone and, allowing a comfortable lead, runs the cord through the abdominal strap. He undoes the right shoulder strap, swings the machine around, and flips the toggle to Record. He stares down his metallic proboscis at the volume meter. "Mosquito. Whoa–." The needle slams against the peg then eases back into the black numbers. He tries again, this time keeping his voice floating just above a whisper. "Hello there. Hello." The needle just grazes the red zone. This might be tricky, he thinks. "Moss Quito. Mosque Eat-o." Hmm. He swings the machine back onto his back. "Okay." Carefully enunciated, "Let me find the spot, here...". He retreads over long strips of words he's already transferred to the similar strip of magnetic tape, words partially erased by his own recent footsteps.

"And away we go..."

The green whale was the green room I'd been told about. It was vast. One wall consisted entirely of enormous glass panes, exposing a view that stretched from the flatlands of the south bay, wrapped around the Golden Gate and continued up past Richmond and Marin. This must be the brow I'd seen from outside, I thought. The walls were of hammered earth dimpled with quarter-sized titanium buttons. Stretching out over everything were the largest wooden beams I'd ever seen; each one bent and twisted slightly differently from the others but all sweeping gracefully toward a sort of large oculus. The space reminded me of a grocery store, except for the ceiling, which was more like a planet-of-the-apes-style cathedral. I noticed that there wasn't a single ninety-degree angle in the place other than on the floor, which was covered in black and white stone tiles about seven feet square. Each square was a single piece of stone. It took me a minute to notice that there were other people in the room. The other applicants, I supposed. Some were talking to each other (there were a few clusters of three or four scattered around), but mostly they were wandering around by themselves and staring. I was reminded of what my driver/guide told me about being able to freshen up once we got there. I had been thirsty for a while and I wanted to splash some water under my armpits before joining the competition. I turned to ask where the sink was, but the man was gone. On the far side of the room I could see what looked to be a bar with a walkway sliced into the wall behind it. Must be the way to the bathroom, I thought, before tingling involuntarily with the heavy, manic idea that I might be able to get something like booze from the bar. A small group of people was gathered in front of it promisingly. One drink would actually help with the interview, I decided. Just a little one. It was after noon, after all.

There were several people in suits, some clearly less comfortable in them than others. There were a few manual laborer types in button-down shirts—unbuttoned at the neck to show a crescent of t-shirt—tucked into jeans (or, in one case, paint-

er's pants). There was a guy with long greasy hair, mint-green gabardine suit and dress socks he seemed intent on keeping an eye on; there was a woman with long salt-and-pepper hair and facial muscles trained to scowl who I bet myself had a pair of steel-toed boots waiting for her outside. There was a young woman who reminded me of a stripper on a visit with her grandmother. Her cashmere sweater buttoned only at the top, her Olivia Newton John-in-Grease dress struck me as costume. She was holding her sweater sleeves with her thumbs. She looked at me through her copper bangs with a combination of boredom and mild contempt. Her eyes looked tired. The sinewy old man sitting next to her had his short sleeves rolled up to above his biceps. His hair was dark for a man his age (I guessed around sixty-five), and was pomaded into heavy parallel furrows. They made a funny pair, sitting together. They weren't talking. She stared while he pretended to work on his gloved cuticles with his gloved thumbnail like some old badass waiting for his parole officer. A balding man in a grey suit was talking to a young Chicano in starched Dickies and blue-and-grey Pendleton shirt. Both gave me that chin-thrust 'what's up' nod as I passed. I 'what's up'-nodded back at them, wondering what the hell kind of job this could possibly be as, at least in my own experience, people applying for a particular job weren't generally cut from such dissimilar cloth.

I noticed something about the windows. As I passed any particular pane, it would warp the light in a way that would magnify the view it contained; like a moving fish-eye lens, only with much subtler distortion. The rest of the view, seen through the other panes, remained static. As if I wasn't moving. I got the uncomfortable sensation that there was some kind of optical illusion being employed, that what I was seeing behind the glass wasn't what was really behind the glass, but was somehow reflected or transmitted onto it... a hard thing to describe. I'd never seen anything like it. I thought about the 580 freeway below us; I'd driven that hundreds of times going commuting to sub jobs near San Jose, and plenty of times I looked up at the hills, but I'd never seen anything like what this room must look like from down there. The sunlight coming in through the windows was natural, authentic sunlight that seemed to emanate from the direction suggested by the view. Was that even possible? Of course, why would anyone go through all the trouble and expense just to distort a view? I detoured to the windows wearing what I intended to be a perplexed look on my face, one that would advertise to anyone who might notice that I was someone who paid attention to things and acted to get to the bottom of them. A self-conscious pantomime, just in case someone was taking cues, or notes. Or filming me, which I felt reasonable in suspecting was actually happening.

A man wearing a white Sikh turban stood in front of one of the panes looking out at an impossibly detailed downtown Oakland. Through adjoining panes the whole East Bay was laid out in front of him like a model or, better yet, like one of those anatomical diagrams illustrating and making simple the complex, interweaving systems and organs that keep a body viable. A tartan pattern of houses, small businesses, and churches fanned out toward the glaring downtown; beyond that the container docks thrust out into the bay and the new eastern span of the Bay Bridge swept toward Treasure Island as elegant as a logo. Far off in the distance—past a washed-out San Francisco skyline and floating above the haze—I could just make out Sutro Tower. It hovered and shimmered, over-sized and cheap looking, like some monster-movie Burning Man. The Berkeley Long Pier was a ruled pencil line drawn onto the bay, breaking up then and vanishing like the vapor trail of something headed toward land. I sidled up next to the man and he turned to give me the same expression I felt was on my face. His eyes were intelligent if a little rheumy. I cocked my head toward the glass and furrowed my brow. He kind of wiggled his head and held out his hand in exaggerated disbe-lief, then looked down at his own palm as if he were holding a shrunken head there. "You ever see anything like this before?" I asked him. He looked at me, then smiled a half-friendly 'stupid question, stranger' smile and vibrated his head at a longer frequency.

"I'm Dave," I said, holding out my hand. "Wow. Everyone here is here for the job listing?" He gave me just the same smile again and a quick nod of his eyebrows, then shook my hand. Smug fucker, aren't you? I thought. "You know what it is?" Same look. "Wonder if it'll involve talking..." I said with a smile.

"What? The job listing?" He squinted, pulled his lips over his teeth and turned away.

"Okay, Buddy," I said under my breath. I'm not here to make new friends anyway, I thought to myself.

I turned and made a beeline to the bar; with purpose, trying to project a lack of concern regarding my company. The bar itself was bean shaped and, as I could see by its construction and placement, not a permanent fixture of the room. Standing in the recess-part of the bean shape, with the bar wrapped around and the room spread in front of him (basically the spot from where a bartender might operate), stood a large man in his fifties laughing toward a couple of people about half his age. His coloring was like that of a medium-rare steak; his high, damp forehead and his neck tucked into his too-tight collar were both grayish green, while his face was flushed as a blister. As I walked up he seemed to be explaining to his audience the "not so bad" -ness of being a sales associate for a plastic injection-molding machine manufacturer.

"No offense, man. Sales. Especially that kind. I'm sorry, it just sounds…I don't know. Sad, I guess," said a young man with swinging hammocks of flesh for earlobes; the result of having trained them around ever-increasing sized bars and disks for a committed period of time. I wondered why he thought it better to leave his disks home today. "I couldn't do it." I peered over them to an array of plastic cups that seemed to be holding a good swallow or two of white wine apiece. I looked at the salesman as if to say "this is such an unusual situation that I think I'll do something unusual for me and drink just after noon at a job interview," reached around the guy with the earlobes and grabbed a cup.

"Huh! What's this, a party?" I said incredulously. The older man looked at me like I was something he didn't want to recognize, and said

"Yeah. How's about that?" Then he turned back at the younger guy, whose attention seems to have wandered from the man. "You couldn't, huh? Know something? Looking at you? Your whole getup there? Your whole... trip?" The young man half giggled and glanced down at himself. "With the tribal shit and the belts and hardware? Know what I see? I see salesmen. And lots of them. Now," he leaned toward the other guy, "is that sad?"

"Dude? That just shows... I know the guy that makes—"

"Sure you do. Hey, listen: more power to you. I don't make judgment calls. Like I said, that's what I do is sell. I'm just saying, my eye, looking at you, sees salesmen on the other end of your...deal. Look. There's a whole room full of people here. Why do you think you're talking to me? Huh? Think about it."

I finished my drink in a long sip and spied the bathroom just behind us. I put my cup down and in the same motion grabbed another and walked away, making sure not to look back.

While my urine stream strafed the shaved ice lining the bottom of the artfully oxidized pisser, I downed the other cup of wine. I gargled some sink water and stared at myself as I spit it out. My eyes looked dull. I tried to squeeze some intensity into them using my facial muscles, but that only made them beady-looking and brought my attention to the puffiness in my face. I had grown a beard a few months back but decided to shave it just the day before. I knew it was a bad idea to shave it; I knew that days ago when I first started entertaining the idea. Don't you dare decide to shave just before you go on that interview, I told myself. Your skin will look like hell. But I knew I would do it. That crazy feud between my self-perceptions! They were almost like fully formed personalities sometimes, like parts leeching the wholeness from the whole. The 'whole' that's always left to clean up the mess the parts leave behind. Like a beaten civilian population in a war-ravaged country, left only their lingering animosities and grudges. I could feel like that sometimes; like a people. One of those skills that just doesn't come in handy in the day-to-day. No shortage of those!

I walked out of the bathroom patting my raw chin, and looked back toward the bar. It was empty, but the formation of cups was still there. I could feel the wine just starting to massage my circulatory system. That friendly feeling got me to think that maybe I'd just go ahead and have a good time with this whatever it was, and not worry necessarily about getting the job so much. It was a short-lived consideration, however; as I'd made only one step toward the bar before hearing a terse "Mister Edwards." I looked toward the middle of the room, where everyone seemed to be massed in a bunch. Most of them were looking at me. My driver was back. He stood between the group and me, holding an octavo-sized computer notebook. He motioned me to join them by using all four fingers of his hand, which, alongside his martial glare, made him look like he was scratching the jowls of an invisible Doberman. I pivoted a little too boisterously and walked over.

"While you were freshening up," he said, staring me right in the eyes, "we've gone ahead and begun the applicant processing process. I'd like to thank you all right now for responding," turning to include everyone, then back to me. Are you going to thank us or not? "I was explaining that the way we'd like to begin is by having everyone arranged to occupy a single square." He traced the outline of his own black stone square with his toe. "Now we have..." pretending to study his computer "...35 respondents. I've asked that potential applicants arrange into four rows of eight. Mister Edwards. Since you were not available to participate, for the time being you will take a seat," pointing with his whole hand toward a hardwood bench being occupied by a woman in her seventies, maybe not yet frail but getting there. She looked up at me and showed off a smile full of bright, white teeth. When she abruptly stopped smiling she looked like someone waiting in a doctor's office. "Many of you will find our screening process unusual, but it does work for us. You can go ahead and sit down now, Mister Edwards. Today we will focus on the interview portion of our screening, which as you will see, won't take long. Those of you who pass the initial screening will be asked to perform some additional... exercises. Some of you may be familiar with team-building exercises, such as you might find at a retreat—"

"Absolutely," declared a woman with silvery, wire-brush hair and gunmetal blue skirt-suit.

"—and some of you may not. For those who have participated in this type of activity, you may recognize certain elements, though you will find our exercise a little... different, in other respects. For those of you who are not familiar with such exercises, you should not be at any disadvantage, as you will see."

"Many times." said the woman.

He went on: "So what we'd like you all to do is simply mark your position in relation to your fellow respondents. We may be asking that you resume those positions at a later time. Not all of you may choose to participate. As you've seen, we've already had one respondent prefer to not continue..." How long was I in that bathroom? "So—" pointing whole-handed at the old woman and me, "you may well get a chance to participate. Good. When you've committed your position to memory, feel free to make your way through the door at the far end of the room, where we will proceed with the interviews."

A portion of the wall behind him became a set of doors that slowly swung open to reveal another room, with a broad, low ceiling and painted a dark purplish blue. We all kept still for a second, then a couple of people peeled off toward the open doors to be followed by the meat of the group, which shuffled off in a mass. People looked around and made some funny faces, but no one was talking. I helped my seatmate to her feet and we held up the rear. We exchanged names, hers being either Beatrice or Patrice-with-an-accent. Only when we reached the doors could we fully see the interior. The table was the first thing I noticed, as it circumscribed the entire square footage of the room, which I could now see was round. There was an open space in the middle of the table/room about the size and shape of a large conference table, and an open path leading from the swinging doors into the center area. So the table was shaped like a large horseshoe about twenty feet in diameter. To my astonishment, it appeared to be carved from a single piece of wood. We all crammed into the circular area and looked around. As he stood in the doorway and effortlessly secured two hanging leafs, making the 'C' into an 'O', our director told us to please take any available seat (there were low-backed chairs facing outward from the table's inner edge) and open the laptop in front of us. I hadn't even noticed the computers before then, but there they were, one apiece. "Aw, Christ." Beatrice it is, then. "What is this shit?" She did not sound vulgar. In fact, she enunciated 'shit' like a blueblood, with the 't' sound doing a brief pirouette on the tip of her tongue. Maybe she had never been bothered to use a computer before. I looked at her hands. They looked old, mostly. It was hard to tell what they'd done. So as not to leave her stranded, I mumbled: "no kidding." A few people looked at her and, due to our proximity and shared 'bench' status, me. I suddenly felt like I'd just walked into a class I'd been caught ditching. A tall woman looked down her long nose like it was the barrel of a gun. A fat man with a spare eyebrow mustache said:

"'What is this shit' is right." He put his hands into a fleshy fold above his hips, shook his head and let out a sound like a puff of steam. I still had no way of knowing whether I was alone in the dark about just exactly what it was we were applying for, or if everyone was in the dark with me. Could so many people be that clueless about something so ridiculous to be clueless about? I turned around. The doors were closed, and our maitre d' had vanished again. I turned back. There were a few people who hadn't moved but were still rather uncomfortably taking in the scene, like me. But the rest were settling into their chairs, and that included my bench mate. She had taken the seat nearest us and was staring at the screen as if she were driving in a blizzard.

I found a seat, adjusted myself, and stared at the monitor. The monitor lit up immediately, and a prompt appeared asking me to type my name into a box in the middle of the screen. I did. Suddenly a face appeared on the screen. I thought, where do I know that face from? Then I recognized it. It was same guy again; the one who'd driven me 'up' there. But there was something a little odd about him; something that I couldn't put my finger on.

"Mister Edwards," he said, "Thank you for responding to our request for an interview. The interview process will be as follows: We have compiled, with the aid of information supplied by you on your online interview request form, a short education and employment history, as well as some additional information, gathered via public records and internet-based social-networking sites, which may prove helpful during the interview. These documents will appear in the lower left portion of your screen. Please click on the document you wish to examine. After you have looked a document over, please verify its accuracy by clicking on the 'I Accept' button at the bottom of the screen. If there are any perceived inaccuracies, please click on the 'I Do Not Accept' button. Please examine all documents. The interview itself will essentially be face to face. I will ask you questions and you will answer them. My questions and your answers will also appear in the lower left portion of your screen, in written form. You will also be asked to verify the accuracy of the written account by clicking on the 'I Accept' button at the bottom of the screen. If there are any perceived inaccuracies, please click on the 'I Do Not Accept' button. We will move to the next question and revisit, at the

end of the process, any questions which require further attention. At the end of the interview, you will be permitted to ask
any questions you may have." A set of miniature documents
appeared on the screen. The face continued, "When you have
finished examining and verifying your information, we will
begin. And please look directly at the screen when you speak.
You will note the absence of a keypad; the gloves you have been
provided render the use of a keypad impractical. At any rate, a
keypad will not be necessary. Now please take the time to thoroughly examine your information portfolio."

I looked around the room. There were other people also
looking around, some just sneaking glances and others stunned
into wandering stares. I could see every one of the monitors
as they radiated out from the theoretical center of the table.
The face on my monitor became still, though I could see the
head rise and fall slightly in rhythm with a relaxed breathing,
like something floating in a tide pool. The eyes were fixed
on something off screen and the head was bowed to an angle
of repose. I had noticed something strange in the murmur of
voices I heard as I was getting my spiel, it dawned on me
now that I had been hearing a murmur of not voices, but
voice. The same face appeared on every screen in the room but
for a couple which were already displaying their users' histo-
ries. Some were still finishing their introductions. Others were
in the same relaxed state as my own. My stomach tightened.
These people, this whatever-it-was, expected us all to complete
the same canned interview for a job that was still being kept a
mystery. It was a mystery to me, anyway. The only hint I had
was from the initial request. That read something like 'job

training/placement high level cultural/entertainment'. Maybe interviews such as this were not uncommon for 'high level' positions. Maybe I'd just never been in the position to know. The wine had dried out my mouth; leaving a bitter, tannic film. I noticed that there was no water in the room. Suddenly I needed water. But I would have to forget about the water. I had decided while walking to the room that if the interview didn't pan out I would at least have something interesting for the blog I'd been tempted to start writing. People would be interested in this, I thought. Tales of bizarre job-searches or something like that. With that determination, I clicked on the first page of my 'portfolio'. Suddenly the lights came on in the room. It startled me, as it happened at precisely the time I engaged my monitor. At first I felt I'd turned on the lights myself somehow, and set off some insincerity alarm. I actually gasped, something I didn't catch myself doing all that often.

But it turned out not to be me. A chair clattered across the room spinning like a soft-boiled egg. A tall man wearing a bowling league shirt and wallabees, with his pants and shirt a little short and his grey hair coming undone, looking longer than it was probably supposed to, stood over his monitor. He looked like a streetlight with his arched back and hands curled into cups. He looked cornered. He backed up a step toward the center of the circle. "I want to know where you got that—" His computer cut in politely: "Mister Crawford, any question may be asked—" " Well I'm asking now!" He seemed to consider something for a second. "God! Fucking! Damn it! Who the hell you people think you are, having me come all the way... I didn't sign up for this!" "Mister Crawford, you will be free—"

"I'm free now! God damn it!" His hands started tugging at each other. *"I'm free to take these... goddamn..."* tugging, *"... gloves and shove—"* Then all the monitors spoke in unison, each set of eyes following him as he spun around in a pan of astonishment. *"You may want to listen to this before you do anything irreversible, Mister Crawford."* 35 raised voices, all blankly authoritarian in tone, began softening as if they were gently sidling toward us. *"Your disquietude is quite justifiable. Your file does include a certain amount of personal information, some of which, we are aware, has the effect, upon being seen in writing and presented as fact, of creating unease and suspicion, perhaps even fear and anger. Let me say to you that the purpose of including such information, which, allow me to add, is more easily obtained than many of you may realize, is to create, admittedly by means of engendering some initial apprehension, an atmosphere of trust and transparency. You will see what we know, and you may in turn rest assured that such information as we possess is in no way considered by us to be to the detriment of your chances for ultimate success within our organization. I'll say now, to everyone present, that many if not all of you are going to find similarly embarrassing material as you review your documents."* Really? Oh, what the hell... *"I will also say that each and every one of you do indeed have the chance, if you submit to our training exercises and perform them with commitment and determination, to attain, with the direct assistance of our organization, positions both personally and economically... rewarding."* He was practically purring in our ears, now, *"Now if, Mister Crawford, we cannot stop you from removing your gloves, you*

should still understand that without your gloves, you will be unable to operate your controller. In order for this process to be most effective, and to relieve us of the burden of any unnecessary...authority..." And here his voice ratcheted back up, "all respondent files will be made available to all networked machines," and back down, "in order to avoid the development of any artificial advantages... or... disadvantages..."

"Jesus Christ. I'm sitting down. All right? But let me say— I'll say it to all of you—I got a feeling we're getting shook down here. Me, I got a pension coming, so far as I'm concerned you can keep this shit. I don't need it. I spent many, many years as a union rep. So... So uh..." The lights went back off as he sat. The room felt smaller, almost claustrophobic. My monitor resumed displaying the screen I had just brought up. So, one suspicion: the interview was not going to be canned like I thought. At this point the canned interview idea didn't sound so bad. The 'nothing to lose' perspective I had enjoyed was starting to fade ominously as I began digging into my portfolio.

The first file consisted of what I'd provided myself: my history in reverse order. A couple of years of scattered substitute teaching gigs, followed by the carpentry I'd done sporadically while moseying my way to a teaching credential, followed by the 'comparative research' job I'd talked a manic/depressive boss—while he was riding a pill-induced whitecap of a mood—into creating for me at mopedtrader.com, followed by the copywriting I did for the Concrete Critters catalog. I left out my cafe job but included, at the end, the record store job I had when I was a teenager. It seemed silly, I knew, and irrel-

evant and distant too, but I'd included it in every resume I'd written since, and couldn't bring myself to let it vanish into the mists of time. I liked that job. Then my education: four years at Cal State East Bay, (English, with an emphasis on 19th century California Lit) preceded chronologically by multiple bouts with various junior colleges, and finally, concurrent with the record store job, the graduation from high school that I'd long ago decided to claim, even though I had actually taken the GED.

After that was my personal statement, a proclamation of my personification of good employeedom in search of a worthy beneficiary, written in a tone that I both cringed at and felt was perfect.

It all looked fair to me, so I hit the 'I Accept' button. My resume zoomed back into the corner of the screen, leaving center stage occupied by another document. I stared at it for a beat or two before really starting to read. I was impressed on some dark, ancient level by the words there, about me, from somewhere unknown. Then, starting to read, I wondered briefly if I was having a nightmare. I actually hoped I was. My stomach bobbed and rolled like a dead fish, producing a weak and nauseated imitation of hunger. Here was a written examination, exploration, investigation, and 'reinterpretation' of my contributions to the arena of human endeavor, presented in reverse order: that is, chronologically.

"Mister Edwards,

Certain discrepancies exist between the biographical information provided by yourself and that which we have culled—"

...Culled...? "In regards to your educational background, neither South El Monte High School nor the El Monte Union High School District possess any record of a David Dennis Edwards having graduated with the class of 198–. On the contrary, EMUHSD records show that, at the end of your 10th grade year, and after a period of marked increase in scholarly disinterest and truancy, you chose to forgo completion of your studies." *Oh, brother.* "Our own research suggests you spent this time cultivating relationships with various other truants, dropouts and delinquents while engaged in activities generally attached to aimless excursions via the Rapid Transit District bus system, the frequenting of public parks, and 'pan handling' outside of and within various establishments; most notably consumer centers." *Come on! This is impossible. Where the hell...?* "The image below is taken from security footage taken on May 1, 198– from within the Contempo store at the La Puente Mall, with a view of the central balcony and main escalators. Pictured at left, apparently attempting to sell booklets of blue chip stamps, are yourself and another young person." *Well I'll be damned. Look at that! A black and white shot of me—eyeliner and soaped hair, British army cape and monkey boots—sitting on a bench holding those blue chip stamps I stole from my grandmother. In a way it was nice to see, since I had no photos of myself from that period. Standing over me in the photo, frozen in the motion of rocking back on his heels and staring at the camera, was the serpentine figure of a young skinhead. He wore a white Fred Perry shirt tucked into a pair of Levi's that were themselves tucked into a pair of 20 eye Doc Martens that came up almost to his knees. His*

*head was freshly Bic-ed and reflected light from somewhere
out of frame, and his suspenders hung over his thighs like
chaps.* "Incidentally, the young man pictured with you, Arthur
Ramirez–" *oh yeah, Artie was that guy's name.* Crosstop, "was
found murdered at the Chino Men's Correctional Facility in
199–, where he was serving a three-and-a-half year sentence
for aggravated assault. The murder is believed to have been
committed by a member of the–" *weird. So? Why are they
going into–* "Nuestra Familia, though the perpetrator was
never found." *What, are they suggesting I was in some criminal cahoots with Crosstop? I was almost giddy with disbelief.
I had completely forgotten about this guy, this kid, but here
he is all out of proportion to*—"According to the EMUHSD,
you briefly attended Fernando R. Ledesma Continuation High
School during the autumn of 198– before dropping out of
that institution as well. Records from the California Department of Education records indicate that, on June 15, 198–,
you took and passed the California High School Proficiency
Examination and in the following autumn began your college
career by attending two semester courses at Pasadena City College." *Oh yeah, that's right. Not even the GED...* "You completed a total of 8 transferable units there before taking a six
year hiatus from higher education. After resuming your studies
at Merritt College in Oakland, you took another five years to
complete your transfer requirements, as opposed to the three
years stated by you." *Fair enough.*

"In reviewing your employment history, we noticed a gap
dating from June of 198– to May of 199–. In the process of
gathering an accounting for this period, we discovered that,

in addition to infrequent and uncompensated forays into the desktop publishing industry, you availed yourself of a number of short-lived and often menial opportunities within the service sector. The longest held of these positions was that of espresso machine operator and cashier for the Ground Under Cafe then located at 2112 Folsom St., San Francisco. It was brought to our attention that during the greater part of your employment there you were engaged in at least one scheme involving deceitfully secreting assets belonging to your employer. Though there was no disciplinary action brought at the time, as indeed it is unlikely that the ownership of Ground Under Cafe was ever made aware that such schemes were taking place, and therefore no public record of this activity is extant, we have obtained the oral statement of one Charvel 'Loaf' Jackson detailing the arrangement." Before I registered those last words the sound of a voice, deeper in timbre yet more hollow than the one I dimly remembered (while still wrought with the same bargaining cadences) emerged from the computer speaker:

"What we'd do is I'd get on his line in the morning, okay… with all the business people who'd be lining up to get their coffees and what he'd do is he'd have all these coffees already ready, all the special drinks for the people he already knew what they wanted, so he'd get a head start on them. And so he'd yell like "double macchiato" and then he'd just have to point to it and then the whoever it was would just leave his money on the counter and be gone. So what I would do is see I couldn't pay the prices for the fancy coffees back then but I did like them. But I was around, you know, and so people knew me. So he'd know, so what he would do is he'd make me something,

what I liked as matter of fact those days was those double macchiatos, and what I would do is I just drop a, say like, a, dollar or something, maybe not a dollar, whatever it was I had to spend, see, in his tip jar he had there. And he'd point at it by looking at it, and I just grab and go. Now that in itself must've come to a good hundred dollars over time, but what it really was I'd notice is now when I'd go up there and drop my change in, or my dollar or whatever it was, is he'd have that register opened up, and he maybe would ring up, like, half, half of what he took...no he'd ring up most of it, but not all of it. And all them business people they didn't bother paying attention just wanted it fast so they could be busy, already getting it done. They liked how he was doing it, it got them all charged up with efficience. Efficiency. That's all true enough from what I saw."

And that was the end of that. Stunned, I laughed to myself self-consciously and thought: who could possibly have the kind of resources necessary to waste on such low-ball old intelligence. And why– "We are aware that there are episodes in all lives which may not be fit to include in an autobiographical sketch written for the purpose of serving one's own interests; we have included this particular episode primarily to remedy the lack of information provided by you for a notable period of time. A vacuum, if you will, to be filled. As an illustration of the sincerity of our position, we have not included similarly... incriminating episodes from subsequent periods for which you did furnish us with at least some information. We would note, however, certain patterns that emerged as we researched your employment history from May 199– to the September 200–

commencement of your teaching...career. During this time, you appear to have developed a compulsion toward arriving at your workplace at such a time as to force supervisors and others in authority to make difficult judgment calls re the practical definition of the word 'late'. You also appeared to have developed a tendency evolving toward dissatisfaction with the interpersonal dynamics and organizational structures inherent in all workplace environments you chose to become a part of, opting eventually to 'quit' from almost every position you have held. Now then:

For the period dating from September 200–, to the present, you list your occupation as 'Teacher'. As this most recent period is naturally of primary interest to us, we have done thorough research in order to reach an accurate determina-tion regarding your activities in this capacity. Owing to the irregular employment practices peculiar to the occupation of substitute teacher, as well as difficulties with certain union representatives, information tended to be decentralized and often elusive. However, we did manage to amass a good deal of anecdotal analysis regarding your performance. This series of recordings begins with an evaluation taken by the principal of Green Oaks Junior High School in East Palo Alto. It took place on November 30, 200– and refers to your November 24 assignment teaching Adolph Nolting's 7th grade class."

Another sound track faded in then, right on cue with my eye reaching the end of the last sentence. The recording was of remarkably high quality; too high, I thought, to have come from one of those armored Ford-era workhorses you generally find in broke schools. The eagerness to discuss Mister Edwards *was palpable in the atonal preteen voices:*

"He was kind of a mess."

Oh yeah. That quiet kid—

"Yeah he looked like a homeless guy."

"You mean smelled like."

"You're so mean. He was nice, I—"

"And member he flew the door open—"

"We were waiting for like—"

"And it hit Calvin on his butt—"

Laughter.

"Yeah and he said 'Oh… shoot.' But, the other word."

"And he called him Man."

"Oh yeah he said 'Oh, s-h-i-t, sorry Man.'"

"He was like lost the whole time pretty much."

"Like, he made us read Flowers for Algernon—"

"Even though we said, we told him, we don't read that yet."

"We told him that's an eighth grade story—"

"And then we passed this one book around and everyone had to read like one paragraph."

"And he was just like, he wouldn't answer our questions when we were like 'what's that mean', or something."

"He just sat there, like with his thumbs pressed in his eye sockets."

"Yeah. Member when he said, 'fuck?'"

"*Travis!*"

Impressed giggling.

"*But he did.*"

I don't think he really said that, Miss Roswell."

"*I do.*"

"*I thought he was crying.*"

"*No, he wasn't.*"

"*No really, I saw his eyes were watering.*"

"*I think that was cause he was hung over April.*"

"*Duh–*"

"*That's what Justin and me were like, after. We were like 'he was like, drunk, or something.'*"

"*Yeah he smelled like …*"

Then, after a stylish cross fade, the seventh graders receded into the aural distance as the strident, DMV-clerk voice of a certain type of principal emerged.

"*Ideally, we like our subs to arrive early, okay? Maybe get a look around? Mister Edwards showed up (extra beat-you-over-the-head-with-it tone, each word a separate blow) After The Second Bell. He should've been In Class. I'd say he seemed nervous… and he was I would say not At All communicative when we met. He would Not Look Me In The Eyes. Not a once. And slow to respond to questions, you know? Now we're used to subs being a little lost. Okay? But he was downright flustrated…*"

Another cross-fade– "Now I don't know the man. He may be a fine teacher… on a good day–" a different principal-type here, the kind with a fondness for one-way conversations and phrases like 'end. of. discussion.' and 'aahhhh, no.', "–but let me say this. The day he came to My school? Mister Edwards had no business– NO business– leading a classroom–"

In what was most likely an involuntarily triggered physiological defense mechanism, my focus suddenly shifted to my surroundings. So thoroughly humiliated was I that the last of my verve was abandoning me by way of audible grunts and moans. With grim relief I noticed I wasn't the only one grunting or moaning. I could hear similar expressions of agony floating around the room, to the accompaniment of a multitude of recorded testimonials emerging and receding, bouncing off each other like bubbles in a sulfur pool. A couple more principals added their voices to my particular bubble; I just kind of let their damnings wash over me without paying much more attention to what they had to say. At some point it stopped. I didn't look back at the screen for a few minutes. Instead I went into a sort of a 'take a mental snapshot of this' exercise. I regulated my breathing. I concentrated on my pulse until I could feel my whole body dully throbbing and could see my acid-lined stomach pulsate through my shirt. Then: So what was this? What was going on, exactly? It was far and away the most nakedly Kafkaesque situation I could remember being stuck in. Part of that aspect, the 'good' part, was that nothing had actually happened yet. I had the feeling I would get sometimes on airplanes, where I would come out of yet another anxiety attack/reverie/preënactment of a violent and horrifying *midair disaster to realize that the plane I was on was actually still doing just what it was supposed to be doing, which was hurtling through the thin, frozen upper atmosphere, being kept aloft by a collective faith in math that I must certainly be breaching, with tragic consequences for everyone, with the sheer electromagnetic power of my panicked skepticism... Cold comfort, in other words, but comfort nonetheless.*

I closed my eyes. The ghost image of my monitor dimmed and was swallowed by the myriad darting multicolored particles animating my inner space. My own personal share of big-bang residue; a terrifying space in its way, but mine alone. I thought, 'what are they going to do to me, anyway?' They showed nothing here that would interest law enforcement (although I suspected they must've come across something on my countless half-pint-down forays into nocturnal Oakland...—cold flash - driving...) and I couldn't imagine them capable of doing more damage to my teaching career than I had already done (I had wondered if the substitute gigs I wasn't getting had to do with me personally, knowing, but not knowing... Now I knew). But still. Fuck them. Fuckem! My pulse raced, causing a layer of those particles to surge upward like a school of jellyfish. 'My wife already doesn't talk to me,' I said to myself. I know it's only her vestigial Catholicism keeping her from divorcing me outright, and as it is I'm wracked with guilty anxiety whenever we bounce into each other... So fuckit! Who cares!' The exercise was working. I was talking myself out of giving a shit. 'I'll just find out whatever this operation is here and...blow the whistle on it. Whatever it is!' I opened my eyes, grimly fortified. I skimmed through the rest of the document without really reading it, instead keeping focused on not focusing by muttering aloud. "Blabitty blabitty blah, blabitty blabitty blah..." I figured there must have been some sensor detecting my eye movements in order to cue those miserable sound tracks. Well, they weren't getting any more of that satisfaction! They made their point. I reached the bottom, where I was again prompted to verify the 'accuracy of the written account...'. I thought about this for a minute, and came to a helpful realization. When our host spoke of 'accuracy' he meant it terms of marksmanship. Martially, perhaps, but more likely... hunterly, which, I thought, put me in a position analogous to that of a deer being asked whether the shot lodged in its brain had entered at the spot intended. Looking at it in that light, and understanding that any denial would just serve to resume the onslaught of anecdotes that, exasperatingly devoid of fair context as they were, were, on the surface at least, true. And then there was what the guy said to Mister Cramden, or whoever...Crawford. So I hit 'Accept'. Another document popped up. In glancing at it I recognized, buried in type, the name of my next-door neighbor. I jerked the cursor to the bottom of that one and Accepted it as well. Whatever. 'Whatever.'"

5

The tape announces the completion of its reel-to-reel migration with a regularly-spaced but arrhythmical 'slapslapslap'; startling Stevie, who has worked himself into something like a meditative state. He stops the machine and looks up. In the hours he's been out here on the trona he's been watching the sunlight. More than watching, actually, as he is in the middle of it. It has mellowed from the morning's uncompromising, sustained flash toward more mature, conciliatory tones. Brown shadows have filled the lines, sharpening and clarifying the print. In his reverie, Stevie had experienced this as from a sort of accelerated, Koyaanisqatsi-type perspective; as seasons—years, even—of light working on paper; aging it. Now, as Stevie takes in the whole scene, the words appear to go on forever, embossed into the earth like an endless, illuminated manuscript. By first settling into a sort of comfortable lapping-at-the-shore, then just listening passively, as if to the words of a calm stranger, he's become spellbound by his own voice. Distinct phrase and word meanings slipped away, simplifying into a language of tones and subtones. At times the words may as well have been (or even may have been) written in the some Mongolian yakherder tongue or something. That's how it seems to him now, anyway. He also may find out later that he was there after all; and the 'voices' he has given to various and varied personages might be deemed, upon further scrutiny, to be 'spot on'. Who's to say?

Stevie is suddenly, almost violently hungry. Lately Stevie's been in the habit of dismissing nutritional sustenance as something of a secondary concern. Now—like some timid debater who's about to lose an argument with a boor, and so in desperation and frustration awkwardly over-asserts himself—hunger lunges at him. With wobbly legs Stevie makes his way back to the squad car. He finds Officer Tales splayed across the front seat, head back, snoring. Stevie spies a perspiring cube of loosely saran-wrapped carrot cake stuffed into a cup holder. Where'd that come from, he wonders. He grabs it—Fairytales be damned—and shoves the whole thing into his mouth. Officer Tales wakes to the sight of the ensuing gag, scowls, and pulls himself up.

"I tell you you could have that?" he grumbles through a yawn. Stevie just stares at him; momentarily at a loss. "So you done or what?"

"Uh-uh," Stevie says thickly, through the cake. He points to the machine. "Ran out."

"Of course you did. You know that's it for tape…" as if Stevie had screwed up, somehow. "And you're not done."

"Not even. Not even close. This is going to take like– I don't even know how long!"

"Get in the car." Stevie does as he's told, still in a reflective frame of mind. Ah. Why is it that there's something almost cozy about the inside of a cop car? Stevie wonders to himself as he settles in. Is it the competent dispatcher cadences? The big leather seats and the sounds they make? If only Fairytales would pull that blackjack out of his ass...

"Now I'm going to have to go through the whole store room myself," Officer Tales complains, still put-upon, keeping the metaphorical stick firmly in place: "I'm going to have you report direct to the chief. And then you're going to stick around after you're done. You got that? I don't want to have to go–"

"Man– I mean... Gary—Officer Tales sir—I got to eat something."

"And that's my problem?" he laughs, insincerely. "What do I look like?" Then, just to rub it in: "Work's a bitch. Get used to it."

"Yeah. Well if..." Stevie stops himself. No use trying to whistle into the bluster of a cop; especially this one. He keeps quiet while Officer Tales mumbles to the steering wheel. Eventually he whips the Crown Vic into its spot next to the wheelchair ramp.

"I'm not seeing his truck," he declares. "You go in and make sure. I'll be back. And remember what I said. Don't make me have to come looking for you."

"Aye aye." Stevie salutes, jumps out of the car, and trots up the ramp.

Officer Tales gets out himself, slowly, seat and belt leather groaning, keys jiggling. Smart-ass twerp. "Ay!" he yells after Stevie, but Stevie's played deaf just long enough to slip through the door.

Officer Tales stares for a second then turns and ambles across Whitney to the gas station food mart. While selecting his three-for-a-dollar hot dogs from the warming tray, he hears sniffing noises coming from the chips aisle, followed by Lee's heavy-tongued voice:

"You smell something?"

"Shut up dumbass."

"I smell bacon."

Tales peers over to see Keith and Lee turn toward him. Keith is sort of smiling while clutching a large bag of Lays like some cartoon burglar, while Lee, shirtless, his flip flops splayed out the sides of his feet, absently rubs his belly.

"Oaohhhh. It musta been those hahhht dogs I smelled," Lee says, in a burlesque of dawning comprehension.

"Hello, Officer," Keith chirps, "how's business?"

"Business?" Officer Tales stares a smile-melting stare. "You want to be in my business?"

"I just meant about that thing that Stevie Lud–"

"Oh, you just meant about that thing. Yeah, well how's about you don't worry about it unless we say so. How would that be?"

Keith shrugs. Lee brushes past Officer Tales, belly to belly. He clicks his tongue.

"Ossifer."

* * *

The mummy lies upon a stack of large acoustic tiles. Guy had the tiles made just after he built the COA (which now holds both tiles and corpse, centered under its dome and illuminated by a column of diffused late afternoon light—like a poor man's Lincoln-in-state). The idea at the time was to introduce orgone accumulation to the mass market by merging it with state-of-the-art drop ceiling technology. Unfortunately for Guy, by the time he got the whole thing rolling the drop ceiling craze had come and gone, at least among those who might be willing to pay a premium. He ended up having to build another shed just to house the tiles. In the twenty-five-odd years since they have sat—never molding, mildewing, discoloring or taking on odors of any kind. With Chief Officer Hill needing a place to stash the mummy while he does "some cogitating on the matter," Guy is more than happy to volunteer the COA. Guy assures the chief, who voiced some mild concern over what happens to the air in there when nobody's looking, that atmospheric conditions inside will be more than suitable.

"It is not only dry inside, Cherief, it is even drier," is how he puts it.

* * *

Stevie opens the door to what Raylene likes to call the greeting area. The glassed-in porch serves mostly as a buffer zone between the too hot or too cold or too dusty or sometimes just too shitty air outside and the constant 68 degrees of the Golden Empire Cafe. Stevie walks through quickly, opens the inner door and peeks around the restaurant. Ray, Candy and Nuncia are gathered around the corner booth. They're soldiering through a mournful rendition of 'Happy Birthday To You' that's aimed at a transparent-haired and heavily rouged old woman who sits, sunken and hemmed in, in the booth's elbow. She looks up at them from behind a candle-spiked cupcake with a blend of embarrassment and irritation on her face and makes semi-voluntary rolling 'hurry it up' gestures with her speckled, translucent hand. Ray shoots a glance in Stevie's direction then turns away slowly. So she'll let him stay, he gathers, so long as he behaves himself thoroughly. He squishes into a puffy vinyl barstool, and, inviting another glance from Ray, grabs a menu. But she's got nothing to worry about. Stevie is in no mood for scribbling. Wrong chemistry entirely, today. His stomach twists with hunger, and he's developed a nasty crick in his neck. He doesn't even read the menu. He's just holds it. He knows what he wants.

After a minute or so, Stevie sees Candy's long forearms rest on the counter. She leans toward him.

"Hey Stevie."

"Hey Candy." He nods brightly, like she's a great idea that just popped into his head. "How come you're working the bar?"

"Just for this morning." She motions toward the birthday party. "That lady goes to Nuncia's church, and it's her ninety-ninth birthday. So me and Nuncia switched."

"Interesting." Dull. Right now his mind is an Etch-a-

Sketch being vigorously shaken.

"It's better for me." Candy lowers her voice. "I've served her before lots of times. She's a nightmare." She laughs at herself. "I know. It sounds so mean." Stevie giggles. Candy leans in closer. "She complains about everything. I mean everything. I'm like: You eat here why? And–," she measures a space of about an inch with her thumb and forefinger, "–she tips in nickels. A little stack, like that."

Stevie laughs. "Wow," he says, again unable to think of anything better to say. Here we go again, he thinks, having to start from scratch, from a total blank, and go from there. Sometimes it's a ridiculously hard thing to do.

"Are you eating today?"

"God yeah. I'm so hungry. I've–"

"Hey! Want to do me a favor?" Candy's clear, turquoise eyes (working on Stevie—to Stevie—like a gravitational tag team of Uranus and Neptune drawing the scattered space-debris of his gaze all the way down deep into their twin atmospheres...) fix on his.

"Probably."

"It's not a big one. It's just– I just talked Raylene into putting veggie burgers on the menu, and so far nobody—nobody local, I should say—has ordered a single one, besides me. So..."

"So..." Cheeseburger dream starting to fade—"Will I, I mean, do you think they're good?"

Candy raises the pitch, but not the volume, of her voice.

"Actually I do." She smiles and bounces her pencil, eraser-side down, on the counter.

"What the fork," he says, "gotta try anything once." What the fork? What the dork, more like. Gotta try anything once? Jesus...

"Oh, goody. Curly fries or regular?" She whispers, "Get the regular."

"I'll take regular. And a Coke. Please."

Candy drops into her work voice; mental muscle memory.

"Let me grab that for you."

Stevie tries not to stare as she spins away, all neat in her white button-down blouse and navy-blue gabardine skirt. He watches her reach to lift a beet-red plastic glass from a tall stack of identical beet-red plastic glasses, one panty-hosed heel slipping out of one sensible shoe as she stretches. How much longer till she leaves all this behind? Months, probably. Enough time? No. Enough for what, anyway? Weeks, maybe. Maybe a dozen more chances. Chances for what? And what good has time done? None, that's what.

It's been over seven months now since they took that long walk together, swung on the swings, then sat on the bench till the end of the night, talking.

Stevie has replayed his memory of that night countless times; so many that it has achieved a sort of constellation status within his own interior cosmology, like some heroic event distilled and enhanced by oral history. Something majestic and embarrassing, like: 'A trust grew between them, and together they (focused, determined) dove head-long into the dark, and together they threw light at it, and some of that light undeniably stuck, and he was who he hoped he was, and she was who she was, and nothing was off limits, and nothing was left out, and they aimed straight for that other, more elusive thing, and for a second they had it…'

Not surprisingly, the conclusions they reached were pessimistic, and their assessment of the human condition even more so, but it was joyful really, and he'd never felt more hopeful in his life. They didn't make out or anything, but by the end of the night they'd intertwined their calves and were facing each other well within whispering distance. Up close she smelled like night-blooming jasmine.

He saw her next the following Monday. She was walking by herself to school. Stevie thinks about this from time to time in the same way he might suck on a cavity, just to make sure it still hurts. In some grand mal display of nervous paralysis, Stevie couldn't bring himself to acknowledge or even hint that anything at all had occurred between them. Nothing. Even though (or more likely because) he'd been thinking of nothing else since he left her that night. The silence was like some mental garbage disposal that turned his anticipation into mush. It had taken him two blocks of speed-walking to catch up with her, to just grunt "hey" and walk next-to-but-not-really, stare straight ahead and in increasingly panicky silence for two more blocks before pantomiming that he'd forgotten something at home and running—yes, he ran!—down Whitney and away from school. The confusion she hid behind her smile when he just kind of waved, he could still see it... He must've walked twenty miles along 395 that day; and it was that very evening, while dragging himself back towards town, that he first encountered his mysterious benefactor, his speed-demon death-angel. What a day.

He made some attempts at reconjuring that state of grace in the following couple of weeks, but the spell was broken that morning. Just like that. His attempts at ingratiation were clumsy at first, then became increasingly feeble, and finally took on a reek of self-defeat. Meanwhile, what started as a serendipitous, indeed almost magically facilitated opportunity for self-destructive indulgence had grown into a full-blown garden-variety meth habit. No, the latest stretch of time hasn't helped any. The speed-fueled mutation of intentions into the menu-scribbling has really been a form of throwing in the towel. Become a clown, come to expect that hint of pity he sees in her eyes. Or is it disappointment? And which is worse? Maybe if he told her what he was up to today...

She sets the Coke in front of him.

"What're you reading these days?" she asks.

"Huh?" The question throws him further off. "Uh..."

Before Stevie can put together an answer, Candy spins off toward the kitchen window. Order up, then another. His own order comes up. The first thing he sees is a bun top tilted over a puck-like patty. The whole thing looks like a rivet, or a squat mushroom, he thinks. It's kind of small, isn't it? Green? Wimpy... Is it Tuesday? Whoa, it is Tuesday. Would Wimpy consider... wait. It's not Tuesday–

"What I tell you?" It's Chief Hill's voice. He must be talking to Fairytales. Great. Of course! First real meal in days and –

Candy greets the officers with a quick smile, then ever-so-briefly narrows her eyes at Stevie as she sets down his plate. 'It's not what you think,' his eyes try to say. 'What-ever you're thinking.' Hey. Are those carrots in there? Oh no...

"Ray know you're here?"

Stevie looks up at Officer Tales, then to Chief Hill.

"Am I on the clock right now?" he asks earnestly.

"Eat your lunch, son." Chief Hill says. "You're fine." Stevie takes a large bite of the burger, chews it deliberately, then takes off the bun. He dumps the contents of a small, pleated paper cup of special sauce onto the patty, finally squeezing the cup—toothpaste-tube-style—to get every last bit. Chief Hill looks down at the plate. "What in Sam Hill are you eating, there?"

Stevie reassembles the burger then he stares at it himself.

"Well? It's a veggie burger." He looks concerned. "No cheese I guess..."

"That what that is? How are those things?"

"Um..." He takes another bite. "Um, it's pretty good, actually."

The chief looks at Stevie, smiles and sits in the next stool.

"Yeah? Well, they're supposed to be better for you. That's what they say. Good for you. You're braver'n I am."

Stevie looks up at Gary Tales, then—like Gary's face is the sun or something—quickly redirects his gaze. Officer Tales is staring back at him, his eyes expressionless. Stevie tries to focus on his lunch. He chews the burger self-consciously, trying not to masticate too audibly, wishing someone would start talking. He is so eager to finish that he almost overdoes it on more than one swallow, resorting to the use of his soda as a sort of esophageal Drano.

The chief waits until Stevie gets started on his fries before speaking again.

"Officer Tales here tells me you all had a productive morning. That right?"

"I guess so."

"Yeah? How's that old workhorse holding up?"

"Fine." Deja vu? No... "Except, it's super big so it kind of hurts my shoulders after a while. But it's a pretty cool...I mean... I like it, as, like, a thing."

"Do you. Good, I'm glad to hear that. Cause it's what we got. It is big."

"Mm hm."

"How's it sounding out there?"

Stevie wonders if this is a trick question.

"Well the levels look good…you know…on the meters…"

"You didn't–" Chief Hill flings a glance at Officer Tales. "That's okay. I'll show you. So Officer Tales explain to you about how this is gonna work now?"

"A little. He said you guys might be putting me–"

"No might be. You're officially on police payroll for this, son. You okay with that? You know what that means?"

"Means I got to get an ID for one thing, I know that."

"More what I'm referring to is whatever you learn out there is—what do they say?—strictly confidential."

"Strictly…"

"Keep it to yourself is what I'm getting at."

Stevie fishes a soggy French fry from under some fallen lettuce.

"Well… And you guys." The chief smiles.

"You got it. So I hear you went through a whole roll of tape today."

"A whole reel, like three hours worth…"

"We found some more tape for you." The chief nods at Officer Tales. Officer Tales grunts. "And you find anything funny out there you don't mess with it. That's what Officer Tales is there for. You find anything like that?"

Stevie shakes his head.

"Well anything unusual you bring straight to the attention of Officer Tales here, or me, hear?"

Stevie looks over at Officer Tales, who shifts his weight.

"I'll try."

"Otherwise," the chief looks over at Officer Tales, "you let him do his own job."

Stevie bends his mouth into a tight, ironic smile.

"Right," he says. "Ummuh… Can you tell me, not like I plan on telling anybody anything or anything like that, I'm just curious, am I like legally bound– "

Chief Hill, as if just now recognizing the impatience emanating from Officer Tales:

"You want to see what's up with that eleven twenty-six?" Officer Tales fires a last look at Stevie, turns around and walks out of the diner.

"So help me out here, son. What should I know?" The chief wipes imaginary crumbs from the counter—sort of an "Aw shucks" shoe-scuff, only with his hand.

"What should you know?"

"That's what I'm asking you. Something you seen out there? Something you read, maybe? Why don't you give me a little run-down of what you've gathered? A synopsis."

Sometimes Chief Hill reminds Stevie of Columbo; how Columbo would act all rambly, like he was thinking simpler thoughts than everybody else, but in reality had all sorts of other stuff going on in his head. Only Columbo always let everybody know what's what, eventually…

"I don't even know. It's mostly like some guy talking

about a job interview."

"A job interview? What sort of a job interview?"

"He doesn't say."

"Hmm. All right. What else?"

"It's a pretty weird interview, from what I can tell. It's all done on computers, and there's all these other people interviewing at the same time... and they go through like this dude's resume..." Stevie thinks for a couple seconds. "It sounds like it's probably a true story, cause so far it's just like rambling. There doesn't seem to be any point to it."

"And that's it?"

"So far. Well, it's a pretty weird place, it sounds like–"

"And names? What about names?"

"Yeah. David, David something."

"That's the guy being interviewed?"

"Uh huh."

"He's writing about himself?"

"Yeah. Just like... about the interview so far... Honestly, it was really hot out there, and I kind of started zoning out after awhile."

"Okay. What about the tone of the thing? This David, does he sound depressed? You get anything like that?"

"Maybe a little bit like a... sad sack?"

"A sad sack."

"Yeah. Seems like he might be having a midlife crisis or

something. Probably an alkie, too."

"An alkie." Chief Hill thinks for a minute. "That reminds me," he says. "You saw what was out there–"

"The mummy?"

The chief continues:

"Listen, son. You understand we could be dealing with some kind of crime scene out there, don't you? More than could be; I'd say it's likely. Now what troubles me, what I got to be concerned about, is how it seems– well, first off, we got this big old operation going on out there, but nobody around here sees a thing. There's one thing that don't make no sense. Here's another thing. Way we find out is we get you coming in, all hopped up on drugs, telling us how you just stumbled acrost a body and all the rest of it while– what'd you say you was out... wandering?" The chief leans in closer. "I want you to consider something for a minute. I could've done a lot of things. I could've sent you off on your merry way, or told you to go get your head checked. Or, I could've run you in. Nobody would've held it against me, considering. But I didn't. I'm trying this instead. Fact is I'm inclined to believe you. Only you don't make it so easy, do you? You been making some pretty bad decisions lately, son; dropping out of school with a month to go, and then getting yourself mixed up with that speed... You don't need me to tell you where that's gonna wind you up. You're smart enough to figure that out for yourself, I hope. Least I think you are. But you ain't there yet, are you? Now what worries me is you going around running off at the mouth, or–" Chief Hill picks up a menu and waves it like a little flag "– scribbling in menus for any body might stroll in here. You get where I'm headed?"

"Yeah…"

"Yeah. What do you suppose we should do about that?"

Stevie says nothing. The chief changes tack.

"So." He winks at the boy. "How's old Gary treating you out there? Fair?"

"What do you want me to say to that?"

"You said it. Friendly as a seed bag full of hand grenades, isn't he? Yeah… well. That Middle East must be something else, I'd imagine." Chief Hill's tone is familiar now, confidential. Just one local shooting the breeze with another, that's all.

"I guess."

"But…" as if he's just thinking out loud, "can't blame him for looking out for his sister."

Stevie squirms in his seat. The chief gently presses the point.

"Some folks are better'n others for keeping their own counsel, but nobody's immune to peer pressure."

Oh brother, not that peer pressure shit again… The chief continues while Stevie's toes curl. "Youngsters especially. Hard to believe, I know. It's one of those things, though. The more you think you're immune the more you ain't. For instance, even someone who might be careful about who they take a shine to… if they watch someone they do admire, watch that person go and toss aside all what God give 'em? Give up without a fight? That's bad advertising. If someone sees things like you do–"

Stevie can feel the nerves of his elbows where they contact the countertop. Bouncing almost. He feels like he's hooked up to a drip of electrical current that, although mild, if not turned off will eventually do some damage. Might as well say what's on his mind. Stop this.

"Okay. I do have an idea."

"An idea?"

"You asked what we should do. I'm just going to be honest."

"That's all right with me."

"Okay. Just for the sake of…whatever, I'm not saying it will necessarily, but let's say that… shit finds me–"

"It finds you?"

"Let's say I find myself… Actually, you mind if I start over?"

"Go ahead."

"It was really hot and dusty out there today. Right?"

"I won't argue with you there."

"So, what if you let me take the recorder thing myself then that way I could go out there when it's cooler. I actually think I could get more done–"

"You mean at night? By yourself? How you gonna get

out there; walk?"

"I don't mind."

"Son, I can't have you–" the chief shakes his head, "and you're talking about you don't know if you might end up getting drugs? Going out there like that?"

"Well, no. Not necessarily. I'm hoping actually that I get out there off the street before anything happens–"

"Off the street."

"And I'd like to say that I'll do that for sure but I know myself too well. Which sucks. It doesn't matter what I say now, or even what I'm sure of in my head. My thinking changes. I don't know what else to say. But if I got a... a plan in place... and no matter what, you wouldn't have to worry about me blabbering to people around here, because I'll be out there. Right? Again, not that I'm planning... you know..."

Chief Hill studies Stevie's face.

"I appreciate your being honest, Steve. And I have to say there's some logic in there somewhere. But I'll tell you I'm also starting to think maybe this ain't such a hot idea after all; keeping it local that is. And trusting somebody who can't trust themself, well... that's never been a good idea."

"I get that." Stevie takes a swig of soda. It burns his neglected teeth. "I'm trying to be trustworthy right now. I can do a good job. I'm just going off of why I think you got me doing this in the first place. Plus, I think better at night, most the time. And as far as me being out there by myself, I'm always off somewhere by myself at night anyways, so what difference would it make other than you knowing where I was?" Stevie stops, somewhat surprised at his own determination. The chief pinches his lower lip and stares out the window, through the traffic, toward the lake. Stevie takes this as a cue to keep pushing. "You want this thing done as quick as possible, right? Well? So do I. Not to sound weird, but I'm into this thing."

"As a thing."

"Well it's interesting, and it's kind of like, amazing to think someone did that, don't you think? And it looks kind of, I don't know, beautiful I guess when you look at the whole thing at once."

"Beautiful, huh? Let's see your eyes."

Stevie laughs nervously and continues,

"And whoever did it, I mean you can tell they put a lot of effort into actually writing it, actually..."

"And you appreciate that sort of thing."

"Well–"

"Sticking something through, having something to show for your effort. That what you mean? Well let me ask you then–"

"I know what you're going to say. Can I tell you something? I had all my required reading done by Christmas break. I read the whole Literature textbook, and the whole World History one, too. Way more than we were ever even supposed to."

"So then you what, give yourself a diploma?"

"I know."

"You know, huh? That right? Then why'd you do it?"

"I don't know. I just... oh I wish I could say."

"Mm Hm." After a pause: "I've been meaning to ask how your aunt's been doing..."

"My great aunt."

"That's right. How is she?"

"I don't know. I'd say not that great. You know. She stopped going to bingo after her friend Ruthie died. Now, she doesn't ever even go out of the house, hardly... except for to the store sometimes."

"Hmm. How would it be if I paid her a visit?"

Stevie considers for a minute.

"Maybe you get her to go to her doctor's appointments," he says, with emotion more genuine than he intended, or even expected.

Chief Hill laughs mildly.

"I was thinking I'd tell her about your throwing in with the forces of good."

"Oh." Huh? Oh. "Yeah, she should know, but I don't want her to think I'm trying to become a cop. No offense. It just wouldn't make sense to her. Cause I don't–" at this point Stevie senses he'd better get back to the point before it dissolves. "Don't get me wrong. I think it's cool that I'm going to get an actual paycheck. My aunt will definitely like that. And since I got to get an ID anyways, maybe I can get her to take me for my driving test so I can get my license. I got my permit already. Might as well."

A discouraged (and, to Stevie, discouraging) look passes across the chief's features.

"And that's another thing that works well with my idea." Stevie says enthusiastically. "You could keep track of my hours just by how much gets recorded. That's a cinch. You don't even have to worry about how I get—"

"Then what? Take the day off?"

"No, but it would be better to start later. It's super bright out there in the morning anyways," Stevie says, "and Officer Tales wouldn't have to sit in his car all day long."

"Never mind all that." The chief is silent for a solid minute, silent in a way that strongly suggests to Stevie that he should keep his own mouth shut as well. They both look out the window, then Chief Hill turns to Stevie and looks at him. They stare at each other, the chief in repose, Stevie uncomfortably resisting the urge to focus on the chief's haphazard eyebrows, or the topography of his nose. Finally Chief Hill leans back.

"Full moon tonight?"

"Tomorrow. I think. Or maybe it is tonight. Yeah, I think you're right—"

The chief smiles, pushes himself up off the stool, finds Ray's gaze, points at Stevie's plate, then at himself, and waves. Raylene screws up her face in a friendly way. He turns back toward Stevie.

"You know what's a blessing, son?"

"Um...?" Stevie pulls some money from his pocket, feigning confusion about the bill. The chief motions him to put it back, which Stevie does, after taking a five-dollar bill and sliding it under his unused knife.

"Being a bad liar. That's a blessing." They're at the door to the greeting room, bracing for the heat outside. Stevie turns around and smiles at Candy. She smiles back and raises her eyebrows curiously. Chief Hill holds the door. "Atta boy," he says. "Never trust a man who don't tip." When they get outside, the chief, his arms crossed, again silently assesses Stevie. Sensing this as more of a formality than a real examination, Stevie stands up straighter than usual anyway. "I want you to pay more attention next time," the chief says at last. "Maybe write down any details you think I might find interesting. Names and places. Think you can do that?"

"Yeah. For sure."

"You ever drive a ATV?"

"Not really."

"Well you get to learn."

6

Stevie waits. The sun has dropped behind the mountains; the remaining light is what ricochets off of a metallic overcast somewhere behind them. The moon that just moments ago rose pale as a dandelion puff is now the brightest thing in the sky. Crows shout back and forth like factory workers in a parking lot, calling it a day.

Chief Hill's gone home by now, Stevie imagines. Most of the cars have their headlights on. There doesn't appear to be any less activity around the roadside scattering of buildings in the middle distance, yet this stretch of highway sure seems to be getting quieter. Quieter? Since there's no less noise as far as Stevie can tell, does that mean there's more silence? The cars that drive by can be heard coming (maybe 'heard' isn't quite, or completely, accurate) from farther away than during the day; and after they pass, the sound seems to linger longer. A higher contrast, and a broadening of the event horizon in both directions to indicate a widening of all such cones, from precognition to memory, surrounding all events? Even the hidden ones? And there goes another soap-bubble perception. Pop.

The ants are coming out. Stevie watches as populations of them, rush-hour citiesful stream from tiny holes in the ground. In the area where he sits—limbs folded against the chill, blending into the shadow, waiting—the ants are countless, a seething fabric that stretches... He looks back toward the town. He can see the inside of the Golden Empire, which tells him they must be about to close for the night. They always close right at dark. Stevie's theory is that it has something to do with an effect the interior lighting has on Raylene: how as it drives away the world outside—replacing it with a reflective-yet-exposed box for a habitat, and with Raylene's own reflection displacing the expansive dead-lake view from the plate-glass windows—it impels her to undergo a corresponding psychic shift toward reflection and introspection. Or something like that. And she doesn't want to go there. In other words, she must be lonely. That's the hunch he's developed over these last couple months of this waiting; a hunch based mostly on how Ray never seems to stop for air during business hours. It could be for safety's sake, of course; Ray not wanting hers to be the only place open this side of Independence. But Stevie doubts that somehow. If it were him he'd want the only open place this side of Independence.

He turns back toward the strip of dark and empty road to his right. Waiting. Waiting for that noise to emerge and grow, for that rush of certainty. Waiting—like in line, like for the bus, like for the shower water to heat up... for as long as Stevie could remember waiting has always got him thinking the kind of thoughts he might have to physically force from his head. Inevitability. The future. And this particular waiting—having become more or less ritualized— is generally the worst. The dimming of light, the growing quiet (the meetings have always taken place just past dusk, regardless of the time); these things surely explain a part of why that is. But isn't the main reason (and he concludes this anew every time, doesn't he?) because of what he's waiting for? The sound that will grow, and soon? It will be soon. He will show. He always shows. The sound of that engine, that car, what it brings. Just like Chief Hill says. It's no secret. He knows what he's waiting for. Stars start to appear, starting with the closest. Closest in time, that is, and moving back from there, right? So much time up there.

Stevie turns his gaze back down to the ants. So many ants. So many little holes. He extrapolates the distribution of ants and holes immediately surrounding himself onto all the land in town, all the land he can see, then all the vast volcanic land beyond. If we paid attention to everything going on around us we'd all go nuts, he thinks. If people only realized what we share with... like Cartago at dusk belonging to these impossible numbers; they come up from God knows what kind of world while the few of us stomp around oblivious, every dumb move of ours a killer. We have no choice though, do we? There are just so, so many of them. And if evolution happened the way they say it did, then buried within all of us must be some residual ant-memory, some ancient relationship with thoughtless, arbitrary... Hmm. And yet we pretend not to understand paranoia. Seems perfectly reasonable to be paranoid if you're paying attention (isn't there a bumper sticker that's something like that?). Maybe it's the paying attention part that's unreasonable...

Stevie hears it coming now, still minutes away. Now for a

different kind of waiting; too acute for introspection. First he 'hears' the cold, hypersonic whine somewhere near the top of his head, to which a more visceral buzz gets gradually added; then the aluminum crackle—all throat and no heart—joins the mix. He can see the headlights now, icy blue and alien. He turns around and looks back toward the black-and-white Polaris Scrambler lent to him by eccentric old Guy. He finds it surprisingly well camouflaged by mottled moonlight and creosote shadows. He stands up. The bruise-yellow Nissan is close now, and going fast. Looking until the last second like it will fly right by, the car cuts across the opposite lane and stops dead in front of him with that sound like a giant vacuum cleaner whose cord has been ripped from the wall.

The exchange doesn't vary from ritual. The driver's head is turned away as if forever assessing the passenger-side mirror angle; so all Stevie can see is a very blonde, very close-cut flattop. The head says "enjoy" while a muscular arm reaches out and snaps a paper bindle from out of nowhere, it seems, into its manicured fingertips. Stevie takes the bindle and awkwardly offers some bills–which get waved away as usual, with the head saying: "I'll get you next time." No price has ever been agreed upon, though on occasion the man has taken what was offered. A quick rev of the engine and the car rockets off–its manifold sucking atmosphere like some mini black hole while that white light coming from where the license plate should be etches his retinas. Next time, Stevie thinks as he turns toward the ATV, I'm going to change things up on that guy. Next thought: Yeah, just like the last time about this time, and then the time before that... followed closely by: Oh well. Stevie kneels in the shadow of the vehicle, carefully opens the bindle and pours the contents into a bullet-shaped plastic speed-dispenser. He tests it then vacuums the bindle with his lungs and lips. The moonlight immediately brightens. Stevie feels suddenly exposed. "Time to get." He starts up the ATV then immediately cuts the ignition. The two-stroke engine racket sounds like pitched battle. He freezes, expecting the town to spill out of their doors, wondering what the hell... but nothing happens. After a minute of listening to his heart rate rise and fall, while convincing himself that all that internal combustion wasn't as loud as he thought, he restarts the engine and creeps—hardly more than idles—toward the hidden bay.

* * *

Chief Hill gets his pills ready while the microwave counts down the last seconds on his Healthy Choice pot roast. Apricot—a fluffy, ill-humored Himalayan cat—half-heartedly tears at the dining room's rattan wallpaper. While he walks back to the living room the old man considers sending the cat spinning on its haunches, but ends up leaving it alone. Better it shreds the wallpaper than the chair, he reminds himself.

He sets the dinner on a tray in the living room right next to the chair and in front of the TV then goes back to the kitchen for the pills and a nearbeer. On his return trip he pats the cat with his foot. Delores named the cat Apricot, and insisted on a soft-A pronunciation that playful-pain-in-the-ass Jim Hill, her husband, would never give her the satisfaction of using. He would eventually refer to it as Ape, which Delores liked to pretend really ticked her off. In the three years since Delores died the cat hasn't heard either name. Jim Hill looks at the cat. Looking a little brittle these days, isn't it… Judging by what he's been finding in the cupboards lately, he's come to conclude that the old cat has gone into retirement. He laughs to himself, remembering how it was for getting rid of vermin that he agreed to live with a bat-faced malcontent of an animal in the first place.

Chief Hill turns on the TV (by hand; it's one thing he never could get used to using the remote for), sits down and passes over a couple of police dramas in search of something funny. Having settled on an episode of Frasier that he suspects he may already have seen, he's leaning over his dinner tray when he hears a sports car accelerate from a dead stop. He's just about to wash down some heart medication with his O'Douls when he hears the ATV start up, stall, and start up again. He thinks about Stevie as the sound dies away; wonders again if it's such a great idea to rely on a foolish… an unpredictable kid to do his work for him, if it even is his work. He wonders if maybe all things considered haven't caused him to lose some or all perspective himself. What should he do different? Call in the guard? Let the Rio Tinto boys run their tanks all over it? And he knows enough to know that just keeping it between him and Tales, what with Gary so quick to be so sure of things, would be too claustrophobic, deduction-wise. So the thought loop ends the same way again: Yes; this is the best way. For now, anyhow. Bright kid. Likes to read; honest enough. Might've picked him for the job myself it he wasn't picked for me. Strange thing, isn't it? Sets up almost perfect...

But there's another thought—another whole way of thinking, actually—that's been an unwelcome guest in his head all day long. Something that's got him questioning his own judgment a little bit. He tugs at the afghan that Delores (or maybe it was her mother?) made when they were young; the same one that he used to avoid for how it tended, because of its loose, yarny weave, to coil itself around his feet like some boa constrictor; he pulls it up over his legs and stares at the TV screen. The little dog has evidently done something that's hilarious to the studio audience but not funny at all to Frasier's old man.

The troubling thing is this: when Delores was near the end, Jim Hill had given her a couple of reluctant vows to go to her rest with. One of them was he'd try and get to know Jesus better, try and listen for God's voice instead of always his own all the time. A personal relationship. That's been slow going. As he sees it, he's been on sort of nod-ding-acquaintance terms with God (or Jehovah, as Delores liked to call Him—and wanted Jim to too but he never could do that either) for so long that it feels uncomfort-able, ridiculous even, trying to be pals with Him now. But he's trying. Like the living better; whatever that means. Or: he'll attempt conversations with the Almighty, even though he's always had an aversion toward talking to himself. He'll even ask for advice sometimes, but —logically enough, he supposes—it's always Delores he hears answer him then.

When he'd made that promise to her, Delores said she could see the doubt in Jim's eyes. She told him that she knew—she knew!—that Jehovah would reveal himself, and that if he only prepared himself the best he could, he would know the sign when he saw it. All the doubt would fall from his eyes, and he would know the word of the Lord. Chief Officer Hill couldn't wrap his mind around much of that then, and still can't now. Still, he can't shake the notion that this whole mysterious writing in the desert business seems like just the sort of thing God might do if he was looking to knock some revelation into the mule head of somebody like himself. Downright and undeniably Biblical. And what kind of denial would he have to be in to pretend it can't be seen that way? He can't ask Delores' advice on this one. He knows what she'd say. He suspects that part of the reason he got old Guy involved is that being around the old frog and his flighty ideas makes it easier to keep his own thoughts closer to the ground. After all, he is the Chief of Police, and as such, has to do his job the best he can. Though, in all honesty he hasn't had to do much, or hasn't had much to do that requires much concentration, job-wise, for longer than he can readily recall—a fact which he's not too proud to suppose might be contributing to his present confusion. What more, what better could he do? Even Jehovah couldn't argue with that.

Then there's that other promise. Jim Hill wonders if he didn't slip up on that one today, over at the cafe. "Hell," he says out loud, "am I supposed to pretend the world ain't here?"

* * *

Keith, Lee and a thirteen-year-old seventh-grade dropout who goes by the name Flyball, who will show the tattoo to anyone who asks why, sit in a treeless field of patchy grass. They're all sitting Indian Style, arranged as vertices of a stoner triangle. Keith is being clumsily passed the joint when he hears the ATV.

"What a fucking dick," he says.

"Who?" Lee asks.

"Fucking Stevie."

"Who's fucking Stevie?" Flyball asks.

"Nobody. Somebody who's getting paid to read shit into a fucking microphone who said he'd try and get me a job. But watch."

"Who'd hire you?"

"You don't want to know. Just some joneser. Who the fuck– what did he do to get that shit?"

"Who?"

"Dude, I just told you. Give me that."

Flyball drops the roach into Keith's palm.

"It's my fucking joint, don't forget."

"How old are you, man? Like fucking eleven? You're

gonna stunt your growth you know that?"

"F.T.W." Flyball replies. It's his mantra.

Lee lays back.

"That's Stevie?" referring to the slowly descending and diminishing engine noise. "Is that why you're saying–?"

"I'll bet you."

"We should go out there and fuck with him."

"Yeah we should."

"What's his name again?" Flyball asks. "Keith or some shit?"

"I'm Keith you fucking– dude, are you fucking brain-dead? Why don't you go sniff some glue?"

"You know what?" Flyball says, getting up but not bothering to knock the dead grass from his clothes, "I'm fucking out of here is what I am. Because…"

He walks away, trying to pull up his pants; a task made difficult by the muddy ribbon of pant cuff strapped around his heel. "…you guys are trippin'."

* * *

The sound of his own two-stroke cutting through the atmosphere finds Guy busy, scissors in hand, bisecting a pair of old slacks.

"Give it some gas, hey?" he shouts.

Jeanne's in the back room, chain-smoking her Vantages,

doing some research on the internet.

"Hear that?" he yells. She doesn't reply. The door must be closed. He smiles to himself while making the last cut, then holds up the front piece and declares:

"Okay. That will do."

* * *

Candy closes her bedroom door, lights a stick of incense and waves it around the room. Gary is in the kitchen frying himself a cube steak or something. Whatever it is, it's giving off a sour odor, bringing out the worst in whatever that tater-tot smell is it's mingling with. Straight from the freezer to the pan. No seasonings. Cooked till grey. Candy doubts if he knows if that's how he likes it or not. She suspects it's more like he just does it like that. That he doesn't even pay attention. After serving up bacon-cheeseburgers and sausage gravy all day, Candy could really do without having to come home to the stench of cheap cube steak. Would it kill him to throw a chopped onion in there at least? Come on, brother. Candy hears a pop. God, how much oil is he using? Seriously, how can he eat that? Why? And why's she got to be the only one thinking about it? Flesh... demolished and reassembled... frozen... heated to kill but not remove, right? It's still there, right? The bacteria? Candy lets herself get carried away sometimes; lets the magma get close to the surface, as her mom used to say. But wow. So incredibly disgusting. Why would anyone– Candy stops herself. Candy—having lately come to the realization that people are sure quick to call you self-righteous, then there's nothing you can do; you just lose—makes a point of keeping her opinions to herself these days. Still, the way she sees it, her very restraint should give Gary more reason to show some respect for who she is. Instead of just being sarcastic. She's only been vegan for five years already; would it kill him to register that fact? That that's a real thing? There again, though; that requires paying attention, and Gary doesn't pay attention. It's like he refuses.

She flicks a lever on her record player and the needle glides into to her mom's old copy of David Bowie's *Hunky Dory*.

So right on, it is a godawful small affair. The caveman, the lawman, beating up the wrong guy is in the kitchen, cooking his steak. She lays back on her bed and without letting her eyes focus, stares at the frosted, leaf-etched, and coved-to-square glass bowl that covers the overhead bulb. The song builds toward its string-soaked crescendo while for Candy the light becomes a supernova; shimmering, teeming with clean new worlds. The song ends. She hears a purring sound, far away; thinks maybe it's some test coming from China Lake. Now she lets her eyes focus. Cobwebs hang like lace—no; like lacy deserted Martian ruins—from the sparkle-flecked ceiling. She sits up and looks out the window. The next song begins (a campy cabaret number; not her favorite, though there's one lilting cadence in there that she's quite fond of...) and she thinks: this could not be made here—this music—in a place like this. She lets her gaze drift down the wall to the flimsy aluminum-sashed window, and rests it at a spot where the corner bead has curled to create a fault-like crack that runs the length of the narrow—the uselessly narrow—sill. Candy is not a snob. She's for the underdog if she's for anything. But does everything around her have to be so cheap?

Candy tries not to ask herself anymore: what am I doing here? But she still does wonder: what is anybody doing here? Candy is not a snob, she likes to reminds herself, but there's something about these thin desert walls that makes her sick to her stomach. She can't help it. She can only imagine the world, the habitat that produced, for instance, this music. Only imagine. She imagines a large room full of silver lamé, glossy faces with high cheekbones and wildly drawn brows. Frothy, bleached permanents. Self-conscious excess in all its forms. And surrounding it all: massive Rococo walls of cream and antique gold. Candy would have to say she's against decadence as a rule. But if they were all just faking it, like she would be? What if what those thick Rococo walls protected them from was the pressing, depressing mediocrity of their own kind? When all you want is for everybody to do better, to try harder?

Why is that like the worst thing ever?

Or a wall is a wall is a wall. Don't let's get carried away…

Candy can imagine herself being in that world she imagines, but maybe not entirely of it. She can see herself. She can see herself enjoying a languid conversation, draped like an overcoat across a Turkish pillow that seems to float on the mirrored floor. She's nodding with genuine interest as the... Mussolini impersonator makes her friendly, sedated case for... Ezra Pound's something or other. Soon Candy will attractively, eloquently and elegantly countervail. She will steal a glance or two at the gigantic gilded birdcage that's swinging from the ceiling. Slowly rotating, it will shed goose-down feathers; it will send them to drift around like theater snow. But does she imagine herself up there slurping around in the pile? Not really.

Candy used to hate her name. Her mom named her for Candace Bergen. The actress. Candy has seen Carnal Knowledge, and the Sand Pebbles, and her share of Murphy Brown episodes, but she has never figured out just what her mother saw that would make her do that. To name your daughter after a particular person, when that person is famous and alive and someone you don't know is odd enough. But if you're going to do that, to choose Candace Bergen over every single one else is just plain weird. Candy used to despise the name Candy; it made her feel white-trashy, not to be taken seriously. Over time, however, she's developed a defiant fondness for it. Candy is a great name for a desert waitress; no doubt. And that's fine. But Candy can be other things. The way she sees it the letter on her bed is both proof of and a chance to prove this fact.

* * *

Gary can't find the spatula. There's not enough oil in the pan, now the damned patty's going to fuse with the damned pan before he can—there it is. Wouldn't you know it; dirty in the sink. Damned spatula. Gary pours a good bottle-gulp of Crisco into the pan then hastily washes the spatula. He doesn't bother to dry it; instead he slips it into the now hot oil.

Tiny water droplets leap, burst, explode from the oil, producing a hot, pyroclastic drizzle. The rain singes the top of Gary's hand. The rain sprays the stovetop, making a mess. Magma. IED. The patty is stuck. Gary scrapes, flips, and endures another burning drizzle. "Bitch!" he says, addressing pan, patty, spatula, and oil. He barely represses the urge to slap it and splash hot oil all over the place. Smash the whole damned thing.

Fuckin' shrinks! He'd talk, if shrinks weren't all creeps and quacks and leeches. But they are. That's just how it is. Like the one that Prometheus hooked him up with. He tried to talk truthful to that guy, didn't he? And what did he get for all his effort? What did that fraud leech do? Give him a prescription for pills! Just pushing drugs. Hand out crutches; that's all they do. Show them weakness they'll make you weaker with it. Anybody who can't see that is a fool.

Going to Iraq was supposed to make Gary stronger. That was the whole point. The prescription made it as far as the lobby trash can, along with the card that showed him when his next appointment was.

He won't make that mistake again.

Gary fishes the cube steak out of the pan, then spits into the oil. The spit pops, sizzles, bubbles away. Gary watches.

Gary was still in Kirkuk when he got word that his folks

disappeared. Just three weeks previous to that he was called to the scene of a particularly grisly mortar attack. He had held the head of a translator; held it together in fact. At the very instant she died, he was checking out her tits. Not a damn thing he can do about that now. Not now, or ever ever, ever...

It had been three weeks since he first endured the nightly turbulence—with its attendant spasms—that made it impossible for him to get to sleep. And a week since he'd seen the doctor. In all honesty, the disappearance of his parents was welcome news. It struck him as just another one of their flighty granola stunts, like the obsidian hunting or the petroglyph mapping. You never knew with them. Volcanological research, they'd told Candy. Volcanological Gary's ass. Since when? Eventually they'd show up, he figured, and most likely act all surprised that ever a fuss was made. Like carefree children. He would give them hell for making him drop everything to deal with one of their wild hairs, again. But he'd stay. When he submitted his resignation—listing the reason the fact that we was now acting as sole legal guardian of his seventeen-year-old-sister—his superiors were very understanding, and willing—eager even—to help. Prometheus gave him a pay and medical package (which they didn't have to do, he reminds himself) and welcomed him back any time.

Gary pulls the tater tots from the oven, squirts some ketchup onto the foil, harpoons the patty with his fork, drops it onto a saucer and starts eating. He eats standing up. He chews to the sound of the ATV. Must be Stevie

Ludich. Didn't he turn out to be a loser. Weakling. It's not Gary's fault Stevie's a weakling. No, that was already there. Like two plus two equals four. It was bound to come out sooner or later. While strong people have to kill and die... Ludich is damn lucky things aren't worse for him, as far as Gary's concerned.

* * *

The 1989 Subaru wagon belonging to Linda and Gordon Tales was found up by the Long Valley Caldera, near an area where CO_2 concentrations from underground vents create an atmosphere that's deadly toxic to trees and mammals alike. One theory, the one Candy subscribes to, is that they got trapped in some toxic vent, or maybe fell into some superheated sulfur pool. A fatal accident; in other words: they're dead. To hear Candy talk, you'd think they ascended bodily up to heaven. "They died doing what they love" and bullshit like that. Of course Candy doesn't remember—hell, she wasn't even born yet—when Dad quit his engineering job and followed Mom to Shasta for the damned Harmonic Convergence. Left Gary in summer camp for three extra days then told him when they finally picked him up how happy he ought to be; told him that they were about to make big changes as a family. Good changes, they assured him. Gary was eight at the time, and going into third grade. He had his friends and all that. He wasn't looking for big changes. But they never asked his opinion about it.

Yeah; no. What could Candy know? She grew up with

the New Linda and Gordon Tales. They filled her head up with their romantic bullshit from day one. Self re-creation with the emphasis on recreation, far as Gary could ever tell. Voyages of self-discovery; all self-this, self-that. But Gary remembers. He doesn't believe in reincarnation. People don't change. A twenty-year vacation is what they're on, and people don't die on vacation. A twenty year play-act, an extended pretend session is what they're on, and they can't die while faking it. Fluid self–? No. Death sets identity like concrete. No. Gary knows who his parents really are. Sometimes he wonders if they disappeared just to get him home from Iraq. He wouldn't be surprised at all. And it worked, didn't it? Got to give them credit for that. No. He'll stay and he'll wait, and he'll make sure Candy does the same. And when Gordon and Linda do come back he's going to let them have it. He'll snap them out of this for once and for all. When he tells them what he's seen and done, and why, and what he knows... he'll make them come clean. He'll make them come back for real.

7

My screen went blank just long enough for me to release my breath.

"Okay, so where were we…" Stevie kneels next to the reel-to-reel and adjusts the straps on the respirator/microphone contraption to accommodate the vinyl headphones supplied to him by Chief Hill. He rewinds the tape a revolution or two by hand, then flicks a toggle. "…where were we." The playback is a little muddy and a little hissy, and his voice sounds more immature than he was expecting it to, but the words are easy to understand. He repeats the process to check the VU meter. It seems fine. He throws the pack on his back and finds the spot. He pulls a pad from one pocket and puts it into another pocket. He takes another toot from the bullet and flicks the toggle again. "Ho-kay! Let's see… where were we… ah yes yes yes here we are. Yessirreebob. Sirreeboppitybop… andabopbo-paloobopalopbam…"

My screen went blank just long enough for me to release my breath. A bead of sweat broke free from my underarm and tumbled, tickling my ribcage on its way down. Another one rappelled along my biceps before coming to rest in the crook of my elbow. Then the now-familiar petrous features of our intermediary (or whoever he was) reemerged. He was almost smiling, and there was something in his acid-yellow eyes that was almost caring, if not exactly kind.

"Mr. Edwards." The voice was so resonant, self-contained, and crisp as the sound of officiously shuffled paper that the top of my head tingled. It was like he touched my pituitary gland and my scalp, like some tide-pool creature, contracted around the contact. "Mister Edwards, you have finished reviewing the full contents of your file, and have verified the veracity—" did he say voracity? "—of all textual and... extra-textual information. Is this correct?"

"Okay," Stevie editorializes, "so this guy just looked at this file these other people, well I don't mean exactly people, but you know what I mean. I'm just gonna say people. But more like a company. They know all this weird stuff about the guy and he's kinda trippin' because it's all pretty much out of the blue and I think he thought he was just going on a regular job interview. Don't ask me. So I'll continue now, and whoever's listening to this just so you know I won't keep interrupting I just wanted to, um... Well anyways, here we go:"

"It is," I said,

Stevie: "This is the guy talking, not me...um..."

"It is," I said, modulating the last syllable as if to imply "but...". I left it at that.

"It is..."

"Uh...correct?"

"Okay," stressing both syllables. "Good. Now then..." He looked me right in the eyes; that is both of them, simultaneously. "You must have questions. Questions as to our methodology, as to our intentions perhaps, or perhaps as to the ultimate aim of this process. Who are we? What do we...do? I'm sure you are aware that you have been given no obvious clues as to what, exactly, the position is that you are seated here in hope of securing. That brought you to this room. Why is that? And many more questions, I'm sure. Questions as to the data we have collected; as to how it has been presented to you. Why this and not that? Perhaps you feel the need to explain–"

"You know as a matter of fact I have to say one thing. That skinhead guy?"

"Mister Edwards, let me as–"

"I mean why that guy? You must've figured out–"

"Let me ask you something." A half-measure of authoritarian tone again, eyes literally flashing, "Mr Edwards."

"Nn-kay."

"Why do you think your history looks the way it does? You think it's because you're lazy, or unfocused? We don't think so. You may find it...unfair of us, to present you to yourself in the way we have. Let me assure you, we possess much more information than we have provided here, and are not unaware of the...circumstantial complexities, extenuations, and so on, which surround and inform your actions... But all of that is inconsequential to what we are hoping to illustrate to you here."

"Can I just ask is this really leading to a job offer somewhere?" My throat felt like a leaky valve– "Because honestly I'm just not seeing, I don't see how– "

"Do you consider yourself a...humanist, Mister Edwards?"

"Well, in what sense? I mean–"

"In the broadest sense. Would you assert that the process of attainment... of the realization of full human potential— Aristotelian excellence, if you will—is the, if you will forgive a metaphor, the 'best game in town'? Or the only game, perhaps? Would you assert that the maximal degree of opportunity being given to the maximum number of human beings is intrinsic—even necessary—to the self-realization of the isolated individual? Would you assert that this is the highest aim to which a society can aspire?"

"Well..."

"Speak frankly."

"Okay, welp... I would say... if I understand you right... there doesn't seem to be any... well sure. I suppose I would."

"Yes..."

"Yes what? You want more?"

"Please. Keep in mind, Mister Edwards, that we are quite aware that the clear articulation of your thoughts on this subject, particularly within an unfamiliar context, is a difficult task. That is our intent."

"Okay. You want me to explain...I mean, I'll try but... I'm not sure I can. Honestly, I'm not sure I want to try, but I will. I mean, you're talking about relative consciousness here, right? And that's kind of tricky, cause, you know, you take some of those ideas about what a 'higher consciousness' might be? All that jealous God stuff, or the um... Medieval Lord stuff? Taking everything personal, and so much in the wrong way? Going around dispensing rewards and punishment to His, um... inferiors? Being anti-logic and reason? All that? I actually don't see much sense in...you know, I just think that makes for a pretty twisted view of human potential. I mean, if you think this world is just like a waiting room for some exclusive club in some other dimension, well...well I don't really see that. But it does seem like our best conceptions of... of, like, say, transcendence, or illumination? Best to me I guess I should say; well sometimes I think that could be our... our aim, for ourselves, for someday... Like a species project; does that make sense? And we use God, maybe, as like a blueprint." I paused. "I know I'm not being clear enough, but you asked... you know I've got to say this really is hard...I mean, for a job interview?"

"Have patience with yourself, Mister Edwards. Please continue."

"This might sound, uh, I don't know..." playing right into a weakness of mine, aren't they? "...but maybe our compulsion about becoming like God? Well, maybe we can do it." I stopped to catch my breath. "Even if there isn't one. Yet. You know what I'm saying? Is this at all answering; what was the question?" Silence. "I'm not explaining..." Silence. "Well it does seem to me that we're the only animals trying to become something else all the time. So that might be what we do. Because it is what we do. I mean, it's not like I see chimps being able to ever... but then; I guess no one really knows what dolphins– "

"Do you like people for that, Mister Edwards?"

"I'm sorry? You mean–"

"In the objective sense. The people you encounter in your normal, everyday life, read about, and so forth. The people that exist. With their distractions, their thoughtlessness, their willful ignorance. All the pettiness with which they–we–conduct ourselves. Their willingness to settle. When you dream about what humanity could be capable of, do you ever really ascribe–to the real people you interact with on a daily basis– that potential?"

"Oh, I see. Well, I don't know. Not everybody... I could see us being like one big organism, right? A liver cell isn't a brain cell, but they're both human. And anyways, that's where education–"

"Do you like children, Mister Edwards? Your students, when you have them? Do you look at them differently than you would, say... their parents? Are they different? Is it a future... different from your present that you see in your student's faces? Or detect in their cruel rehearsals? What do you really see, when you glimpse the adult in the child?"

"*Actually, there is the occasional kid—*"

"*—and what can you offer the occasional kid? Your theory of transcendence, your 'willing God into existence', while it might be hopeful enough to ward off nihilism, if only just... it is a bit tortured, isn't it? A theory that requires the primacy of theory? You offer up a pregnant chicken, Mister Edwards; you've dusted off the Biblical concept of 'word made flesh'. But you are a writer, aren't you?*"

"*Again, I'm not sure what you're getting at here. That's what I meant by tricky. Everybody's ideas are different, and... are... each one in constant flux. I'm not saying I'm right, but that's the view from where I stand right now. I mean, you can't believe everything—*"

"*No? Hmm. While you've brought up the subject of religion—*"

"*Wait a minute. It was you that asked me to—*"

"*—you mustn't fail to mention the simplest explanation in considering its utility. As something for the—not your new brain, Mister Edwards, but rather the brain opposite that one...the old brain, if you will—to attach itself to. And attach itself not in order to change, but in order... not to change. In order to remain just what it is. With the rest being merely window dressing. The evolutionary process? Simply a refinery of efficiencies; more consultant than priest, if you will forgive me another metaphor. Is there something about simple explanations that causes you to avoid them, Mister Edwards? Because, as you well know, in this capacity religion has a proven track record. Nature itself seems to prefer surety of mind, and pays*" *no mind to theoretical elegance. An action defines its reaction. But a dimly imagined ideal of humanity? A theoretical exercise, with actual oblivion awaiting every individual in the meantime? Come now, Mister Edwards. If it were possible for you to believe in anything else, anything with something in it for you, would you not leap at the chance to do so?"*

All right, I thought. So this IS some sales pitch. Maybe the Mormons got some computer out in the desert that—

"As it is, you appear to have become dependent upon a chemical facsimile, not even of personal salvation, but merely of an absence of... absence. Lack of meaning. You think the world would be a better place if everyone thought more like yourself? Or let me put it this way, Mr. Edwards. Is the world a better place with you thinking like yourself?"

"Hey wait a second. Is this some sort of a... an intervention?"

"Do you ever feel, Mister Edwards, that what you have to share may do more harm than good?"

"You know? How much of this do you expect me to take? You're full of shit. I'm sorry. I came here to interview for a job, not to have you scour my soul. If this is some conversion attempt... job or not, I really don't need some, whatever, telling me..."

"No need to get excited, Mister Edwards."

He's right. Don't show these fuckers any emotion. Try— *"Okay." Breathe. "What's your point?"*

"Bear with us here—" the 'I'm in your ear' voice again,

"while I make some... educated guesses... about you. Certainly there's no harm in that."

I exhaled dramatically. "Shoot. What the hell."

"Respond freely, but, please, continue trying to be honest."

"Go ahead?"

"I'm going to suggest some things to you, then I'm going to tell you something that might surprise you."

I shook my head in hopes of expressing annoyed bewilderment. He went on, not appearing to notice:

"Our assessment of your... personal outlook suggests a certain amount of angst and uncertainty. A certain amount of what might be called... existential suffering."

"And what possible difference could that make to you? So what? I can't imagine what any of this could have to do with anything. I think you should probably mind—"

"Here's what we think. You tell me if we're wrong. Somewhere far beneath your surface pessimism and anxiety; the seed, if you will, from which your philosophy of open-minded futilism initially grew; is something of a martyr complex. You watch those around you blithely going about their daily lives in a cloud of self-satisfaction and ignorance; while you perceive yourself as being in possession of a truth you suspect most of them are incapable of living with, of suffering the possession of. Mister Edwards, do you see yourself as shielding them from this truth? You once told a friend—in a bar, January of 199–, I quote: "...where's the sacrifice if you know your ordeal will get you into heaven?"

Does that sound like you? You went on: "What God worth its omnipotence wouldn't see right through that? The motives are selfish...", and so on. This, I suggest, you do believe. I also suggest you possess an amoral moral superiority, a self-image built around a certain nobility of purposelessness. An exceptionalism; perhaps even a...chosen-ness, if you will. Or, to put it in terms you may be more comfortable with, a mutual empathy with a mortal universe—a mutual affinity, even— beyond the reach of mere human endeavor."

"Seriously? I would say...honestly? That you guys were singularly, um... wrong? Psychotic? And maybe any purposelessness, as you say, you detect? That's coming from this horror show you call an 'interview process' or whatever." I wasn't lying then, but at the same time I knew he was right. That was how I felt, to a degree... if I was truthful about it.

"And what would you say if I told you," he said, "that you were right? Yes. You are right about it all. Your exceptionalism... your chosen-ness, Mister Edwards... it is real. It is the truth."

"Um, I would say you—whoever you are—you're even crazier than I just thought you were a second ago. Honestly." Not entirely honestly.

"Let's examine your job history, your career choices and/ or lack thereof, in this light. I would suggest that the same dynamic is at play here. Perhaps you've seen... oh, countless individuals I would imagine... people who do not share your... depth of awareness... seen them achieve outward success merely by limiting the breadth of their experience and

choosing instead to focus on a simple... you would probably say shallow... game plan. Or perhaps they pick from among the previously existing templates for a life, and merely retrace, or stencil it. It is hard to deny the effectiveness of that approach; wouldn't you agree? Society does tend to reward what you might, in a strident mood, consider cowardice, or at the very least, monomania. Perhaps you've wondered: is this not only the most that seems to be expected of you by your fellow man, but the most that might be tolerated by him? Whereas you, on the other hand, your inner life is far too vast, isn't it? Too profound to be limited by the banalities of say, career, or... or any number of similarly artificial constructs, for that matter. You operate within an arena of ever-unrealized potentiality, as the prince of a delicate, crystalline palace of thought. You protect this inner life of yours like it's your only child, and react with defiance to anyone who would assume authority over even a small portion. Perhaps you perceive this to be the... the only valid approach to truth. And the difficulties this characteristic brings you can be explained simply as resulting from more ignorance and weakness on the part of your fellows. They would be lined up to enlist you to their aid—"

"I wouldn't say I'm nearly that, um, paranoid."

"And what if I were to tell you that—in this also—you have been right in your approach? What if I told you that you have acted with rare nobility of spirit, Mister Edwards, inscrutable to all? Well... to all, that is, save for us."

"Okay. Well, I don't really know what to say to that. I actually don't think I agree, but I'm not... maybe at one time...."

I wasn't sure of much at that point. My head felt like it was filled with hydrogen. My thoughts revolved around each other without touching. "Again. Even if everything you say is true, how would any of that pertain to me getting a job, is what I'm wondering." Which was true.

"Attached to the back of your computer, you will find an electronic pen. If you would like to participate in our training program, take that pen and ascribe your signature to the last document in your file." A document appeared onto the screen.

The letterhead read: PISR, 5 Paradigm Dr. 94616-0005. That was it. The body of the document read: I hereby agree to participate in the Special Career Training Program. Information gathered during the course of the program may be used by PISR for research purposes. Signed,

"Upon signing, you will be asked to read the statement aloud while facing your monitor. At which point the sum of one thousand dollars will be automatically transferred to your... Union Bank? ... your Union Bank checking account, and made immediately available to you. We have arranged for this and all further payments to be tax-exempt. You will then be directed to take—"

"I'm sorry could you slow down a little bit? What's that about research? What kind of research am I submitting to?"

"Nothing...sinister, Mister Edwards. Nothing so sinister as... well... as yourself. As a matter of fact, our research will require nothing of you outside of your participation in the various interactive exercises which will comprise your training regimen. You will be asked to bring this laptop computer home

with you—it is yours—and your gloves, which you will use while operating the computer while away from our... facilities. The gloves will also serve to allow you to enter and exit from our facilities. As I'm sure you've guessed, the gloves you have been given are outfitted with certain biometric sensors, and should never be tampered with under any circumstances while you are off-site. Now—"

"Wait a second. I'm confused. Is this the job? A thousand bucks to submit myself—"

"Merely the training, Mister Edwards. I'm sure I explained that. Further compensation will be made in additional thousand dollar payments automatically transferred to your account at the conclusion of every twenty-four hour period in which you are in active participation in our program." Wait. What?

"That's a lot of money, isn't it?"

"No, Mister Edwards. It is not."

"Well." This must be some kind of a trap, I thought. I didn't know any more about the place than I did when I got there. "It's legal, whatever it is you're doing?"

"Perfectly."

"Okay, well can you tell me who you guys are now? Or how this money is tax-deductible? Whether or not this is some sort of a church at least?"

He smiled. "You should understand at the outset that a degree of patience will be required of you with regards to our training. You will be...illuminated as to our...aims and means in a manner consistent with your progress—"

"Okay, if not you guys, then you? Yourself, personally?"

"That, I'm afraid, I also cannot disclose to you at present. Permit me to suggest to you—and I realize the meaning of my suggestion cannot be fully...comprehended by you now—that our mutual purposes will be best served if you are able to perceive...try to follow me here, Mister Edwards... to metaphorize me as a function of, how shall I put it, your own subconscious. Do you follow?"

"No. Not at all."

"No. Of course you don't. Mister Edwards, if you do indeed agree to participate, as I strongly suspect you will, you will be required to set aside an uninterrupted amount of time—say, a quarter-hour, perhaps after your wife retires at night—to be spent in correspondence with me via the laptop you have been designated. It is important—please try to pay attention here—that you assign no particular identity to me during these sessions, as that may... compromise the integrity of our research data. Naturally, you may deny the reasonability, or even the possibility, of this request, as you have undoubtedly already gathered certain perceptions, individualized me in other words, which you may feel yourself unable to... deperceive. But we insist that you try. As you will find, we have certain... applications...that will make this task quite less than impossible. Again, we find that the simplest way for you to furnish us what we require is for you to conceive of our dialogues as... monologue, if you will."

"I beg your pardon? And what exactly will I be furnishing that's worth a thousand dollars a day to you guys? That song and dance about me being, like, some singularity? I think a lot of people must feel that way."

"So we were correct. And yes, those notions are quite common in persons given to certain forms of... introspection. They are generally mistaken. Not always, of course, but generally they are. Now we are by no means completely certain about you, Mister Edwards, but here's what we suspect, and why you are here."

Wait. Didn't I find them?

"What may set you apart, and this is more than we anticipated sharing, may not be so much your relationship with society, but your relationship with... time. We shall see."

I snorted, "Well, that clears things up, right!"

"I would suspect not. But you asked what we should expect of you during your training period. And I have responded honestly. What we expect, all we desire from you, for now, is your time."

There was a predatory flash in the way he said that that made me uncomfortable. "Don't worry, Mister Edwards." – the gloves must've picked up something– "There is no danger. Just the opposite. I grant you, the training process may seem... unusual at times, but you will get used to it. Of that much we should be confident. You enjoy unfamiliar circumstances, do you not?"

"Only to a point."

His eyes became sunny. "So. Do you give it a shot? I'm afraid we have to 'wrap this up' now. Again, assuming y agree, after you sign the form and state your affirmation, you will take this computer with you and exit through the doors by which you entered. You will not reconvene with your fellow candidates today. In the Green Room you will find an escalator. Take that down. It will connect you to a moving walkway, which will convey you a distance to another escalator. Take that up. It leads to a short corridor, at the end of which is a door. Hold out your gloved hand, and the door will open. You will find yourself at the head of a short trail leading to the gate through which you entered this morning. When you reach the gate, hold out your gloved–"

"What if I'm not interested?"

"If you choose not to participate? You will be asked to remain in the Green Room. After a short wait you will be driven to the gate... and released."

"What about my shoes?"

"Your shoes will be waiting for you in an alcove located to the left of the door leading to the exterior pathway. You will leave your slippers there in the alcove."

"And tonight? How do–how would I–"

"Simply turn on your computer. After a moment–"

"Any time?"

"Any time before two AM."

"Well, shit." I looked around. The doors were open. When
＋ happen? Most of my fellow applicants had already
I could have some time to think it over."

"*Time? Take a moment. But you must decide, one way or the other, before you leave this room.*"

I leaned back. On the one hand, the whole experience had me feeling somewhat degraded and somewhat more creeped out. And in my head I had already sacrificed the next day to that night's getting smashed on airplane bottles of Jack Daniel's and sifting through my drawer of note paper scraps and post-its to see if any of those old flashes of inspiration still made any sense. Or maybe I'd just add to the pile, like usual. It sounded like an impossibly good time, actually. But then it occurred to me that they may already have guessed my plans. And they didn't seem to care. But was that a good thing? Could any of it be good? Are there any 'good' organizations willing and able to pay thousands of dollars to people like me? There was, of course, the thousand dollars. A thousand dollars a day was a good thing. For training, though? With no strings attached? It was too good a thing.

"*All we're doing is some team-building exercises, you said? And late-night computer meetings? That's it?*"

"*That's all you would be agreeing to at this time.*"

"*And what about later?*"

"*You will be made aware of any changes to the program as it evolves. You will be asked to do nothing to which you have not already agreed. You may rest assured of that.*"

Creepy.

But: a thousand dollars a day. A thousand dollars a day.

"*And my time away from here is my own?*"

"You are free to do as you please."

"Well." I knew there was no real question as to what I was going to do. I had the internal debate, to make myself feel better. Now–

"Well I'm going to do it."

"Very good, Mister Edwards. Excellent. Now just sign the statement, and read it aloud while looking directly at your monitor."

I did what he told me to.

"Okay...."

"You are free to go. You will be returning tomorrow at nine AM. In the meantime, we will talk for a few moments tonight. Good afternoon, Mister Edwards. And good fortune."

"Uh...okay. Thank you, uh...–"

"Mister Edwards."

"Yes?"

"Or you may call me David, if you prefer."

"Are...—oh! Wait a minute! You mean... You're kidding, right?"

"You are under no obligation to address me by name, Mister Edwards. But should you choose to... no. I'm quite serious. Oh, yes... and please refrain from conversation with your fellow candidates on your way out." I stared at him in disbelief. "And Mister Edwards? You may want to keep in mind that not everyone has been given the same manner of compensation as yourself."

Before I knew it I was outside and alone. The road disappeared around a bend below me and reappeared several hundred feet further down. I could see the fat guy from the interview room stomping his way across a bright patch down there, shielding his face from the sun with one arm. The other arm held what I guessed was a laptop, but his girth caused it to angle away from him in a way that reminded me of a discus thrower. There were no cars, and no one else on the road that I could see. Maybe the place had multiple exits. Who the hell knew? It wasn't me. I lurched stiffly down the hill, slapping the balls of my feet on the asphalt, till I reached the spot where I'd glimpsed the man. There was a clear view to the west from there. The sun was being cupped by the suspension cables of the Golden Gate Bridge, and the sunlight was drifting toward the red end of the spectrum. I must've been in there for hours, I thought; but it didn't feel like any particular amount of time had gone by. It was a funny feeling.

I figured I'd work my way down to the BART station and check the Union Bank ATM that was across the street. I'd hit a liquor store when I got back to my neighborhood. I looked back up the road. I could see no sign of the place I'd just come from. The eucalyptus trees around me had that cat piss smell to them. Ammonia. I had drank about a gallon of water before leaving, and with all the sloshing around it was doing as I sole-slapped my way to the flatlands, a cramp was starting to form like a tropical depression in the area of my kidney. By time I reached the bottom it was at full force. I had my fingers pressed up behind my ribcage. It didn't help. I squinted up the block of faded bungalows on my right, then the block of worn-out apartment buildings in front of me. At the end of that block I spied a moldy-looking white plastic store sign, dimly backlit. There was a 70's era RC Cola logo on it, and—in black-faded-to-grey letters—S&M Liquor. The ampersand was of a do-it-yourself type, a backwards 3 bisected by a lower case L. Fuck it. Get something for the walk.

When I got to the store the metal door grate was locked. A note was pierced by one of its galvanized metal spears. It read: back in 15 minutes. In an apartment above the store I could hear a man chanting. Evening prayers, I guessed. Should I wait? I looked up the street. I couldn't see any signs of opportunity for at least the next couple of blocks. What an annoying note! How was I supposed to know how long ago it was put there? A pair of black teenagers showed up on bicycles and began silently orbiting around the intersection. They were both wearing oversized, bright white t-shirts. Quite possibly bought from that same liquor store. I could see them for sale behind the register. One of the guys rode a beach cruiser with silver strips woven into its spokes in an apparent attempt to simulate auto rims. The other guy was on a girl's ten-speed. They kept circling. I had already stopped, and obviously appeared to be waiting. I felt exposed. The battered, anonymous neighborhood suddenly became a barren plain, and I was a forsaken herd animal with nothing to do but watch as the predators and scavengers gathered around me. A thousand bucks a day. I could rent a car for that. Take a cab at least. I was still holding my new laptop, and I also held a fleece pull-string bag that contained my supergloves. Sky-blue, with PISR printed on it in white block letters. Oh, brother. The chanting *stopped. I relaxed. A few seconds later an old bearded man opened the grate, turned around and shuffled to his perch behind the counter. I walked over to the register and peered beyond it to where the miniature liquor bottles were usually found. Postcards of Yemen hung from a shelf filled with 50ml bottles of E&J Brandy. Ugh. "You got any of those little Jack Daniel's?" I asked, helpfully supplying a bottle measurement with my thumb and forefinger. The man looked at me and shook his head. The combined odors from a dozen varieties of cheap incense disturbed my sinuses. A bouquet of tiny glass tubes—each tube containing a gratuitous cloth-and-wire rose— balanced on the register, partially obscuring the proprietor. "Jim Beam?" "Only this. E and J." He pointed at the brandy. I gave him an "I'm really stretching the old self-loathing here, partner" look and said, sighing, "let me have two of those then I guess." He looked back at me—in the way my grandma might, were I trying to buy bad booze from her—and said "You know, you can buy from somewhere else. I don't mind." Well, I thought, No use pretending here. For the purposes I had in mind, cheap brandy would serve just as well as anything else. Even better, perhaps, more to the point. "No that's all right. I'll take 'em."*

As soon as I got outside I reached into the small brown paper bag and pulled out a bottle. The guys on the bikes were gone, and the sunlight had begun to shift from orange to purplish grey. It had gotten darker in the five minutes I was in the market. I squeezed a bottle from the bag. I twisted the aluminum cap from its seal-ring and poured the brandy straight down my throat. I let out a quiet moan and choked back a dry-

heave. "Oh, Jesus," I said out loud. The stuff was miserable. I made it about a half a block before draining the second bottle. It went down more easily than the first, but hit my empty stomach like corn-sweetened battery acid. "Oh Jesus," again, but with less conviction. I wrapped the bag around the bottles, shoved them into a hedge I was passing, and ran for one step. Out of sight out of mind. My eyelids relaxed, and my senses became slightly less edgy. I covered the next few blocks with pointless determination. I'm going to have to cover this taste up with something, soon as possible, I thought. I kept meeting my reflection in the passenger-side windows of the parked cars I passed; each time I gave myself the same look of chronic disappointment before sheepishly averting my self-gaze. What a pain in the ass this is, I thought. So much work...

I popped into another liquor store on the same block as the bank, and successfully acquired four little bottles of Jack Daniel's. As I quickly emptied the first of those, an escaping air bubble caused some of the liquid to splash from my mouth while a burning rivulet formed to travel, pachinko ball style, or like quicksilver, through my stubble to the collar of my shirt. I thought about it but didn't bother checking to see if the rivulet reached its destination or—like the Colorado River being gobbled by the circuitry of sun-belt sprawl, never to reach the Gulf—got dissipated en route. Dissipated en route. I looked around. It was a busy intersection; cars were peeking out from between buildings, turning on headlights and inching their way across sidewalks full of elderly Laotian ladies being ballasted by reused bags of strange greens. A pack of strangers huddled together in a hive at the bus stop. They waited anxiously—

buzzing into the street by turns—for an accordion-type bus that was stuck, folded into another stop up the street and unable to work itself into the flow of traffic. All of it was acquiring that alcoholic 'things moving in a fluid' quality that, for some reason I never could figure out, made urban navigation so enjoyable. I walked over to the ATM. Shit am I still holding— Okay, yes. Can't forget… I decided to get a hundred dollars cash first; then I'd look at my balance on the receipt. Heighten the suspense. I gave my card to the machine and typed in my PIN with a gust of nervousness. What if I'd been played? What if I couldn't take any money out? I spent all but my last dollar and a quarter on the whiskey. Not enough for BART. I'd have to… I didn't know what I would have to do. Panhandle seventy-five cents? Walk home? A dollar twenty-five would get me one more of those E&J's, I guess…

Then what do you know? Modern banking's Great Affirmation was given: 'Please Take Your Cash'. Card? Check. Receipt? One thousand, six hundred seventeen dollars; eighteen cents. There it was. What a pretty number. $1617.18. That morning I had $726.19 in my account. So with the bank scraping $9.01 off the top (unexplained, of course; and so consistent with that customary obliqueness which should make Byzantium look like a barter faire by comparison), I luxuriated in a vision of the penny being channeled to some robot war chest somewhere before relegating the thought to my 'used flashes' stockpile. There it was. I'll be damned. There it was. I folded up the receipt and put it in a pocket of my wallet. Just in case. Great! Now whatever happens, I win. I got a thousand bucks from those people! And all these people around me? None the *wiser! Look at them. Look at them! Noble, clueless... trying and failing, trying again... You poor people!*

Wishing to make the most of my mania while knowing all too well what tended to replace it, I walked around the building to its parking lot and downed another bottle. I was on top of the world. I shoved that bottle into a bush in one of those curb-reefed streetlight islands, thinking: who cares who sees me? I looked at the glove bag. Who cares what they see? They asked for it. We're all connected like that.

I took this darkly carefree attitude with me onto the BART train. I spent the next few minutes with my forehead pressed to a window that looked like it had been bombarded at high speed by millions of abrasive particles and watched as the chiaroscuro reflection of my face morphed through an evolution of grotesque masks. Every so often I would get disturbed and blink, thereby resetting the spell/process.

When I got off the train the sky was the color of a blood plum. A desert sky got lost in Oakland. The air was still and full in the way it is just after a windstorm, but there had been no windstorm that I knew of. The moon was somewhere—also full, or almost—but I couldn't find it. There was a windy sound coming from the freeways, but I couldn't see those either. Lights were starting to take their time transiting my field of vision, darting and elongating a bit. Falling into my singularity, I mused. But still comfortable. Not the frantic torquing yet. Not yet. I got three more airplane bottles for home, had one for the walk, so...four. Rattling around in my pocket like bamboo chimes. I wrapped them tightly with a bag and tucked that into the inside pocket of my jacket. Oh shit did I...? No, okay. I got them. I enjoyed the eight-block walk in that stage of blooming intoxication, in boyish awe at wonders like over-lapping angles of rooflines silhouetted behind ground-cover-hugged retaining walls, or the multiple-light-sourced shadows falling over the curb. All of it important and remarkable, and me the man to bear witness, etc. Before I knew it I was home. The traveling carnival ground to a halt at the bottom of my stairs. That was awful quick, shit. Was I running? Not pre-pared... I cleared my throat and, holding my eyes open a little wider, walked in. My wife was sitting in the living room, reading. She looked up at me slowly, stared for an excruciating three or four seconds, then returned to her book. I couldn't see the title, only a pen-and-wash drawing of a caged bird on the dust jacket. Something with some shitty man in it, no doubt. I stood there dumbly, at a loss as to how to proceed, then dumbly held out the laptop and bag. Then, finally—

"So I had a weird day," pathetically.

"I'm sure you did." Not looking up, voice dripping with contempt.

"I did, actually. I don't even know where to start—"

"What's that in your pocket?" My pocket? I stared at her damply, damning myself.

"My pocket?"

"Your pocket!" slapping herself on the chest. I just kept staring, trying to feel offended while my chest pocket bulged and a little flap of serrated brown paper peeked out of it like an idiot's handkerchief. I was the convicted man, watching the

judge's mouth for the sentence.

"You know what? Can you just fuck off? Leave me alone."

That was just the sentence I was hoping for. But no. Not yet. Hopelessly, perversely: "You know what?" What? What the hell was I going to say? "Maybe you could try and not be so...I don't know. I mean, maybe—"

"Are you really going to make me get up and leave this fucking room, now?" Her eyes were white hot. I did my punctured-tire impersonation. "No." Deflating..."I'll be downstairs."

"Surprise, surprise." Slinking away, I worked on piecing together a logic that would put the blame on her. It was there, I knew. As usual, I only tried to find it when I was drunk and obviously, directly guilty. When it wouldn't cohere. She should treat me like a man! I thought. So it's not true...so? It could be. But she refuses to cast the spell? The exercise always seemed to be too much trouble when I was sober; to say nothing of pointless and unfair. There's a definition of irony there...

My writing area was in a moldering corner of the garage. It consisted of two filing cabinets supporting a blanket-wrapped length of plywood upon which sat an outdated, beigy computer amidst various scraps and filmy stacks of paper. The space was enclosed on two sides by rough-framed redwood siding that had been marinating in oil and dust for decades. I could see moonlight through the rotten siding boards, and on the studs were black-moldy patches, freshly irrigated from a recent rain. I took out another bottle then got down on my stomach to shove the bag under an old magazine-covered sewing machine console. As a child I used to escape the summer heat by lying out on the garage floor, where the concrete slab always stayed cool. I was reminded of that every time I performed the bag-hiding ritual in my area, and it was soothing; though at times the floor could be so cold there as to feel wet on my cheek, and would eventually begin to hurt. The bag joined some others (also empty-bottled), which I would sneak into the garbage can on the night before trash day. I curled my tongue into a tube and poured the whiskey. It cascaded down my tongue like water in a waterslide to the pool of my throat while I, in an unformed sort of way, imagined myself as young and care-free, riding the chute. For an instant I was ecstatic. Then the instant was over.

I was sitting in a cold garage staring at composting piles of old inspiration in a lot of creativity gone to seed. This is what I was looking forward to? At times like this they struck me as vaguely nauseating, those piles. I would get this feeling while looking at the obsessively rendered, hyperlineated draw-ings made by schizophrenics, for instance (the more techni-cally astute the draftsmanship, the more horrifying, generally), or while watching the chaotic finger movements and darting eyes of some bus-bound, mid-episode unfortunate. It was like a glimpse at a certain dark secret about the nature of things. Inner...brokenness, made manifest in the world of objects, assaulting the necessary illusion of, the possibility for... mod-eration, maybe. Not only man-made manifestations either; obsessive design in nature would give me the same feeling. Too many eggs in one sac, too many sacs... too much going on in that flower if you looked too closely. Too many stars. I sus-

*pect that that was the secret behind the mild horror I would
feel while looking at my own display of uncontained fertility.
Nature itself, unfolding in a realization of... insanity.*

*Ugh. "And that's why you drink, son," I said out loud, in
what I noticed was my father's voice; in what may have been
his father's voice. "Oh kay," in my own voice, "pull out." I
looked at the clock, pulling out. Nine-thirty. Okay. I resolved
to take another stab at organizing my mess of unfocused con-
ceits, honest and half-honest attempts, pretty unfettered sentences, beginnings of epic works; other abortions. 'All these
little bits of proof. Proof that you did not indeed drown in
that pool on that day; that no vehicle rushed in to occupy at
least one of those spots on the wrong side of that mountain
road on which you too often found yourself, trapped in the
back seat as your old man's girlfriend in her whining Subaru
Brat determined to take the straightest possible line...' Sure.
I would do that. Edit. Just like the last time I 'tried', or the
time before that. Edit what? There was no way of organizing
all of these undated abstractions; nor was there any reason
to bother, really. No one ever saw any of the stuff but me. I
would get it into my head from time to time to piece a bunch
of it together into some formalized compendium, with stories
here informing aphorisms there as all parts played off of the
whole, maximizing the profundity and beauty of the work
and—by extension—of my mind. The Dave. But what always
really happened was I'd get drunk and read my own stuff
(again!) and sort it into piles according to however any particular thing struck me at that particular time. Like there might
be a cringe-inducing pile, a good workmanship pile, an 'I*

totally know what I mean!' pile and so on. Then I'd come back to it after a while, on a different drunk, and start all over again. And in the meantime the piles grew. On receipts, photo and printer paper, the margins of old crossword puzzles, notebooks whose purposes tended to devolve from specific to general, post-its... Then there was all the stuff on the computer hard drive, which I would have to treat like an alien, imponderable world if I wanted to get anything accomplished at all. Either that or some mental input overload breaker would trip, and I would end up more or less paralyzed, staring at but unable to comprehend my own words. And trying to transfer those notations and scribbles onto the computer? There was a bleak exercise! Just the thought of it had me on the floor, my hand sweeping like sonar for the heaviest bag, empty bottles rattling like bones. Ugh!

Refortified, I thought: this time it's different. Thousand bucks a day for me. Cause? Because I 'got what it takes'! Whatever it is. That takes... a unique specialness; a special uniqueness. And here was my proof. I'd written things I'd never read before. But then just about everything I'd read before was actually published, whereas...hmmm. There were piles just like mine, unpublished, all over the world. Must be. Maybe we're all working on the same thing! In communal isolation. And ignorance. Writing the Great Unread Thing. Wow; then; nah fuck that. I'd let them read it. Who knows what's useful after all? So what if I couldn't see redemption in it? Someone might! Right? Who was it that said writers should keep in mind that someone might be reading them on their deathbed? Aw well. What are you supposed to do? Lie? Write lies and dress them up as truth? Isn't that the opposite of fiction? That's a sin even an atheist can get behind. Or against, rather. Ah, screw it. Why do I have to be all these other people? Why can't there be any, 'you know, I'm just a dumb writer. Let someone else do the figgerin' part...' Hell, they say; no, they usually write, don't they, that nobody even reads anymore, but then writers are still expected to be responsible for Everything. All right. Fuck it. No more thinking. What have we got here...

It turned out that I was in a narrative mood. My poetry was getting on my nerves. Too much self-conscious meaningfulness; too much romantic hiding in the mist. I became overly aware of a mawkish quality in everything I wrote. I fell into one of those moods where I wasn't too impressed with my work, and I could see the problems with it too clearly; they were too obvious and fatal to be bothered with. I really hated that mood. But there was nothing I could do about it; I never knew how I would respond to myself until I started reading the words. That's all right. Soldier on. There were some little stories I had set apart, some long-ago A-Team. All right, let's see what's wrong with these. Let's see...here's Russ (c. 199–), sitting on the tail gate of his '78 Chevy Luv, throwing acorns at the far curb. Waiting for his coke dealer. Here's Scott (c. 200–), my mooncalf 16-year-old alter-ego, sitting on the curb at a suburban bus-stop, waiting an hour in the heat for a ride to Pasadena. Tiana (c. 199–), elevenish, sitting on another curb, sharpening a popsicle stick on the pavement. Not even waiting. Jesus! Come on, people! All these back stories, but nobody's fucking doing anything. Nothing's happening. Screw these guys. Let's find some action! We got Harvey (c. 200–)

here; what's he up to? Oh yeah, Infinity Fever. Pass. Scott again (c. 199–), wishing he could roll the world into a ball and hold it. Pass. Somebody training his nostrils to smell in stereo. Mmn, nah. Description of a sunrise? A guy trying to use telepathy to get a bee off his face? Lonny and Ronny? Hetrix? (c. 200–): "Darksome…"…ugh… Scott again, with Infinity Fever: "he realized HE was a matter of time…?" Sheesh. Oh, yeah…that dismal old style, of sentences like "…as a wet night may cause a certain blending of parts subject to contact with its effluent medium into a more cohesive and yet not so definable or delineable environment, an arena suitable for elemental interplay inherently symbiotic (due partially to the wonder of that most gregarious of molecule in its gifts for both bonding and transmitting…" just to describe reflection? Oh, Brother. Scott again, saving sow bugs from pincher bugs? A description of a sunset? How about a field? A road (Joe (c. 199–); waiting while moving)? Drunken love-letters to cigarettes? Pee Wee hanging from the semaphore, working arcane equations? No. No. No! Snippets of conversation? Okay. Sure. I'd set those aside. Let's not make this a total waste.

Was I looking for something in particular? No. In general? Well… it had occurred to me that certain themes and subjects orbited around the whole… whatever it was. I had been developing the same ephemeral 'concepts' for all the twenty years covered by that pile of jottings. A boy leaves home, in order to 'leave home.' An adolescent is disillusioned to muteness when he figures out he's been lied to by society. A young man sees himself as an old man looking back at his life, thinking about how precocious he once was. An old man, receiving the mes-

sage that he as a young man had sent to his future, transmitted along the lines of mental notes-to-self like "remember,
the alarm clock is broken and you got to be up by six-thirty,
so, if it's six-thirty, get up," but on a macro scale, over years;
strong initial signal, a path subconsciously kept clear… Little
nibbles at the nature of time, about how perspective shifts with
context, and how it doesn't. And, as far as the writing went,
it hadn't. I'd written the same thing over and over with dif-
ferent-ish words, different structures. It occurred to me that,
since I didn't like anything I had done at that time anyway,
I would try to organize the stuff thematically. Maybe if I saw
everything about 'leaving', say, or 'trains', all together, some
hidden thread of meaning would show itself. Something hard
to get to; something worthwhile, maybe. I got excited by the
prospect, excited enough to grab two more bottles. That left
one. Would I get more? That was a secret I would keep from
myself. No. No way. Be strong. You know what happens. You
don't need to go wandering the streets again, making those
sick rounds. Hitting liquor stores you've stayed away from for
a couple of days. Mixing 'em up, letting the proprietors think
theirs is the only store you patronize, hint at that being the
case. Hmm. Maybe they all know each other. Did they know
my game, and pity me as a lost cause? Or cash cow? No. I
wouldn't do that tonight. Then, of course: Yes. I will probably
go. I plan on being up for a while. The sooner I stop the sooner
the hangover arrives. The sooner I stop the sooner tomorrow
arrives. Yes. No. NO! Yes. Who knows? I gargled another shot,
and threw everything back into a single pile.

The next hours were spent in a blurred, slippery haze. I sat *on the floor and started spreading papers around. Just to over-whelm myself I noted all the different times, all the different contexts and states of mind and body before me. It was like looking at the stars on a dark, clear night, and contemplating how each little dot of light began its trip toward me at a dif-ferent point in time, and how what I'm really looking at is all this time, all these times, converging at me... I began building piles of themes that would evolve into other themes. Time seemed a good place to start, but turned out to be too broad. It all seemed to be about time. So, here's 'time as river'... Okay... rivers. I found some 'memory as river', which branched out (I had the paper physically branching out from the source), other stuff about memory. Plenty. I started reading all this stuff about memory, written at different periods of my life. Dif-ferent ideas as to what it was (memory), or what it was to remember, memories accruing contexts through past remem-brances, and similar stuff. And again, it all seemed to be beating around the same bush, one I'd never managed to iden-tify. I was surprised by that... that murky consistency that still somehow was consistent in all this far-flung production. Some-thing very strange was happening to me. I found myself being transported to the time and place from which each 'piece' ema-nated. Not just imagined myself to be transported, but there. Really subtle things, like atmospheric pressure, or the taste in my mouth as I wrote, all that I was aware of; but there was something more than sensory input I was getting. I was getting everything, all of the context; like, what I was looking for-ward to the next week, or whatever thoughts I couldn't get out of my head, or what bills were overdue at the time. When I got* to: "...*eyes aflutter, he reached beside him and from the top of a large box of fruit pies, grabbed a copy of 'Paradise Regained'*...", *for instance, not only could I smell that the cheese-bread cooking in the toaster oven was about to 'ding', and see the precise shape of that mote-sparkling parallelepiped the afternoon sun was transmitting to my tabletop, and hear the scrape of the outside gate as it dragged against the sidewalk, but I also gathered that I was sick of cheese-bread, and would make sure that for dinner I would get something healthy, maybe a nice soup packet from the health-food store and definitely not let myself be lazy and get pizza slices for dinner; and that the beam of sunlight was then transporting me—but only in a dimly perceived way—to my grandmother's house, when I was five or six, staring at another dusty ray of sunlight terminating at her oversized, amber glass lamp, and that I hoped the person who'd opened the gate and was about to bound into the house was the Mike that would have weed, and not the Mike that was going to want beer. I could sense the contours, my vista on the past and future, what shape the past was making, what was emerging and what was receding and with what character were these things emerging and receding. What Doppler effects, what overlapping influences... It was a very intense experience, one I would call spiritual even, if it wasn't so cold. As to the river pile: I had strayed from whatever focus I had to begin with; there were 'branches' all over, and they were moving away from each other like a universe bound for heat-death. In addition to the more metaphysical suckers on the trunk, there was one for 'train tracks and trains' (via 'rivers of men'), which became 'roads and 'the* road"; then bits on traveling that all seemed to belong connected. Another for actual rivers being actually experienced which went nowhere. Or rather, it went, briefly and out loud to: "why is this all based on rivers anyways?" while the foundation for that branch had me off in another direction. This one started with something I wrote while sitting on an old couch left by the side of some small river in a regional park up North... Boring. I found the first few pages of this piece I had worked on for a rainy season of brown sugary lattes (c. 199–), that (in synopsis) starts with a boy (Mason), standing on a dry, chaparral-covered hillside, overlooking a scene that included a long reservoir being held by a dam. Next to the dam was what looked like some giant obsessive/compulsive erector-set creation, sitting on what looked like a massive pile of dirt. That was the switch garden; I explained how it took the power released by, or inherent to, moving water and transmuted it to a different kind of current (electrical) which flowed by way of cables strung over enormous transmission towers. The line of towers followed the canyon down to the beigish-grey, heat-shimmering valley below, tracing closely the path once defined by the river. The canyon itself was the result of the power now being sent in sort of an obverse manner, to tributaries and then on to silicon capillaries so small that the electrons flow in single file. Meanwhile, above him on the hillside Mason sees the figure of an old man doing something with a disc. He goes to investigate. The old man turns out to be a sort of Ishi, the last of the band of Chumash Indians that used to inhabit the area, and the disc is a polished obsidian mirror, an effigy stone, which the old man is using to map *out, with green and blue pigments, certain star patterns; but in reverse. They get to talking, and the old man tells the boy about how the Chumash saw themselves as living in a 'center world', balancers of power between the Sky People and the Nunasis, who lived in the lower world. The Nunasis were Dark Beings; they were misshapen, evil and harmful. They were also capable of coming to this world—at night, of course—and were known to take the form of humans. It turned out that the old man was a mysteriously anointed shaman charged with the noble and completely dispropor- tionate task of restoring a certain cosmic balance, the devia- tion from which was somehow evidenced by the dam. He explained how he used the mirror image of the heavens to plot out the terrain of the underworld. At this point the air around them begins to vibrate suspensefully. What starts out as an ionic disturbance more felt than heard builds to a deafening electromagnetic C# hum. Here the scene suddenly shifts to the inside of an observatory, where a beautiful young woman, a grad-student/dominatrix type, is busy coaxing a scientist to name a star after her. The rest of the story was missing. "Didn't I finish this?" I whispered, though while reading I sensed clearly what I had intended to happen next. Had in fact hap- pened, somewhere. I was on a dripping park bench in bright polarized November light, everything around me wet and fiercely reflective, the breaking clouds especially...the specter of the future, of days beyond the millennium, having the dim, greyish-blue aspect not of hell but of an older underworld; a hades, or maybe an Elysium... I found some notes that I 'decided', now in High Stupor, somehow seemed to follow, like: (c. 199–) "... those who have developed their sense of will to an extent that it controls the destiny of masses of people and things. They point their mirrors away from themselves, never looking directly at them...", comparisons between the fall of the druids and ancient Germanic magical techniques, mirrors and the destruction of collective memory and PRECOGNITION, an explication on the superstition regarding mirrors sucking the souls of whomever looks into them, the use of mirrors to sell ourselves to ourselves and, as with large glass office buildings, to DRAW MASS GAZES. Tezcatlipoca—the God of the Smoking Mirror—and its association with a sacred lineage of people. The Black God of the north, god of witchcraft and black magic. The God of time, ancestral memory, and the embodiment of change through conflict who, by looking into his mirror, controls the deeds of men. Electronic mirrors, mirror imagery on lapidary stone in the Mayan tomb of Lord Pacal the Great, and finally: (c. 199–) "...look, you got all these wonderful ruins to play in, yeah beautiful old stuff we don't really have too much use for anymore—tell you what; let you in on a little secret here... NOW is your last remaining relation to time, regardless, unfortunately, of how it suits you. As you may have read, the workings of collective memory have been fully mapped out. These processes can be accelerated in any given case to where by mere contextual injection any action can be altered almost immediately to one suiting us. Therefore your past is nonexistent—rather, irrelevant—except with respect to your own private entertainment which, of course, is no secret to us. [illegible]. But of course we [illegible] that's the whole idea, and it's easy to do. So if you feel subversive you know, go ahead. The ratios have been stabilized [illegible] got your place to fill as far as we're concerned, and you can fill your [illegible]." When did I write that?*

It was at this point that my stupor began losing altitude; the here-and-now reasserted itself, and the more prosaic thought processes marched in to reestablish their predominance. Another revolution put down. I was starting to think more clearly but I was at the same time no longer capable of capturing, of sensating the contextual essence of what I read. The last bit of writing no longer seemed to belong where it was. But, like waking from a dream that immediately slips from memory, I snatched enough from the void to know something was there. It was quiet; I could tell that Hope was asleep. The room was a mess; and it was cold; colder, it seemed, than it should have been. The whiskey was gone. All drunk up. At some point, presumably in order to keep warm, I had put on the gloves. They really were comfortable and warm. But it gave me the creeps that I couldn't remember putting them on, or how long I had been wearing them. Not often did I black out and back in the same night. Usually I had until morning before that bill came due. Perhaps this was a sign of advancement, and not the good kind. And, as usual after drunk driving down memory lane, I felt a little banged up; sore. Suddenly I remembered my teleconference. I didn't look at the clock. I knew that if I waited any longer it would be too long; the exact time didn't matter. I grabbed the computer and threw it open. There was that short electronic crackle; then the machine ramped up with an ascending turbine-like whir. The black screen became, for an instant, somehow blacker, then bam! There was the face of my new employer, or my new employer's representative, or whoever the hell he was. I couldn't tell if it was my sloppy vision, but his features seemed a little softer, not quite so stony. Maybe he'd been doing a little tippling himself. "Ah, Mister Edwards. Perfect timing." I looked at the clock then. Eleven eleven. "You've been busy, I see." There was something different in his voice as well. He sounded extremely relaxed; not loaded exactly, but more like someone enjoying the effects of tryptophan at the end of a long Thanksgiving Day. Doubting that I could pull off professional, I decided to be familiar:

"So are you just like, waiting there—"

"Not waiting. But here."

"First of all I got to say," I said, as soberly as possible, "there's just no way I can call you David."

"Mister Edwards, please. Suit yourself. Point one seven."

"I beg your pardon?"

"Your blood alcohol content. Point one seven. Falling. You were wondering—"

"Wait. You can read my mind now?"

"The gloves are a great help. They're equipped with… sensors. You must have guessed—"

"Yeah but—"

"Mister Edwards, try not to jump to any…illogical conclusions. Of course I cannot hear your thoughts. That is impossible." Did I sense a shade of regret? "But at the same time that is not a condition necessary for me to…read your mind, as it were. Consider, Mister Edwards. One can only read what is written. If you will." His eyes scanned the space around me. "You write words, Mister Edwards. Though...your production has slowed a bit?" I looked around as well and, sitting there Indian-style, pulled my shirt out over my crotch. "Words. Yes, look at them all. What you've done with them. My. Could you tilt the monitor slightly, so I can get a good look?" I did. "MmHmmm."

"Okay... So...?"

"You received the bank transfer."

"I did." I waited. "And that's great—"

"Tomorrow morning you will be introduced to your co-respondents. A number of you will indeed succeed in your... training. But not all. I sincerely hope you are one of those who do. I would urge you then to act with determination and clarity of mind, as there may be difficult—"

"What? The drinking? You know, I could—"

"Mister Edwards," cooing again, "patience. That is not your problem."

I was starting to get tired, weak, and annoyed. I needed food. "Do you think you could be a little more cryptic?"

He smiled. "Mister Edwards. You write. You... explore... with language. I'm surprised you don't understand," looking back at the paper schematic surrounding me, "You must have heard it a thousand times. Nothing is cryptic; there are only the... alphabets... you have never learned."

I sighed.

"So is that it? I mean, I don't mean to be rude but are we just chatting here? Talking unlearned alphabets? And how you can kind of read my mind?"

"I reiterate: only what is—"

"I know. I heard you. That's great," trailing off, "clever."

"Mister Edwards?"

"Nothing. I apologize, but I really need to get something to eat. Shouldn't we, don't we need to talk about—"

"Mister Edwards, why do you suppose you never finish any of these," sweeping the room with his eyes. Mine followed.

"I don't know. I get to a point and then—"

"Perhaps you understand more than you think you do, Mister Edwards. Perhaps you realize that...that one must be careful what one writes. That in some...in some way, what one writes all does seem to be...true. We have come to understand that nature abhors surprises. That our world and everything it contains is—indeed, must be—expressed. Have you never sensed that? Consider. Rather, let me give you a simple example. Earlier today, you hinted at your opinion of certain Biblical interpretations. While you might mock those who live in expectation of, shall we say, the actualization of the written prophesies of John the Revelator; dismissing them, perhaps, much as you did during one particular Community College 'rap session' held in April of 198–, as: "a horrific, base, primitive and bigoted creation... a senseless, destructive hallucination..." perhaps your underlying indictment of Revelation is not that it is a lie, or even the ugly product of a troubled mind, but rather *that it is…irresponsible? That, having been written, it can not but be true? That there are no lies? You understand that; don't you, Mister Edwards? It is clear that you do. It's written all around you."* I looked him in the eyes, or rather I looked at the eyes on the screen. They rolled and dipped, but stayed still. Sickening. I blinked to refocus. It was true. My characters all at some point stopped acting. They would gather their identities only to a certain point; generally, just to when they attained a volition separate from my own and, strangely, when they should have been able to 'write themselves'. Their first, and only, demonstration of free will was invariably a choice to stay put, suspended in medias res. It wasn't that I could think of nothing for them to do or nowhere for them to go. I had written many clever plots full of causes and effects. But the plots always remained oddly uninhabited. It was as if my 'creations' all had one thing in common: they would refuse to go, to do. They would not let it be written. It was as if they knew…

"Yeah." I'd never looked at it that way before.

"Not so cryptic. Simple. Frustrating, though; I would think."

"Impossible." I felt like, I sounded like someone talking to a shrink, though I'd never actually gone to a shrink before. I'd imagined it, though; many times.

"You know something, Mister Edwards?"

"Hmm?" My eyes were watering. I wanted to explain things, but I couldn't. My forehead felt like it was tied to a water balloon.

"Not impossible. Maybe what you're doing here," again with the sweep of the eyes, "is just what you think you are doing."

"Can you please—"

"Let's assume that you set out on this task of yours tonight in the hope of reaching some revelation which might enable you to transcend your stunted narrative. Of conjuring a burning bush moment, if you will."

"Sure."

"Look around you. What do you see?" I looked at the paper form I'd created; the thematic generality of the 'trunk' splaying, branching out, realizing into specifics.

"What?" Uh…huh! Yeah, it did— "A bush?" He smiled again. "Are you suggesting that I burn—"

"I'm not suggesting anything. I'm merely… reading. Rather, we're reading. Mister Edwards, get your food, and some rest. Remember. Nine o'clock. Tomorrow promises to be a long day."

"Yeah, okay. I've got to tell you, these chats of ours really take it out of me."

He kept smiling.

I woke up the next morning on the basement floor, cold and slightly damp from the concrete condensation that had formed overnight. I had been sleeping with my arms wrapped around my chest, and as I came to, it was with an unpleasant sensation wherein any point of contact from one part of me to another—whether it was arms across torso or, as I masochistically confirmed, fingertip to fingertip—came with a sickening *reflection of mass. That is, I felt gross. Gross as in I was taking up space; I was a thing coming into contact with another thing; this other thing also being me, and also having the same nervous experience. It was accompanied by that creepy 'can't make a fist' feeling, felt over my whole body. I literally shook that feeling off, then stood up and walked my fingers from my temples to the top of my skull, feeling along the furrow where, when I wasn't so dehydrated, I could feel my blood flow. I took a couple of deep breaths before looking at the clock. Eight-oh-five. "Well, that's good," I said, looking on the good side of sleeping on a slab of cold concrete; that it did not let me oversleep. I marched upstairs and turned the coffeemaker back on. Hope had already left. God, I thought, how does she do it? Why does she do it? She's got her good job, good solid education behind her, all these good decisions in her past. And then she's got me. I must be looking a lot like a lapse in judgment to her; I know that's how I would feel. But she leaves me some coffee...*

It was hard to make sense of it. "...that problem won't be yours..." Is that what he said? What was that? I took a shower while the coffee reheated, drinking no less than twenty full swallows of warm water straight from the showerhead. I brushed my teeth, scrubbed my tongue, chewed up and swallowed some toothpaste. My tongue felt like a blimp in a hangar. That feeling again. Ignore it! Get moving! Visine. Hat...no hat. I combed my hair with my fingers. Shit! I dragged myself to the dryer and opened the door. My clothes had been sitting there since the morning before and they had gotten deeply wrinkled. I pulled all of them out except for a pair of fading black chinos and a maroon button-down shirt. I cranked the machine to Cotton and stood there watching it as if it were a toaster. A sketchy outline of the night before started forming in my mind. I clearly remembered starting to go through my writings; then being drunk. Lights and images darting around in the air, splashing; lights tracing, streaking by like sardines, carrying familiar things. No details, of course. And just little bits of the conversation I had over the computer. But those memories, such as they were, were suspiciously fantastical in their nature, and I had the feeling that I must have dreamt at least some of what ran through my mind. Well, Christ. Again I would wait for today to tell me about yesterday. What a lousy way to gather information! "Well, there you go." I dressed quickly. It was almost eight thirty; it felt like it was taking five minutes to get through a thought. I downed a cup of coffee overcooled by too much half and half and got myself outside.

Stevie unburdens himself of the recorder pack, unmasks and sits down on the words he's just read.

"Enough of that," he says out loud as he looks down at the list of impressionistic snippets he's jotted down:

written first then transcribed?Waitingtoo much detail for?

interviewer CREEPY!

legal?

definitely a drunkused to be a teacher

$1000.00 / day!

so what?
way too wordy for?
wannabe writerwriting about his own writing
Reservoir
????????!!!!!
Self-indugentneurotic
paranoid (good reason? what is job?)
CIA? corporate? mystic? identity thief?
Jesus complex?
word made flesh
Nunasi
Can relate to time stuffinsanity stuff?
TOO MANY
Doppler effect for events!
Was just thinking that 2nite!
name of company?
who is this guy?

That's all I wrote—Stevie thinks with alarm—in how many hours? I just blew it. There's hardly anything here... He rereads the page. This disjointed list might be helpful to the chief, but from where Stevie stands now it's sure hard to see how. It doesn't say anything. It's nonsense. If anything, it blurs Stevie's own memory when he reads it over.

When he started he really thought he was focused, and really expected he was about to do a bang-up job of things. Of course in retrospect he can recognize that what felt like concentration to him then was just the speed improvising with his synapses; noodling. It occurs to him now that once he got into it, and settled into a rhythm, along with forgetting to take real notes he forgot to keep taking pops. Now he's exhausted, sleepy even. He considers taking one now. He pulls out the bullet and looks at it, flips it over like an hourglass. Imagine how that would be, to be some middle age dude, lying to his wife and himself because even after all that time being alive he still can't get it together. No, thank you. If that were me I think I'd just kill myself. Why bother at that point?

It is you.

It's a feeling, more than a voice. It comes up from somewhere deep within him, somewhere not only beyond words and such, but probably the target area at which those things are trained. And speed'll get you there–he snaps his fingers into the dead-of-night air–like that. Funny, Stevie kept noticing little parallels between himself and the writer while he was dictating, but now has a hard time remembering what they were exactly. Well, the doing a weird new job-thing, for one...

"Can relate to time stuff"

What was that? It was something...

Stevie sighs heavily and returns the bullet to his pocket. Being tired isn't so bad right now. Then there's tomorrow. Got to stop borrowing from the future, Stevie; you know It'll be broke when you get there.

Was that you?

Stevie inhales deeply; he fills himself up to the throat with clear, still air. He lets the breath stall for a second, imagining a roller coaster at the top of the chain lift, then lets it out slowly. He savors his slowing pulse and the smoothness of his exhalation. He tilts his head back, lets his jaw go slack and breathes some more. He finds a satellite and follows it until it vanishes into the light of the setting moon. There is no wind at all, and not a solitary ripple of sound reaches this particular spot. The mountains, backlit now, look to Stevie like they're receding—like a giant, slow, and white-capped wave passing in some open sea. Making its way to some western shore, at last to break...

8

Stevie wakes at dawn to find himself slouched over the handlebars of the ATV. He clenches his sleepy fists and examines some indentations the handlebars left on his forearms. He stretches, casually scanning the area around him. He scans the area a second time, this time more intently. Okay. Where the fuck's all my shit? His stomach tightens.

"What the fuck?" he asks aloud. He reaches into his pockets. Empty. He pats his pants. Empty.

"What the fuck!" he repeats.

Not that I necessarily want any now—mid-whirl, in the thought equivalent of a whisper, while looking around for the third time—but still, where the hell is it? And how did I wake up here? This isn't where I remember... He looks off to the north, where the evanescent pink of predawn has just this instant been supplanted by gaudy yellow sunlight. He walks, then jogs off in that direction, still careful about where he steps. Where's the recorder?

"Shit shit shit shit..."

He sees something glint and runs toward that thing. As he gets closer he sees that it is the recording device, sitting just where he left it.

"Aww... thank God!" There's the microphone, lying across the respirator's upturned rubber facepiece; there's the large smudge on the lakebed where he must have fallen asleep. There's the spent reel—filled under that enormous moon halo that served for him as a celestial reflection, or archetype even, to his flashlight beam—tucked into a cracked vinyl pocket. All shadowed surfaces are covered with the merest of films; the fallout from that moon ring. Stevie bends down over the machine and flips the toggle to Rewind. It rewinds. He unsnaps, peels back the padded vinyl sheath and examines the back of the case. 10 D batteries. No shit. That's pretty good. Stevie turns around and sees a set of footprints (his own) heading back toward the ATV. I must've really been out of it, he remarks to himself. He tries to remember. He sees no sign of the plastic bullet. He stands up, spins around, swings the pack onto his back and spins around again. Nothing. He circumnavigates the spot searching for some magic perspective, some revelatory shift in shadow or light. Nothing doing. The lakebed could be the surface of Mercury; how naked it seems, so inhuman in this light. Stevie retraces his unrecollected steps, swinging the microphone back and forth like a metal detector. To keep his focus, Stevie does his best to ignore the fresh words materializing like a scroll in his right periphery; even so he reaches the ATV without finding anything more than the occasional lost, doomed brine fly.

Stevie unloads his pack and takes a seat. He hesitates at the ignition and considers retracing his steps yet again, while his confusion and frustration merge into something resembling rage. It can't just be gone! It's got to—

"Bah!" he barks out loud (a self-directive translating to "stop thinking for a fucking minute and get gone!"), starts up the machine and gets moving. He opens the throttle. The engine noise tears at the silence like a predator. The print-filled bay quickly curls away, the volcanic promontory swinging across it like a closing gate. When he finds himself in the open Stevie closes his eyes and lets himself feel the clean morning air buffet his face and chill his hands. It's a singular thrill; of course Stevie knows nothing can happen, since there's nothing but trona in all directions, but—as he tells himself about twenty seconds into the exercise—you can never be a hundred percent sure, right? Ninety-nine-point-nine, sure; but never a hundred. He holds his nerve like he might hold his breath underwater; to the limit of his comfort and then just beyond. When he finally opens his eyes Stevie sees that he could have gone many times as long as he did. Cartago is still well off in the distance. Stevie can just make out the exhaust plumes rising from a pair of warming semis parked alongside the highway. The corrugated metal quonset huts by the old potash plant glow with reflected light. There's someone walking. It looks like they're making their way across Lake Street. Now whoever it is appears to have stopped, and appears to be looking in his direction.

The air is quickly heating up. Stevie finished his water sometime during the night. The relentless push of air is drying out his eyes and causing them to itch. He's having to blink every other second or so. The blinking makes it hard to keep a focus on the stationary figure on the far shore, but as he moves gradually closer he's able to glean that whoever it is holding their left hand across their forehead, like an awning, in order to see him more clearly… and in their right hand, some kind of sack. Is that Candy? The figure is still too far away for Stevie to make out even char- acteristics as easily discernible as sex or approximate age, but something—the shape, maybe?—tells him anyway… It is Candy. He can see that now. She doesn't wave. She stays perfectly still until he gets close enough to see her eyes, then starts wading out towards him. The sunlight reflects both black and bright from her black and straight as a nun's habit hair. She's wearing Levi's and a T. Rex t-shirt, and a pair of boy's tennis shoes without socks. She stops at the same creosote bush where he'd parked the ATV while waiting for his man, and steps into its shade. Stevie lets go the throttle and coasts in the last hundred feet wishing he had something to put in his mouth, along with something caffeinated to wash it down with. Then–like some kind of genie or something–Candy reaches into the bag and pulls out a plastic thermos.

"Hey Stevie," she says in a way that also says "I expect information", as he cuts the motor. "Ice coffee?"

"Ice coffee!" Stevie cheers. "No way!" He faces her with a curious look to match the one she's giving him. "What are you doing out here?" he says. What time is it?"

"Almost seven. I came out to see what you're doing out here. Here." She hands Stevie the thermos and the bag. Inside the bag is a half-loaf of pull-apart bread.

"Oh my God. Sweet!" Stevie says (did he just say 'sweet'?). "Let me- just–" Stevie unscrews the cup from the thermos, unscrews the thermos lid and pours himself an ice cube-splashing cupful of coffee. He takes a big swig. "Ahhh. Thank you. This is, um, obviously a surprise. What'd you say you're doing out here, again?"

"I asked you first."

"Should be ask first tell first–" Stevie tears off a piece of bread and lifts it to his mouth "–don't you think? I never under–"

"I heard you take off last night, going out on this–" She points to the ATV. "I didn't know what it was at first. When my brother said something about babysitting you out here yesterday I figured it was you. But then he wouldn't tell me anything else. When I heard you again this morning..." she points to the thermos, "I made that coffee last night, so–"

"It's good."

"Is it?"

"You want some? Here." Stevie offers up the plastic cup, but Candy shakes her head.

"That's okay. It's your turn now. So what's the big secret?"

"That's what he said? Babysitting?"

"Something like that. Are you trying to change the subject, Stevie?"

"Subject? Oh, uh, well I'm not supposed to, what's the word? Divulge. I'm not supposed to divulge what I'm doing, although I guess your brother is free to–"

"Wait. You're–" Candy rolls a ball from the bread in Stevie's hand– "you're working for the PD? Like actually working working?"

"Just temporarily. If it was..." Stevie huffs, "believe you me I'd... love to tell you. Only thing is Chief Hill, and your brother–"

"What, are you, like, undercover?"

"Hardly."

"Wow, how do you like that? There really is a secret. And I thought I was joking. You're really not going to tell me?" She's smiling, and the mountains are reflected in her eyes. "Something actually interesting happens and–"

"It's not that interesting, actually..."

"Yeah right. I can tell it's something, Stevie. Just by the way you're acting I can tell." Candy peers into Stevie's eyes and narrows her own just a little. Stevie figures he must look particularly stricken, because after a second or two Candy furrows her brow (making her gaze for an instant even more penetrating) and lets out a short, friendly laugh.

"Oh, don't worry about it, Stevie. Seriously; if it makes you uncomfortable; that's not what I meant to do that at all. I just came out here... I was just bored, and curious; thought it would be fun to see what you were up to." She takes another chunk of bread, using both hands. "You know–" she takes a bite, "you know you'd be curious too."

These last words create a shift in Stevie's perspective,

or at least cause him to question it. Why exactly wasn't he telling her again? Wouldn't Candy be the first person with whom he'd choose to share an interesting and secret thing, and the last person he'd choose to be the first one he wouldn't tell? It's probably true, what she says about it making no difference. And he didn't exactly swear an oath or anything...

While these thoughts work their way around Stevie's increasingly unsupportable resolve, Candy wipes her hands on her pants and says:

"Well that was fun, but I think I'd better get home." She pauses and says: "I'm meeting with someone from DeVry before work today."

"DeVry?" It takes a second to sink in. "Seriously?" Stevie pauses again. "Nuh uh."

"Not really. But I am expecting a call. You can bring the thermos by the cafe any time. If I'm not there you can just leave it at the podium there. By the way, I do think it's cool that you're–"

"What are you doing tonight, Candy? Do you know?"

"I haven't really thought about it. Why?"

"Well, maybe when you get off work, if I go– if I do– maybe– I don't know–if you want to come with me–"

"You don't have to do that, Stevie. I don't want you to... to compromise whatever it is you're doing on my account. But come by and tell me all about it when you can. I'm sure it's fascinating."

"No. I really want to–I want you to come–I mean, it's not that big a deal, I don't think. Maybe just think about it–and I can come by your work this afternoon to drop this thermos off–and see if maybe–maybe if you change your mind… or you can decide then if you want to…"

"Okay. Let's just see. I really do have to go, though. See you, Stevie." Candy takes a couple of steps backward, still facing Stevie. "I'm glad–" she begins, before turning and walking away. Stevie is left there wondering how it ended up after all that with him beseeching her to do the very thing that she seemed to want in the first place. Go figure with that one. Still, once he's parked the ATV in his aunt's garage and gone inside; after he's flopped down on the matted loveseat and closed his eyes, Stevie's feeling pretty pleased with himself.

* * *

"Steven? That you?" Stevie opens his eyes.

"Yeah," he yells. "Hi auntie. I'm just resting for a minute." About a minute goes by. From the back bedroom:

"Come here, Steven."

Stevie pulls himself up, walks down the stained hallway, grabs the last doorknob, turns it and holds it like that.

"Don't let the cats out!"

"I know." Stevie opens the door just enough to slide through, while using his legs as a sort of moving wall against which an aggressive and well-orchestrated feline escape attempt once again comes to nothing. The cats beat a retreat. "Watch the water," Aunt Jody says. Right on cue Stevie kicks the bowl. The bowl sloshes off in a short zigzag pattern from the middle of the room to under-the-bed, tossing off water with each change of direction. "Jeez, Auntie. It's so dark in here." Stevie looks over at his aunt. She's half-laying, half-sitting on a pile of pillows. Her dingy cotton nightgown merges with the sheets. A paperback lay open next to her. Its glossy, embossed cover tells Stevie it's another one of Aunt Jody's romance books without him even having to read the title. Where's she get those things from?

"Don't turn on the light. I've got one hell of a migraine."

"Again? Maybe you shouldn't be reading in the dark."

"I can see fine. Why didn't you tell me you weren't coming home last night?"

"Uh–, I didn't know until–"

"Listen to me, Steven. You might be eighteen but that doesn't mean I'm not still your aunt."

"I know."

"You've been off somewhere almost every night lately. Steven, are you listening to me?"

"Mmhmm."

"It's ever since you got into that trouble. You better not have been lying that that was just that one time. It's been almost every night since that you've been off somewhere."

"..."

"You got a girlfriend you're not telling me about? Ever since you took that test. I swear, Steven, I'm starting to wish I never agreed to that. And what ever happened to signing up for community college like you told me you were gonna? That was two months ago."

"I know. It's just that... it's all the way in Ridgecrest, though. How am I even supposed to get there? Actually, auntie, that reminds me of something–" She interrupts:

"Honey, would you do me a big favor? Turn on that air conditioner for me?"

Stevie walks over to the swamp cooler.

"You mean this one?"

"No, the other one. Smartass. Then come sit over here by me."

Stevie presses his face as the paddlewheel churns into action. Warm, humid air blows through the slits.

"Let me go turn on the hose real quick," he says. "The water's hot."

"It'll cool down. Come here." Stevie turns toward the bed but remains standing. Jody Comstock reaches across her body and, like a crane, slowly lifts a glass of water from the end table and transports it to her lap. "So let me guess... Honey would you grab those pills for me off the dresser there? Yeah, those ones.... You were about to tell me you need to get your driver's license, right?"

"How'd you know that?"

"Your new boss, from what I hear. He gave me a call last night. Nice man. That Jim Hill. He told me he's got you working on something. Some dictation, is that right?"

"That's pretty much it. Just, like, temporary work."

"He told me they want to put you on the books."

"Yeah, but—"

"But nothing."

"Whoa." Stevie holds his breath and waits to find out where she's going with this.

"I'm not stupid, Steven."

"Who ever said you were—"

"None of your family's stupid. Is or was. That's never been our problem. And you know, you're not stupid either."

"I know that, Auntie."

"Maybe you know. Don't you want anyone else to know?"

"Yeah," Stevie says, a whine creeping into his voice.

"You going to get a job over there at the police department of all places, just so you can stick around here and keep me company? That your big plan?"

"Well, honestly Auntie... that really isn't my plan."

"Because you don't got a plan. You better get busy coming up with one, Steven. You're not going to be eighteen forever."

"Auntie?"

"Steven? I'm serious. No more excuses."

"Auntie Jody? I'm sorry. Do we have to talk about this right now? I really was working last night, and I really am super tired."

Aunt Jody takes a long breath.

"I just don't want you... drifting off into something that's not you. You understand? You don't need to be ashamed of who you are."

"I know."

"That Jim Hill said he helped you with getting your license taken care of. Said he even let you drive his truck around to practice for the test, and you did real good. I thought that was really nice of him, to do that. Now if I was to let you use the Maverick, you got to promise me again you'll enroll yourself into school. I mean first thing."

"Right off the bat I'd say that sounds great, Auntie. But can we talk about it a little later?"

"You always liked animals, Steven. Go study animals. Remember how you always wanted to be a veterinarian?"

"That was when I was ten."

"What, so that don't count?"

"That's true..."

Stevie smiles and glances around the dim room. The dusty bureau, the vanity with its model city of abandoned make-up containers, the walls... at some point in the distant past Aunt Jody must have professed a fondness for lion cubs, because ever since Stevie could remember the default

Christmas or birthday gift for his aunt was just anything with a lion cub on it. Porcelain and pewter figurines, bobbleheads, stuffed animals and wind-up toys, framed prints. A thought strikes Stevie. She probably didn't choose one thing in this room herself. Then again, there is that wood carving–life-size and delicately rendered–of two frolicking cubs that hangs above her bed. He always wondered where that came from...

"I'm gonna go lay down."

"Come give me a smooch."

Stevie leans over the bed and gives his aunt a kiss.

"You'll always be my favorite nephew." An old joke; he's her only nephew. "If you turn on the TV keep it low. I've got to get this migraine to go away."

"Kay."

Stevie slips out the door. If she only knew, he thinks. Then: if she only knew, what? Who knows what she really knows.

* * *

Guy grabs a spade from the tool shed and carries it, cement-caked-blade-side up, to a steaming patch of saturated dirt back behind the hotel. He scoops out a few shovelsful then reaches down and pulls out the pair of jeans along with the front half of a pendleton-style shirt he picked up years ago for the Bishop Mule Days parade. Both articles are caked with dark volcanic mud; which may be what's holding them together now, as both articles also got thoroughly worked over with a belt sander the night before. Guy holds them up to the sun admiringly, like a prize fish. He carries them over to a rusted old T-bar clothesline anchor, gives them a good whack against the pole and drapes them over the horizontal bar to dry.

Jeanne appears from the other side of the building. She's got on some turquoise overalls, and she's smoking a Vantage. Her long, straw-grey hair is pulled back tight. She peels a spider web from her handsome face and says "Which one you want to use, babe?"

"Maybe put some primer on that petting zoo one?"

"That's the one I got out." She disappears back around the corner of the bungalow.

Of the two of them, Jeanne Valleroy has definitely got the harder features. More than one person has remarked that she bears an uncanny resemblance to Bruce Dern, the actor. Guy is crazy about her. Has been from day one. To him there's no mystery why. Jeanne likes a happy man; in Guy's experience a rare trait not to be confused with the more common 'likes making a man happy' which by definition requires liking an unhappy man. Even better, she enjoys herself besides. Those silver, lashless eyes of hers can go softer than velvet; you better believe it. She's sweet as maple pudding when she wants to be, but she won't fake it for anybody. Most of all she's up for anything. Always has been. She'll lead the charge, too. And she can dance like *Salomé*. *Crisse de calisse*, can she do that!

Guy stomps the mud from his boots and walks through the back door and into the kitchen. He pours himself a glass of tap water and sets it down to settle. Then he opens the sink window and peers down the wall to where Jeanne has already leaned the old sign. She's slopping onto it a heavy coat of primer.

"Not so thick, maybe," Guy says. "It takes so long to dry."

"Hey! You got your project. This is my project."

"You want for me to—"

"I don't want you to anything. How do they look?"

"The clothes? I think good. We'll see."

Guy keeps watching. After a minute, Jeanne stops painting and looks up.

"Go on! Get out of here, would you?" She laughs. Guy winks, gives a squat thumb-up, retracts his head from the window and heads out back to finish his compound cloud-buster.

* * *

Keith and Lee, ignoring the 'Please Wait to be Seated' sign, help themselves to the first available window booth. The previous diners' dishes have yet to be cleared. Lee stares at them, heavy-lidded. Keith watches Lee. A stretched peloton of black bikers grumbles by on the 395.

"How'd you already wake and bake?"

"Huh?"

"I haven't let you scrape my pipe yet," Keith elaborates. "How'd you smoke out already?"

"You remember the last resin you gave me?"

"You told me you smoked that shit up last week."

"I did."

Keith lets Lee's comment sink in.

"Fucking Lee, man. You're a fucking mutant. Resin resin?"

Lee lets Keith's comment sink in, in a way, before replying.

"Mutanto," he says at last. Keith shakes his head.

"Damn, you're a stupid motherfucker."

Lee smiles proudly.

"It's all good."

He picks up a menu.

"What are you gonna get?"

"You said you'd buy me anything I wanted."

"I know. I'm just trying to figure out what I should get."

"Bitch, what do you think? We're sharing?"

"I want to make sure I get my money's worth, that's all."

"What? That doesn't even make any fucking sense. Where'd you get money from anyway?"

"I scrounged it."

"You scrounged it?"

"From my mom's."

"You're fucking buying my resin with your mom's money? Damn, dude. Does she even know you took it?"

"I'm not buying your resin. I'm buying you breakfast and you're letting me scrape your pipe. There's a difference."

"How old are you? Like thirty?"

"Stop trying to...fucking... ruin my high."

Candy approaches their table. Just at the last second she turns slightly and walks by. "Be with you guys in a minute," she says absently. Candy's all business all of a sudden. She doesn't look at them or even slow down. Her eyes are on the front doorway that's presently being occupied by Raylene. Ray walks in, snaps her purse closed, lifts her gaze, and immediately detects more than the usual degree of dysfunction. Candy reaches Ray just in time to absorb a steaming interrogation.

"What the hell's going on around here, Candy? Why are these dishes not getting bused?"

"Geronimo–"

"Where's Eduardo?"

"He's in back. Washing dishes."

"Why? Where's Gerry?"

"He hasn't come in yet."

"Are you shitting me? Did he call? Where's his number?"

"No, no, and it should be in the book."

Keith and Lee listen in as the workplace drama unfolds. Lee makes a feline clawing motion with his hand while Raylene pulls a binder and telephone from the lectern shelf. She finds the number and dials. While she waits for an answer, she covers the mouthpiece, points to Keith and Lee's table and mouths: "get this cleaned up."

Candy looks at Lee, then Keith, then the dishes. She bites her tongue and starts stacking while Lee shrugs, Keith winks, and Raylene, speaking in a strained semi-whisper, accosts Gerry in boss-Spanish:

"¿Dónde demonios está, Geronimo? ¡Son las diez menos cuarto!"

…

"Mm hmm."

…

"Por lo que no vienes a trabajar. Mm hmm. Mm hmm…"

…

Candy finishes all the stacking and piling before acknowledging Keith and Lee.

"I apologize for the wait, guys," she recites to them as Ray hang up the phone, "and I'll be right back to take your orders."

"He quit."

"Huh?"

Raylene is standing next to Candy now, at Keith and

Lee's booth. Now she's talking more or less to them all.

"Go tell Eduardo to come out here, Candy. I'm sure he knows someone who could use a paycheck. On second thought, never mind. I'll go do it."

"Did Gerry say why he quit?" Candy asks, hoisting the dishes, saucers and cups from the table.

"He was talking so fast I couldn't catch half of it. Something about a sister in Frisco? Or a cousin, maybe? I don't—effing know." Raylene removes the remaining water glasses, silverware and napkins herself.

"Slice of pie on the house for these two," she says, addressing Candy's backside. She follows Candy into the kitchen.

"There you go!" Lee says after they've gone.

"There I go what?"

"Didn't you hear what she said?"

"What? Dishwasher? You must be high. I ain't no fucking Mexican."

"Free food."

"Fuck that noise."

"Well okay. Why don't you run for fucking mayor then?"

Keith points at his chest, as if referencing the breastbone of the stylized skeleton printed on his hoodie.

"Bitch? Do I look like a–"

"You're the one who said–"

Keith blows a straw wrapper at the window.

"Fucking Stevie!"

"Stevie again. What's he got to do with it?"

"There he goes. Lookit." Keith point the straw towards a squat silhouette off in the distance; a black pixel floating across a field of light. Lee turns and looks. Candy, approaching their booth with order pad in hand, slows down and looks also. Keith continues: "That motherfucker! What a dick! Finds some shit out in the desert and gets a job out of it."

"How come you keep–"

"He'll smoke my weed, though, huh. Lurpy-ass mother-fucker."

Candy reaches their booth.

"You guys know what you want?"

"I did, but it's been so long I forgot."

"Yeah. Again, I apologize for the wait. You heard what happened."

"Don't trip. Just give me some French toast with bacon. And a fucking Mountain Dew."

Candy turns toward Lee.

"And you?"

"Biscuits and gravy, please, ma'am. Make sure you put a lot of gravy on it."

"I'll inform the chef. You want a fucking Mountain Dew,

too?"

"Fuck yeah I do."

"All right, guys. Let me get this in and I'll get your drinks out to you."

"Good."

Candy rolls her eyes and walks off to put in the order.

"What a bitch," Keith says when she's gone.

"Who, her?"

"Who the fuck you think, dumbshit, Dena? Of course I mean her!"

"Dude, that's the one whose parents disappeared."

"So? That gives her the right to act all stuck-up? Fuck that noise." Keith looks back toward the lake. "He should've never took us out there. That's where he fucked up. He had to go–"

"That was your idea."

"That's what I was about to say. He had to take us out there."

Lee ponders this.

"You still want to go out there later on?"

"I'm thinking about it. I think I know how we could do it."

"You really think that was a bo–"

Candy returns with the drinks and a condiment caddy. She takes her time setting them down, hoping that Lee will choose to ignore her and finish his thought. Instead, Keith puts up his hand and Lee goes quiet.

"Your food's coming up, guys."

"Shit, don't tell us that. Or at least wait till we eat it first."

Candy laughs an artificial 'I'm laughing in spite of myself' laugh and asks:

"Where you guys going later on?"

Keith looks at her differently.

"Why?" he replies, "you want to hang out?"

"Um. I just kind of overheard…you guys…saying something about…"

"Us? We ain't doing shit, huh Lee. Damn, where you been? Haven't you noticed there ain't shit to do around here?"

"I was just wondering."

"What?"

"What what?"

"What the fuck were you wondering? Damn!" Keith says damn a lot when he's flirting.

Candy smiles.

"Don't trip," she says. "Just making conversation."

Candy walks away. Keith watches her go.

"She's pretty fine, huh? I'd fuck her. I'd fuck her in a heartbeat."

"If you're into that shit." Keith looks at his friend.

"Into what shit? What the fuck you talking about?"

"Whatever she is."

"What–"

Candy returns with the plates and sets them on the table. She asks Keith and Lee if there's anything else she can get for them.

"Whatsername said we get some free pie," Lee says.

"Ah, right you are."

"This guy thinks you're a witch."

Lee, loud and, for him at least, squeaky:

"That's not what I said!"

Candy laughs again, this time with incredulity.

"Not that I know of. But maybe–" nodding toward Lee but addressing Keith, "he knows something I don't."

"Whoa. See? Maybe you're right, dude." Keith addresses Lee but keeps his eye on Candy.

"I never said that," Lee repeats.

"So what's up?" Keith addresses Candy this time. "You wanna chill, or what."

"Uh, the answer to that question would be what. Let me bring out your pie, and I'll just leave the check then if that's okay." Candy smiles. "Take your time, though. Pay up front when you're ready."

As Keith and Lee finally get up to leave the restaurant

(after devouring two enormous slices of two-day-old lemon chiffon), Keith reaches into the condiment caddy, takes out a packet of sugar, tears it open, dumps the contents onto his pie plate, grabs a pen from atop the lectern, writes down his name and phone number, and leaves it under the salt shaker in lieu of a tip.

9

Chief Hill stares down at the page of notes Stevie left along with the latest reels of tape. He reads it and rereads it while absently tearing off the tiny bits of paper detritus left behind as the leaf was ripped from its wire-spring binding.

What exactly is he supposed to make of this?

Chief Hill took the morning off to go to church. Not that Kingdom Hall out in Tehachapi where he'd drop Delores off all those Saturdays, but the one in his old Oildale neighborhood where he used to go as a kid. He'd found the building intact and being used as an outreach center. Jim Hill spent over an hour—dressed in street clothes and sharing the front steps with a pair of sleeping borrachos—waiting for the doors to open so he could... So he could what? Just step inside, and be enclosed by that space, he guessed. Breathe the air.

Turned out that out no one ever came to open the doors, so he ended up taking a stroll around the old neighborhood before coming home. That air hadn't changed a bit. Some of the small, boxy houses were built after his time, but they were no departure from what had been there back when. The streets were in the same state of relative neglect. Not any more or less poor; just as more or less poor.

He comes back to this:

Jesus complex. Word made flesh.

Stevie also left the chief a note to help explain the notes, but it's not much help to him either:

'I came by while you were out. I think I got more than halfway done last night. Sorry these notes don't make much sense. Neither do the tapes. David Edwards drinks and writes, and lives in Oakland. I think he thinks he's the subject of mental experiment disguised as a job interview. Not sure why. I paid attention for company name but never found one. Maybe he already said it and I missed it. High-tech operation pays him $1000 a day for interview. The interviewer guy seems to be digging into the man head or using computer to read mind? Hard to follow.

I'm going back out there for a little while right now. Then back again tonight if that's OK.

Steve Ludich'

Chief Hill takes a deep breath and pulls himself up from the chair. It's an effort. He stares out the window for a minute then grabs his keys. You win, Delores. Kingdom Hall it is.

* * *

Stevie's back on the lakebed. He throws the pack onto one shoulder and starts walking. He traces his earlier steps from the ATV to where he left off reading last night in hopes of finding the missing speed. Stevie assures himself that his only aim is to figure out what happened to the bullet, so he can at least rest assured that it's not just floating around out there in the unknown, where it might cause who knows what sort of trouble. That's how it's feeling now, anyway. The thought of doing a pop this morning, out here on this exposed and sun-beaten sheet of minerals, in this heat, strikes Stevie like a big whiff of dead dog. Of course that could all change if and when he finds the bullet. Knowing what he knows, Stevie does what he can. He tells himself he will crush the bullet; he'll grind it into the trona when he finds it. The notion makes him feel better so he repeats it to himself as he scans the ground. He repeats the notion not as an affirmation so much as a bulwark against other, even more unhealthy thoughts coming to the fore.

No matter. Again Stevie reaches his destination without having found a clue to the whereabouts of his drugs. Stevie straps on the respirator. He's surprised and further irritated at the level of his own irritation. It's not just the speed, though that's got him frustrated enough in its own right. He all of a sudden doesn't feel like being out here any-more. The novelty of the situation has vanished. It's just hot, and too bright; and this setup is heavy, uncomfortable, unwieldy; and his shoulder hurts and he's got no shades, and...

What was that? Working's a bitch, ain't it? Fuck Gary Tales. But he's right. This is work. Stevie turns toward the glaring sun. The hidden town is at his back. In this light the only way Stevie can read is upside-down; otherwise he can't see the words. It's almost like they're polarized. Oh well. It's just the sun. Best to get to it.

"Here we go again," Stevie tells the microphone. He

reads a few words silently. "Okay. Looks like the guy's heading back for more. Here we go again."

The sky was bright and creamy but the air was still cool. I headed toward the bus stop, figuring to shave a couple of minutes from the walk to BART. I walked fast, watching buildings as I passed, passively observing all the closing and opening angles. I heard the pressure release of the bus's hydraulic lift a half block away and cut through a gas station to head it off. In open pavement between the two pump islands one of my hard-soled shoes hit a slick patch at the extreme of my stride. I slipped backwards with surprising suddenness, just barely getting my hands out to break my fall. I climbed back up and resumed my chase with the palms of my hands throbbing and a big metallic ball of adrenaline dissolving in the pit of my stomach. Whatever I'd slipped in was stubborn and I slid on my shoe for several nervous steps. I had debated whether or not to wear something more comfortable, but went with the dress shoes because they were already in my hands. Whatever.

I caught the bus running on my toes. When I reached into my back pocket to grab my wallet I was reminded that both my hands were smeared with that petroleum/grime mixture. Now so was my pocket. Fine, fine, fine. One good thing, though; somehow the shoulder bag containing my computer and gloves swung forward as I fell, and landed unmolested on my stomach. It figured. I sat in my molded plastic seat like I was showing off stigmata to a doubter. No one sat next to me. I stared at my hands. I couldn't wipe them off on the plastic. I would have to wait. Gasoline. Whoo! It occurred to me that I didn't remember whether those papers were on the floor when I left home. It didn't seem like they were. Did I clean up last night? It didn't seem like it. I hoped so. "Now that's going to bug me all day..." I mumbled.

It was nine on the dot when I got off the bus. I took the hill; alternately running, getting lightheaded, walking until my vision normalized, jogging, panicking and running again. I rubbed my hands on a still dewy lawn then immersed them in a pile of decomposed granite left over from some roadside landscaping. I stopped at a bay tree, pulled off a bunch of new leaves and worked them in like soap. These aerobics are going to settle into a headache, I thought. Should've taken something... At the gate I smelled my hands. I couldn't tell what they smelled like, other than not good. I was breathing too hard. I put on the gloves. They tingled. I placed them in front of the gate, which opened toward a verdant path. During the short shady walk to the peoplemover, I tried to relax. I regulated my breathing and straightened up my clothes. The peoplemover was not moving, so I was forced to break into a speedwalk. I had been dry as I made my way up the hill, but once I got inside the building my compromised cooling system decided to catch up with events. I started sweating in rhythm to my pulse, with each heartbeat forcing perspiration through my pores. It was in this state that I came up the escalator into the green room. Throbbing, sweating, stinking of sweat and everything else, I popped up in the no-man's land between two groups of people; each standing to face the other, now all (from what I could tell) turned to face me. I felt like I was being raised into a dystopic arena. Everyone had masks on, or rather everyone had on a kind of headgear—like a full cranial wrap of some hi-tech fabric—complete with a perfectly round grey screen covering the face. The screens were almost (but not quite) opaque, and looked like they were made from some superfine kevlar-y mesh. I walked backwards a couple of steps on the escalator, which just served to freeze the disturbing scene. "It's nine-nineteen, Mr. Edwards." Where'd that come from? "Go back and remove your shoes." The escalator reversed direction and began to take me down. I turned around headed toward my slippers, which were—along with one of the masks—sitting in a plastic box at the bottom of the escalator. The mask was in a plastic bag. "Remove the house shoes and helmet from the receptacle! Now place your shoes and bag in the receptacle! Now—"

Damn, dude! "Hold on? Jesus." As I changed into my slippers I for the first time that day gave a thought to what an odd and uncomfortable thing I'd agreed to. In my rush to make it on time, while simultaneously working to suppress a half dozen symptoms of hangover, I hadn't let myself remember how badly I wanted to get out of there the previous afternoon. How I'd been half-coerced into doing something that I didn't want to do, and didn't have to do, but had agreed to do. It wasn't the money–. I stood up, my stomach growling sickly. Or the creepy praise. No-. I stretched the mask over my head. I agreed to return because that meant first I could leave. I'd convinced myself that somehow I'd be able to stretch the interim interminably; that today could be deferred indefinitely. How many times have I done that?

Stasis...

What was that about my writing? Didn't I figure something out last night? What was that? God, was that stuff on the ground this morning? Did I see it before I left? Just didn't seem—

"We've already begun". I was back in the green room. "Time is not yours to withhold here, Mr. Edwards. You are A-five." A-five? I scanned the floor, trying to figure out just what the voice was talking about. While I could see everything quite clearly, looking through the mask was a bit like viewing the world through a really good cell phone camera. I saw that everyone was standing in their own stone square, and that one of the squares—a white one at the front, probably five-eighths of the way down—was unoccupied. I took my chances and occupied it. "It would have been better for you to have arrived at the agreed upon time. Unfortunately, Mr. Edwards, there is no time to repeat for your benefit what we have already covered." Where was that voice; who...? "Let's continue. Mr. Zuperba?"

"Hem...ooh kay...soo, ...oh, it's Gus..."

"The roller disco," someone said, impatiently.

"Yeah so that was all what happened with that. I bought the Rolar Eclypse oh, what was that, ninety-one?"

Stevie twists his arm back to reach his notebook. It's jammed deep into the tight vinyl pocket on the back of the case, and it takes Stevie a contorted few seconds to retrieve it. Names and places. He writes:

Virtual reality helmets?!?
Gus Zuperba
Rolar Eclypse 1991

"But yeah; that's what they did. Said it was gonna be a what was it? A bus, uh, a transfer station. But you drive down there you won't see nothing but a empty lot. No, come to think of it. They got a big billboard up there now. But you look close, look in the back of the lot, you'll see them. Yeah. Still there. They just piled 'em up there, in a pile. They're just all covered with weeds now so uh..." As I tried to locate the speaker—the voice coming from within my helmet, but with some sophisticated acoustical effect 'suggesting' its spatial source as coming from somewhere at the far end of the group opposite me—I noticed something very strange about the masks we were wearing. While I wore mine the others no longer looked like grey screens. They seemed to be reflecting the image of whatever the wearer was facing. Then I looked more closely. There were some people whose masks suggested they were scanning the room, looking around; but their heads stayed still. It wasn't what they, we! were facing; it was what we were looking at. Not only that, but in the 'reflected' image, the faces of the other participants could be seen as clearly as if their masks were made of glass. So if you wanted to see someone's face, you'd have to find someone else who might be looking at them and look at that person, while of course not being able to see that person's face at all...

"Let's move on," the voice, from everywhere at once.

"Whoa," coming from a reedy-sounding voice to Mr. Zuperba's right, "oh, wow. Okay...? Well my name is Wyatt Timmons? So...well that was for practicing law without a license?" What the hell was he talking about? *"Okay well I'll try to list them all. So...research subject? Just kidding; uh, okay Art gardener, triple-jump coach, proofreader? ... bush surgeon? ... cab driver, ball collector, secret shopper? Let's see... entomologist, etymologist, methane diviner... organizer, okay, chocolate maker, wine taster, tea buyer? Vermiculture, high steel... steam engineer, fiddler slash auctioneer..."*

Stevie adds: Wyatt Timmons. He will leave some blank space below the name.

I was trying to follow, but after a while my mind began to wander; and I turned from the absurd scene to stare at the windows, at a diluted blue sky that may or may not have really been there. What's this guy's deal? There's no way anyone could have this many, and varied, jobs—by accident. Drifters and dabblers usually settled around some general area of endeavor, it seemed to me. Even people cursed with chronic indecision have periods where they at least try to follow through for a while, or they get stuck in a rut and end up doing something for a while just out of listlessness. But here was something different. This guy was driven. This wasn't just a random series of jobs. This was a career. No; it was a calling.

"My name?" It was a different voice. Did the other one fade out? I couldn't remember. I turned back. The light from

outside was not being reflected by the masks. I was, here and there.

"Okay. My full name is Yvette Ynez Yninguez Ybarra."

Stevie adds: Yvett Ynez Yninguez Ybarra YYYY

"My story is I'm from a little town out in the desert, called Cartago."

"What's this?"

"That's where I was born and raised. It's on the 395 if you're like, going to Death Valley from Bakersfield that's where you turn off to the 190. I'm like fourth generation from that area. My family used to farm there, when they had Owens Lake. Now everybody I know pretty much works at Crystal Geyser out in Olancha. Or for Rio Tinto. That's where I used to work too. At Crystal Geyser I mean. And that's where I was when I started thinking about this thing my Grampy's friend told me a long time ago. Helping fill these little water bottles, you know, for people in L.A. Right there next to the aqueduct that's the same water that's in their toilets is the same water we use. I don't even know why it's there. They used up the lake a long time ago. So this is what I was thinking about. Back in the old days when there was no town called Cartago, the town there was called, um, Carthage. You wouldn't know it though. There's no signs or nothing, to tell you. Because who

cares, right? Carthage and Cartago. I know. This is what I was thinking: both those names are after a city the Romans burned down then covered in salt so nothing could grow there. You guys know that story, right? But Carthage is the English. And I started thinking that, that's actually pretty, I don't know, weird if you think about it. Because I think when they called Cartago Carthage? That was back when there was a lake there. But then when the aqueduct came, and L.A. started taking the water, and the lake started shrinking, and the dust storms started coming, and the salt, then they changed the name to Cartago. They abandoned Carthage and put Cartago right next to it. Or maybe on top of it, I don't even know. That didn't seem right to me. Know what Cartago in ancient times meant? 'New Town'. Sometimes I think like the Americans wanted to forget what the name meant, but they didn't care if, you know... we remembered or not. Or maybe they did care. I wonder that sometimes too. But anyways, now if you go there there's mostly just a big old dry lakebed, white, like a ghost. And that's what it is actually, is a ghost. They mine TSP out there now. Sometimes we'll get these dust storms from the lake, and sometimes they're even poison. Like, they got like minerals in them that cause you cancer. So that's what I was doing, putting little bits of water in little plastic bottles for like, joggers in Hollywood. And I thought about how the Crystal Geyser plant was part of like a extra little diversion, you know? And it kept us there by that big old ghost lake to get sick. And so I thought you know what? What if we changed the name of the town back to Carthage? I started talking to my work friends about it, but it was hard to explain what I meant.

They thought I was stupid. I think they figured all I cared about was like for the, you know, the Anglos to know there was a Carthage in California; like to make them feel guilty or something. Who cares about that! Like most Anglos know there was a Carthage anywhere, you know? I doubt it! Mostly what I was thinking was how when it was Carthage, it must have been nice. That's all. And maybe it would help the town if it had that name again. You don't know; it could. That is really what I was thinking. Carthage means 'new town' too... but—"

Stevie turns off the machine. Yvette Ynes Yninguez Ybarra? Under her name he writes CARTAGO! and circles it. He stares at his notebook. He writes 'Crystal Geyser Olancha'. Under that he writes 'Mexican bottler Roman history water history? Carthage? Carthage/Old Cartago. Change name to Carthage?' He stares some more.

She said she grew up here, didn't she? Yvette Ynes Yninguez Ybarra? Who the hell's that? From here? He writes 'Carthage = new town?'

Stevie thinks about stopping now, going back and telling the chief about this while it's still fresh in his mind. He looks back at what he's just read. While what's still fresh in his mind? It's gone. Annoyed, he restarts the machine.

This was interesting. It reminded me of something, but I couldn't put my finger on what it was. I'd been on 395 before, but I didn't remember any Cartago. I'd never even heard of it. What did she say her name was? Yvonne? She pronounced her name like a declarative sentence. Rising and falling, then stamped at the end. Her voice retained a fair amount of youthful clarity, but it also had a serious edge to it. It was tempered. I guessed she was a couple of years older than me. I generally liked people a couple of years older than me; I always have. I made a mental note to ask her what else she knew about 'the old days', if not 'ancient times'. That is, if we ever were allowed to speak normally... That might make a good story, I thought. She went on:

"...so then after they let me go I came up to San Francisco to visit my cousin. But then my cousin's boyfriend got hurt at his work and so she went to stay with him in Fremont and asked me would I stay at her apartment. And I said if I can find a job. And then she's the one who actually saw your ad, and she sent it to me on the computer. So now here I am. And now, well, this is so strange—"

"Let's move on. Mr. Rubottom?"

Mr. Rubottom proceeded to tell a story about the trophy store he used to have. He said he'd owned it for thirty-six years. Since the year I was born. He said it was next door to a Carpe Tile on El Camino. The way he said that, "CarpeTile on El Camino," it was like one long word he'd said a million times. He talked about how back in the days when the CarpeTile was doing good business he had a steady stream of business as well. "Soccer teams, beauty pageants, bowling leagues, you name it," he said. "Talent shows, tee-ball, you name it. And those people boy, they loved their trophies. I'd have coaches, pageant organizers, why sometimes they'd unpack those trophies before they even got out the door. See, they'd have to spend a minute or two in admiring them, be the first one, you see." *He explained how people would hold the marble base with one hand, "holding the trophy hand higher than the other one. Like they were weighing something. And hell if they didn't run their thumbs over that figurine every time. You'd think they'd gotten ahold of Aladdin's Lamp. I kid you not. And those days, CarpeTile was always chock-full of shoppers. Whole families of them; they'd park out front, peek through the window when they walked by my place. I'd see them in there, running their fingers through the different piles, kids rolling all over the place. Breathing in that new smell, that what was it? Anson 4 Nylon. Sure. I'd go in there myself sometimes. That was a good smell. That Anson 4 Nylon." He chuckled like he just told himself a joke. Then he cleared his throat. "After while things got slower, and slower, and slower. And the CarpeTile wasn't bringing them in like they used to either. And after they opened up that place up the street, forget it. 'Flooring Solu-tions', they call it. I supposed people must've stopped sitting on the floor. Is that true? Who wants to sit on a flooring solution?*

Well, to make a long story short, they closed down the old place. Took down all the signs. Covered up all the windows with brown paper and that blue tape. Now who wants to have to look at that ugly thing all day long? When it rained you started to get that mildew smell come from over there. Well, my business just flat croaked. Now I look at it like: would I want to get a trophy from some old place next to a great-big eyesore, that smells like mildew? Might not be my first choice. At the same time, lots of the old guys were retiring, see? Gone fishing, or moved out to Vegas. And there just didn't seem to be so many talent shows anymore. On top of that, you see people like to use the internet these days. Mail order. Get everything delivered to you. Besides, I suspect that's where the kids are getting their trophies from nowadays, is computer games. Super powers, what are they giving them? Anything they can think up, I suppose. Boy, that's great. Kids just sitting there on their folks's flooring products." He chuckled again. "Video games. They got them winning the war single-handed, I suppose. Then they turn the damn thing off and walk away why they've already forgotten whatever the hell it is they'd just done. Sure. Some trophy, boy. But what are you going to do?"

To kill time between customers he took to doing Sudoku puzzles.

"I got pretty good at them. I got started with the Daily Journal there, then I started picking up the Chronicle and doing that one. Pretty soon I was buying those Sudoku books. I got to where I was working on the Mensa puzzles, hardest ones I could find, when they started giving me this feeling. Whatever you'd call the opposite of accomplishment. Now I would concentrate while working on them, see, and I could sharpen my focus. But then, soon as I'd see the solution there, a wave would just, engulf me. You know? Like: what a waste of time, see? At least with the crossword puzzles you're getting some vocabulary; you're getting some current events you might not already know. Something you could maybe share in conversation. But Sudoku puzzles? What's there to say? Now I don't know of anyone giving out trophies for Sudoku. Maybe I'm wrong. I sure as hell hope not.

It got to where I went an entire month without a single customer. Not a single one. Now I owned the building outright, so that wasn't a problem. But see that's not taking into account the property taxes and utilities, and zero coming in was not going to cover those. So at that point...at that point I'd got to feeling pretty low. Almost as bad as when... Well, let me say I'm not one to stay like that forever. So I went through my old cabinets, looking for something I'd seen years back. And I found it, in a rotten old catalog of mine. Tell the truth I was surprised that someone was there to answer the phone. But they were still in business, and I got what I was looking for. And boy, was that baby nice. About yay big, forty-five pounds give or take. Had four tiers, with different types of columns going up. Corinthian twice, then Ionic, then Doric on the top. Always my favorite, that Doric. All silver-plated. You had the muses laying around, hanging off the corners there. Silver-plated. A real beaut. Base was Pakistani green marble with egg and dart carved trim. White gold bunting. You get the picture. Up at the top I had them custom make a special Winged Victory. Eighteen inches to the top of her head, and above that she held another itsy bitsy version of herself, up on top of her own little pedestal. A trophy holding a trophy, see. The plate at the bottom I had anchor-bolted into the base. Not a drop of glue on that baby. Uh uh. 35 years, that's all it says. I paid for the whole thing out of my own pocket. It was a lot of money, too, and the first time I ever had to pay for a trophy. A few weeks later I got it. Cleared out my front window display, I had built some nice glass shelfs some years back, I took all that down. Then I brought out this little antique display table

I had in the back, and I put the trophy up there for whoever might want to see it.

By that time my block of El Camino had turned into one of those that people don't even see; they just drive through to get someplace else. The street outside was looking more—how can I put it?—generic by the day. That's what happens. The old details fade away. It was dissolving, you see? As far as traffic went, well there was as much as ever, maybe even more. Only difference was it was going by much faster than before, ever since they retimed the traffic signal there.

But after I put my trophy up in that window, see, I start noticing cars slowing down as they passed by my store. Not anything dramatic, but some. And as a car would go from say, forty down to thirty, right in front there, when I felt like it I could always get a good look at the driver's face. Every once in a while I might recognize someone from around town. Most of the time though, it was strangers. But I could see their faces, always. It was almost like they were lit up for just an instant. Captured in time, almost. I figured the trophy must be catching a reflection off the sun, or could have been the floodlights coming from the shithole equipment rental place across the street, excuse my French. Those Vietnamese left those damn things on all day and night. It's beyond me why they did that...

So, to make a long story short... it must be flashing in their eyes, I figured. I imagined it must be quite a surprise getting that flash, looking over and seeing a golden statue. On that block especially, you get what I'm saying? Now I never drove *by my place on El Camino. I'd always parked off the alley in back. So I never did find out for certain.*

Now after about a month goes by a fellow comes into the store. Things had picked up a little bit. Not much. Mostly one-offs, special orders. Different kind of business from what I was used to. But this fellow, I could tell straight away that here's someone who's looking to make a real order. He was sure professional in his demeanor, good posture, pricey looking briefcase, the whole bit. So he explains that he's there on behalf of a developer, and asks me would I be interested in selling my property. Well naturally the thought had crossed my mind. So I ask him what kind of development. Mixed use he says. He opens his briefcase and pulls out an artist's rendering of a retail strip, one of those you see with the apartments hanging over the stores, and a parking garage underneath. They're putting them up all over, you've all seen them. You don't need me... Anyhow, in the drawing there's foot traffic. Families. Pedestrians. A row of Japanese maples to block some of that southern exposure. Now while I'm standing and looking at the future there, the fellow lets drop the price they're willing to pay. It was more than I'd've figured by an easy hundred thou. I started to explain how I wasn't sure I was ready for retirement, that this here was my livelihood and not just some property. Then I had a good look around, we both did as a matter of fact, and I'm thinking about what it was I actually did all day. Not much, is what. The man says to me now what if he did some asking around, talk to people he knew, suppose if a position could be found, something not too boring, maybe, and not too strenuous, would that change my thinking any. I took a good look at that drawing. It looked nice, I'll tell you. I looked up at that old eyesore rotting away next door, just going to shit out there in the sun. Place sure as hell wasn't doing anybody any good. Someone needed to tear that thing down, and it sure as hell wasn't going to be me. So how selfish would I have to be to say no? And as I said, the price was more than fair, however you wanted to slice it.

One more thing, the man said. Your trophy there in the window? That's part of the deal. I says to him I beg your pardon? What do you fellows want with that? Just what business could you have with that, I say. Well, the man tells me, we would like to incorporate your trophy into our final design. We envision the corridor leading from the parking garage to the sidewalk as exhibiting an archive, he says; a sort of museum dedicated to the history of the location. A nod to the past, he says. Understand, he says, a connection to local history is important to the condo buyer, and a gentle psychological spur to the shopper. And of course your trophy would be the centerpiece...

Well who could argue with that? I made the deal right then and there. The idea of my trophy, in the place they'd put it in that drawing; to have it enshrined there... well that did it. I couldn't resist the idea. From there on out everything went smooth. No reason I can't live comfortably for the rest of my life, far as I can see. That was last month. Last week I get a call, then a letter in the mail on the same day inviting me to be a part of this—they called it a— opportunity. That's what the letter said, anyhow. Let's just say this isn't exactly what I'd had in mind.

Still haven't been by the old place, so couldn't say if they got started yet. Don't know what's going on there. Hell, one of these days I might drive by, someday, maybe after it's finished. In the meantime, I'm still trying to figure out what the hell kind of opportunity has got—"

Mr. Rubottom was cut off by the omnidirectional voice. Whew. I thought the guy would never finish. He must not get to talk to people much, I guessed. I crooked my arms behind by back and worked my spine. Oh man, were we going to have to stand all day? Then a woman's voice; crisp, with a little undertone of desperation. I recognized that voice from the day before. The skirt-suit. I was starting to wonder if I was even with the same group of people. The woman launched into a description of her area of expertise. Once she got started she went on as if were she to stop throwing new words in front of her then the ones piling up behind her would knock her down. I couldn't follow it. Something about monotone comparative statics and endogenous outcomes and exogenous parameters and of using sensitivity analysis within a dynamic model on account of how useful it was for solving optimization problems and so on… She said something about how comparative statics usually requires fewer assumptions and usually it just gives an ordinal rather than a cardinal answer, simple up or down in other words and in contrast to the implicit function theorem, which gives rates of change… "Lately," she said, "I'd been seeing something else there, implicit in the data. My colleagues couldn't see it, or wouldn't. They didn't, at any rate. Before I knew what hit me I was removed from my group. I worked in isolation while they figured out what to do with me, then finally I was asked to take a leave of absence..."

Next up was a man with one of those warm, bottomless, Paul Robeson-type voices. He told us his name was Curtis Proctor. Then he said he was a buh buh bus driver. That since he was buh buh born he was a buh buh big guy buh buh but never wanted to do manual labor like his father. Buh buh because even as a child he could see that he had extraordinarily buh buh beautiful hands. I could feel his cavernous chest quake as he tried to get through this introduction/explanation business. "So, coming up, I was like the buh buh blacksheep of the family". It was a coincidence, no doubt, but he spoke those four syllables, buh buh blacksheep, with the same melody as the children's song. I grunted to myself in recognition of a curious and pleasant thing, in this case a magnificent, rumbling baritone. Once I heard it it ran over and over in my mind. Buh buh Blacksheep... He was talking about how he had been trying to break into the hand model business. He'd paid a studio photographer to do a series of shots of his hands, and he sent those pictures out to agents and agencies. Someone would be interested; later they would talk over the phone and that would be the last he'd hear from them. He gave his brother a few dollars to deal with the phone calls. He got a few gigs that way, but when he'd arrive at a shoot he could see, in the faces of the people he met, what they were thinking. Who's the gorilla. The rest of him maybe wasn't so pretty as his hands, he said. Like that made a difference, he said.

The comfortable rumble of Curtis' voice was interrupted by a loud staccato shriek like an old bus hitting a glass wall. The tonal shift sounded almost choreographed.

"I am Anh Thai," she yelled at us. "First I will say that I am not a quote unquote conceptual artist. I know some of you like to call me that. And to me, you're the worst. The worst! Because you think you understand me, don't you? Or at least you let all your stupid friends think you understand me. That's what gets me," she said. "Because you let them think that. But then you don't think anything! You don't. You just fake it. Everything is a joke, right? How convenient for you. I wasn't trying to be cute. I don't think it's cute. I'm serious. But those of you who would call me an arsonist? You're just as bad. Yes, I am a guerilla. Yes, I am a fighter. But I am not a criminal. And convicting me of something I didn't do will not make me a criminal." Holy shit. She was pissed. And so theatrical. Who's she talking to? I heard someone giggle. The group perked up a bit. People started shuffling around, looking around 'at' each other, trying to get a glimpse of her. "I've been told to tell you I'm currently serving at the Northern California Women's Facility at Stockton," she said. "That I am here as part of a work furlough program. But this; whatever this is is the joke, I say. Bad, bad, bad joke. Whoever thought this up is… it's bad art. That's it. I get it. I'm done." Then, after a pause, "no I don't care! I told it all in court. Have them come get me then!" A longer pause. So this was a job for retirees and work furlough people? "Fine." … "Fine I said!" Back to addressing us, she said: "You want to know what happened? What really happened? Again? Okay. Here we go again. I'm just minding my own business, doing what I call rebranding, and I get a call from this guy. On my cell phone, right. He says he's from this arts group out in Manteca. There's this thing they got *going, where they're working with the city to turn this old run down part of town into like an artsy neighborhood. Partners In Strategic Redevelopment or some bullshit like that. One of those things where they're trying to bring the white people back to downtown, right? I should have told them to go fuck themselves. But I didn't. Because see? There you go. I can be just as bad as the rest of you! So they got this art day thing planned where they're going to close off the street to traffic and have artists and bands and shit like that. Apparently somebody'd seen this rebranding thing I did off the 101 where I projected slides from a rooftop across onto an American Spirit billboard. Still shots of worms and lynchings. Yeah yeah. You've seen it if you pay attention. So they tell me they got this old movie theater that used to show Mexican porn but got closed down. And they asked me if I'd be interested in doing something in there. I don't know if they thought I'd do a slideshow, like slides were my thing or something. I don't have a thing.*

But I got this friend that does welding and electrical, and he helped me rig up a bunch of the theater seats with all these clapping machines that I could control from outside. Yeah, with knobs. Then I recorded this porno film we found in there—the noisiest parts—and made loops, and hooked that up to this big PA; and I had that running to an iPod so I could control that too. After I got it running I locked all the doors so no one could get in. You could hear the movie from outside, only you couldn't tell exactly what it was. I ran the clapping machines so sometimes you would hear a big like, ovation; or sometimes just a few claps, or little spurts of applause. People kept walking up and trying to open the door. And they couldn't do it. And some of them got pretty pissed. Even some of the people who got what was going on still had a hard time walking away. Then what started with a few people just standing around pretty soon got to be this big line of people waiting to get in. With nobody saying anything. See, that's all I was trying to do. That's all it was going to be. Pretty mild stuff, if you ask me. For me it was definitely subtler than what I was used to doing. Well that's when we started to smell smoke. And that's when I realized I'd locked myself outside with everyone else. I bolted all the front doors from the inside, and went out the emergency exit. How was I supposed to know the door locked automatically? Okay, so I should have checked first. No shit! So then now no one could get in. When we saw fire coming up people started freaking out and yelling like there were people inside, like 'fire! there's a fire! get out of there!' I mean, wasn't it obvious that no one was in there? But it was like they didn't care. People were trying to break the doors down to get in. The fire department came right away, though, and put the fire out. My clapping machines were still going until they put them out with their hoses. And that was another thing. I had all my stuff in there! All that work! After they did their investigation they said they found an accelerant had been used to start the fire. So it couldn't have been an accident, they found. Totally ignoring the fact that there was no one in the fucking building to start a fire in the first place! And all my stuff was still going until the firemen came, so I don't see how, even if it was an accident... What matters is: they decided because I was the only one who knew what I was going to do then it had to have been me. Now, was I the one collecting insurance money? I don't think so. Yeah, I was the one who could tear that place down now, do whatever the fuck I want to with it. It's so obvious. And here's what really gets me: those fucking losers who said that without the fire my installation would have been pointless."

After Anh Thai finished we were given one minute to stretch. I spent it sitting down on my square and staring at my gloved hands, trying to get them to stop shaking. We started again. A carny named Coop gave us some vision of him falling to hell through the floor of a port-a-john he found in the middle of a dry riverbed outside of Hemet. He was fervent about it. Then a girl named June; and something about how everybody thought she dressed like she was from the sixties but she actually dressed like someone from the eighties dressing up like someone from the sixties. Then this other guy that did solar system installation and energy auditing, and how honestly he got most of his auditing business through talking to people at job interviews…

I couldn't concentrate. It was getting closer to my turn. I'd always gotten unreasonably nervous in situations that included sequential introductions. Like watching a fuse burn toward a bomb, the bomb being me; and by time it got to me I'd be so overwhelmed with self-consciousness that my heart would be slamming like a pile driver, and invariably I'd end up warbling something in one anemic breath without even filling my lungs first…

The guy next to me started talking. Now I could see my face in the masks of the people as they looked across at him. Some of them skipped ahead and looked directly at me. I looked to myself like a pat of warm butter, soft and yellow. My mind was starting to flutter around, shut down a little bit. Then from out of the fog of my anxiety I heard the guy say: "I moved up here about fifteen years ago. First time I came to San Francisco I said 'this is the place for me'. People out on the street, talking, hanging out. Jaywalkers walking right in front of cops. It was great. Just... interaction, you know? That's why I had to get out of L.A. I felt like that place already had my future figured out. Working, taking the freeway everywhere. By myself, listening to the radio. Making special trips to see people. Never talking to strangers unless at least one of us is getting paid. I was pretty idealistic back then. It seemed to me that the only way anything new was ever going to happen was if we, like people, got together and dealt with each other in person. Of course it's not like I knew what I wanted to happen specifically. Everyone just to have fun together, I guess. And that just didn't seem possible where I'm from." I tried to get a look at the guy, but none of the angles were adding up. He had his head turned away from me and was looking toward the windows. There were a couple of people who were lined up in the direction he was looking, but they wouldn't look at him. I think one of them was asleep. I really wanted to get a look. I was relating to what he was saying. It could have been me. He sounded like he was about my age. He had a funny drawl to his voice; like a mildly effeminate surfer. But just a little bit, and just every once in a while. "So, anyway," he went on, "I came up here, bounced around for a while, went to a lot of shows, met a lot of people. Had my fun. I did some paste-up for an auto trader magazine for a while, and I worked at a postcard place in North Beach for a year or so. I played in a band for a while, and we played shows around town. Back then I used to go to the park and write a lot. Look at girls. I actually met some interesting... ones that way. But it was fun to just make eye contact with them, while I wrote. I loved that eye contact business. So did they, I think. Like I might immortalize them in my pad. Then, you know, going out every night. Parties and shows at first, then more and more just bars. Just getting drunk, bringing drunk girls back to my apartment. It started dawning on me that just hanging out and partying wasn't working for me. It sure wasn't making the world a better place, or anything like that that's for damn sure. It was getting boring. And lonely, too, and kind of gross. I was becoming just what I'd been trying to avoid, you know? I started not having so much fun going out and getting loaded, and it was starting to show. The old saying about staying too long at the party? Literally and figuratively, right. I was getting unpleasant when I was drunk. Not violent but just, I don't know...embarrassing. Creepy. So I thought, why don't I go back to school, do something worthwhile before it's too late? I went to City College and took all their writing classes, then I transferred to State where I majored in English. That's where I got into the transcendentalists. Ralph Emerson, Hank Thoreau, Margaret Fuller; you know, those guys. I figured well somebody's got to do it. What good was that going to do me professionally? Or financially for that matter? I didn't even bother to guess. The answer, it turned out, was none. I concluded that the only thing that was really available to me anymore—to affect change as they say, and make some change for myself—was to become a teacher. To work with kids. Huh! Easier said than done... Anyway I got my credential and started substituting last year..." What was going on now? This guy was basically telling a variation of my life story. Could it possibly be a coincidence? No. Nothing in that place was a coincidence. I would say I had a healthy enough mistrust for paranoia; I was normally careful not to let myself be seduced by its... charms. But I couldn't help succumbing then. And paranoia seemed to be somehow wrapped up in the whole point of the exercise, which made me even more paranoid. 'And all this boozing's tearing up your nerves, too,' I thought. Nice work. Instinctively I brought my hands up to massage my eye sockets, but when the gloves touched the mask I was hit with two overlapping splashes of electronic light. The splashes scared the shit out of me, and I couldn't see for a few seconds. They also shocked me into composing myself a little bit. To remind myself that nothing's happening, really; that the plane's still in the air...

"Tell them the truth."

What was that? Was that...no!

"Just tell them." Yes it was. That was my own voice coming through the helmet audio. Well, that's it. I've just lost it, is all. This isn't happening. There is no plane in the sky. I'm going to wake up drugged in some psych ward any minute now. Fine. I'll just ride it out. Like the time I took those mushrooms at the Big A...

"Let's proceed," I heard from somewhere far away. "Mr.

Edwards." Then it came to me; from some murky nonverbal area of my consciousness; a suggestion that it might be a slightly saner course of action, if one finds oneself hearing voices, to not do whatever it is the voices recommend you do. No evidence was offered, of course; as a matter of fact a more verbal thought process synchronistically concluded that it's probably all the same difference, you're crazy either way, and either way ain't pretty. And at the same time as that, another part of me mused: 'so this is what 'cracking up' means. Your identity literally shatters into its component parts. Interesting...'

"What the hell," I said out loud.

Yvonne's Owens Lake story had reminded me of a documentary I'd just seen about efforts to restore bird populations. The show ended on an up note, with a couple of success stories. I said: "my name is David Edwards. I was—" I said, "until recently that is, a... an avian veterinarian." Then I just ran with it. "Avocets, American avocets. American Avocet... vaccinations, actually," I couldn't resist, "was my vocation." Everyone was looking at me now. I could see my face being reflected from a dozen different angles. I thought of cubism, and kaleidoscopes, and compound eyes. I thought of my own recently shattered identity staring back at me, reconfiguring me. But my mind ran like mercury. It crackled and sped. I didn't realize it until then, but I had picked up a thread: there was something a little tilted about the stories I'd been able to pay attention to; they were a little tweaked in the cause-and-effect department. So I continued, confidently, convincingly: "See, for many years the American Avocet population was in serious decline. Finally it became clear that if we did nothing *we would lose the species entirely, and a concerted effort was made to stabilize the remaining population. A vaccination program was undertaken because a lot of the birds here in California were coming down with, um, sterility caused by... well, basically a virus. So any time they would come across an injured Avocet they would call me, since I was the only, you know, American Avocet vet-vaccinator... available. To get to the point, I guess you could say I was a victim of my own success. The Avocet population has rebounded nicely in recent years. Of course nothing could make me happier, but it is ironic because now there is not so much concern for the health of the individual Avocet. Not like the good old days. I'm being facetious, of course. But seriously, as a society we don't seem to mind the odd sterile Avocet anymore. What are you going to do? And besides, todays Avocet population seems to have developed a natural immunity to the, you know... virus." I chuckled as if the thought just occurred to me. "Also probably as a result of our program's success. So, uh, voila. There you have it. And here I am." I waited. Nothing. Silence. Everyone just stared. I smiled wide, the way kids do when they're showing off new teeth, and all the reflections smiled back at me. I puffed my cheeks and crossed my eyes. I mouthed the words 'oh, yes' as creepy as could be, just to see myself do it.*

Stevie peels off the respirator.

"Ho, Jesus."

He rolls his head, closes his eyes, pinches the bridge of his nose, and thinks:

Is this guy for real?

Stevie makes his way to the ATV. After setting the reel-to-reel on the rack behind him, and cinching it with a bungee cord, he sits down. He grunts '...so tired. So tired this evening'. He peels an orange and squints back at all he's already read. The bay looks like it's been lined with a brassy foil. It gleams metallically. Stevie's having a hard time focusing. The long, smeared lines resemble the gentle rippling that reveals a breeze on water. The eastern mountains are a dingy blueish wash hovering in the distance. A cirrus cloud formation sprawls high above the mountains like some enormous Ichthyosaur skeleton, or even better like some giant hanging mobile of an Ichthyosaur skeleton with each component part rotating and shifting almost independent of the others, but somehow not quite.

What is this?

Stevie looks at his notes. They confirm what he already knows; namely that he wrote nothing after 'Cartago = new town?' Nothing about the trophy guy; who Stevie pictures as a sadder, older and smaller version of Chief Hill. Nothing about the crazy artist chick either. And then: what difference does it make again? Anh Thai? Come on. Either this guy is off his rocker or he's making shit up, right?

There's more dust in the air today. Stevie takes note of this. The blue of the sky looks faded. And there's that hunger again, making up for lost time. What a nuisance. Stevie guesses it's around three-thirty, maybe even four. He's more or less forgotten about the missing speed for the time being. He's thinking about a triple-decker peanut butter and honey sandwich and maybe even a nap. He's too fried to talk to the chief now; he'll go see him later... after dropping off that thermos, maybe.

Candy's been popping into Stevie's head all afternoon; the thoughts just rolling around up there like milk in water, twisting without direction. Clouding up everything. What was that all about? Bringing him coffee? Why, the uh... the uh...

A couple of times Stevie has gotten so lost in reverie that he'd forget to comprehend what he's reading, and would have to reset. Pour out another glass of milky water and refill with fresh, sparkling, delicious.... Okay:

Look at the word. Say it.

Concentrate.

In a way, Stevie supposes he suspects that whoever listens to his recording will be able to tell, just by listening, the times when he, Stevie, had been engaged with the words he read, as opposed to when he was merely transmitting. That would be cool to know.

On his way home Stevie watches the tendons of his hands vibrate on the handlebars as he tries to get something to congeal. She said she was just curious; is there any reason not to take her at her word? There could be. Or not. Some reason, sure... No?

There you go again, he thinks at himself, with that thought vortex! There are no answers there. Stevie coaches himself: stick to the business at hand. What will she say? Hmm. Will she say yes right away, or no for sure right away, or would he have to intercede, negotiate or plead? And if she says yes? Then what? Just bring her out here to watch him work? Lay out a blanket on the trona? How's that going to work? Can that possibly be a good idea? How possible? How good?

Or will he be distracted beyond usefulness, fretting the whole time about if he should, how he should get close to her again? And what if he's prohibited from going out tonight? What if it's back to the original plan, with Fairy-tales stuck out here with him like some malignant tumor?

The whole deal is starting to get old. He may have to fake excitement. Just the idea of that is a drain...

A filthy, uninvited thought pushes its way to the fore.

...Come on (so soothing)... Wouldn't you rather fail?

Well? Would he like it if she said no? Part of him would. The coward part, and whatever gland it is that produces regret. Will that part end up vibing it all away? That would be an unforgivable act of self-sabotage. But he has no idea. He's so exhausted... he just doesn't know...

"You'd better not!" he says, slamming an imaginary door on the waif-thought. This line of reasoning is no better than the last one, he thinks. That was a whirlpool; this is a toilet bowl. Stop it. The thing to do is to not think about it. Duh! Everybody knows that but you, Stevie. Like in sports. You always blink when you swing so you're blind when the thing happens. How come you do that? Same reason. It's not a bomb, you know. It's not a universe. It's just a ball.

Not even that, Stevie thinks. It's just another metaphor. Those things must be contagious, and whoever this 'flustrated' writer is, he's been hacking them for days. Metaphorically, of course. What good are they? What's the point in replacing reality with what it is not quite? Stevie examines the question. He thinks of himself as a child, alone in his room, creating a universe literally from what was at hand. The blanket, for instance, with its topography of hidden regions and great, free expanses became a theater, a land, a country, effortlessly assuming whatever form the story required. Each object, each relationship between objects, each color and sound, each synesthetic fusion was free to express its own... charismatic identity. Nothing was decided yet. The shape-of-a-six, cowering under the aggressive shape-of-a-nine, asked for (and received) sympathy and protection. The vaguely nine-shaped form of a weatherhead on the roof next door—lined up with the window so as to be seen from under the bed at a submissive angle, looming over his room-world with severity, majesty and latent oppression—was not to be trusted. The sorrowful face repeated in the wallpaper, and the wryly smiling one, were sometimes welcome and sometimes most definitely not. The corner behind the bed...

So is that it? A way to get at, what did the guy say, my own personal big bang residue? A way to tap into that energy as it was before things got settled; when the laws governing my universe were still in flux?

Stevie is more than halfway back to Cartago. The quonset huts are just starting to reflect the afternoon sun.

It occurs to him that someone ought to put solar panels on those things. He decides to take his time for the rest of the way in. He listens to the engine cough as he lets off the throttle. Clean energy, he thinks. Is that what you're getting at with the metaphors, dude? A purer, more undifferentiated psychic energy? Closer to the source? If you tap into that stream-of-consciousness, do you also divert it? Do the laws of thermodynamics apply? If it is diverted, where does it go? Into the story, somehow? Into the ether? Into this tape?

Stevie suddenly recalls the part he read toward the end of the day. What was going on with those masks? And was that a panic attack that David Edwards was having? A psychotic episode? Or is he describing an energy transference of some sort? Careful, Stevie, Stevie tells himself. You don't have to relate to the guy too much. He's probably at least partly nuts. Come to think of it, how could he not be? To come all the way out here, to do this without even knowing it would be read? Who knows... maybe it was never intended to be read. Maybe it's out here because this is a good place to get ignored...

Stevie reaches the old lakeshore and Lake Street. He eases his way toward the 395, having left his esoteric reflections on the trona. He reaches the highway. Opening the throttle to cross, he makes a point of not turning his head toward the police station, just in case the chief—or, worse yet, Fairytales—happens to be looking his way. No chatting, now. That will have to wait.

10

Candy is sitting on a folding chair at a plastic table behind the Golden Empire. Eduardo's friend Xavier is heaving rubber kitchen mats out the kitchen door so he can hose them off. A mat flops in the air like a fish before hitting the patio with a wet slap. Another flops onto the first, then another, then a fourth that causes the stack to quiver. Xavier follows the mats out the door and stands there next to them. He might be staring at Candy. Xavier has a sleepy eye, so it's hard for Candy to know for sure what he's looking at. Candy's halfway through a Marlboro Light. For the record, Candy does not consider herself a hypocrite for smoking, despite her brother's incessant suggestions to the contrary. She tells herself that smoking helps keep her from succumbing to self-righteousness; she tells herself that smoking allows her to say 'nobody's perfect' when she has to, and mean it. Besides, Candy likes smoking. She likes herself as a smoker. She likes the way she imagines herself, smoking. But she doesn't like to be stared at during her smoke break. She frowns at Xavier and points at the cinderblock enclosure that holds the dumpsters and gas meter. She takes an earbud from her ear.

"What's up?" she says. "The hose is over there... Take them over there?"

Xavier smiles a little, nods, then drags the entire stack

from the doorway with a single, extended strongman pull. Candy hears Stevie gunning the buggy he's borrowed as she pushes the earbud back into her ear. The motor sound grinds against the plaintive guitar notes that fall into her other ear, and completely drowns out those first, tone-setting syllables. She's always felt a connection to The Velvet Underground's "Candy Says", for all of the obvious reasons. It's her song.

For the record, Candy has not come to hate her body. Still, she would admit that the process—the coming-to, the getting-there-from-here—intrigues her. Something about the wisdom of dissipation is attractive, no doubt about it. It sings her song. But it only sings to her now; it does not sing about her. Must it then, eventually, sing about her? Is that the deal? Or can she get close to the sound without being swallowed by it? Can she enjoy the weary glamorous knowledge of what It Requires In This World without having to hate? It's a mystery; Candy knows there's more than she knows.

Candy looks over her shoulder and watches as a large, blue-legged bird lands in the long, melancholy shadow of a telephone pole. A couple of crows swoop down and chase it back into the air. Candy loves the way the lonely backsides of storefronts, the service areas, the rarely-used alleyways, and the power company right-of-ways make her feel, especially at this time of day. These places, touched just enough by humans to be rejected by nature (the landscape equivalent of that baby bird she tried to save when she was a little girl, only to find out from her mother that by picking it up she'd only sealed its fate) are home to something else instead, something Candy feels at times only she can see. It lingers on the rails after the train's gone by. It leaves places strange.

Candy used to bring a 35mm camera to work. She would sneak in a few shots during her breaks, looking to capture that, that barely, carelessly human essence of ignored landscapes. Or the non-human essence, or whatever it is. Whatever it is has turned out to be nothing if not elusive. But it's almost been captured before, she'd remind herself. Edward Hopper found some of it hiding in the city. Whatsisname de Chirico spied its Old World cousin. And it's thick here, elaborate even. Native. This is its dominion. It doesn't take a dead man to see that.

So Candy might love the quiet places, but she doesn't like them very much. They are stingy as well as strange. Whatever it is is mistrustful.

Candy lights a new smoke with the butt of the old one. Candy knows that she will take these half-places with her. She will use them, if they will let her. They will become part of what will be her allure, what will make her fascinating. They will become part of her mystique in those fabled circles where mystique is given its due, so she pays close attention to their demands as well as to their unarticulated promises and takes what she can get. Because if these places are going to see the light of day through her, it's going to be on their terms. That much is clear. If that's Candy's end of the bargain, then Candy is more than willing to hold up her end of the bargain. After all, that's why she stopped taking photos. Presuming to direct the stuff—with the necessary ignorance of some elements, the pretentious coaxing forth of others—began to feel tawdry, like selling out cheap; not to mention altogether too unsubtle, verging on parody, and maybe even insulting. Whatever it is simply ducked into that barely-ignored region just outside the frame and teased her. She wanted to walk away from herself then. She'd jumped the gun. In that sense, she has since realized, she was disrespectful. She blabbed the first secret she was told, instead of waiting, instead of trusting that there was more. She even tried using her video camera once—tried filming fifteen-minute movies of nothing happening, going for a landscape equivalent to Warhol's headshots. She imagined framing the projection screens like still photographs, hanging them on a clean wall in a dirty neighborhood somewhere in Manhattan or L.A.—somewhere urban, somewhere seen. Somewhere seen on purpose. But when she tried to watch the movies she realized there really was nothing there, as opposed to the something-in-nothing that she was expecting, or at least hoping for. There was no poetry. The light itself seemed bored. She decided that her photos were better.

Candy pays extra close attention to the light. The first of the last days.

She applied for a departmental scholarship at UCLA a couple months back. She didn't expect anything to come of it. She'd included some of her better photos with her application; just for the heck of it, just to see what would happen. When she received a request for an interview, Candy's first reaction was disbelief. She called the number right away. She didn't want to give them time to reconsider, or realize their mistake.

They returned her call this morning.

With the last note still ringing in her ear, Candy stubs out her cigarette. She remembers telling Steve Ludich about her photos once, and about what she saw or thought she saw or wanted to see. She recalls now how it felt then, how his eyes widened, with a sort of bliss in them, as he told her how right she was. She wonders whether Stevie will come back. She hopes so. She wasn't going to take him up on his offer at first, but overhearing those assholes talking earlier may have changed her mind. If he offers again she's pretty sure she'll go. And why not? What's the worst that could happen?

As far as Stevie goes, the worst that could happen is he gets corny, or clams up and makes things uncomfortable. But so what? To Candy, even that stuff contains its own dorky charm. And Stevie looking like a teenaged Peter Sellars doesn't hurt. Not at all. She likes that. Actually the worst thing Stevie could do is to show up all spun out. That would be bad. If that happens she will obviously say no. But Candy doubts that he'd show up like that. Actually, if she had to bet on it she'd say he'll probably just get preemptively weird and not show up at all.

Candy walks through the kitchen to the dining room. The dining room is empty save for Trucker Dan, in town for his weekly danish and barstool catnap. Candy pushes the coffee pot to check its weight, then she grabs some tongs and sets about rearranging a dwindling supply of pastries in order to more evenly distribute them within the display case. Ray likes them done this way; she thinks it gives the illusion of there being more there than there is. Candy would prefer to do the opposite: let the area shrink while leaving the density alone. That, she feels, is the more effective means of retaining or, at least, conveying the quality of the morning's plenty. It keeps the pastries from drying out, too. Spread-out looks to Candy like making-do, like a scattering of mobile homes instead of a quaint Swiss village. Spread-out is too much like Cartago. But it's Ray's place, as Ray so often points out.

A quick shot of dread flashes through Candy's system. She's got to talk with Ray about maybe staying with her sister in Hollywood if and when she goes to L.A. She's not looking forward to it. It seems to Candy that the most delicate way to broach the subject of her possible departure is to ask for Ray's help in pulling it off. But it's still going to be tricky, and she needs Ray to be in a good mood. Ray's in a funny mood today, hovering around all afternoon, not really doing anything. And what's with the dress?

Candy closes the pastry case and opens the cash register. There will be one more busy spell when the lunch-for-dinner crowd shows up. Candy makes sure there are enough ones in the till and shuts the register. Trucker Dan stirs on his stool. He lifts an eyelid and peeks at her.

"You all right over there, Trucker Dan?"

"Dandy. I'll take a cup of coffee when you get a chance. No need to rush, Sissy."

"We got one more Napoleon if you want it."

"All right. Set it aside for me, would you? If you don't mind? I'll have it in a few." He winks. Trucker Dan is a winker.

"You got it."

Trucker Dan loads his chin back onto his chest and closes his eyes.

Candy pours the coffee. Trucker Dan's all right. Candy imagines he's got a nice family in Modesto or some place like that, some place where he's just Dan. Trucker Dan calls Candy "Sissy." He thinks Candy's a dead ringer for Sissy Spacek, or so he says. Where he gets that idea from Candy can't even fathom. Candy suspects Trucker Dan's got Sissy Spacek mixed up with somebody else. Loretta Lynne, maybe; but even then... Anyway, she doesn't mind the name, even though it has, once or twice, triggered reflections upon how much waitressing has in common with an even older profession. She brings him his coffee.

And why did she bring Stevie that coffee this morning? Candy's been asking herself this question all day long. Certainly, plain old curiosity had something to do with it. She has to admit she was surprised at Stevie's hesitance to share what he was up to. She expected him to gush. But seriously, what could be out there, anyway? Candy's asking herself a rhetorical question, and she knows it. Candy hasn't tried to imagine anything. She knows the reality—if it's anything like the rest of the reality around here—will only disappoint. And Stevie's been put in charge of whatever it is? Sorry, Stevie, but that says something right there. Says it can't be that big a deal; says the bar for out-of-the-ordinary is set pretty low around these parts.

That's all, probably. But Candy does want to know, like the song says, what others so discretely talk about. Or is it souls? She closes the opens the display case, takes out the Napoleon and puts it on a saucer.

Was it to thank him for ordering that veggie burger yesterday, just a paying-back in kind for a simple consideration? No. That's a copout. That's too easy. It might be closer to the truth to say that that ATV way out there on the dry lake was just about the loneliest sound she'd ever heard. It sounded like he was trying so hard. It just went on and on and on...

Candy knows she doesn't belong here. Not permanently, anyways. That was never the plan. It was her parents that brought her here, and–. She can look through their eyes, but not yet into their eyes. They are gone; yet they will end up staying. Gone; staying. Strange. Candy knows that sooner or later she will have to face it all. It'll hit her. But it will not hit her here.

Candy's been saving her tips. She's got eight hundred dollars of her own money literally socked away. There's still some money in her parent's bank account that she can access if she has to, and at some point Gary will have to deal with the life insurance. Candy would rather not think about that, though. No sense in even theoretically relying on anything outside of her own portable capacities.

But what about Stevie? Where's he going to go? All he really knows is one shitty place that doesn't want anything to do with him. It's no wonder he reads so much. No wonder he likes her, too. Sad thoughts can be so clear sometimes. Stevie's problem is he's so a part of this place that he sees himself the way the rest of them do and he treats himself just as indifferently. That's practically obvious. Candy's moved around a lot in her life; she knows what it's like to not have a best friend. But somewhere along the way she learned how to be her own ally; if not, indeed, friend. If she could only teach Stevie that trick...

Candy is staring at the display case. Is that going to be you, Stevie? Can you get out? Or will you just keep doing what you're doing; estranging yourself so you can dry up like every other thing around here, living or otherwise? You should show up, Stevie.

11

Guy and Jeanne haven't even finished pouring the footing before their sign draws some attention. A pair of wispy-bearded Dutch hikers has pulled their weather-beaten Leganza to the side of the road. The sun is behind the sign, which they attempt to read by the red pulse of their hazard lights. The driver rolls down his window.

"Excuse me!" he yells.

"Okay," Guy shouts back. "You are excused."

Jeanne smiles and shakes her head.

"No, no," the young man says. "I meant to say, you are Valleroy?"

"We are both Valleroys," Guy says. He points to the sign. "The apostrophe is correct in its place."

"I got it from him," Jeanne adds. Guy smiles at his wife.

"Like rabies," he says.

The driver and passenger share a look and a nod.

"Oh," the driver says vaguely. "Can you tell us how far to the Mt. Whitney trail?"

Jeanne fields the question.

"Whitney Portal?" She points through the sign. "You just keep going till you get to Lone Pine. That'll be the first decent-sized town you come to. You're going to want to swing a left when you get to the sign there. You'll see it."

"And in Lone Pine–"

"That road'll take you to the trailhead, but you still got the whole hike from there." She glances toward the sun, then at Guy. "You boys should've started in the morning."

The driver nods toward the sign.

"What is this organ hut? There is some food there?"

"Talk to him about that." Jeanne laughs, pointing her thumb at Guy. "He'll tell you all about it."

"No organ hut! Org-own Hut. You can see it there." Guy points his shovel handle at the dome, now in full silhouette. "See? It is properly called a Communal Orgone Accumulator. It attracts energy. Good vibrations."

The driver opens his door and hoists himself up for a better look. The passenger does the same.

"And who is this Ambrose Bierce?" the passenger asks, pointing at the sign. "He is a performer? Why do you punctuate him with a question mark?"

Guy begins to answer but Jeanne preempts him.

"If you guys want food there's a place right up the street. No organs, but their biscuits and gravy are famous out here."

The passenger perks up at this.

"Famous biscuits," he says cheerfully.

Guy peers at the hikers. First one, then the other. He takes over the pitch.

"Maybe you want to get an early start tomorrow, you can stay at our hotel tonight and be the first to see him, maybe."

The hikers trade a couple of comments over the roof of the Leganza:

"U wilt blijven we hier vanavond? Zie wat dit ding is?" The driver nods meaningfully. "Misschien eten de rode paddestoelen? Huh?"

"Boete bij me. U bent de bestuurder…"

"O.K."

The driver turns back toward Guy and Jeanne.

"And this restaurant is close to your hut?" he asks.

"Of course. It is very close. Maybe a one-minute walk."

* * *

Officer Tales has his cruiser backed into the shoulder and shielded from the road by the same clump of creosote that hid Stevie's Polaris the night before. His radar gun is trained on the northbound lane, and he squints down its length like a sniper in the brush. A pickup truck—in the process of an abrupt deceleration from eighty-six miles per hour—slips by. Officer Tales follows the truck with his gun and watches as the driver glances back at him with anxious eyes. He lets it go.

Gary's been paying attention. He knows that the source of his power isn't found in the law that he is charged to enforce. That's merely ammunition, the potential for power. Authority maybe; but not power itself. The law acts just like a shifting pile of sand, only you can't see it, and you can't touch it. It's just words somewhere. It doesn't actually do anything, and it's so weak that it doesn't even have power over its own existence. EMT Tales witnessed that first hand in Tikrit, where Prometheus made up its own laws, often on the fly. It's clear to Officer Tales that anyone who confuses the law with something right or true is a fool. Enforcement is everything.

That's where Gary fits himself into the equation. There may be no real power in the law, but there is plenty in its enforcement, or more accurately in the distribution of that enforcement. In the how, where, when, and most of all the to-whom the abstract law becomes a material fact. Another useful thing he learned from the good folks at Prometheus. Every third car speeds down this stretch of road, and Officer Tales couldn't catch them all if he tried. So like a sniper he selects his quarry. The law is the bullet; he is the gun. His judgment is real. It is through him that some will be condemned to relative hardship, while others enjoy absolution. He and he alone determines who gets what, and why, and how much, around here.

But the chief seems to have his own plans lately. First the stupid Stevie Ludich duty, then the damned goose chase trying to pin down that eleven twenty-six. What's he trying to pull? Wasting time is supposed to be some exercise in humility? Some wise-old-man teacher bullshit? A whole morning spent trying to pin that thing down with nothing to show, nothing to trace even. And there's not a tow truck in town big enough to drag it off with.

"Do I look like a babysitter? A goddamned janitor?"

An antique Dodge Dart station wagon passes, doing about seventy. The rear end sags under the weight of what looks to be instruments, amplifiers, and supine musicians. A cardboard cutout of William Burroughs' head has been affixed to the Dart's long side window, and on the quarterpanel below is stenciled: 'The DeadBeats'. Officer Tales tosses the speed gun into the passenger seat, turns on the lightbar and creeps out after it.

* * *

Lee watches. He reaches the mouth of the alley just as Officer Tales hits his lights. He ducks behind a bottle-brush tree while the cruiser peels away, then cups his hands around his mouth and loudly clears his throat.

Upon hearing the signal Keith jumps from his crouch, wraps his hands around two of the wrought-iron spears that crenellate the cinderblock fence, and uses them to hoist himself into Doyle Gomez' back yard. Lee scrambles across the alley and follows him over, scaling the fence with respectable agility considering his flip-flops, not to mention his gut. There is a light on in the front of the house that barely makes it through the back window. Keith puts his finger to his lips and points to a small, crumbling stucco outbuilding; sort of a midget garage in the corner of the yard. Lee flaps over to the structure and tries to peer into a small window along its fence-side wall.

"It's–"

"Shhhh!"

Keith delicately skirts the side of the house until he catches sight of the Gomezes bickering in sign language over what looks to be Judge Judy on the T.V.; as the closed captioning under the judge's astonished face reads 'What in God's name is wrong with you?'. Keith looks down the driveway. Mr. Gomez' pristine '79 Mercury Monarch is parked half in the driveway, half on the sidewalk. The big sliding driveway gate is wide open; still there isn't much clearance between the car and the chainlink fencing on either side of it. Keith rolls a dirt-heavy, plantless planter from the pathway leading to the back then sneaks around to meet Lee. Lee has a nail in his hand and is attempting to use it to score a line around the window sash.

"What the fuck are you doing?" Keith manages somehow to shout and whisper at the same time.

"It's painted shut." Lee explains.

"What's wrong with using the fucking door?" Keith grabs the nail from Lee's hand and throws it at the window. "Your fat ass ain't going to fit through that shit! Come on!" Lee slides around to the front of the structure and lifts the door just enough for Keith to squeeze through from the side.

"Hold it from in there. Right where it is. Don't let it fucking spring open." Keith slides under the door and Lee lets it close behind him. The space smells of lawn chemicals, old dust and corkboard.

"I can't see shit." Lee whispers.

"That's because it's dark, dumbass. Close your eyes for a minute."

They stand there for several seconds, in the dark, with their eyes closed.

"All right open them. Now look for a light." They grope around, looking for wall switches or hanging chains. Lee discerns the outline of what turns out to be an old metal desk lamp of the kind that requires the ON button be held down while the fluorescent bulb primes itself. On his third try Keith figures out the trick. He bends the flexible metal cables to send a dingy half-light into the center of the room. In the midst of a mess of paint cans, roller cages and tarps sits a go-kart; one of those miniature grand prix racers, liberated two summers previous from the Ridgecrest Family Fun Center.

"There she is," Lee says admiringly, "in all her glory. How'd you know it'd still be here?"

"Where else would it be? You think he took it with him?" The 'he' Keith refers to is Doyle Gomez, who recently cleaned up his act in trade for a job out in Ridgecrest selling stereo equipment right next door to the go-kart track, of all places. Keith locates a gas can, inspects the contents, unscrews the cap from the go-kart's gas tank, gives the tank a sniff and pours it full.

"Let's try to start it."

"Here?"

"Why not? They're both fucking deaf, dude. Anyone else'll just think it's a lawn mower."

"Oh yeah. No shit, huh?"

"Huh."

Keith puts his foot on the spoiler next to the engine, flicks the toggle to RUN and yanks the starter cord. Nothing. He pulls again, and again, managing only to fill the space with the smell of uncooked gasoline.

"Where's the choke on this thing?" Keith says. Not bothering to look for the choke himself, he yanks the cord again. This time the engine sputters into a phlegmatic idle and the go-kart begins inching forward, slowly compacting the scattered paint cans against the back wall.

"Shit!" Keith turns the toggle and the engine dies with a hack, leaving the air thick with exhaust. "Fuck dude. I'll bet this thing doesn't even have reverse." He peers under the steering wheel. "Yep. It's just gas and brake." He looks over at Lee, who is thumbing through an old Life magazine.

"Put that fucking thing down and let's get this bitch turned the other way."

Lee holds up the magazine.

"This is from the week I was born."

"Trip out. Now put it down. Let's get the fuck out of here."

"That's pretty coincidental though, right?" Lee marvels.

"I just picked it up for no reason, without even thinking."

"No shit? Without even thinking?"

"Tssss." Lee tosses the magazine. He walks over to where Keith stands, bumping him slightly while pretending to examine the go-kart. "You want to drive this thing out of here?"

"You want to carry it?"

"So… so what do you want to do again?"

"You'll go first and make sure the coast is clear. Then you're gonna open the door and I'm gonna drive this thing out. Simple as that. The only hard part might be getting past that piece of shit in the driveway, but I think we're good. You just watch me until I get to the sidewalk, then you fucking jump on and we'll take the alley back. And fucking pay attention."

"Back where?"

"Esther's backyard. Where did you think?"

"Why my house? And I wish you'd stop calling my mom by her name, man. It's fucking… nasty."

"Esther's house is closer than mine."

Lee stands with his arms crossed, trying to protest with silence. His defiance fades quickly, though, and he circles the go-kart again.

"Jump on where?"

"Who gives a fuck? Anywhere." Keith looks behind the bucket seat. "Stand up right here."

They get the go-kart turned around. Keith, after aiming a kick that sends the wafer-like remains of a pack rat skittering across the concrete floor, climbs into the machine. Lee starts the engine then shoves himself out through the door, pinching his hand in the process as the torsion spring he's using as a swing bar bows against his weight.

"God damn it," he says matter-of-factly to the blood blister developing at the base of his thumb. He does a hasty perimeter check, then he runs back to the outbuilding and throws the door open. The go-kart's engine nearly stalls as Keith applies the gas, but it recovers and he zigzags toward the driveway while Lee, flip-flops slapping the concrete pathway, lumbers behind. Upon reaching the driveway they realize that the Monarch has moved. It's been pulled further up into the driveway, and the long gate has been shut behind it.

"Fucking open it! Quick!" Keith yells, desperately easing his way along the car's length. Lee tugs at the gate, but he's only got one good hand and it's on the wrong side. He runs over to the end bar and pushes it with his shoulder. Slowly, squealing and shuddering, the jammed gate wheel scrapes along the track for a couple of feet before sticking again.

"It's hard!" Lee whisper-yells.

"Well I can't get out!" Keith shouts, abandoning any pretense of whispering. "I've got to hold the brake!"

With a sustained, pressurized grunt Lee muscles the gate open. Keith bounces through and takes off down the sidewalk. Lee watches him go then slowly bounces down the sidewalk after him, staring down at his palm and muttering.

The Gomezes watch the entire scene from their porch. When it's over Mrs. Gomez goes back inside while Mr. Gomez trots down the front steps to the sidewalk. Mr. Gomez is not an interior monologue kind of guy. He signs what's on his mind. He stands there facing Lee's retreating form, and gestures:

"Good! Get that fucking thing out of here. You good-for-nothing punks. Ha! It's your problem now!"

Then he walks over to the driveway gate, lifts it, gently slides it closed, and padlocks it.

12

Ray sits down at her desk and turns toward the west-facing window. A philodendron on the sill filters honey-colored sunlight, softening it before it reaches her features. A small swivel mirror sits atop an unsteady pile of receipts, spreadsheets, and unopened envelopes. The old Gateway sits dormant on a folding table next to the desk awaiting its time of the month, which was scheduled to have arrived the day before yesterday. Ray does her best to ignore the computer by focusing instead (shifting her position slightly and tapping the mirror just a smidge) on getting her face lit just right. It's an act of defiance, her ignorance. Ray has yet to figure out what the big benefit is in putting all this shit into the computer when it's already on paper. Other than to her tax accountant, that is. And he'll cut her a break on his 'professional fees' because of all of his work that she's now doing, of course. Yeah, right. That'll be the day.

Don't get started on that.

Raylene plugs in her hair dryer and opens her purse. She takes out a compact and an eyelash curler. She heats the eyelash curler with the hair dryer and brings it up to her face. She squeezes carefully and holds it like that, while eying through the device the reflection of her same lidless eye, eying back at her like a snared animal. With her free hand she clicks on the clock radio. Anne Murray's version of "Danny's Song" seeps into the office as she repeats the procedure on her remaining lashes. She unplugs the hair dryer and plugs a curling iron in its place, then opens her compact and applies her makeup by tapping, rapidly, at her face with the pad. She sucks in her cheeks and purses her lips. With her free hand she takes her curling iron, grabs the clump of hair closest to her face, flips it like a patty on the grill and holds it there while she examines her reflection.

It's been a while since Raylene has eaten someone else's food. She tells herself that that fact alone is cause enough for celebration; and she might as well look her best. Ray isn't letting herself think about old times, though. No, no 'why now?' now at all. But it's still nice to be surprised every once in a while. She adjusts her bra strap with her thumb while seizing and flipping another portion of hair. She directs herself to stare tenderly at the reflection, almost softening her features into an expression of confusion. She relaxes those facial muscles she's worked so hard to develop; lets them fall and rest, and looks deeply into her own round eyes.

13

Chief Hill winds his way through Red Rock Canyon, thinking: that makes oh-for-two in the entering of places of worship today, don't it. And a tank of gas to boot.

After driving all the way to Kingdom Hall he never made it past the parking lot. Of course when he arrived it was with every intention of at least stepping inside the building, but truth be told he hadn't really thought it through much to that point. At the last moment, sitting there in the truck, he changed his mind. Turns out there was just no reason for him to go in there. The big beige box still makes him think post office. So he pulled his truck from the parking spot and brought it around to the drop-off area instead, over to where he knew he could talk. And talk he did. Not out loud, of course; but still, he made sure he chose his words carefully. He explained everything he could as best he could. He told Delores how he felt she might be trying to tell him something. He told her that he hoped - he felt he knew what that thing might be. He told her he under-stood why she would ask of him what she did, after what he did. He told her how it seems to him that the pain he'd caused her all them years ago was left here, with him. As that seems to be the case, he said, he told her he was hoping that now that she'd shed her mortal coil and all her positions on those things might have changed. He told her that he hoped that was the meaning—or at least a meaning—of the sign, if indeed a sign's what it was, or is. He told her he was sorry again, and thanked her for understanding about... about how no one should be asked to die alone. He told her that he knew she loved him, and forgave him, and could never—especially now that those things could no longer matter quite like they once did—ever wish that upon him. He told her that he loved her too, every second of every minute of every day, and for every one after that.

A couple of stray raindrops—must've been blown over from the cloud that just peeked over the pass, he thinks—hit the chief's truck just before he pulls away. Big drops; drops big enough to gather into rivulets and slide fitfully down the steep glass slope of his windshield.

Now with the sun going down and a great big humid bag of ribs and fixings riding shotgun, the chief wonders if he was right. Maybe he should have talked to her first. Ah well... Maybe, maybe, he's starting to sound like Guy! What's a man to do? What's done is done, besides. And God? God, you got to know it's near impossible to be sure of anything these days. That's a natural fact. And that's how it's supposed to be, by appearances...

The chief is still trying to converse in this way when he spots the sign.

"Well I'll be god damned!" he says aloud, slowing down to read it. He apologizes: "Beg your pardon there, uh... Jesus? You know how these things are. They take time..."

14

The hot water is just about to run out. Stevie hears it before he feels it—a subtle, high-pitched ring in the pipes, similar to that pre-sound that tells him his dealer's coming on fast—and so has time to brace himself.

How long has it been since Stevie's taken a shower? A week? Easy. More. If Stevie could say for sure he probably still wouldn't. He shuts off the hot water and lets the cold shock his system for a five-count before jumping out and into a waiting towel. Man, showers are great! he thinks to himself, I really ought to take them more often. Really–

Stevie gets dressed slowly, and into clean clothes. He brushes his teeth and, using his fingertips as a comb, combs some conditioner into his hair. He looks at himself in the mirror, gives his face a couple of slaps to get the blood flowing up there, tiptoes past his aunt's room, and heads for the kitchen sink. He washes the thermos, sniffs it, and washes it again with a new sponge. He grabs a plastic bag from under the sink and heads into the living room.

Today's tapes are on the love seat next to the front door. As he looks at them it dawns on Stevie—for the first time, really—that he will actually be getting paid for what he is doing. Better yet, for what he's already done. Real money already made. Here's his timesheet, right here. Working for the man. What strikes Stevie now is how easily he came to be working for the man. Just by doing what he would've done anyway. Nothing. Is that how it works? You just fall into these things?

Stevie walks into the dining room and turns to face his reflection in a wall of gold-veined mirrored tiles. It feels good to be clean; to be smooth and not sticky. To be thinking at a reasonable clip: it feels comfortable, like a blanket almost, or like he'd imagine a massage to be. It's nice, isn't it? To let things soak in a little bit, or soak into things instead of scampering around their surface connections all the time.

Also being reflected is the twilight coming through the living room curtains behind him. The light's got that alluring quality, Stevie notes to his relief. The Golden Empire'll be closing soon. Stevie gives himself a mental pep talk. Look at that light! Let's get in it! You ready? If you're going to do it you've got to do it now, and you're going to do it so go do it. He walks back into the living room, throws the top three tapes and the thermos into the bag and steps with it out the door. When he gets outside he takes a deep breath and lets the sweet magic-hour air course through his system. This is how eighteen is supposed to feel, he tells himself. At least how it always feels in books. Sweet. Memory-sweet. Sure feels good when the air is like this. And a full moon's coming too, right? Good.

Things are starting to happen, Stevie. You're being set in motion. Weird acceleration. Here goes.

The fluttering in his stomach adds a strange bounce to

Stevie's step as he cuts across the dyed gravel of his aunt's front plot. He walks down the middle of the empty street in order to take in the more expansive view it provides. Breathe it in. The bag swings at his side. He reaches the 395 just in time to see Chief Hill go by in his pickup. Stevie, who hasn't yet decided who he wants to talk to first, doesn't advertise his presence, and the chief drives by without seeming to notice him. Actually there's something in the way the chief keeps his eyes locked on the road in front of him that suggests to Stevie that he—the chief, that is—is also looking to blend into the background a bit. He watches the truck go by then takes his gaze up the road to where a set of round, passive-looking headlights are inching toward town. They swing from side to side and bounce, almost twirl; they remind Stevie of an old anthropomorphized cartoon jalopy. Strangely, the chief, rather than showing any curiosity himself, instead makes a left turn just before the police station and disappears behind the mobile home settlement. Well that makes things easier anyway. Stevie can just drop off the tapes with another note. Include something about this Yninguez-whoever-she-is. Save the conversation for later. Besides, that's going to be a tricky thing to explain in person. But at the same time that means no more possibilities for excusal, no hanging late with the chief, no "...just couldn't... got waylaid, hanging with the chief..." He looks off to his left, beyond an old pile of mine tailings to the inhuman-scaled colonnade of transmission towers. You're being set in motion, like it or not. Potential energy will become kinetic energy, whether or not you know or care how. Stevie takes a deep breath, then another one. Smoke the beehive in his stomach. He looks to his right. Looks like Valleroy's hit the jackpot tonight. A funny-looking assortment of cars are scattered around the courtyard, and there are lights on in a couple of the rooms. "Hmm," he hums to himself. When was the last time he'd seen that? He turns back toward the head-lights. They're pulling into the police station parking lot, leading an old station wagon that takes the right-hand turn keeling like an old ship. Just as the car's rear end smacks the driveway ramp, Stevie gets a glimpse of Gary Tales in the driver's seat; smiling. Man! Stevie thinks. A lot can change while you're in the shower!

That changes things again, though. Now he's got to deal with Fairytales. Stevie slumps, straightens himself up. Fuck him, he tells himself. I'm just doing my job, right? He reaches the station and takes the stairs to the front door. Gallegos is behind her desk. She glances up from her monitor when he walks in, then ignores him. Gallegos has never, so far as Stevie can remember, ever said an extra word to him. Sure, she's handed him forms to fill out, paperwork; she even gave him his stuff back when he was arrested. And the necessary information was given on those occasions. Nothing more. Seems to Stevie that when she looks at him it's like she's not really; it's more like she's got some picture in her mind of something not worth bothering with, and the look on her face is in response to whatever that thing is. She wears a uniform. She's got a big brass tag pinned to her pocket that doesn't include a first name. Just 'Gallegos' in stamped capital letters. Stevie hoists the bag for Gallegos to be able to see if she were to so choose, which she does not. There is a table and chair set up outside of Chief Hill's office. Stevie sets the bag on the table and sits down to pen his note. He overhears Fairytales doing his smug and contemptuous routine from the processing room across the hall:

"...shoulda thought of that before doing seventy in a fifty-five mile-an-hour–"

"Officer–" a nervous-sounding voice that Stevie guesses is the driver's says, "the sign said seventy–"

"What sign is that?"

"The uh, the speed limit sign–"

"And where was that sign?"

"You mean like where on the side of the–"

"I'll ask it again. Where was the sign?"

"I'm trying–"

"You're in a fifty-five mile-an-hour zone if you can read that sign."

"Aw, give me a break!" It's a different voice; sharper, louder. The first voice says:

"Dude, Tania. Be cool."

"Yeah, Tania. Be cool. Like cool Kelly here." Laying it on thick tonight. "Kelly..." Gary pauses, "...how do you pronounce that?"

"Co..." ahem, "Colacky?"

"Kelly Co–lacky. You sure? Okay, Kelly Co-lacky, let's see what we got. I got you in violation of vehicle code 26708 A, which states that you can't have any object or material placed, displayed, installed, affixed, or applied upon the windshield or side or rear windows. I got you for doing fifteen miles an hour over the posted speed limit." Stevie can practically smell the asshole smile on Gary's face. "And I got you for no insurance. Top of all that, you can't even prove to me that you own the vehicle in question."

"But I told you–" the driver again, his nervousness fermenting into a mild panic "–I just bought it off a friend of mine. He was supposed to… he said he was going to the DMV this week to pay off some parking tickets… or he's got to pay off the tickets with the DPT, city of San Francisco then go to the D… I forget exactly; all I know is he signed the pink–"

"This? This is nothing, Kelly. You could've done this while I was approaching what you're calling your car. Am I right?"

"I don't know." The voice sounds beaten. Kelly is going under.

Fairytales goes on:

"That thing shouldn't even be on the road."

There's a pause. Stevie guesses that Kelly must be adequately shaken, as Fairytales shifts his sights to one of the others:

"And you. You're in possession of a controlled substance.

In case you don't realize, this ain't Buzzerkeley. We take drugs seriously around here."

Stevie clears his throat with comic timing. He hears Fairytales push his chair back, stomp a couple of steps, crane himself out the doorway, scowl, throw Stevie a dry "surprise surprise", and shut the door while, inside, a female voice begins explaining in tones of patronizing patience, as if she were talking to an actual idiot—

"I happen to know…"

Stevie tries to focus on writing the note. He tears a piece of paper from his notepad, writes: 'Found some–' then stalls. Found some. Found some what? And what did Gary Tales mean by that, anyways; surprised to see me here? He sits, stalled, for several seconds before popping up and walking over to Gallegos. He asks for and receives from her an envelope and a tape dispenser. He tears the short page of his most recent notes from the notepad, puts it into the envelope, licks the envelope shut, tapes over the seal, writes "Chief Hill" on the front, tapes the envelope to the topmost reel, walks the stack into the chief's office, drops it onto his desk and walks out. Gary Tales is not on his list for anything tonight; he'd just as soon be gone before this trial adjourns.

Gallegos pushes another envelope at Stevie as he's leaving. This one has his name on it; or rather it has his name peeking through its plastic porthole from some interior document. He takes it from her, folds it into his pocket and exits the building. A second or two later he walks back through the door, heads straight to the hallway, grabs the thermos from the table and walks back out again. With the notebook framed by his left arm, and thermos hoisted by his right, he does a pretty good accidental impersonation of the Statue of Liberty for the benefit of any curiosity Gallegos might have.

Stevie separates himself from the station by way of the handicap ramp, and takes his time in doing so. He listens to the air. The big, soft whoosh of it fills his head. He looks across the 395; from his vantage point the white ghost is veiled by a sheet of streetlamp light through which it looms in the distance like some featureless, dark presence. A semi pushes up the road, moaning and hissing. An orange-blue glow lingers in the northwest; it looks to Stevie like the lights of a far-off metropolis.

Without giving too much thought to the matter, Stevie decides to avoid the highway. He'll just take the cozier route down the alley and collect his thoughts without distractions. He cuts across the parking lot while looking down at his shoes; he watches as his feet negotiate some weed-broken, apple cobbler asphalt that's dissolving into a hardpan field, barren but for a few patches of stubborn, anemic crabgrass. He scrapes his way through this field, plowing his shoe-tips into the dust, alternately imagining these as meteorites and bombs, while illusory lines of print form and dissolve in his peripheral vision. He reaches the alley and heads toward a floodlit clearing. The clearing is yet another crumbling asphalt expanse back behind the Golden Empire where the truckers occasionally idle their rigs. Stevie described them once as 'light-encrusted beasts'—a description that has managed to stick in his mind ever since. At first the lot looks to be empty, but as he gets closer and the angle-curtain is drawn, he spots the chief's pickup tucked behind a cinderblock wall, with only the hood peeking out into the light. What's up with the chief tonight? He's doing some weird– A funny thought occurs to Stevie. Funny and chilling at the same time. Funny because it's ridiculous, chilling because it's not impossible, actually... that being the thing about not knowing...

What if he found my drugs?

That self-administered little prick of a thought, impossible though it is in reality, has nonetheless reminded Stevie to get nervous again. Sneaky!

Is he going to ask her out on a date or what? Get all like that? No idea–

Making his way more or less toward the kitchen door, Stevie curls around the dumpsters and comes around behind the pickup. The truck faces the kitchen door, and the chief sits inside, also facing the kitchen door. He sees Stevie through his rear view mirror, and Stevie sees him. The shape of the chief's eyes, framed just so by the mirror-shape, look a lot like the headlights from that old station wagon. The chief gives Stevie a cool little two-fingers-off-the-eyebrow salute. The reflection is aimed at Stevie, but the chief's actual fingers point from Stevie to the door as if to say: "You. In there."

Fine by me, Stevie thinks, as he does like he feels he

might be being told. It is interesting, though. He had approached with some trepidation, and a bit of hope perhaps, expecting to be called over for an impromptu chat that would no doubt end up revealing—or at the very least precluding the possibility of—his still unformed plans. But the chief seems even less interested in conversation than Stevie himself. Stevie eases his way through the door half-wondering if the chief is on a stakeout, and is startled to see a new guy mopping up inside. He nods at the guy, who looks just as startled as Stevie is. The guy jerks his head up and keeps it there, standing his ground. There's something odd about the guy's eyes that Stevie can't put his finger on.

"Candy here?" he asks.

"Candy?" Inscrutable. Stevie tries again, touching his face in a sort of inexplicable descriptive plea.

"Candy?"

"Mmm." The guy finishes his nod and points toward the dining room. He resumes his mopping. Stevie exhales as he tramps over the bleach-wet linoleum tiles, leaving a dashed trail of reddish smears behind him.

He spots her from the griddle. She's scraping some change from the edge of a tabletop into her hand. She looks up as if sensing eyes upon her, glances around, and finds him. He braces himself as thoughts start making their way, quickly, to the exits. Luckily the look on her face tells him she's genuinely happy to see him. Delighted, even—if he's reading it right. She motions him toward the big wraparound booth. It's empty, but Stevie is surprised to see many of the other booths are occupied. He holds the thermos up, head level, as he stiffly makes his way over. Candy pulls some napkin-wrapped silverware from her apron and smiles.

"Oh, good," she says, "I don't know what I was going to do without that thermos."

Stevie gives her a smile that promises a witty comment; a smile that morphs into an anguished grimace when the hoped-for witticism fails to materialize. She waits, briefly caught in the tractor beam of his panic.

"Mamihlapinatapai."

Candy looks across Stevie.

"Huh?"

Stevie turns around. The remarkably bright-eyed occupants of the pair of stools directly behind him swivel in unison to face the space between him and Candy.

The one closest to Stevie, through a mouthful of veggie burger, repeats:

"Mamihlapinatapai."

"What are you talking about now?" Candy asks, slightly more amused than annoyed.

"I just read this word," the man says in an accent Stevie correctly guesses to be Dutch. "It means, how can I say? When two people face each other and wait for the other one to say. But no one can say. You know *El Ángel Exterminador*?" The man's eyes flash like disco balls, and his smile is pressurized.

"He is too much in love with words," the other one says, looking at Stevie.

"That is not true," the first one says fiercely, "I hate them."

Stevie smiles at Candy, grateful for the opportunity to establish a camaraderie of any sort.

"Hate them?!" he says, oddly.

"Oh yes. There is only one word I say... I mean I say there is only one word, and that word does not exist." He leans back, satisfied. "Oh, no!" the other one shouts, "Not you again!" He looks to be literally gathering a head of steam before venting: "Thief!" His own eyes shimmering, he looks at his partner but addresses the others in a hoarse whisper: "This is what I say about numbers! Exactly this!"

"Yes, but you are a liar!"

Another man; older, vested, with something in his upper lip suggesting a recently shorn beard, appears out of nowhere complete with an air of patiently waiting his turn.

"You aren't by any chance referring to the Platonic Ideal?" he asks.

"Ik zou neuken de platonische ideaal! I would fuck the platonic ideal!" the first Dutchman barks, breathing fire from his eyes.

"Excuse me?" the man replies, shaking his head back and forth involuntarily.

The Dutchman almost answers the man; he turns to him

and starts to, but yawns it off instead. Then he fills his mouth with food and leans into the face of his friend.

"Ja. Het is waar."

"Hah! You wish!"

"You wait!" the first one says, "Sir!"

The Dutchmen start giggling.

"Dief!"

"Liar!"

They snicker uncontrollably. Stevie turns from this strange display, smiles again at Candy, and crinkles his eyebrows.

"Holy smoke." he offers earnestly, leaning in.

"I know." Candy also leans in. "Late rush, too. And Ray wants me to close up tonight."

"Oh ... So—"

"—Scary. She's making this big deal about it, like I'm her like, successor or something."

"Really?" Forget smooth. Smooth is out. "So have you, um thought at all about what I asked you...what we talked about..."

"Yeah."

"So you're probably too busy? We should just skip it?"

"Well... you don't think you can wait a little while..."

"For what?"

"For me to close up here. Do you still want to–?" She looks closely at Stevie, smiles. "What conversation were you having?"

"I– I'm here. I mean I hear you. I'll have to run home and pick up my stuff. That won't take too long. That all right?"

"Are we taking that off-road vehicle thing?"

"That was the plan, but–"

"In that case you think you take me back home first real quick so I can change my clothes?"

Stevie's pulse quickens. He holds back an extra second before answering.

"Yeah. Sure."

"Cool. It'll take me like an hour to finish up. Should I bring anything from here?"

"I don't think–" and for the next extended instant his statement proves demonstrably true. Finally he peels off and scans the walls for a clock he knows isn't there. "An hour, you said?"

But Candy has started walking away. Representatives from two widely separated tables hold their checks in the air like bidders at a livestock auction.

"Hey Candy?" She turns and hurriedly steps back toward him. "Um… I haven't really eaten. Think I could get some biscuits and gravy real quick? I'll eat them outside."

"Outside!" Candy laughs. "Why?"

"I don't know; I—"

Candy pulls a napkin-wrapped silverware bundle from her apron and lays it on the large table in front of them. She pats the large vinyl booth.

"Just sit here. I don't think Ray's going to care."

Stevie shrugs, sits down and spends the next minute and a half sliding back and forth across the seat, trying to decide if it is less ridiculous for him to sit on the edge of the thing or in the middle. He settles on the middle, and when Candy comes back with his biscuits the smile on her face immediately tells him he's made the wrong choice.

"Don't pay for it." Candy slides a large oval saucer across the kidney-shaped formica plane. Stevie eats quickly, surveying the batch of strangers peopling the Golden Empire tonight. An older woman sits by herself, nibbling at an assortment of side dishes. His eyes wander to the far end of the diner, where a very clean-cut man sits taking small sips from a delicate china cup. Have I seen that guy before? Stevie wonders.

He finishes eating and releases himself, with some effort, from the booth's spongy grip. During the walk home he takes special care not to break a sweat. Damn, I just took a shower, he thinks, and I can smell myself already. He couldn't smell himself before the shower, though. What to make of that? Stevie doesn't own deodorant; now, for the first time since he was still impatient for puberty, he wishes he did.

15

Officer Tales loosens his collar and adjusts his belt. He's feeling good. He'd had those kids thinking they were headed to Lompoc before he got to waving his magic wand around. What a bunch of skittish slackers they turned out to be. He looks down at the CD they left him (as a gift no less!) but doesn't bother picking it up. DeadBeats, huh? Sounds about right. He could tell just by looking at them that they play that whiny, emotional crap like Candy listens to. That's obvious. And that chick might the toughest one of the bunch, but come on... she's the drummer? Yeah; no. Gary doesn't think so.

When he explained that though he had decided not to hold them pending receipt of authorized documentation concerning ownership of the vehicle in question etc. etc.— in contrast to what a less magnanimous arresting officer might very well and properly do—he nonetheless saw no choice but to impound the car, well, they practically congratulated him. Sensible thing to do, they agreed, considering the circumstances. What a friggin' riot. They actually thanked him "for everything" as they pressed into the doorway, each more intent than the rest to be first to flee. He had to bite his lip or else he would've laughed out loud. They reminded him of peasants or something; all thanking and shuffling, waving and grimacing. All except for the girl, whose defiant silence betrayed an unmistakable current of disappointment no doubt related to the parents she was so insistent upon dragging into her troubles.

So Gary thinks: I know they'll go back to their little urban-playground fantasy, tell all their trust-fund-blowing, SSI-cheat friends about their run-in with ignorant redneck law, but they'll leave out the thank yous. And sure, they'll try to forget about what really happened tonight; but the letters, telephone calls, the court dates looming in their collective futures—collective due to a spirit of fairness that led the bassist and toy-pianist toward a full disclosure upon the subject of socialized marijuana holdings—should keep it in their heads long enough.

Fact is, they agreed. Events led them to a choice and they chose. They chose to see that the best way to see things was his way—betraying their own convictions, indeed self-perceptions, as evidently inferior to his own in the process. They can say what they want later on, and their friends might believe it, but they won't believe it. In that way—as Gary knows full well—they are and will remain his.

The driver receives a speeding ticket, along with a fix-it for the impounded car's missing registration, which should give him a good headache when he finds out what will have become of said piece-of-shit. Gary strolls casually around the room, stopping to pretend-examine an old M.A.D.D. poster while giving time for the driver to finish filling out the release form for the band equipment. It works better if they don't see him again in a... different context. If he was perhaps a bit more honest with himself he would say he'd rather they not see him out there interacting with Officer Gallegos, getting his authority diminished by that haughty attitude she has with him. And that look on her face like he's just another punk.

Who's she think she is, anyway? Just a glorified receptionist, as far as he can tell.

* * *

Stevie's back outside with the remaining tapes in his hands and his aunt's parting "be good" punctuated a fraction of a second too soon by the sound of the door closing behind him—ringing in his ears. He walks around the carport to where the ATV is parked. He sits down, changes the batteries in the reel-to-reel and calms his nerves with a solitary exercise of dead-battery-into-trash-can throwing. He makes the first nine, badly misses the tenth, starts the engine, swallows, and hits the road.

He reaches the highway in time to catch a group of people in the midst of transporting equipment from the police station to... Valleroys'? Jeez. First thing he sees is a large bass drum coming at him from that side of the street like the world's smallest parade. As he passes the drum, Stevie spies a pair of fish-netted calves and a black... is that a paper dress? He tries to get a look at the face, but it's turned toward the lake, so all he can see is a curtain of shiny black hair. Following several paces behind is a doughy-looking figure, wobbling under the weight of various bags, items of luggage, and a high-hat stand that incongruously appears to be the primary source of his difficulties. The doughy guy peers at Stevie. Stevie looks back, thinks 'big toddler face', makes the briefest eye contact before the guy's eyes dart off like... bosons, is it? The guy puts his head down and keeps walking. The big toddler's going bald. Stevie thinks about the impression he must be making; some desert weirdo in a button-down shirt rattling down the middle of nowhere on an ATV, outdated surveillance equipment riding shotgun. You might avert your gaze too, Stevie, if you were he. Imagine that. Being scary....

A few yards straight ahead of him are two more black-clad figures busy ferrying equipment from the station side to the other, darker side of the street. Tiny-wheeled swivel casters cause the amplifiers and speaker cabinets to bounce and rattle all over the highway's degraded asphalt, making for some slow and tortuous crossings that are periodically illuminated by the headlights of oncoming cars. Stevie can see that one of the figures has got on a black suit jacket and—what's that? Are they wearing matching turtlenecks? And are those matching black berets?

Well what do you know?

The one with the suit coat has got on some oversized work boots, while the other one appears to be wearing some sort of wraparound moccasins. Stevie reaches them just as they ford the highway for a final time. He slows down and shouts:

"Hey! You guys want some help with that?"

"Um..." they hum in unison, circling their gear like

homesteaders in hostile territory, before the booted one settles on an answer.

"Naw. I think we got it all right," he says with a put-on heartland accent.

"You could throw that on here somehow, I'm sure–"

"Like we said, we think we're good." the other one replies with evident consternation. One of his wraps has sprung loose, rendering him immobile, rendering him as a guy who's got one foot in a leather bag. Stevie keeps on.

"Don't you think it'd be way easier than–"

"Can we just... not... do that?" the booted one says, in a way that could put someone in the mood to smack somebody. But that someone wouldn't be Stevie, who instead attempts to illustrate their prejudicial error and impress them, too—after all it's not every day you get beatnik bands around here—by replying in his most self-composed and mockingly reasonable tone of voice:

"By all means, then. Suit yourselves, gentlemen." He points back down the road and throttles jerkily forward. "But you might want to... well, you'll see. Good luck to you." If they reply, Stevie doesn't hear it. He does feel their eyes on his back, though, as he cuts a path across the highway to the Golden Empire.

Okay, there's Candy. She walks—steps full of purpose—along the plate-glass front windows. Double-checking something or other, no doubt. Save for her, the half-lit diner appears to be empty. A rig rests, purring, in the back lot. Stevie can't see it but he can hear it. A car flashes its brights at him then flies by at easily twice the speed limit. Whatever, dude. When he looks back at the place, Candy is no longer visible. Seconds later, as he watches, the building goes completely dark. A few seconds after that, Candy hops through the door, locks it behind her and immediately peers between cupped hands back through the glass. Satisfied, she turns toward him, already waving.

Okay. Remember how much better things go when you breathe, Stevie. It's no big deal. She's just another person; just like—well don't get carried away... just pretend you don't think, you haven't thought–

"Perfect timing," she yells when she decides he's close enough to hear. He coasts up to the entryway where she waits.

"Hey Candy. Hi. What'd you just say?"

"Huh? Nothing. I just said perfect timing–"

"Oh. Cool."

Candy looks down at the seat.

"Ah. You got that thing again."

"So... Um. I was thinking maybe you could keep it on your lap? I don't know if that would be..."

Candy walks over and lifts the reel-to-reel by one of its straps. It takes both hands.

"Jeez."

Stevie snorts, "Tell me about it."

Candy sits down, sets the machine on her lap and studies it.

"So what exactly am I looking at?"

"It's a tape recorder. It takes these." He holds up one of the reels.

"Jeez."

"I know."

"It really is heavy."

"Yeah, it's old."

"That's what it looks like."

Stevie laughs. "I know. You know what?" He lifts the machine from her lap and clumsily swings it onto his back. "I can just wear it."

"No. It's fine. You don't have to–"

"I'll just– It'll be good. Anyways we might be going over bumps and—can you hold these?" He hands her the tapes, along with the mask/microphone. He walks over to the other side, climbs on and hunches over the handlebars. "Oh yeah. It'll be totally fine."

Candy settles into her end of the seat with a wiggle.

"I got to say I'm intrigued," she says.

"Yeah?" Stevie relaxes a little, in a way. So far so good. Candy's hair whips in his face as they drive to her house. He leans toward her just ever so slightly; more like a suggestion of a lean than an actual physical thing. Still, he feels a resistance that does not give way, yet doesn't push back. "So then you said you want to, uh, change, isn't that–?"

"Yeah. Just get cleaned up a little bit. Is that cool?"

"Fine by me. Is your, uh, brother going to be there?" Stevie flashes back to what he heard at the station earlier, then of his encounter with the beatniks. He probably wouldn't be too friendly either, if he was them. Fairytales. What a tripper. Still, they didn't know he heard all that. Far as they know he was just trying to be cool, which he was. They didn't have to be... Eh. Oh, well.

"I'm hoping he's still at work," Candy replies, "but we'll see."

Oh great, Stevie thinks. That's the last thing I need is to explain any of this to him. Shit. Why didn't I consider this before? He spends the ride working on a not-too weird excuse for waiting outside, all the while preparing to coast in so Gary doesn't hear the engine.

"It looks like we're in luck, Stevie." The bungalow is dark. There's no sign of Gary. "You want to come in for a minute?"

"Well I don't want to leave this out–"

"Cause of my brother?"

"Why don't I just–" Stevie tries to suggest that he could just go around the block a couple of times but she preempts him:

"Oh, just come on in, Stevie. We'll take our chances. I'll

just say you gave me a ride, and I'm showing you some of my photographs. No biggie. Anyways, what? It would be better if he finds you wandering around out here? Because that wouldn't be strange at all, right."

"Aahh…"

"Come on."

"All right. But let's not stick around too long, 'cause…" You got someplace better to be, Stevie? "Yeah, you're right. I'm not worried about it."

They pull up to the stoop and dismount. Candy opens the front door while Stevie unloads the pack onto the porch. She flicks on a light and they step inside. The living room walls are off-white, and mostly bare. There is a print of a river—one of those long-exposure images where the water looks like a vapor trail—on one wall, a calendar and some family photos on another… and that's about it. There's a bookshelf full of guidebooks and eighties-era hardcovers, with a few more snapshots propped up here and there. A couch, a TV, a recliner and an upright piano complete the scene. Not that Stevie was expecting anything in particular, but the furnishings surprise him a bit. It smells good, though.

"Do you remember how you said you wanted to check out my photos sometime?"

"Oh, yeah! Of course," Stevie, a little too eagerly, replies.

"Here, you want to look at some while I jump in the shower?"

"Sure." Stevie follows Candy into her bedroom. So she is going to take a shower.

"Here's some of my better ones. I think." She pulls a shallow box from her closet, along with a blouse and skirt. She lays the box on the bed and goes to her dresser. Stevie watches from the corner of his eye as she grabs some tights and a black bra. She looks at him and he throws his gaze at the box.

"So these are the ones you were talking about?"

"Yeah, some of them. I sent my very best ones off—recently."

"Oh yeah? Where to?"

"Oh, just… here, hold on. I'll be right out." She tosses off her shoes and ducks into the bathroom, leaving Stevie alone in the room. Record player. Books. Cameras. Papers. Bed. Dresser. Some records on the floor. Nothing on the walls.

He reaches into the box and picks up the top photo. It's a black and white 8x10; black with a little brown in it. It's a view of the road looking back toward Olancha. The lakebed reaches in from the left edge and arcs around the top of the frame; it glows white, and looks frozen. A late-afternoon shadow cast by the cafe windows fills the lower-right-hand corner region, though the cafe itself isn't visible. The road leans off to the right, but its vanishing point can still be seen, more or less meeting the tip-edge of the lake at a point marked by a distant cinder cone. The asphalt is finely detailed; the most sharply focused part of the photo is the road. Between the road and the lake is that one old cottonwood tree, and the rotten adobe wall there next to it.

Stevie wonders briefly if that's Carthage, there. A triangular shard of arrow forms—telephone poles and their shadows—slices into the scene and comes to a vanishing point in the trona. In the middle-far distance—between the big slag pile and the cluster of dwellings way out there by the honey store—a tall, solitary figure walks off. He's slouching, and his hands are deep down in his army-jacket pockets. Stevie picks up the next photo. This one's also dark-brown-and-white; it shows the view from the back of the restaurant, looking toward the front, and though it seems to be a wider view than the last one, the overall angle is more straight at the lake. The cinderblock wall juts in from the lower right; it casts a chair-shaped shadow that appears to be loomed-over, pressed down upon Nosferatu-like by the shadow of an unseen telephone pole. The pavement here, particularly the parts covered in shadow, their intricate elaborations of aggregate looking almost staged, is also shown in very fine detail. In the middle-right distance, the late-afternoon sun again shoots right through the door opening of that bunker out there, highlighting the window opening on the other side of the roofless enclosure against the relative shadow of the interior wall, revealing the view he knows all too well. Stevie hears the jingling scrape of the shower curtain being drawn. So she'd be stepping out of the shower now, then, and—he listens. There are no sounds coming from out front. He starts thumbing through the stack of photos. They all seem to be taken at the same time of day. They all seem to be very well done, and they all share a– not spookiness, exactly, but something... old, is it? Even the ones with cars in them, or other modern things; it's like they could be from a hundred years ago, or even older than that. Is that it? And the people, that one in particular–

"You see that's you in that one?"

Stevie jumps.

"Oh, Jesus." Embarrassed, he adds: "That was fast." He looks down and realizes that the figure in the top photo is— now quite obviously—him. "Wow. I didn't even notice." Candy's behind him now, fully dressed, and just needing to comb out a few knots before she's ready.

"You're in a couple of them, actually. Hope you don't mind. You got a way of finding yourself–"

"These are really incredible, Candy!" Stevie interrupts enthusiastically as if he's just seeing them for the first time, steering the subject from his roadside wanderings.

"You actually think so? Oh, good! I've hardly shown them to anyone–" Candy cuts herself off, not wanting to get on the subject of the letter, but Stevie's distracted anyway, busy trying to come up with some way to follow up 'incredible' in appraising her work.

"You remember when we hung out a few months ago, and you told me you can see beauty in even ugly things?" She looks at him. Stevie thinks: she's impressed that I'd remember. And I paraphrased, thank God, which is way less creepy. Must be careful...

"Yeah...?" She replies cautiously.

"Well it seems to me you can see the personality of the person who takes the– the photographer, you know, to bring out the beauty... like it isn't necessarily there for sure..."

"I don't think I get it," she says to him, though something in her voice tells him she might just get some of it. "What are you trying to say?"

"Okay. I'll try..." Stevie picks up one of the photos, muting the voice that's telling him to quit while he's ahead. "Like this one. Let's see, it's got a dumpster, and the oil drums, and the bathtub full of oil it looks like, and a field. Well I'd say, if you took like, just some asshole and gave him a camera, and put him in this parking lot, and left him alone thinking his, you know, asshole thoughts, and he took a picture of this, well it would probably just be ugly. Know what I mean? But you... I mean... these are beautiful."

Taking the compliment as having more to do with the quality of her soul than that of her photographs, Candy replies:

"That's such a sweet thing to say," She says it sadly, almost ruefully. Stevie catches her drift. Sweet? That's a dead end. A key change is clearly called for.

"And, I mean, they like, capture something, but I can't put my finger on it."

"What do you mean, capture?" He's regained her attention; now he sort of wishes she'd let him off the hook.

"I don't know. It's like this *thing* that's there."

"Hmm. I always feel the opposite, like there's something that's *not* there. Something I expect to be there but never is."

"Hmm. Well maybe that's the thing I see."

"But I don't see it."

"I do."

They stare at the photo for a few seconds in silence, with Candy's leaning over Stevie's shoulder making his neck tingle.

"So you're saying that the absence of that presence I feel–"

"–comes across as the presence of that absence. You know what, though? I'm sorry. We should really get going."

"What do you think? Should I bring my camera? Or does that even make sense? I don't know–"

"Oh. Hmm. Actually... I don't know if it does, actually," Stevie says, a little sick at the idea of tickling fate more than he already has. "I don't know..."

"Yeah, I'll just leave it. You'd know, right."

"You know what?" Stevie says, "Bring it. Bring your camera."

"Are you sure?"

"Yeah. It'll be fine."

Candy smiles, takes the box of pictures, and asks Stevie to wait outside while she does one more thing real quick. Feeling more-or-less pleased with himself again (presence of that absence and all...), Stevie strolls down the hall to the living room. He wanders over to the bookshelf and stands there facing the books. He starts running his fingers over their spines. He does this thoughtlessly at first, like he's running a stick along a fence. He stops at a copy of 'Creative Visualization Made Easy' that has caught his attention. He's pulling it from the shelf when his eyes land on the framed 5x7 photograph propped next to it. He lets go of the book and picks up the picture. This one's also black and white, but more of a blue black than the ones Candy took. In it, about fifteen or twenty people—mostly men but a couple of women—pose in two rows, smiling stiffly while a large armored troop carrier towers behind them. They all wear matching tee shirts emblazoned with the word: 'Prometheus.' Stevie spots Gary. Sunburned, standing with his hands behind his back so his shirt can be read in its full, in-your-face glory. He's not the only one like that. They all stand this way, all except for the two men flanking the group. They've got their arms crossed over their chests, almost Run DMC-style, or... now there's something about the blond one on the right that reminds Stevie of something. He looks at the photo more closely. His initial confusion becomes a mix of recognition and disbelief that focuses to a nauseating surety. But how is that possible? Not in his deepest forays into speed-paranoia would he have… He looks again. There's no doubt about it. That's him. He'd recognize that buzz cut anywhere; and those forearms, those biceps clipping the ends from the name on the shirt and leaving only the middle four letters like some twisted superhero logo.

"Okay." Candy walks past him. "Shall we?" Stevie turns around and they look at each other. "What's with the face, Stevie?"

Stevie almost asks her about the picture, but then thinks better of it. Instead he asks:

"That video camera I saw in your room; do you ever use it?"

"Yeah. Sometimes."

"Why don't you bring that as well? Get more bang for your buck." Candy laughs.

"Is that what I'm looking for?" She runs back into her room and grabs the camera, leaving Stevie standing in the front room feeling like one of those old percolator coffee pots. His pulse is hot and audible in his head.

At the last second, Candy picks up the letter and, like an impulse shoplifter at the checkout counter, slips it into her pocket. She finds Stevie staring off into space so she startles him again and points him to the door. They bang through the screen and load up the ATV; Candy leading a dazed Stevie by a pheromonic leash while the next-door neighbor's dog barks at them from behind and half-beneath a low, wood slat fence about a foot or so from their feet.

As they pull away Stevie sees the asphalt of Mojave Drive brighten behind them.

"So here we are," Candy says. They've just passed the last streetlight, and are about to dive into the white darkness of the lakebed. 'We Got Tonight' inappropriately worms its way into Stevie's head. He shakes it off. He's having a hard enough time focusing as it is. His palms are sweating, making it difficult to hold his grip on the accelerator. His leg muscles are too tense, so they shake. He hopes the shaking is imperceptible. Their knees keep touching, though. For an answer he turns his body around like a bush pilot checking on his cargo, though most of this cargo is on his back. He yells "hang on!" and opens the throttle. It's too loud to talk as they speed toward the distant bay. This fact suits Stevie just fine. For the next few minutes he's Marlon Brando on a three-wheeler. All he has to do is exude competence and coolness. And: it's even too loud to think too much. He looks at Candy. She's got her eyes closed. She opens them and looks at him. He turns away first, then wonders whether it's just his imagination telling him she's still gazing longingly in his direction. He doesn't turn to find out.

Candy soaks in the scenery. She's hiked out into the lakebed a bunch of times but never at night. She's never been this far before. The moon is by itself now, rising like an air bubble from the eastern hills. It's smaller than it was a few minutes ago, smaller but brighter. What was just gold has turned to a distant white; its light coats the surrounding landscape with a spooky Surrealist patina of polarized blue-blacks, silver-blues, and metallic browns. It reminds her of a Max Ernst landscape just before the creatures arrive. Hiding in the wings, still. She imagines the ATV's engine sound, loud as it is, and the headlight as being localized abnormalities. She thinks: we are the creatures, Stevie and I; we are the strange objects in the foreground. How phenomenal! She lifts the 35mm from her lap and takes a couple of un-aimed shots at the breeze. She can't shoot the moon from here, small as it is. She holds the camera at arm's length and points it straight ahead and down. She twirls the camera in her hand and points it back at Stevie. He pretends not to notice, and tries not to focus on the warm pressure of Candy's left shoulder being applied to his own right shoulder and arm. He holds still. The same wind-whipped lock of her hair keeps grazing the back of his neck. He can feel it even when it's not there. It doesn't feel random. He has to remind himself that it is. Candy lowers the camera and tilts her head back to let the wind reach behind her ears. She arches her back slightly and nudges toward Stevie just a bit but perceptibly and enough to increase the overall surface area where they touch. She closes her eyes briefly and smiles. Stevie takes a longer look at her face. She's wearing lipstick that looks like pearl in this light, and her eyelashes shine too. She furrows her brow curiously and opens her eyes. Stevie watches her focus from just to the right of where he now pretends to look. She turns to him and holds a smile long enough for him to glance, smile back at shyly and turn away from twice.

"This is just fantastic!" she yells.

"I'd say we're about half-way!" Stevie replies.

"Wow." Candy twists around to look at the dimming lights of Cartago. When she turns back she and Stevie are no longer touching. Stevie pretends not to notice this either but after allowing a couple of seconds to pass he lets himself lean forward to take some of the weight off his back. He looks down at the front fender and the trona spray being thrown from the tire. Now he swivels around and looks behind them. He looks at their wake. He thinks: soon that wake will vanish. It's not only water that gets absorbed. Maybe everything does that.

* * *

Chief Hill opens the door and slowly rolls out of the truck. He's been sitting behind the Golden Empire for an hour, lurking like he's on some sort of a stakeout. He clicks the door shut, stands up and stretches. He looks at the back door of the diner. The place has been dark for several minutes and, from what his ears tell him, the chief surmises that Stevie's out using Valleroy's buggy as a taxicab. He's not surprised. Matter of fact, the chief reckons he might've even given the kid the idea... without meaning to, of course. Not that he considers it a good idea either by any stretch, she being Gary's kid sister and all. Course it could occur to Gary that those two got a lot in common, him and Stevie; not the least being they got... well, they all three got that in common. Course Joyce is quite alive, he thinks, if you want to call it that. Chief Hill locks the truck door. What a shame. She was a bright kid, too, but impetuous from the get-go. Always a little wild, she and her sister were. All that carrying on of theirs... But Joyce, she got downright feral before they carted her off to Atascadero. No one ever did figure out what finally sent her around the bend. He looks down at the wad of keys he's holding. He tosses it, spins it in his hand with the deftness of a safecracker till the right key falls between his thumb and forefinger. But Stevie's all right. Chief Hill wonders how much Stevie knows about himself. Might make him more careful to know. Or the opposite could be true. Who's to say? He looks to the left, right, then left again before crossing the shattered concrete pad to the back door of the Golden Empire. It disconcerts the chief to think he might've been doing some projecting with the kid, what with his own not knowing—

The chief heard the chaotic combustion of Valleroy's two-stroke gunning across the road. Headed out again, the sound gradually dropping in pitch with... reasonableness. The chief got a cold shock in his gut. It's that uncertain feeling again. He's been getting a whole lot of that lately. Stevie's all right, he guesses again. He's been doing a lot of that lately, guessing. One thing he does know, as he steps into the dark kitchen entrance and sets the bag of barbecue on a stainless-steel sink counter: Stevie's putting some miles on old Guy's buggy. The kid's doing his work. That old frog, on the other hand...

16

Jeanne pushes another complimentary "Orgone Hut" postcard across the lacquered countertop. She slides the two twenty dollar bills toward herself. She holds them in her lap, peeks down at them card cheat-style, tosses them into a box, reaches behind her, grabs an unnumbered key and spins it back toward to the man.

"And which room is that again?" She hasn't said.

"Just look for the silvery doorknob," she says now.

"The silvery—"

"You'll find it."

The man thinks to say something, but instead turns around slowly, snaps his watchband on the underside of his wrist and wanders away. Guy ducks past him in the doorway and, smiling broadly, approaches Jeanne.

"Guess" he says, his eyes glinting.

"Hmm?"

He doesn't answer her verbally. He walks around the counter, takes her hand in his and reaches behind them to flip a light switch. She looks up at him.

"Really?"

"One more is parking. That's it."

"And they're all here to see it?"

"Curiosity. Of course. Why not? And I think the road is not good on the pass, maybe. They are coming in wet."

She raises her eyebrows.

"The peoples?"

"The peoples!"

"So no one else."

"Not for tonight."

"So? When are we going to open it up?"

"Soon. Let them relax, maybe. It will be very dramatic for them to wait. And then they will see. And then they will feel."

"And the Sheriff? You talk to him yet?" Guy pivots and gives her a wide-eyed freeze-frame pose.

"He was here?"

A tall figure fills the doorway behind Guy, preannounced by the sound of rattling metal and boot heels on the wooden plank floor. Jeanne is immediately reminded of Clint Eastwood in some spaghetti western; Guy thinks Leone too, but instead of Eastwood his mind flashes to Henry Fonda in *Once Upon a Time in the West*; Frank entering that adobe in Harmonica's memory. The man's eyes have that same lifeless quality, suggesting either utter self-possession or something maybe more pathological. As Guy's own eyes peel away and down he sees that it isn't cowboy boots he heard coming in but English riding boots and spurs. The man acknowledges Guy as he walks up to the counter.

"I would like a room, please," the man says, addressing Jeanne now. His voice suggests nothing.

"Unusually busy tonight," Jeanne remarks as she hands him a card to fill out. "You got the last of them."

"Did I?"

Jeanne drops her smile and looks him in the eyes. It's been a long day and she's in no mood for bank shots.

"We got one more room," she says coolly. "It's yours if you want it."

"Of course," he stretches his lips into something resembling a smile, "I'll take what I asked for." Jeanne watches as the man folds the card and slips it into his front pocket. He pulls two crisp hundred-dollar bills from the same pocket. As he hands her the money he says:

"I'd like to see my room first." He taps his pocket. "I'll fill this out when I'm settled, if I might be permitted that... accommodation." Jeanne looks down at the money, then back at the man.

Jeanne pins up her cheeks to expose her canines.

"This is a motel. It's got motel rooms in it. It ain't the Frontenac." She lowers one cheek, raises one eyebrow and says: "All right. Just be sure to bring it back. Don't make me chase you around for it." She glances at Guy. Guy glances away and freezes, like a cat, as if freezing renders him invisible. Jeanne takes the money and hands the man a key. He examines the key, thanks her and walks out of the office, his spurs tinkling like castanets to the flam beat of his boot steps. He doesn't ask for a room number. Guy and Jeanne give each other looks. Jeanne's says: 'you sure this is a good idea?' while Guy's says 'no'. Jeanne frowns.

"Well you got your peoples, Guy. But I'd feel better if you talked to Jim about this. I don't think he had this in mind when–"

"Who could have this in mind? Not me, Jeannie. For sure. I'll talk to Jim Heel. But it is better, maybe, for now…" Guy searches for the words, "It's a roadside curiosity, Jeannie." He calls Jeanne 'Jeannie' when he's uncomfortable. "…that is the genius thing. Who will believe that the little brown thing in the outfit is what it is? No one is who. It is better than trying to hide it. Who would imagine so many, but… it's good! It's good, Jeannie. You'll see. They will come for the Ambrose Bierce, and stay for the communal orgone, eh? And…"—as if he's the one who needs convincing—"we only charge for the rooms, Jeannie. Not the accumulator…"

Jeanne loosens up. She says, "Well, I guess we'll have to just see what happens, right?" With all his maybes Guy's rarely unsure of himself. He's unsure of himself now and she doesn't like it. "Quite the clientele, huh? D'jou notice? What do we got… a rock band, a professor… and one woman said she hadn't–"

"No cameras."

"What's that?"

"No cameras inside. I will have to tell the peoples no cameras while inside the accumulator. Can you write a note for me to put on the outside? Just: 'no cameras'?"

"Why? Where are you going?"

"I'll just be checking to see..."

"Take those towels, would you?" Jeanne points to a stack of stiff, abrasive towels that's leaned against the water cooler. "I didn't get a chance to put them in the rooms yet." Guy turns and addresses the stack.

"Okay," he says to it, retreating– "but first I need to check..." as he drifts out of the room like he's being summoned, leaving Jeanne alone with the towels.

17

Stevie eases the machine around the large rocky outcropping.

"You should get your camera ready, Candy. We're coming in to it now." Candy peers out at the moonlit bay; what she sees is acres of parallel lines tilled into the trona. She's more confused than overwhelmed.

"You planted something out here?" she asks.

"Not me, but yeah. Somebody did. I'm more like harvesting."

"What can you plant in salt?"

"Check it out." They've reached Stevie's 'bookmark': an orange peel marking his last night's parking spot. He takes a hard left turn and cuts into the bay. The ATV rides the edge between read and unread as Candy points, films the rush of oncoming words. Stevie cuts the engine and they coast to where he left off earlier. Candy lights a cigarette and starts fiddling with the still camera.

"I don't know what to say," she says. "What is this?"

"Honestly? You got me. I found it the other night. They got me reading it into this here." He pats himself on the back. He plugs in the mike cord. "With this." He reaches for the mask, but it's snug in Candy's lap. He just points at it. "My invention. During the day it gets pretty nasty out here."

"Okay…" Candy responds. Suspecting she's coming across as more narrow-minded than she intends, she almost chirps: "so this is the big secret." She peers up and toward Cartago. She can't see the town; only unread words that spread out wide and merge in the distance. Beyond that, the heavy clouds fingering their way through the peaks and ridges look just like a giant phosphorescent squid.

"Check that out," she says, pointing with the mask that's still connected to Stevie.

"Here. Let me see that real quick?" Stevie pulls the microphone from the mask. It makes a popping sound. "We don't need this." He addresses the clouds. They look to him like a wave crashing against a seawall, or opposing wave. Staring, he attempts to mimic the apparatus' popping sound with his thumb and cheek.

"Whoah…" he replies at last. He turns to Candy. "Well, I could try to tell you about it or we could just start reading… or here… I could read and you could take pictures, or film or whatever. What do you want to do?"

"Yeah, let's just start, I guess. I'll just follow you with the camera. But wait. First," she points at the mask, "think you can put that back together for a minute just so I can get some shots of you wearing it? It ought to look amazing out here."

"Sure." He does, and pretends to start reading as Candy figures out the lighting. Amazing, she said. After a minute he yells:

"Does it look amazing?"

"Yeah, that's good." Stevie dismantles the apparatus again and turns on the machine to start reading in earnest. Candy walks close behind him so she can listen while she shoots, and see what he's reading as he reads it. The moon shines crisp in the clear eastern sky as Stevie begins:

...No one appeared to notice any of this, of course. I couldn't say how long we'd been standing there when finally the voice said, "Let's move on then. Ms. Donner?" Ms. Donner moved on. I was having a hard time paying attention to her. It was almost as if her volume had been turned down. She was saying something about editing songs for cheerleader competitions. Something about her days being broken up into two-minute, thirty-seconds-long episodes. Not a second more or less...

Someone had been staring at me ever since I finished my bullshit spiel. They wouldn't take their eyes off me; or, my eyes, rather. I decided to stare back, give them a taste of their own medicine. While I did that I started thinking about what I had just done. My mind seemed to have put itself back together. While not actually hearing my voice coming from the helmet it was a lot easier to imagine it all as some kind of trick. The exercise was obviously part of some sort of experiment, and God knows what they could be measuring. I hoped that I had put a wrench in their works. What did they expect, anyway? You got to be clear about your parameters. If you allow for a possibility then you got to accept it when it happens. So stick that in your equation! But then I wondered about the money.

I decided that, starting that evening, every day I would withdraw the daily maximum, figuring that if the whole thing goes up in smoke the smoke is likely to include my new bank balance.

At some point during Ms. Donner's ordeal I stopped listening. It was getting harder and harder to hear through the helmet, so I really had to strain to follow along. The stories ran together. I fell into a sort of narcotic trance, not feeling my head or back, not thinking anymore about how long I had been or was going to have to stand there on the stone floor. Not thinking anything, really. I was startled when the host voice broke through the drone.

"When I call your name, please exit by way of the escalator. You are free to go for the day. Any arrangements we have previously made concerning further communication should be adhered to. When you reach the exterior door you will find your shoes, bags, and so forth in an alcove marked to correspond with your position here. For example, if you are standing at A5, yours is alcove A5. Please place your helmet, as well as your slippers, into your designated alcove. Now then. We will do this alphabetically. Vroyer Arcasian…"

The dismissals were spaced a couple minutes apart, presumably to give the person leaving time enough to get out of their getup and back on the street without being recognized. I was grateful for my name being toward the front of the alphabet. I couldn't say what time it was, but I would have guessed around two-thirty. Everything else aside, the schedule was shaping up as one I could live with. I had forgotten how tense

I was, even in my stupor; I was only reminded of it by the sheer elation I felt as I descended the escalator. I could feel the dopamine permeate my nervous system. It felt (and almost tasted) like my brain was a thick pancake being drenched in warm, amber syrup. My gloves seemed to notice it too. They got warm and slightly tingly. I left them on as I made my way out of the compound. I was a little optimistic in my estimate of the time, but not by much. I had been instructed at some point to keep my phone turned off while 'at work', though I couldn't remember when that directive was given. It was three-thirty when I turned my cell phone back on. I was starving. The best time for whiskey, I thought. Close as you could get to slamming liquor. Then I thought: No. Let's not take that ride today. Let's get some carbohydrates in our system before we change our mind. And get that three hundred dollars out of the ATM before they change theirs. If they haven't already, that is. A nervous spasm hit my empty stomach. Time to find out if I screwed myself with that avocet business. It occurred to me that there was bound to have been someone in that room with enough related knowledge to know I was full of shit. And certainly he—'he!' knew. 'Now what did you have to do that for?' I scolded myself. 'You could have told them anything!' Then: 'now now, we don't know anything yet.' My gloves had gotten cold. I took them off and put them in my bag. I took my time walking down the hill, framing imaginary photographs as I went. No one else was on the road. No fat guy further down, no one coming up behind me as I loitered in spots along the way. I hoped that Hope would be in a 'take what you can get' mood towards me, and I could finally tell her about what weird shit I'd been up to. And the money I was making. That meant no drinking. I reached the bottom of the hill. The idea of a civil, shameless conversation put a spring in my step. The spring lasted for a few blocks, but by time I reached the ATM I had myself worked up again; again convinced that there would be nothing there. Once again I let my anxiety fester for a minute before putting in my card, and savored it. What fucked-up games I play with myself! I even wondered, while standing there: Is there something I'm actually getting out of these games, this self-administered psychic harassment? A weapon for killing time, is that it? Is that all? I wondered: did these games even have a winner? And if they did, was it ever—ever!—me? I couldn't see how. Why, then…? And: couldn't a definition of a 'loser' be someone whose most private mental scenarios tend to play out as unwinnable? And: is that our core identity? Those private loops? Like some melody that gets played out, like so many cover songs, in our actions? Like some thought/action-equivalent to a genetic stamp?–… –that thought train was derailed the instant I saw my balance. The money was there. Okay. Back in the saddle. Now, time to get some grub. Maybe I'll buy a present for Hope, I thought; give her a pleasant surprise. Hmmm… What would she like? I couldn't think of anything. I decided to find a Chinese place that had sizzling rice soup and think it over while eating. Soup is good thinking food, I told myself. And who knows; maybe we'll end up going out to dinner or something. So keep some appetite, just in case. As of now, though, it's hard to think when you're running on fumes…

Just as that thought crossed my mind a cloud of exhaust

rolled up my torso to linger at my face. It came from a derelict onetime school bus, downshifting as it ground its way to a stop at the light. Barely blue in color, with a long stripe of house primer where the school's, or could've been a church's, name used to be. It rattled there in front of me like a neglected steam boiler. I took a look at the driver as I passed the accordion doors. The driver was a large, bald black man. I stared at him, wondering. He looked back at me, and we locked eyes for a few seconds until the light turned green and his right arm, with the surety of muscle memory, swung the gearshift into low. I stood and watched as the bus dragged itself through the intersection and shuddered to a stop across the street, bleating like a distorted tuba. A head and arm appeared out of one of the windows. It yelled at me, "Hey! You!" I pointed to myself. "Come here a second!" The arm made an exaggerated motion toward the bus. The voice was a woman's, and it was no squeal either. I jogged toward the bus. It dripped raw fuel from its tailpipe. I reached the window where the woman was. She had thick, tightly curled copper hair and large, glistening eyes. She squinted slightly, smiling, and said "Hey did you come from—" She turned around and asked someone I couldn't see something I couldn't hear. Then, back to me: "—up there?" She pointed in a random direction.

"I did…" I said.

"We're going to go get something to eat. You want to come with?"

The doors opened with a loud 'psssshhhh' and the bus bowed down slightly, camel-like.

"*You guys came from up there, too?*" *She nodded.* "*What were you thinking? …about food, that is?*"

"*Well Curtis said he knows a good barbecue place down by the Coliseum.*"

"*Hmmm…*" *I rarely ate meat, and most barbecue places didn't have many other options. Even the vegetables usually had meat in them.* "*Aww, what the hey. Why not?*"

I climbed onto the bus. Curtis nodded at me. He still had his gloves on.

"*Hey. How you doin'?*" *I said, nodding back.*

"*I'm doing. Hop abuh-board.*"

"*Thanks.*"

I turned to take a seat. Most of the seats had been removed. There was a set where the curly-haired woman sat, and another set opposite those. A young woman occupied both seats of the opposite set. She had her feet up on the inside seat, and she stared out the window like she'd been on the bus for days. At the very back of the bus was a vinyl-upholstered bench. It was empty. There was brown carpet covering the floor; on the carpet two men sat cross-legged. One of them was the guy with the earlobes from the day before, and the other was the smart-ass in the turban. I said "howdy" as I took a seat on the floor, not looking at anyone in particular but rather taking in the overall scene. The paneling had also been removed from the interior of the bus, leaving all the support bracing exposed on the upper walls and ceiling, and making the bus look even older than it actually was, like something from the industrial revolution. The smell, a mix of pressboard and gear oil, added to that effect. "So," I said, leaning against a diamond-plated wheel well, "I'm Dave." The two male passengers looked at me, deliberating whether or not to speak. The girl continued to stare out the window.

The curly-haired woman broke the short silence. "I'm Sophie. And that over there is, um, June." June moved her head slightly in our direction. And, Amin—"

"Amen," the turbaned guy said. "Not Ay-men. Ahhmen."

"And, Deiter, right? I got that right; right?"

"Hey hey."

"Hey."

"Deiter." Sophie repeated. "Deiter. Even I couldn't forget a name like that. That's cool! That, is that German?"

"What about Amen?" Deiter asked, deflecting the question. "Is that like the prayer? No offense, but do Muslims say Amen?"

"I believe Muslims say Ameen, if I remember right. You should ask a Muslim. But to answer your other question: No. Not like the prayer. Amen's not my full name. It's an abridgement."

"Oh yeah. Sorry dude. Duh. Muslims don't wear turbans. I knew that. But abridgement for what, if I might ask?"

"Amenhotep."

"Whoa. Right… Like the Pharaoh. That's pretty intense."

"Yep."

"*He was just over at the De Young, you know. The museum. I–*"

Stevie turns back toward Candy. She smiles and says: "Weird." Stevie smiles back. He should really be writing this down, but how's he going to–? And what would happen if he told her about the body? Not now. Maybe later. He turns back around and continues:

Arriving to mingle with the pressboard and oil came the smell of patchouli. It crept up my nose. Patchouli was funny to me. When some people wore it it smelled gamey, like animal sweat. And it always smelled like dirt. And gamey dirt is close enough to a description of shit; so I generally considered myself not a fan of patchouli. But sometimes, when certain people wore it, it could smell like a meadow, basking in the sun. Sophie was one of those people. She said:

"*So what do you think?*"

"*Oh, Jesus. I think I ought to get some food in my system before I start thinking.*"

"*I hear you Dave,*" *coming from Curtis.* "*You like 'cue, Dave? You like ribs?*"

Actually I'm kind of a, well, I don't really eat meat, but that's all right–"

"*Well, you like catfish?*"

"*Uh, yeah. Sure, catfish–?*"

*This place we're going? They got catfish; whooo, Dave! ...
gonna knock you right out of your skips..."*

*"Is that right?" Drawn out, maybe more than I normally
would. "Dynamite!"*

*The bus had no suspension to speak of, and we rattled
around in it as it groaned and clattered through the Oakland streets. Curtis' big, bulbous AM radio was transmitting
'I Want to Make It With You' through what looked like drive-
in movie speakers. He didn't have the volume up enough to
pick up whatever bass might have been in the original signal,
and a lot of the mid range remained trapped within the metal
speaker boxes. That left only a foil-y sizzle of high end to buzz
around the bus's hull. No one seemed to know where to take
the conversation. More small talk suddenly felt inappropriate,
even rude, somehow; and as far as a serious discussion was
concerned there was no easy or even sensible place from which
to launch that. So we all sat and listened to those mildly sleazy
whisperings in silence, mostly avoiding each other's gazes. We
made our way out of a residential area and into the industrial part of town. We weaved around and under various off
ramps, overpasses, and freight trestles. Curtis described tiny
conductor-baton motions with the first two fingers of his left
hand—his left thumb hooked at high noon over the wheel—
as he drove. We bucked our way over dead railroad tracks
and rattled through reverberating corridors of corrugated
steel, and inched our way along alleys lined with semi trailers.
Finally we stopped in front of a worn-out, asbestos-shingle-
covered Victorian duplex. It was tucked between a scrap yard
and a day-old bakery outlet. The house was set back from the*

street and was surrounded by a chain link fence. The fence was woven with fiberglass strips so you couldn't easily see through it. Curtis led us through the gate.

"Ayyy! There he is!" A man in overalls smiled from behind a wall of rising smoke—it looked like an inverted waterfall—pouring from the bank of oil drum grills that surrounded him. He gave a friendly wave with his huge, sharpened fork. A few weathered picnic tables were scattered around on the gravel in front of him. The only plant life I could see came from a tub of corn sitting just outside the door to the house.

"How you been Bubba! How those hands of yours?" Curtis walked up to the man. The rest of us followed, more or less in single file.

"This here's Mr. Daniels," Curtis said. "He's the pitmaster. You just tell him what you want. Dave, you go in that door there. She's gonna set you up with some fish. Three different bu-bu-batters to choose from, Dave. You like snapper?"

I told him I did, but I'd probably go for the catfish.

"Don't tell me. Tell Mrs. Watkins, inside there. Do it up, Dave. I'm a rib-b man myself."

"Gotcha." I went to the door and peeked inside. An old woman was sitting at a little chrome dining table playing clock solitaire. She looked up at me. "What can I get for you, baby?" she asked. I inched forward.

"Umm…"

"Step on in here where I can see you!" she scolded me, "don't be shy." I did as she told me.

"This is where I get catfish?"

"What kind of mud you want him in?" she asked, pointing to the big white bowls next to the fryer.

"I'm sorry?"

"You want him nice and juicy on the inside, don't you?"

I told her I did.

"Okay then. You want the cornmeal batter. Keeps it nice and juicy on the inside. You outside?"

"As far as I know. No; yeah I am."

"Go on and sit down then. He'll bring it out to you. You gonna want something to drink? A beer or a Coke?"

"I think I'll have a...beer."

"Tell him outside then that you want a beer."

"You mind if I wash my hands?"

"Go right ahead! Use that sink right there. Just don't touch nothing."

After scouring the gasoline residue from my palms, I walked outside with an eye out for 'him.' The rest of my party was sitting at a table with styrofoam plates of ribs and sliced wheat bread already spread out in front of them. A man was orbiting the table, dropping off cans of beer. Each can wore a flimsy plastic cup like a comedy-drunk wears a lampshade. As I walked up to the table I heard Deiter say to the man:

"Could you not call me boss, please?"

I sat down and asked if I could get one of those beers as

Deiter glowered at his food. "Damn," he told it. Deiter seemed to have a hard time relaxing. I'd noticed that about him the day before. One of those guys who's always out to prove something to the world, but can never quite pull it off. I put him at about twenty-five. He looked up at me; suspicious. That's cool, I thought. There's plenty to be suspicious about. Just pick your battles, though...

"You asked about my name." I was in the middle of asking the beer guy for a beer, so I held up my finger as if to say 'hold on a sec...'. He narrowed his eyes. I let him wait.

"Wasn't me." I said, finally. Then, deciding it'd be best not to encourage his persecution complex, I added: "I think she did." I pointed at Sophie, who looked up at us.

"It means 'army of the people,'" he yelled.

"What does?" Sophie asked through a rib.

"Deiter."

"Oh yeah? Deiter does, really? Huh..."

"Yup. I–"

"The Germans?" June asked.

"Huh? Naw, It's just 'the People', you know? Like–" he held up his fist, palm-side out, "power to–"

"German, right?"

"And that has to do with anything...how?"

"Take it easy, Deitruh." Curtis said. "Buh-buh-be a gentleman, now. She's just asking you a question."

"You don't like Germans?" the girl asked.

"I don't–" Deiter stopped himself, looked up at the sky and smiled a frustrated smile.

My fish arrived on a slice of wheat with a side of cole slaw and a squirt bottle of hot sauce. I took a bite and looked over at Curtis. He had taken off his gloves to eat, and I could finally see his hands. I was half-expecting them to be strange and delicate, somehow out of proportion. They weren't. They were substantial. However, they did seem to possess a certain sensitivity. They had presence; maybe you could even say they emoted. I looked around at the rest of the party. Everyone but me had gotten ribs, and their hands were all covered in sauce. But Curtis kept his hands clean. He ate with skill and casual concentration, yet he dispatched his plateful of ribs faster than anyone else at the table. My fish was very good, particularly when I added the hot sauce. It was juicy. After a few minutes of our slurping, punctuated with regularly spaced "mmmm"s and "oh, this is soo good"s, Amen spoke.

"So what do we say about this interview thing?"

"What, you mean the little experiment they're doing on us?" June said, her words looping spookily in the air. She looked up as she spoke, and as she did I got my first good look at her. Her face was framed by a perfectly symmetrical, perfectly black bob hairdo complete with bangs she must've used a ruler to cut, and her already pallid skin was complemented by white eye shadow and lipstick to produce an almost solarized effect. While she wasn't unattractive, she was repellent in a studied sort of way; her decision, in other words. Her nose and ears were almost translucently pink.

"You think that's all it is?" Sophie asked, dipping her sleeve into her sauce as she leaned forward. "Let me ask you guys are you getting paid already? Cause I got like, money, put straight into my bank account. And that was for...?" In her body language "I don't know" looked like an imitation of a rising muffin.

"Yeah... how much?" Deiter asked. She looked at him. We all looked at her.

She raised her eyebrows and kept them there. "All right, you guys. Let's do this. If you got... Why don't we on the count of three let's all say the amount of money we all got yesterday. You want to? Just to get it out of the way?" I nodded 'sure' uncertainly. She continued, "I haven't checked today so just for yesterday, okay?" She looked around again. "Yeah? On three. One. Two. Not on three, but after. Onetwothree then GO... Okay? One?... twooo?... three—" Sophie, along with Curtis, June, Deiter and myself, croaked "thousand" or "a thousand"; although Deiter waited an extra beat before chiming in and added "dollars" at the end. "Dollars" hung in the air. Amen remained silent.

"Oh, no!" Sophie laughed. "You're not going to say how much you got, Amen?"

"I didn't say I got anything."

"Well... okay. But did you?"

"I'm not sure it's such a good idea to say. Anyway what's the point? I was specifically warned about...talking about this stuff, as I'm sure you all were too, am I right?"

"By who?" June grimaced at him. "The guy up there? Dude, maybe you're into freaky authority trips or whatever, but that's on you. Fuck that guy. I'm sorry, but we're not in his little lair right now. Maybe you—"

"Well look," I said diplomatically. "You obviously got paid something."

"So you're really not going to say?" asked Sophie again.

"Now, that's you asking us do we want to talk," Curtis mused. "And here you don't want to say anything to us at all. Come on, now?"

"I didn't know we were going to start out talking about THAT," Amen said defensively. "See? And now here you all are, pressuring me. Just like...but you know what? Fiiine. I got a thousand dollars too. Everybody happy now? Like it matters? We all could be lying. Who's to say?" He corkscrewed, looking for the beer man.

"You're right. But honestly why would it make any difference to me what you guys got," I said. "What's that going to change for me? If you think about it, none of us got any reason to lie."

Amen leaned back in his chair and looked at me. "And you're the 'avian veterinarian', right? Wasn't that you?" I stared at him. I could feel my eyelid twitching. "Uh huh," he said sarcastically. "I know you—"

I made a quick decision. "That's not right," I said, struggling not to break eye contact. "I'm a substitute teacher." He winced.

"YOU are?" Sophie asked, shaking her head. "Didn't you say your name was—"

"I don't know what to tell you," I said with a big hint of desperation. "But that's the truth. I am a, or maybe I should say I was a sub—"

"You know what." June said. It wasn't a question. "Who really gives a shit. I mean, seriously. What about all the weird shit they got us doing in there? Like those masks, for instance. What? The. Fuck! And that creepshow doing his fucking psychoanalyzing…ucchh. Psycho is right! I'm assuming you guys had your own little chats last night?" I nodded. "I mean, I'm almost like 'is it even worth it?'!"

"Almost, right?" I said. I smiled.

"Hey, Guy," she said in a chilly mock-laid-back sort of way, "maybe for you it's different—"

Candy laughs.

"Stevie, I think it's 'guy'," rhyming guy with eye.

"Oh right," he replies sheepishly. "You getting bored yet?" He turns around. "How are you doing; you getting bored yet?"

"I'm good. I was just looking at those clouds."

"I know, huh?"

"You want to take a break soon?"

"Yeah. Five minutes?"

"That's fine."

"I mean in five minutes…" She gives him a thumbs-up and takes his picture. He smiles.

"Okay cool. So yeah. Right. Guy."

"Hey, Guy." she said in a chilly mock-laid-back sort of way, "maybe for you it's different. Well," assessing me, "maybe for you it's not. But still, for a young person? Sorry, but a thousand bucks a day is a lot of fucking money." I had made my comment in the spirit of camaraderie, or at least of complicity, but she chose to—and intentionally, it seemed to me—misconstrue my meaning. I shrunk back into my beer. It was my own fault, I reminded myself. Forgetting who I was and was no longer. I spent more thoughts than I cared to think about in peering back at the purpling shoreline of my youth, trying not to lose its contours. It was easy to lose perspective doing that, and forget how small I must look from that shore. I stared down at the table as she continued: "Seriously, though; could it get any weirder?"

"It can always get weirder," Curtis said mysteriously. "But I hear you. Makes no difference if Dave here's full of you-know-what."

"I'm not, though," I said. "I really am—"

"Anyways," Deiter playing catch-up, addressing Amen, "didn't you say you were a—"

"I have a degree in veterinary medicine," Amen, wide-eyed, cut him off, "if that's what you're going to say. A real one." He looked at me quizzically, a little wetly. "And I actually DO *specialize in birds. How's about that? But not in, what was it you said? Avocets?"* He grunted an abortive laugh. *"Vaccinations!"* Then, still looking at me, *"I would like to know where you pulled that out of–"*

I grunted too. *"You... you guys really want to know? I'll tell you. I just totally made it up! But you know what, man?"* I looked back at Amen. *"Total coincidence. I don't know you from Adam. I don't know what to tell you. Anyways, you guys were in that room! I mean, come on! Was that supposed to matter to me? Who was I even talking to in there?"* I stopped to catch my breath and draw the last foamy remains of my beer. When I resumed speaking it was in a less desperate, more conversational tone: *"Can I tell you why?"*

"Be my guest," Amen said dryly, wetly.

"Remember the teacher by any chance? He spoke just before me? Like just before? Well his story was pretty much identical to what mine would've been. I swear to God. I felt like it would have sounded like, I don't know... it would've sounded like I was copying him if I tried to tell the truth–"

"And you think he was telling the truth?" Deiter asked with rhetorical flourish.

"Huh? Hell if I know. But why do you ask?"

"Nothing. I don't know. It's just that... well it's kind of obvious isn't it? What do you think was going on with those helmets we were wearing?"

"Okay?" boomed Curtis, *"That was hands down the most–"* raising his hands for emphasis, *"–you go on, Deiter. I think I*

got a feeling what you're driving at."

"Really? Wow." Deiter went on, "Well, you can probably tell by looking at me, I mean, I've seen my share of weird shit. No offense, but you guys really have no idea." He took his head in his hands and twisted it with a sudden violent jerk. His neck crackled. June rolled her eyes. "But nothing even close to that shit for just straight like 'is that even possible?' kind of thing, right? Where was I going with this...? Oh, right. Okay, you know how we saw our own face whenever we looked at somebody else?" Grunts of assent all around. "And all that other stuff? Could that have been all that was going on? Like what... like just a super elaborate parlor game? Maybe so. I don't know..."

"Don't stop now," Curtis urged him. "I feel you."

"Yeah," June added. "But please; hit the bullseye."

18

"So you think these are real people? Or's this a story or something? What do you think?" Candy and Stevie sit on 'bullseye.' Stevie slides out of the machine and turns it off.

"Me?" Stevie shrugs his shoulders. "I have no idea. I kind of doubt it, though. I personally think it's going to end up being autobiographic...al."

"Do you?" Candy leans back on her elbows and looks up at the shrinking sky. She stays like that for several seconds, then says: "Can you keep a secret, Stevie?"

"Well...." Candy hands Stevie the letter. He reads it.

"Wow," he says. Too sad-sounding. He tries again. "That's really awesome, Candy!"

Candy, lying down now, asks: "Where's Orion again?"

Stevie looks up but doesn't change position. He points vaguely.

"It's... usually it's... I'm pretty sure it's..." Normally Stevie can find Orion no problem. He found it for Candy while they were swinging that time. But the stars look scrambled right now, unfamiliar. He thinks: not that dumbstruck thing again! Not now! What is it with you, man? He frowns.

"I have an idea," Candy declares suddenly, as she springs to her feet. "Why don't we do it like a play? I'll be—what's her name? Yeah, I'll try to do the girls, and you do everything else. I think I'll switch cameras when we're back by the thing."

Stevie thinks to himself: What's it matter now? You might as well let the old chips fall where they may at this point... like Dave Edwards here...

"All right. We'll try it. But we'll have to share the mike somehow," he says dully, as he sweeps the sky one last time for any recognizable constellation.

Candy can no longer see the mountaintops; only a massive grey smear that's swallowing the stars. She sees what look to be the headlights of a parked car way, way off; but now they're gone, too.

"We'll figure something out," she says. Stevie loads back up and they start walking again, this time with Candy leading so she can read ahead. Stevie begins:

"Well okay. Look. Check it out. This might sound, whatever... but you know all those stories we heard? You know how they all started running together? Well, for me? Not only could I—how can I put this? Not tell one story from another after while, but..."

"I think I know what you mean," Sophie said thoughtfully,

Candy, doing a husky, groovy drawl:

"—but you go ahead and say."

Stevie laughs. Stevie:

"It was almost like my own...yeah, that's it, my own identity got caught up in the mix; like, I was hearing things people were saying and feeling like 'hey that's me'! Not like, you know, 'I'm relating to you' but more like... I'm having a hard time putting it into words..."

Candy:

"You mean like you couldn't tell between your own... self?... and all the other stories you were hearing? Is that what you mean? In a way? That is so crazy! Or maybe I'm the crazy one cause if that's what you mean then I might get where you're coming from."

Amen nodded along, vibrating his head, squinting and furrowing his eyebrows.

They continue trading lines, putting on different voices, laughing as they read:

"Yeah. Pretty much, I guess." Deiter said with exaggerated thoughtfulness. "So maybe Dave—"

"Hm?" I had drifted a bit.

"Maybe you weren't lying as much as you thought you were..."

"Hmmm," I said, mimicking his tone, "Could be." I wasn't convinced. I distinctly remembered feeling like I was lying. After that, though, after I was finished... I couldn't really remember anything.

"Well think about it." Amen grabbed my sleeve. "It would

explain a lot!"

"Like what?"

"Hey, Amen," June said slowly. "It just occurred to me that I don't remember hearing two bird vet stories. If he—" she jerked her head up toward me, "—if he told the one—"

"That's right!" Amen shouted. "I believe that would be Deiter's point exactly—"

"Not exactly—"

"No, it is!" Amen insisted, "That's what I'm saying…"

"Okay." I said. "Say there was more going on with those helmets than we know. Although, I got there a little late today, so I don't even know what all you all heard—"

"Nothing." Sophie declared.

"Yeah you didn't miss any explanations. That's true." Deiter said.

"So let's think about it then." I said. "What would the point be, if they somehow tapped into our… our what? Brain waves? Electrochemical something or other? Our collective consciousness? What are we saying here? They're obviously studying something, or monitoring, maybe?"

"…collecting…" June said.

"What? Information? They seem to have enough of that if you ask me."

"That's not what I mean."

"What do you think, you suppose we all here are jockeying for the same position?" Curtis asked, avoiding the paranoiac *thrust of the conversation. "That make sense to you all?"*

"Position?"

"Yeah, Dave. Job. We're all looking for jobs, isn't that right? Just seems our buh-backgrounds are just so different I guess, is what I'm driving at. Least to me it does."

"Which backgrounds? Whose is what?" Deiter sounded genuinely confused.

"Shit." I said. "I still think this IS the job. No matter what that guy says. We're getting paid, aren't we? And by the way, I did check my bank account today. I got paid again, just so you know. Another grand. But you know what I'm doing? I'm going to start cashing that shit out, because..."

Sophie butted in: "We should like get each other's addresses and phone numbers, maybe. Just in case."

"Just in case what?" Amen asked.

"I don't think what we're doing is the job." June said.

"What makes you say that?"

"Just from what 'the man' was talking about last night," June said. She was holding her gloves, turning them over and looking at them absentmindedly.

"Are we not supposed to talk about those either, Amen?"

"I don't know." I said. "Mine was kind of a blur." Amen gave me a scrutinizing stare.

"Mine too," he said.

"Well then I won't get too into it. But... is commodify a word?

"*Could be.*"

"*Not sure.*"

"*Maybe that's not what he said. But he was going on and on about how, something like 'if you got the right tools and quote unquote "know-how," you can mine anything.' And he said 'not like, um, metaphorically? But for real, like mine mine. Like you can extract from a human consciousness'; what did he say? Elements I think. Yeah. 'Think of them as elements,' he said. He said they're as real as gold or plutonium. Tangible. Capable of being gathered and stored. Why he was telling me this, don't ask me but he was definitely determined to let me know that he was, um, letting me know. If that makes sense...*"

"*Come to think of it,*" *I said,* "*I got the same feeling from him during our talk, if I'm remembering right. Almost like he was trying to let me in on something or, I don't know, even make me complicit in something. Like a secret. I don't think he said what. I wish I could remember what he was—*"

"*That's a trip,*" *Deiter said.* "*Know what he wanted to talk to me about? Self-similarity. I mean, it wasn't like he told me anything I didn't already know, but still. I mean, I've always been kind of into fractals and stuff. Early on, before anybody else I knew was, actually. And if you know anything about—*"

"*Always been into fractals? How do you get into fractals?*" *I asked, the words coming out a bit more cattily than I'd intended them to. It was an honest reaction. Deiter was showing himself to be a know-it-all, and know-it-alls tended to bring out the worst in me. It was a weakness I had at times possessed, but one of the few I tried not to indulge. So natu-*

rally I had a hard time letting anyone else indulge in it either. Either that, or maybe my inner know-it-all just refused to let anyone else play the role of smartest person in the room. Probably some combination of the two. Anyway, I was getting on my own nerves.

"Well, I've read a lot about them, you know," Deiter patiently explained, "I mean, I'm not INTO them into them; no more than a lot of stuff I like to study. I'm into a lot of stuff like that. Chaos theory, shamanism…"

"Please. Stop. Shamanism. I'm sorry but if you're about to get all hunter/gatherer could you just—"

"Dave, come on." Curtis, folding his plate to hold some beans still for his tiny plastic fork, "Relax, now; cut the bu-boy some slack. Sounds like to me he's just looking around? Trying to figure out what's what? Same as you? Same's we all, I imagine. Right, Deitruh?"

"All right. Fair enough." I said. Curtis was right. There was some envy in my irritation, and it showed. Deiter was evidently searching, just like I was at his age. The difference was that he was still hopeful that his esoteric knowledge gathering would lead him somewhere brand new, somewhere hidden from time. Maybe. Whereas, for me, well… I drank every night. Nothing new there. "No offense, Deiter." He shrugged like he was used to it. I spoke in measured syllables: "Now: self-similarity? You want to clue us in? If you would?"

"Right. Primitive. That's funny. So anyway—" pause for 'let's get back to something important, shall we?' effect— "self-similarity is like, for instance, when you look at a tree in the

winter, and it looks just like say, the human circulatory system? which looks just like a satellite image of a river system?; it's that sort of thing. Like a form, like a formal arrangement nature seems to like."

"Water—"

Deiter looked at me. "That's exactly what he said. In this case, what water seems to like. A formal manifestation of a molecular idea that—and I don't quite get this, to be honest, but according to him—we replicate in our behavior as well. That's what he said. That's not exactly molecular, obviously, I told him. Not exactly, is what he said back. Another thing he said? That example; that form? It's just for one molecule. Out of how many... not even mentioning combinations... Our propensity for ninety-degree angles? Sodium chloride. Salt. Another thing we're made of. You know we're basically just water, right?" No one answered; we all figured he was being rhetorical. "Well, we are." I sighed. "But that's not all we are."

"Did he have a point?" June asked.

"Search me. Did he for you? My point is that he was talking like he was teaching a seminar or something, like he was dropping some knowledge on me. What you guys were talking about? With the, the conspiratorial feel of, I don't know, whatever it is?"

"Well now you guys are way over my head." Sophie sang playfully, illustrating with her hand an object arcing overhead. "Hey up there there there!" she pretended to yell, in a false echo-voice that would have made more sense in another metaphor.

"What about you?" Deiter asked. "You guys just played in the shallow end of the pool?" He smiled cleverly.

"I guess so," Sophie replied. "He didn't get all scientific with me. But he did have me read something."

"Was it about you?" Amen asked.

"No." And then, "No, thank God. Nothing like that. No, he actually had me do a Tarot reading. A very strange Tarot reading as a matter of fact."

My stomach lurched inexplicably. "You do Tarot?"

"That bother you?"

"No. Why would you say that?"

"You just looked kind of... disturbed for a second there."

"No, I got nothing against Tarot. I just–"

"What kind of deck you use?" Deiter asked. "I got the Golden Dawn deck at home, and the Thoth deck too. Wait; let me think. Yeah I think I still got that. Yeah, I got pretty into Aleister Crowley, like way before the whole–"

"Can I ask," I asked, "what a strange Tarot reading might consist of? Like, what was strange about it?"

"Well," she said, clearing a spot on the table in front of her with her forearms. "Okay. So typically I might do like say, a ten card spread, like...that, that... that." She proceeded to lay out a cross design with her right hand, pulling and flipping from an imaginary deck she 'held' in her left. "Kay, you got your present in the middle there...you got your recent and your distant past, your outcome—that'd be your best possible result you can hope for... your challenge... Could be any-thing." She was mumbling, talking more to herself than to us. "That there... that here... that there... okay. So anyway, that's a common one. But you can really make any kind of spread. Depending on the question. A ten-card spread is a big one. Well," clearing the invisible cards from the table, "first of all, he already knew the layout he wanted, and it wasn't one I knew. Second of all," scattering imaginary cards all over the place, "it was a seventy-eight card spread..."

I was suddenly reminded of something from the night before, something sensed... then of the writings I didn't remember seeing that morning. "You know?" I said. "I think I better hit the road. What's the easiest way to BART from here?"

"Well it's a little walk, Dave. You want to hang out I'll give you a ride down there when I leave. Any of you guys."

"Naw. That's all right. I like walking." I took an old busi-ness card from my wallet, one given to me by a guy in a bar who offered to chop all my trees down. I put a large X across the front of the card and wrote my cell phone number and email address on the back, then handed it to Sophie.

"Cool," she said.

"Well you just follow those old railroad tracks outside they'll get you buh-back where you'll buh-be... you'll see where you're at. And then you'll know how to get buh-back here again, okay? Now that you met Mr. Daniels. Hey Dave, how was your snapper? It was good, right?"

"Oh, the catfish was great, yeah."

"What'd I say?"

"Uh..."

"What did I tell you?"

"You were right. Mighty good."

"Dave, right?" It was June.

"Far as I know." I was already standing, and poised to start a big group wave-to.

"You mind if I walk with you? Since you're headed that way?"

I looked at her, sucking my teeth. I wasn't in the mood for company. She raised her eyebrows and craned her neck.

"Of course." I said finally.

"Of course... what?"

"I'm sorry," impatiently, "didn't you just ask—" then: "—no, of course I don't mind. But let's hit it, shall we? I got a big date tonight." She looked at me blankly. "With our buddy," I reminded her.

"Yeah, okay, dude." Not easily amused, apparently. She got up, I performed my big wave and we left through the gate. Instead of closing the gate herself, June pointed the U-shaped latch at the post and slammed it shut behind her. It clattered violently and sent a shudder through the entire fence. She seemed pleased with herself. To the right of us an old set of railroad tracks ran down the middle of the street for about a half block before wrapping around a graffiti-covered warehouse. About fifty feet to our left the tracks vanished into the asphalt. "This way, I guess," I said, frowning. "I would have guessed that BART would be over in the other direction."

"There's more than one station."

"R-i-i-ight." This walk is going to be an eternity, I thought to myself. I looked up ahead to where the tracks veered off into a blind cinderblock corridor of foxtails and rusted metal. I fretted: with my luck, I'm going to get my ass kicked while being forced by convention to defend this condescending girl I don't even know from some sociopathic band of thugs lurking in the weeds. I can see it now. Some crappy comment about her makeup or her ass or something, then she barges right in with one of those remarks that works like a succession of insult-waves that, when fully absorbed, will be impossible for us to walk away from. And somehow I'll still end up looking like a—

"Oh, shit," she said, looking down at her shoes. We'd reached the end of the pavement and were about to hit the railroad ties. The damp dirt patches between the ties were packed with star-shaped, burr-stubbled weed blossoms. "I can't go in there." She was wearing white vintage go-go boots over white tights. "I can not go in there."

"Yeah, it doesn't look too cool, does it?"

"Not cool." She was trying to stay calm. "Maybe there's another way." I looked up the street. Nothing but chain-link and corrugated metal fencing, low-lying light-industrial slabs well off into the distance.

"Well, this is the way he told us to go."

"You mean told you to go."

I laughed. "Well, shit! What am I supposed to do? Why don't you go back, then? They're still there, I'm sure. That's totally fine with me. I'll walk you, even—"

"No..."

"No?" I laughed again. "Why not?"

"Just no. Cause I already left."

"Yeah but... All right. You want to stay here a second, let me run up there and see how bad it is? Maybe it's just like this right here."

"That would be good. Thank you."

I hopped down the tracks, thinking dimly to myself about how I'd bet June was the type to defy any notion of a glass ceiling, but still she chose to surround herself, in a refractive sort of way, with glass walls. Funny society we live in, I thought.

The weeds were pretty bad for the length of the building, and the ties were slick with old oil, decomposing grass and slug tracks. But on the other side it opened up, and the tracks headed back in the other direction through a dry sunlit field before disappearing into another alley that pointed in the direction of the downtown skyline. That was a relief. I felt more comfortable out in the open. I turned around and headed back. June was standing in the same place I'd left her.

"It's actually not so bad once you get out from between these buildings. But they're kind of long. Just so's you know."

"I can see that."

"Well?" I said. She stood there looking at me. "You're going to have to do something. I'm not standing here all day long." Nothing. "Hello?"

"How far again?"

"Well, you can see where these buildings end. It's just right there."

"If you could just give me a piggyback ride then—"

"Wait... what?"

"Is it really that big a deal?" No it wasn't, when I thought about it. A piggyback ride sounded like fun, almost, certainly better than hanging out in the street arguing about it. Still, I continued to act put off by the situation for the sake of protocol. Less uncomfortable that way, I surmised. I huffed:

"Oh, for crying out loud. How do you want to do this?"

It was not as fun as I'd hoped. Her skirt wouldn't allow her to use her legs at all, so she just wrapped her arms around my neck and hung there. She felt brittle. I had to stoop over in order not to get choked, and that shifted my center of gravity to a place I wasn't used to. I was also holding our bags. I had already taken one spill at the gas station, and my tense legs wobbled on the slime in a determined effort not to make it two in one day. "This is fucking ridiculous," was all I managed to say. I imagined myself as a medieval pilgrim, then as the guy on the cover of Zeppelin IV. Something in the light matched that image. I stood up straight when we reached the clearing. "That's all you're getting from me," I croaked, when she continued to hang there. I was sore from sheer concentrated tension. She hit the ground with a crunch, abrading the skin of my neck as she dismounted. "Wow," I said, catching my breath. I pointed at her boots. "Hope it's worth it for you, sporting those—"

"Don't say 'puppies'. Please. Or 'bad boys'. I think it's so gross when people call things—"

"Damn, do I come across as someone who calls things bad boys? Wow. That's a drag!" How the hell did that happen? Was I so blind to myself…?

"You come across as someone who would say it as like a little joke. Like 'sporting.' You said 'sporting.' I can't stand smarm."

"Smarm? Well who in the…?" After a second: "Sarcasm is fine, I take it?" We crunched across the field, each in our own wood-soled shoes. I spent the next couple of minutes wondering whether I was really going to say 'bad boys.' Just when it seemed we'd finish the walk in silence, she spoke: "You know, I didn't mean to hurt your feelings while we were eating back there."

"What are you talking about?"

"About the money. About you being, like, a loser." Ouch.

"Oh, yeah; that. Don't worry about it. I got enough grudges, you know? Some as old as you, if you want to know the truth. Believe you me I've got no use for new ones." Then, in an old man voice that was quite believable, "When you get to be my age—"

"How old are you, if you don't mind me asking?"

"Thirty-five, actually…"

"So you still got grudges from when you were a kid?"

"Sure. Some of my favorite ones, as a matter of fact."

"Me too, I guess. Well, just for your information it was nothing personal. I guess that's just how I am sometimes."

"Ain't no thang."

"Eww-uh."

We reached the sidewalk. Our shoes made scraping sounds from the gravel residue left on our soles. I looked again at her go-go boots.

"So let me guess," I said. "You must be the g–... woman with the, what was it, the clothes? The sixties eighties clothes, or the sixties eighties–"

"Once was more than enough for that, thank you very much."

"Well why do you suppose you chose to tell us that? You could have picked anything. Look at me. I just pulled something–"

"I've been wondering that myself."

"Have you? Well let me just say. When I was in high school, when I went that is... I was one of those eighties kids that dressed up like sixties kids."

"You were a deadhead."

"Oh God no. Jesus, do I–? ...Ah never mind. No. It sounds so silly now. Why am I even... do you know what... Mods are? Or were, or whatever?"

"They're still around."

"Really? Well that's fucking crazy. Is that what you consider yourself?"

"No. That's a trip, though."

"I think so."

"But considering yourself a 'thing' is pretty lame. And so dogmatic."

"That's true. I figured that out after while. But if you don't mind me saying, what you said earlier sounds like you're doing something similar."

"To what?"

"Well I think it's all right to be... specific about your image, don't get me wrong... but if you're going to be so bothered about people misunderstanding you, then... I don't know, seems like–"

"What's the point?"

"Yeah. Something like that."

"The point is I like it. Why is that so hard for people? I just don't like the clothes that are made these days. I never have. I'm not trying to be misunderstood–"

"Yeah, but why the eighties-sixties thing? Seems kind of abstract–"

"Not to me it doesn't. I mean look, if I were to just go around dressing like a Mod from the sixties, like you guys did, well, wouldn't that be a real... eighties thing to do? And I'm not in the eighties, am I?"

"But self-consciously dressing in eighties-retro-sixties style–"

"—is not eighties-y at all."

"Wow. So how are you supposed to tell the difference?"

"I can tell."

"I don't mean you."

"You said you."

"By 'you' I meant anyone but... Jeez. I've got to say, for someone who... you sure take things literally, you know that? By the way did you know those guys in the sixties were copping the twenties look? With the bob cuts and the dresses and all that business? It's like a delay, when you think about it."

"A delay? I don't get it."

"You know, like a delay pedal. Makes like an echo? But yeah, what you're saying is not abstract at all! What was I thinking?"

"Well since you're mister answer man, why should anybody care one way or the other what the hell I do?"

"Hmmm. If you're... if you're not being rhetorical, then I'll tell you that I used to wonder the same thing. And I got my ideas why. But wait a second. It's not like you're in high school anymore. You're somewhere in your early twenties, I'm assuming? Why do you care might be a better question. No offense, but aren't you a little old to be worrying about shit like that? What do you do, if you don't mind me asking?"

"Well... I went to school for fashion design."

"No shit. How do you like that? I thought you didn't like—"

"I don't. The funny thing is, that's what made me want to

be a designer in the first place. But it turns out that it doesn't matter. I can't help but design... new clothes. No matter how I try."

"So you don't like your own stuff?"

"I do. Until it's... until they're made."

"Wow. That's heavy."

"Yeah."

"So no wonder, then... And what about your fellow designers? What do they think about your stuff?"

"Some of it they like, you know. But it's not like they get what I'm trying to do or anything. Everything's ironic these days."

"Ahhh... got it."

We emerged from the alleyway and onto a street of Vietnamese shops on the outskirts of Chinatown. Some kids were trying, unsuccessfully, to build a human pyramid in the park. It looked like the biggest one kept insisting upon being on top. We turned another corner and I could see the BART sign up ahead.

"You know," I said, "some people might envy you your future, you know what I'm saying? Older people, I'm talking about. Then they see you... having both the future and the past, too. Their past, you know? They might feel like they're getting ripped off. Stolen from, even. You know?"

"Yeah... maybe I can see that. But who cares? What about people my age? Why should they care?"

"*Well, think about this: what do you think what you do is telling them as far as what you think of them?*"

"*Huh?*"

"*The present that they're living in; they want to like it, you know. Then they see you saying 'Fuck this' and well, that... and you know... but you know what? Some people are just dumbshits. Fuck 'em probably still is the right answer. I wouldn't stop designing if I were you. You never know what might happen.*"

"*Yeah.*" *For a split second I thought she looked at me differently; like an archeologist, or an art restorer uncovering some hidden thing. In that same split second I found myself trying to look back at her, somehow, from her side of the years between us. I told myself, as if in a dream, that I could simply rinse away the puffy old mask I wore and my real face would be there, intact, waiting to be revealed. In that same split second I also knew that I was a monster; that beneath the dusty mask of years was another mask: the vaporous, ghostly visage of the vampire Who I Am No Longer; another visitation; with Who I Am on the business end of a deal made long before. The vampire, having taken what it came for, vanished; leaving the time-scavenging Who I Am once again with only: never again.*

"*But hey,*" *I said, turning from her,* "*what do I know?*"

Candy and Stevie started off by passing the mike back and forth, but have since settled into a more casual room-mike approach. Candy stops. Stevie—whose momentum has stretched a taut step or two out front—slackens back toward Candy. She's looking at him.

"Want a piece of gum, David? I mean, Stevie?"

"Huh? Why do you say that? Is my–"

"No, but here. Take it anyway. I'm going to have one." Stevie takes the gum, resumes:

When we reached the parking lot there were no parting words.

"That's not what it says," Candy says. She turns off the machine. She knows a moment when she sees one. Not so Stevie.

"What'd you do that for?" he asks. "Why'd you just call me–"

"It says," Candy says, pretending to read but not moving, "Stevie gets over himself," turning now to face Stevie, "for once, and..." walking backwards now, tugging him by the shirt...

19

Raylene eases backward so she's sitting on the seat, and rests her back on the Cadillac's dashboard. Jimmy Hill doesn't make a move. He's got nowhere better to be right about now. He watches as Ray slips her arms into her bra straps. He puts his hands on his head, fills his lungs with air and thinks fond thoughts of camping as she gathers her chee-chees, like eggs in a basket, into their cups. The panties he had wrapped around his wrist slide up his arm to come to rest on his biceps.

"I like your new holster," Raylene says shyly. Jimmy leans his head back, closes his eyes and holds out his arm. Sweat gathers in his eye sockets as he smiles. Ray flips onto her back, slips the underwear over her feet and arches gymnastically to pull them up. Jimmy pulls up his own pants with a little effort. Ray hands him his belt. Jimmy arches a little himself as he threads it through his belt loops. Finally he lets out a long, satisfied breath and stares out at the lake. He smiles mischievously, tears some paper towels off the roll and says:

"You ready to suck on some ribs?"

* * *

Stevie does it. He tucks his gum out of the way and does it. After about four seconds Candy places her fingertips on his chest and gently pushes him away. Stevie blinks. I'd like this moment... he thinks to himself, squeezing it, ... to sink in, please... He presses against her fingers and she backs up a step.

"Now that we got that out of the way," she says cheerfully, even jokily, "you read and let me do some filming. Look." The mountains are completely gone, as is most of the sky. The moon is starting to blur. Stevie nods, already trying to remember.

* * *

Guy stands next to the mummy. The stack of tiles upon which it rests is now fully cordoned off by antique velvet rope. The light of the full moon has just reached the skylight and a beam of white light is condensing on the middle of the accumulator. Guy grabs a crank-operated bullhorn from the folding chair and throws open the door.

20

Candy jogs alongside Stevie with the camera as he reads.

June just said she lived nearby and kept walking. I walked down the escalator, determined to get back to the here-and-now. I started thinking about what I would tell Hope about my new situation. I would leave the piggyback ride out of it, of course. She wouldn't like that. She would get the wrong idea. But now, I thought to myself, I would be keeping an actual secret from her; and that would serve to justify any wrong ideas she would—but would not get the opportunity to—get. How do you like that? I thought. Why do things have to always be so mangled?

On BART I found an unfinished sudoku puzzle in a section of newspaper that was crammed into my seat cushion, and completed it just as the train reached my station. I wondered if the trophy guy ever did that. He must've. I popped into a liquor store to get some gum. No airplane bottles, though it was touch-and-go for a minute there. By the time I reached my house I had a pretty good narrative of my last two days worked out in my head, but when I walked in the door I forgot all about it. Something was missing. A certain density. I walked into the TV room. There was a note taped to the couch at precisely the spot where I lay my head most nights to pass out. It was a Word document. It read:

David—

I am going to be staying away for a while. I can't help but wonder whether you are the person you said you were at the beginning. I am starting to believe that was all bullshit. I think maybe you believe that too, and that you resent me for falling for it in the first place. Maybe I'm wrong. I truly hope so. If it is true then I don't know why you would do that. I didn't make you.

I really hope you don't use this as an excuse to get depressed and even more self-destructive. I'm hoping that you will take the time to examine yourself and either decide to do some hard work to make things better, or stop kidding yourself and do what it is you think you should be doing. I truly hope it is the former. I will call you soon. I love you (at least I think I do).

Hope

p.s. there is a check on the fridge.

I was hit immediately by a wave of nausea, followed by a heavier wave of panic. I'm not ready for this, I said out loud. Not yet. Not today. I sped around the room trying to outrun my thoughts. They kept coming. The consequences are here, I thought. The sentence I had been waiting for. Death. And no one to talk to about it! Oh, Jesus! My heart palpitated. I could feel myself dissolving. Oh no; no no! Impossible! I went to the dining room to look for a bottle of wine. The wine was gone. I found a bottle of vermouth in the kitchen and drank that instead. Downed it. What did she think I would do? I couldn't be trusted with myself. She knew that. Her verdict was an impossibility. Even another minute was impossible.

My nerves were sizzling and an enormous weight was pressing down upon my head. I would cave. I could see the future: me, waiting second by second for her call, until the sheer pressure of it would reduce me to a quivering, flinching fetus. I had to have something to water down the fear. Didn't she know that? Then I thought of what she wrote. How could I expect her to know that? Everything she wrote was true. She wasn't stupid. She figured it out. Long ago, I knew, she suspected a flaw in the system, but was willing to make sure, to see the thing in action, before coming to full conclusions. She was reasonable. That's why I did it: that's why I made myself up. I was just another one of my retarded characters. I created a person that a reasonable woman could understand enough to love, and in doing so I had lied to her a billion times; about everything. Every single thing. Had I done that with everyone, always? Myself included? Was that creativity? That unbearable truth that I felt obliged to shield the world from; was that just another one of my creations? Was I some sort of a demon?

The panic was starting to ferment into the more manageable mash of self-loathing and pity. I thought of the countless lifetimes of failure coursing in my veins. I imagined the suicides of my forebears in order to give myself a good cry; to release the tension. It worked. I sat down and sobbed, then I stopped abruptly, exhausted. I swayed for a minute, thoughtlessly, then got up and walked to the refrigerator. The check was taped to the door handle. A thousand dollars. I knew it. I tore the check from the door. She'll notice my not cashing this sooner or later, I thought as I put the check under the sink tap and ran the water. I wonder what she'll think? Will she

*be worried? Then: Goddamn you're a bastard. You're a poi-
sonous pass-ag sadist! Can't you at least gather the decency to
look at this situation the way she's asking you to? Would that
kill you? Don't you have at least that much in you? You got a
better plan? I went back to the TV room and turned on the
television. Nixon's energy policy adviser, holding court for an
audience of schoolchildren and old people on C-SPAN3. Perfect. I lay down and, with my cheek resting on Hope's note, let
the man lull me to sleep.*

*When I awoke it was late. C-SPAN3 had ended their pro-
gramming. Their logo was burning its shadow image onto the
screen. I immediately—almost instinctively—grabbed the laptop.
I didn't even bother looking at the clock. It didn't matter.
If it was too late I could at least tell them I tried. Or they
would just know. I opened it up but nothing happened. Then
I remembered the gloves. I put those on and tried again. The
machine whirred and crackled, and again I was greeted with:
"Ah, Mr. Edwards. Perfect timing." Again, the man's features
looked different, softer than the night before yet—oddly—more
familiar. To my surprise I found myself feeling comfortable—
yes, comforted—in his presence.*

"Sheesh," Candy groans and laughs at once, "this guy's
just not happening."

"No," Stevie agrees, "he's not."

"That's me," I said. My benefactor smiled.

"You've had quite a day."

"You can tell that quick, huh?"

For a split second he looked almost perplexed, while with a cramping, knotted ache I thought of the enormous unknown that held Hope that night. "A fair amount of your day was spent in my presence. I shouldn't think you would need reminding of that."

"No…"

"We were impressed by the level of self assurance with which you… deported yourself this afternoon."

"You were?" I was surprised. Deported myself indeed. "You liked that?"

"We were satisfied by your… composure, Mr. Edwards, as well as by your sincerity. We feel that you displayed a remarkably successful imposition of will; a very worthy exertion; well done."

"Huh." This is interesting, I mused. My anguish over Hope's leaving had left me feeling detached, and the man's mysterious language wasn't holding quite the same power over me as it had the night before. In the privacy of my thoughts I might refer to him as Mr. E, a bad pun on his cryptically evolving image as well as his absurd suggestion that I call him by my own name. I'm getting used to this guy, I thought. What's he got for me tonight?

"Even though I was lying."

"You weren't lying, Mr. Edwards."

"*Right. I forgot. There are no lies—*"

"*Yes,*" he said politely, "*that is quite true. However, I was referring to the polygraphic sensors in your gloves.*"

"*They told you I was telling the truth?*"

"*Yes they did.*"

"*Huh. Well, how do you like that?*"

"*In all honesty, it gives us cause for confidence in your suitability. You are... ahead of the curve, Mr. Edwards.*"

I wasn't thrilled by the fact that he seemed pleased. I felt conned somehow, outflanked even at my own extremities. The vague dread and incomprehension were starting to creep back into my thoughts when an old song popped into my head: 'No Hope! That's what gives me guts!'

"*Well when can I start, then?*" *I asked suddenly, surprising myself.* "*I don't see why I couldn't handle your... the job at this point. Whatever the hell it is.*" *I felt like I might be lying again, but I wasn't sure. I was more sure that it wouldn't do me any good to guess what difference anything I said could make, and I was absolutely certain that I needed a diversion to keep my mind off other things. And, as of that afternoon, I also needed a steady income.*

"*The assessment process is not yet complete. And there is the small matter of your corresponding with your... co-respondents. While we have not expressly discouraged fraternizing in general, we are concerned that the strict confidence concerning our one-on-one conversations be upheld... without exception.*"

"*Are you talking about us going out to lunch? That's not a problem, is it? It shouldn't be, I can tell you that."*

"And would you be willing to share with us some of the things you may have discussed?"

"Seriously?"

"We must take every precaution against fostering a climate of secrecy–"

"Secrecy?" I raised my voice a shade. "Whose secrets from whom? Let me get this straight. You get to know everything about us off the bat while we get to know next to nothing about you or what you want–"

"Mr. Edwards–"

"Hold on. And you want me not to talk to my whoever they are... my peers, let's say... about the highly unusual situation we find ourselves in, yet you want me to tell you what all we said? One thing I won't do for money is be a toady. I hope that's not the job. If I got any grain left at all... that goes against it. Believe it or not; it really does."

"Mr. Edwards, you might be surprised to learn that not every one of your co-respondents share your... reticence." His tone suggested that he was expecting shock as a reaction. It was a miscalculation; a small one, but it was enough to bolster my confidence that much more.

"That's fine. No offense but... whatever, at this point. I'm not surprised. I don't care. I don't want to hear it. If somebody told you something I said, well...? Well now you know, I guess. You obviously don't need me to tell you, right? So if you're training... what do you call 'em... lap dogs? I think

you're barking up the wrong tree. We should probably get that out of the way sooner rather than later. If it's something else, though... I mean it's not like I don't need money as much as the next—"

"Steady yourself, Mr. Edwards. Rest assured; you are not revealing anything that we haven't previously... ascertained. That being said, voluntary self-disclosure is of course never unwelcome. On the contrary, but be that as it may, as close as you are at present to being accepted, some difficult work yet remains. Your stance, principled though it may seem to you right now, might also serve to place you at a disadvantage—"

"I've got to say, with all due respect, I keep hearing this stuff from you... I'll take my chances, if you don't mind. Anyway, I thought you said—"

"Suit yourself. But permit me to make a suggestion to you, Mr. Edwards. When you arrive tomorrow morning at no later than nine, you may want to do so having already eaten a good breakfast, and having left your personal difficulties... elsewhere."

The shift in the power dynamic, subtle as it was, hit me like a swig of champagne. "Okay, boss." I was getting flippant. "I'll keep that in mind."

"You are not under any circumstances to refer to me as your boss. Ever." His tone was so cold that I held my breath. Chilled and immediately, powerfully aware that I'd misjudged something, I stared at the man. I could have sworn his hair was a shade darker than when we'd started talking. His eyes too... "Good night, Mr. Edwards." I waited to breathe until

after the computer shut down. Then I remembered my writings and went downstairs to look for them. The area where I slept had been straightened up since the night before, and there was no sign of my papers. Hope must have done this before she left, I thought. I never had figured out her methodology for putting things away; it seemed things were always where I least expected them to be. So I started looking around; casually and more or less randomly. Nothing. Maybe she took them with her. Then: why would she do that? Just to fuck with me? To read them? What? I had led her to believe that I was working on something saleable. Boy, was she going to be disappointed! Still, I hadn't forgotten that I'd already had a funny feeling about my papers before I knew anything about Hope leaving. Had she left while I was still in a puddle on the floor, and I was in such a daze that morning that I hadn't noticed? Goddamned booze! That old adage about not being able to trust others unless you can trust yourself? It wasn't like that with me. Becoming an unreliable witness to much of anything that happened after dark didn't change my opinion of other people much as far as I could tell. What it did do—which was almost physically distasteful to me—was leave me no choice but to trust other people. Maybe it was that distaste that the adage man mistook for mistrust in the first place. But I had to get my information from somewhere. That made Hope's leaving all the more impossible for me; her reports of my nightly behavior served as a sort of barbed tether that kept me at least nominally connected to a reasonably accurate reality while giving me something to operate with in the daytime world. Now what? I thought. I had an image of a molec-

ular battle going on within me, with 'me' being just dumb terrain. Alcoholic invaders, like barbarians, bent on instilling some murky, bestial disorder. I took off the gloves and went to the computer. I looked up the alcohol molecule. It looked like a horse. Somehow that was just what I expected. The chat I'd just had was already fading from my memory; going direct to sub-conscious in the way some movies go straight to DVD. I thought about that as I boiled water for pasta. I knew that if I were to concentrate, give it some real thought, that something would clarify. I would see something. But I couldn't do it. When I tried to consider the situation—the man, the job, all of it or any of it—while not actually physically dealing with it, I just couldn't do it. My mind, as if bleached from over-exposure, would go blank while my body would get suddenly tired. Drained. That was the only word for it.

I threw all of the remaining pastas into a pot: a few ounces each of farfalle, orzo and angel hair. When it was finished (angel hair the consistency of algae, the bow-ties still hard at the knot, orzo fine) I threw it into a mixing bowl along with some garlic powder, dried oregano and olive oil and brought the bowl into the TV room. I realized that I had managed to not think about Hope for a while, though I also knew that I was just pushing the tide out, probably to feed a tsunami. I ate while a circa. 1990 Dr. Gene Scott—sporting a pair of hats, two pairs of tinted shades, and smoking two cigars— explained from the beyond that until someone got off their ass and called in with a message he would just continue running the same eight-second loop of his racehorse arrogantly turning its rear end to the camera. I considered calling, but instead I just finished eating, took a shower, laid out my clothes for the next day and went back to sleep on the couch. I drifted off to the loop of the horse but woke up at some point to the Doctor illustrating, via whiteboard, how all of the pivotal events in human history were written into the chambers and passages of the Great Pyramid; chambers which, accordingly, were once 'read' by adepts like enormous pieces of language; as "...a book in a sentence in a word...". Other than that I slept fine.

I woke up the next morning to the sound of my cell phone's default game-show-torture ring tone. I thought to ignore it, but I knew too well that I would be subjected to two full verses and choruses to be followed by a sneaky diminuendo and another full-bombast chorus; a solid minute of noise if I didn't at least touch the phone. Even then, if I didn't answer and the other party chose to leave a message then the whole hideous thing would start all over again. I flipped open the phone. 7:48 AM. It was another text message from my phone company, the third that week. It read:

"Dear customer,

#*This message has been sent to inform you that nickel-based batteries, either NiCd or NiMH, DO NOT generally suffer from a phenomenon known as the 'memory effect'. If your battery is charged partially enough times, the battery WILL NOT eventually 'forget' that it can charge fully. Use of the term 'memory effect' to describe any and all deterioration of NiCd and other battery chemistries, including that wherein the long-term and chronic depletion of a phone's 'short term memory', i.e. text message storage, will adversely affect a phone's 'long term memory', i.e. 'charge time', does not apply in this context; and this message is not meant to address that particular phenomenon. In most cases, a nickel-based battery suffering from memory effect can be reconditioned by completely discharging, then completely recharging the battery. The appropriate length of time between reconditionings may vary, but a good rule to follow for nickel-battery cell-phones is to discharge them completely once every two to three weeks, and only when you have a charger available. For offers on the latest, non-nickel-based battery phones, call 1800-5490564 or visit us online at–."

It was completely self-canceling and useless information, this message; with no clear purpose other than to stupefy. I closed the phone. Normally I would have been pissed, but I was thankful for that call. It probably saved me from being late again. If I was going to take the bull by the horns, I told myself, I would first have to get to the ring on time.

I cleaned myself up and was out the door within fifteen minutes. It was clear and bright outside; the only clouds were some faint, tissue-y strips way off to the south. I walked determinedly toward the BART station in case I had to wait for the train, but when I reached the platform the train was waiting for me instead. A few minutes later I reemerged onto the street and wended my way around the fruit vendors and the frantic stragglers left over from the night before. At the corner I decided I'd try a different route, and after a short, uneventful walk through a silent neighborhood I made it to the bottom of the hill. I figured I'd take it easy walking up the hill. For some reason I never was comfortable showing up anywhere early, and if I did I usually found myself wandering around until the appointed time before rushing to my destination, invariably arriving a couple of minutes late. It was one of those things. I liked it that way, and even made a point of not questioning why, though I would invariably curse myself while receiving the inevitable disapproving stares. The sun had just reached the road when I did, and I watched it speed up the hill as I began my climb. Steam rose gently from the thick, uncut grass on either side of the road. The air carried the scent of lemon blossoms. I could hear crows in the distance; I imagined them emerging grumpily from their mysterious sleeping quarters and lazily pushing themselves into the air to yell at the sun. At times I also heard shoe steps up ahead, but again I took the entire walk without seeing anyone else on the road. I made it to the gate with about five minutes to spare. I thought about wandering around a bit, but changed my mind when I looked up at the cameras. Here we go again, I thought, as I put on the gloves. Inside, the peoplemover was in order. I let it glide me along the corridor while I straightened my shirt and made sure I didn't have any tags sticking out. Then I examined the helmet that I'd just picked up from the alcove. The screen felt like sharkskin as I rubbed it against my forearm; smooth in one direction, rough in the opposite direction. I ascended the escalator half thinking I'd be the first one there, as I still hadn't seen anyone else around. I wasn't. When I reached the top I saw a large circle of cushioned office chairs. Most of the chairs were occupied, but I noticed with some relief that several of them were empty. Good, I thought. At least I'm not last again.

"*Helmet!*" I looked around.

"*Beg your pardon?*"

"*Helmet on, Mr. Edwards!*"

"*Whoa,*" I said, thinking: *is that necessary, that barking? I put the helmet on.*

"*Take a seat, Mr. Edwards. Wherever you like.*" *I walked to the furthest empty seat—one facing the escalator—and eased into it. Just like the day before, the masks only showed what the wearer was looking at. In our circular formation the effect was a kaleidoscopic flickering of faces. My helmet felt like it was hermetically sealed. I couldn't hear a thing. A woman I'd not noticed before came up the escalator—already wearing her mask—and sat down next to me. A couple of minutes later the old badass guy with the pomaded hair peeked his head into the room, looked around nervously, mumbled something, then turned back. He returned a few seconds later, helmeted, and threw himself into a seat. We sat around like that for another five minutes or so, in complete silence, presumably waiting for latecomers. I noticed that the group had shrunk a bit. I counted feet. Forty-one. Forty-one? I counted again. Forty-two. Okay. Twenty-one of us. What happened to the others? Had they dropped out? Had they already been hired? The space in my helmet seemed to expand, with a sound like air rushing in to fill a vacuum. Then the voice. Was that the same voice I'd heard the first day? Almost, I thought, but not quite. Not surprisingly, it was more like my own. It said:*

"*To begin with, allow me to thank you all for your continued participation. The simple fact that you are here today* is a credit to your determination. By now you have no doubt begun to familiarize yourselves with the... idiosyncrasies... of the helmets that you have been required to wear. In all likelihood, this will be the last time you will be requested to wear them. Today you will be exposed, or rather, introduced to an additional element of... interactivity. This element may prove difficult for some of you. Perhaps I should make it clear that the helmets you are wearing have been thoroughly tested for safety and... durability prior to today. So you may rest assured; you are not here to test the helmets. Here's how we will begin. You may be familiar with the species of contest wherein a number of people engage in an activity—dancing, for instance—for a period of time sufficient for all but one competitor to... drop out. This exercise will be performed in a similar spirit to that of such contests, but with certain crucial differences. In our experiment the aim is not necessarily to winnow the field to one individual... victor, shall we say, although that also is a possible outcome. Rather, it is the process itself that is of greater interest to us here. All right. Are you all ready?" I looked up at the oculus. Taking pains to mistrust my senses I still couldn't shake the notion that what I looked at wasn't an oculus at all. It was clearly a lens. But even that was beside the point. At that point it made no difference to me, really; because it was also then that I finally realized what was happening to me. I saw it all then; even, I daresay, that which has been wiped from my memory. Even then, as I succumbed, I knew what I would be allowing them to... take. With my last self-possessed thought, in the last second permitted me... as voice in my head, in the mask, deafening, engulfing, boomed:

"Now—"

"Hey Stevie…" Stevie feels a tap on his shoulder.

"Just a—"

"…what's this?" He turns around. Candy is resting the camera in her right arm. Her eyes are narrowed and zeroed in on his face. There's something in her left hand. She points the thing at him. It's the speed-dispenser. The plastic bullet.

Of course it is.

He looks at it in horror, searching for something to say. Candy turns her head, then swings the hand holding the bullet away to her left.

"What is that?"

Stevie lets out a hot, relieved breath and looks in the direction she's pointing. A white dot has appeared on the surface of the trona, far off in the distance. He and Candy are on the ATV side of the bay, so Stevie jogs over to it and climbs aboard. Candy instinctively resumes filming. She's filming Washington Crossing The Delaware as Stevie puts one foot on the handlebars, shields his eyes with his hand and peers out in that same, almost equestrian pose. Stevie (Stevie!…) as Washington as Centaur, or something like that.

From his elevated vantage point Stevie makes out a snakelike form that looks to be emerging from the lakebed itself. It is white and at the same time dark against the trona, black-lit again, like those rides at Disneyland. It seems to be headed in their direction.

"I don't know," he mumbles clammily, "it doesn't make any sense."

"What do you mean it doesn't make sense? Let me see." Candy climbs aboard and assumes the Washington pose. The white snake begins to clarify itself as a long and growing dust cloud. "Well, it's some sort of vehicle," she says matter-of-factly, "and it looks like it's coming out here."

"You think?"

"Well yeah." Stevie takes off the pack and puts it behind the seat. He sits down and starts the engine, then kills it. He turns to Candy and says:

"Does that thing have a zoom on it?" Candy hands him the camcorder and points to a small sliding switch on its side.

"Just push this with your finger." Stevie stands back up in the seat and tries to zoom in on the oncoming vehicle. The image is blurry and swings wildly in the frame. He backs off the zoom and steadies himself for another approach. This time he locks onto it successfully and reels it in as far as the lens will let him. Just before recognition strikes: Thinking about the stars, which by now have all but been brought under one or the other competing influences of stormy darkness and lunar corona, leads to a thought of astronomy which in turn leads to that thought of the Hubble telescope, and about how the Hubble can show us things that happened like billions of years ago... and then light... which must mean that... all lenses look back in time!

"Hey Candy–"

"What do you see?" Not now.

"Oh. Um, oh... no way..."

"What?"

"You know who it is?"

"No. I don't know. Who? It's not my brother, is it?"

"Shit," Stevie spits at the thought. "No, it's fucking..."

"Let me guess. Is it that guy that always wears that skeleton sweatshirt? And that big lurpy guy?" Stevie looks down at her.

"How'd you know?" She puts up her hands and makes a sad-clown face.

"What are they doing?" she asks. Stevie looks up and finds them again.

"They're riding like a... go-kart, it looks like. Huh... Looks cool through here. The... lurpy guy looks like he's got something in his lap." Stevie watches. For several seconds the silence is complete. Now a dim purr can be heard; it also seems to rise from underground. "It's a gas can," Stevie says.

"Hmmm."

"Can you take this?" He hands the camera back to Candy and restarts the engine. They wait as the go-kart disappears into a depression, revealing a topographic feature that Stevie hadn't previously noticed was there. There must be some sort of ridge... "I'm just going to creep," he says, creeping forward. "We don't know where they're going– "

The purr has become a racket that mashes with the clattering idle of the ATV. When Keith and Lee reemerge they are much closer than before. Stevie can clearly see the sweatshirt Candy referred to; the cartoon bones glow cartoonishly.

"Kind of funny" he says.

"I know." Candy lifts the camcorder to her eye and resumes filming. "I'm going to get them." She stands up.

"Careful," Stevie says.

"Ha ha. Now that's funny, coming from you."

21

Keith is unclear now as to how to proceed. He was sure they'd find Stevie alone. That was going to be easy. But now there're two people, and one of them's pointing something directly at him and Lee. It's a video camera. And who's behind that? A chick? Dena? Better not be. He gets within shouting distance and slows down. They face each other now like bull and matador.

"What's up?" Keith yells. No response. "I said what's up, motherfucker!" Candy lowers the camera. Lee waves at Candy. Keith smacks Lee's arm. Now he's really pissed. This is an unexpected insult. "Get that shit ready," he says to Lee, then shouts: "Where's my fucking job, bitch?"

"What are you fucking talking about?" Stevie responds. He holds out his arms, compresses his neck atlas-style for emphasis.

"You heard me." If I don't do something now, Keith thinks, Stevie's going to turn this into a conversation. He turns his attention to Candy. "What the fuck are you doing out here? You a fucking–" he stops himself here. "You like this fucking tweaker? Fuck you too, then." Keith hits the gas, makes a violent left turn and shoots out into the unread portion of the bay. Stevie jerks the ATV forward, pulling Candy into the seat beside him. He runs perpendicular to Keith and Lee, passes them and puts himself and Candy between go-kart and Cartago. He doesn't want to be boxed in if things get out of hand.

Keith tears through the field of words. He fishtails back and forth, a trona fin arching in his wake. He reaches the far end, does some donuts out there and weaves his way back toward the ATV, his sweatshirt skeleton glowing monstrously. It has no head. Lee leans over the backside of the go-kart, dripping gasoline from the can and fiddling with a grill lighter trying to get it to go.

"Read this, you're so fucking smart!" Keith yells as he buzzes by Stevie.

"Slash and burn!" Lee yells happily.

"Man knock it off, Keith. You're being an idiot now." Stevie manages to say. Keith hears this and whips the go-kart around for another pass, maybe some more aggressive action. Idiot?

"What'd you say mother–?" he yells, followed immediately by: "Oh! Shit... motherfucker!"

The violence of Keith's maneuver and Lee's own cantilevered center of gravity have coordinated to knock Lee from the go-kart just as he manages to ignite the gasoline. Burning fuel splashes from the gas can now lodged between the engine and frame, and just out of Keith's reach. Lee picks himself up and begins jogging toward the go-kart. He stops and watches. The engine has caught fire. The go-kart quickly merges into the light of its burning wake. Keith jumps from the vehicle. In doing so he inadvertently spins the steering wheel and sends the flaming, now ghost-ridden go-kart into an ever-widening orbit that sweeps in and out of the unread words, scrambling them into random particles of smoldering trona dust.

* * *

The chief and Ray are up by the aqueduct, parked alongside the service road that overlooks Cartago. They have been to this spot many times over the years and have sat in this very Caddy, top-down and all, looking out together, after… more than once. As there was never any reason to pay much attention, more pressing matters to attend to and all, the chief has never noticed that from this elevated vantage point they enjoy a clear view of the hidden bay. He wouldn't have noticed tonight either, if it weren't for the enormous spiral of fire working its way from its center.

"Holy Jeho–… Jehosephats…" Raylene, who's working Jim's neck, coos:

"You like that, Jimmy?"

"No. That is, yes but–" He takes her by the shoulders and points her toward the bay.

"Jesus H. Christ," she says. "What in God's name is that?"

"I don't know," Chief Hill replies. Ray grabs the top of the windshield and pulls herself up. She watches, almost standing, while the chief struggles to pull his cell phone out of his pocket. He hits a preset on the phone while starting the car and throwing it into reverse. He skids the Cadillac onto the frontage road as a hail ball (what young Jimmy Hill in his marble playing days would've called "boulder-size") lands in his lap.

* * *

Gary is reclining in the recliner, eating waffles and watching the news. He's just had a big glob of syrup rappel from his fork down into his chest-hair. He tries to rub it in with his t-shirt but that only serves to glue his shirt to his chest. Gary doesn't notice. His eyes are glued to the television. The puffy-lipped Mexican reporter chick from KGEL is reporting to anchorman Scott Scott over the same helicopter footage they took when his folks went missing.

Anchorman Scott Scott—looking directly into camera, which in turn centers on his salt-and-pepper eyes:

"And I understand there's something else they've discovered. Why don't you tell us about that, Arlene?"

Reporter Arlene Arroyo, the camera centered on the lovely silver and diamond-chip choker she wears, looks at Scott Scott:

"That's right, Scott. As I mentioned, these petroglyphs [cut to the new footage: dim, flashlit images of a black spiral that appears to have been branded into a large volcanic boulder] were found in the Long Valley Caldera, very near to where the amateur volc–"

"That'd be amateur volcanologist Gordon Tales and his wife Linda."

"Correct. The remarkable thing, Scott, is that scientists here tell me that the caldera vents where these rock carvings were found have, for hundreds if not thousands of years, been releasing so much carbon dioxide that anything needing oxygen—"

"Like me and you, for instance."

"—Or anyone else... can't survive in there for longer than a few minutes at a time; clearly not enough time to carve these, Scott. Now you have to understand—"

"So tell us then; how were they able to find them? Don't tell me they used robots." Scott Scott laughs at the camera while Arlene Arroyo waits for him to finish.

Gary's phone starts ringing. Gary tries to ignore it and tries to let Arlene Arroyo tell him.

"...It's funny you should ask, Scott. Apparently, these were found by a group of student researchers after receiving what they say was an anonymous tip left on their website. And the footage we just showed? The person who took that was actually wearing scuba—"

"How do you like that?" Scott Scott shakes his head at the camera. "Scuba gear!"

Now he addresses the audience directly:

"Anybody out there who's thinking today's kids are...?" Scott Scott shakes his head again bemusedly then nods knowingly. "Scuba gear. Amazing. Arlene Arroyo, great report. Our own Arlene Arroyo. Now let's—"

"Scott let me just add that it still begs the question—"

On the third ring Gary finally relents. Gary's no good at splitting his attention, so he doesn't even bother trying. He turns away from the television in order to address the phone.

"Yellow." He listens to the voice on the other end. "This isn't a joke, is it Chief? Were you watching–" he listens for another minute. He turns briefly, anxiously back toward the television. A weatherman is pointing a stick at a lightning bolt...

"A spiral. How did you... right. Okay... Let me just–"

Gary hangs up so he can get dressed.

* * *

Guy stands solemnly beside the mummy. With a flashlight in hand and dramatically backlit by the shaft of moonlight pouring in behind him, he begins reading to the assembly:

> "Once I dipt into the future..."

The Dutchmen interrupt in unison:

"Yes!"

Guy clears his throat and begins again:

> "Once I dipt into the future far as human
>   eye could see,
> And I saw the Chief Forecaster, dead as
>   any one can be–
> Dead and damned and shut in Hades as a
>   liar from his birth,

With a record of unreason seldom
    paralleled on earth.
While I looked he reared him solemnly,
    that incandescent youth,
From the coals that he'd preferred to the
    advantages of truth.
He cast his eyes about him and above him;
    then he wrote
On a slab of thin asbestos what I venture
    here to quote–
For I read it in the rose-light of the
    everlasting glow:
'Cloudy; variable winds, with local
    showers; cooler; snow."

The DeadBeats, stoned on a stash of sess they'd managed to hide in the Wah-wah pedal, applaud self-consciously. A weary-looking set of parents and their glum preteens stand in front, all arms crossed and all faces sharing an expression that says to Guy that they can't wait to get out of each other's sight. Guy scans the other faces with satisfaction. Good.

"I wanted to read to you first, something from the writer Ambrose Bierce. It is a poetic illustration for his word 'weather', and comes from this book." Guy shines the flashlight on the book cover for everyone to see. "The Devil's Dictionary, with his very own definitions for the words. It is very funny and I think fitting for tonight. Maybe I should tell you now... if you will allow me to–" Guy turns off the flashlight and removes the batteries. Now the only light is that beam coming from the skylight. Guy begins walking around the dark perimeter, working it; allowing his voice to reach the dozen or so people present from several different points. "This building is constructed for to accumulate a... energy what is called orgone. Which is to say, simply no more than life force. Okay. I won't aggravate you with details, okay. Let me just say these walls are consisting of many layers of material. Organic and inorganic both. There are no windows; there is only the one skylight. Because orgone it is life force it is very delicate and it can POOF," Guy says, gesturing like a magician, "very easily. This is the reason there are no electronics or cameras allowed in the accumulator. Thank you. For the same reason we will spend the next fifteen... maybe twenty minutes with the door closed. Okay?" Now for the first time Guy addresses the mummy. "He was maybe buried for a hundred years... right here... in the very same sodium carbonates once used by the Egyptians to mummify their Pharaohs. In the dry lake where he was found... these salts occur naturally. Okay?"

"Okay!" the Dutchmen yell. The woman in front of them turns around. Her t-shirt holds an elaborate silkscreened image of leaves and branches that upon closer scrutiny reveals the eyes of an owl. She glowers at the adventurers. They beam back at her with eyes so wild that she's forced, instinctively, to avert her own gaze. Clearly the highly parasympathomimetic *rode paddestoelen* have hit their stride. Guy, in mid-sermon:

"…who they say killed President McKinley with his pen… because events were caused by his words? Maybe… maybe he 'dipt into the future'… Maybe words travel faster than events? Maybe…"

The Dutchmen nod fiercely. The *rode paddestoelen* is acknowledged by initiates to produce an effect described by first-timers as 'time travel', and by more experienced seekers in terms like 'temporal indifferentiation'… The professor from the diner–impressive now in a charcoal wool sport coat and black v neck–clears his throat. The man's research assistant—a young grad student whom he has already, with the merest hint of sadism, forced to listen to a smug and half-baked lecture on folk sciences during a walk out to the cloudbuster just before that sheet of what looked like rain spilled through the pass and seemed to reach out at them, and whom he now treats as an accessory to his ensemble—rolls her eyes. The Prof, carefully:

"What makes you think…"

They all wait for the professor to finish his thought, while the professor merely evinces that he shouldn't have to do all the mental work again. Guy breaks the spell:

"That is a good question, maybe." He thinks, then answers: "Orgone. Orgone therefore I am!" Now he gets serious.

"No. I will show you." Guy produces a crispy brown leaflet. "This was in his pocket. Can you see? It's a flyer," Guy says, reading, "for the International Workers of the World rally… held in Los Angeles… on Christmas Day of the year 1913." This is a technically true statement, as Guy buried the leaflet in the pocket of the pants himself. "Let me tell you something else. Something about where you are tonight. The year 1913... is also the year Los Angeles opened their aqueduct right here," Guy points across the body, "and began drawing water from the Owens Lake." The sullen boy asks:

"So?" Guy gives the boy's mother time to yank his hair before adding:

"Another good question." He turns the leaflet over and puts it in the quickly dissipating shaft of moonlight. "You see? On the back of the leaflet here? It is written the word Carthage. Now, peoples, this is when we thought for sure. Once upon a time Carthage was a lake town." He points straight down. "Right here. Where you stand now is on the site of the original town centre." Several people attempt to look at their feet. "Yes. You are in downtown Carthage."

Dutchmen nod again, vigorously. They certainly are.

"I will tell you something else. Also in nineteen hundred and thirteen. In this year Carthage disappears from the map of California."

The COA is getting darker by the minute. People start crowding into the center of the room, peering over each other's shoulders and leaning across the rope for a decent look at the body. Guy steps aside and continues his monologue:

"We can only guess maybe. Maybe this gentleman attended that rally in Los Angeles; maybe he was the victim of violence. Or, he was interested in what was happening to the water of Lake Owens, maybe for a story. This mummified 'Ambrose Bierce?' was found on land acquired for the water on top. You understand this? You can walk from here for only a few minutes, and be in the city of Los Angeles. This is where he was found–"

There's a hammering sound on the top of the Communal Orgone Accumulator; followed by another, and another. The moonlight vanishes, leaving the assembly in the dark before any of them manages a good look at 'Ambrose Bierce?'. One of the Dutchmen squeals with terrified delight. He has been swimming in a timesoup of 1913 California, Pharaonic Egypt, Phoenician Carthage, and 1676 Virginia (where he is soon to ingest a tea made from the 'Jamestown Weed' that, incidentally, is the same plant as the jimson weed that waits in his pocket and whose anticholinergic properties—unpredictable as they can be in their own right—are the only known antidote to the far more profound effects of the *rode paddestoelen*). His squeal is soon followed by other human noises as the banging increases to a fury. Guy looks around nervously. The COA sounds just like what the inside of a popcorn popper might, maybe. He hadn't expected the accumulation to be so... intense. Now, as the skylight bursts and a hailball army pours through the breech, it occurs to him that maybe a compound cloudbuster was more cloudbuster than was strictly necessary. Hail ricochets everywhere, driving the assembled guests up against the wall in a fruitless scramble for shelter. It's pitch black now inside the accumulator, and thunderously loud.

"The door won't open!" It's the Dad. "We can't get out!" he shouts. The shout is echoed soon after by another; then another. In no time even those people who had found good spots inside suddenly feel the need to leave. There's a blind crush at the door, but the door doesn't budge. Unseen hail bounces around, pelting everyone and everything. The owl woman screeches.

"Please, peoples. Please. No need to panic," Guy shouts calmly. Guy is preternaturally serene. He felt the communal orgone before it escaped through the skylight. This he now knows. This he did not know this morning. To Guy this means success; no matter what happens now. "Please. My beautiful wife will open the door very shortly; I assure you. It must be very bad outside for her to not come out yet. Be patient. You are safer here. It is drier here."

He's stopped the screeching, at least. He continues: "Maybe we can direct our energies with singing. Ladies and gentlemen, just like Earth itself, the Orgone Hut resonates to G. Okay? We can try?" Guy starts to hum a G. After several a cappella seconds he exhorts: "Come on peoples!" First to be persuaded are the DeadBeats, who have remained relatively dry and mellow. Soon, by some miracle of cooperation, the brutal cacophony of ice on metal—and wood, and metal, and wood, alternately—is augmented by a lovely twelve-part harmony.

* * *

The chief attempts to outrun the hailstorm. Ray urges him on. By the time they reach Cartago, however, it has become painfully clear to both of them that this is a losing proposition. They pull over beneath the first cottonwood canopy they come to. The Cadillac's ragtop is manually operated, so the chief is forced to get out of the car in order to replace it. After scrambling around the car a couple of times he becomes short of breath. He puts his hands on his knees and inhales deeply. The tree where they've parked happens to be located directly across the 395 from Valleroy's compound. Chief Hill, dripping wet and panting, tries training his eyes on the place. He wonders briefly about the sign he saw earlier, but what he sees now clears his mind of that. On top of the squirrelly old frog's dome, up where the glass used to be, is something his daddy used to call an Oklahoma skylight. He remembers the mummy and his heart sputters. He feels a cold sweat mingle with the precipitation. He takes another deep breath and struggles to quiet his nerves. His pulse is chaotic; it races and stalls. Suddenly, and in the middle of what he suspects might be a swoon, Jim Hill hears something. It's a delicate sound, delicate enough to get trampled by the storm surrounding it; but it is unmistakably human. Or it's at least human. It's coming at him from the dome itself, from that hole, as if it's being driven out by the hail. The chief takes another deep breath. That sweet, slightly acrid smell of new rain on dry pavement fills his nostrils. His favorite smell. He stands up straight and nods a sort of 'thanks' to the voice, allowing it to calm the storm going on inside of him.

Raylene sits in the car and listens to the hail drum on her soft top. What the hell's he doing out there? she wonders. Can't see a damn thing out the windshield with all this crap falling out of the tree...

He'd better not be talking to her...

Now she remembers men again. Nothing changes with men. Undependable dreamers, and that's the best of them. That's this one, anyway. She flips open the visor mirror and checks her lipstick. All those years of halfs; of half the truth; of half-lies... just so a man can dream. And let her be satisfied with half...

Raylene lays on the horn.

22

'The Coward of the County' pops into Stevie's head again. He listens to Kenny Rogers sing about his father. Stevie has never met his father. Never even seen a picture of him. All he knows is what Aunt Jody's told him, which is pretty much nothing. He's asked plenty of times too. Not for quite a while, though. Because what Stevie really knows is that Aunt Jody decided it'd be better that he wonder—even with his sometimes overactive imagination—than that he know. It occurs to him that she's probably waiting for him to get his own thing going first, so he doesn't let some dark secret define him before he can define himself.

So the first time he heard Kenny Rogers sing that song, his child mind decided to build a father out of it. A decent but troubled man who wouldn't want his boy to do the things he done. Of course Stevie's elaborated on this imaginary father image—he's given him hair (unkempt, dark), a beard (greying, always about a week old), ruddy skin, sometimes a blurred out hand tattoo... Stevie's own height, eventually—but truth be told the personality of the man he knows is founded on the Kenny Rogers song.

It occurs to Stevie now that some part of him's done the same thing to this scene out here in the lakebed. Attributing it to his imaginary dad, that is. There's an almost-buried part of Stevie that's been waiting for something like this to come along.

Candy sits down. Stevie twists the accelerator at the instant she hits the seat. He maneuvers the ATV around the perimeter of the smoldering corkscrew.

He points it toward the mouth of the bay and Cartago.

* * *

Jim Hill turns to Raylene. He thinks to ask her: "did you hear something out there?" then thinks better of it. Lakes of fire? Hailstones? And now a choir coming from Valleroy's silo? No; he'd best not. If she mentions it, fine. God knows Jim Hill's always trusted his senses, and he's never been let down yet; but there's a first time for everything. Besides, something tells him Ray doesn't want to hear any of his questions right now. The gaining headlights of a Crown Victoria reflect hailstreaks in the rearview mirror as Jim swings Ray's Cadillac onto the power company right-of-way.

* * *

Gary pulls up behind, follows Raylene's Cadillac out on to the lake. At first he assumes the chief must've commandeered the Caddy for some reason, but the sight of a second head stops his assuming. Must be something. It is... whatever it is, whatever...

* * *

Keith and Lee converge on the center of the spiral and watch the go-kart go around and around. Keith cackles freakishly. Stevie hears the cackling and thinks: All that work down the drain. All those words ripped apart so easily, so thoughtlessly. And he's laughing, and you're slinking away. Again?

"Fuck that." In one sense it's the song that does it; he's reached the last verse in his head. But it's something else too; something in all these the words he's been reading, digesting them as he picks them, as he drops them magnetically into his sack; the three things done at once—the words he's now abandoning, the unprotected effort of a stranger that put him here, now, with something to do. Another caution, another 'don't do the things I done,' another shape-of–a-six asking for protection.

He takes the camera from Candy's lap and begins skimming the edge of the unread words, steering with his right hand and attempting to film with his left.

Candy has been watching Stevie since he turned to leave. The change occurred in his face first, pre-expressed there before he made a move. She tugs at his sleeve.

"Let me do it," she says.

"All right. But hold on." He hands her the camera and whips the ATV around. Keith and Lee stop following the go-kart and fix their gazes in the direction of the ATV. Stevie figures they're looking at him but turns his head anyway just to be sure. He spots the Cadillac. It looks like a surfboard with headlights, riding a wave of what looks like… what is that?

Candy turns, turns to Stevie and says:

"I think that's hail."

"I think you're right."

* * *

The chief's got the throttle pinned as the Cadillac enters the belly of the lake. The chief is driving blind. Hail riddles his view. Hail splatters upon the surface of the windshield, splatters spreading into spidery forms as spidery forms overlap and merge to become the surface upon which the hail splatters. The chief strains to see beyond the surface; he strains to see the fire. He doesn't like what the surface is telling him. It tells him: Time is a lunatic that keeps drawing the same circle over and over. Clear through the paper. Keeps and will keep circling; circling the paper; circling clear through and around himself. The all-encompassing is mania, is obsession ever unsatisfied.

And his own life? Is he satisfied? He's managed to get some. Satisfaction, that is. No, Jim doesn't suppose he'd be first in line for a refund, even if there was such a thing.

The windshield brightens. The chief braces himself. The edge is so close he can smell it.

* * *

Stevie gazes out at the Cadillac in awe. Even with the slow motion of distance, he's able to sense the speed; fully gathered speed; violent speed. From within the silence of its approach Stevie can hear 400 imaginary horses pressing, lunging inorganically, bingeing on billions of tiny explosions. He can feel the breath of 400 delirious scavengers feasting upon carcasses picked over millions of years earlier by the tiny progenitors to their namesakes. He smells 400 inorganic horses shitting speed, plunging forward.

He brings the ATV to the middle of the spiral and stops next to Keith and Lee. They nod to one another, as if acknowledging that on some level they're all in this together, and should be dealt with as a group.

* * *

Gary tries to keep up with Ray's old sled but just can't keep the Crown Vic steady. He stays in line behind the Caddy and rides its wake. The cars just manage to outrun the storm before hurtling into the burning bay, the go-kart at one point passing between them like a rocket through an asteroid belt. Cars skid to stops, rear-ends sweep out like wings. The wave hits. Gary peers through the windshield of the Crown Vic. The wipers are going full-blast. They swat at the giant hail like pinball flippers. He sees Stevie hand Candy a film box to use as a shield. Candy. What's she doing out here with him? Then he sees the others. What the hell's she doing out here with them? He grabs his clipboard and puts it between sky and face as he climbs out of the cruiser.

* * *

Stevie turns to Candy.

"Don't worry," she begins to say, "I'll–"

But Stevie's still got that same look on his face. He doesn't look worried.

"I'm not worried," he confirms. He slides the recorder underneath the rear axle of the ATV. "You got that thing you found?" he asks her. She pulls the plastic capsule from her pocket, looking from Stevie to Gary and back.

"You mean this?"

"Yeah." Stevie says. "Let me have it real quick."

Candy gives him a funny look but hands over the bullet anyway. The hail is coming down in sheets now. The sheets sweep across the bay like waves of fever-dream carpet-bombers, pulverizing the trona. Candy watches as Gary and Stevie stomp toward each other, with Gary slowing down as Stevie speeds up. From what she can see through the icy fallout, it looks as if Stevie is about to assault her police officer brother. She watches him walk directly up to Gary and hold out his fist. She hears a sharp noise as what looks like a little puff of smoke escapes from Stevie's hand.

23

The chief also watches Stevie approach Officer Tales. Ray is saying something to him but the sound of it gets drowned out. The hail beats on the convertible top like a million mallets banging on a drum. Chief Hill throws open the door and leans out, fully expecting to see his legs swing out of the car, too. That's not what happens. Something's wrong. His legs feel like they're under water, simultaneously weight-free and heavy. Simultaneously. Something like an internal gravity seems to be acting on him, pulling inward from all directions. He manages to drag himself out of the car through a feat of will that seems to him to take hours, at least, of sustained concentration... at the very same time being well aware that it's only taken a couple of seconds. Barbecue sauce on his fingertips. And that other smell. He puts his arm up and takes a step forward. He sees Stevie raise his hand and both fully knows and will never know what to make of this image. Now he's falling backwards into space; he's sliding down the door and the door's slamming; he's bouncing off the slammed door and onto his knees. He's looking up at the sky. Hail neither falls where he looks nor touches him. The storm is being held back by the thing he sees; the thing he sees is both many things and not any thing at all. It is an instant he sees, an instant he is free to examine at his leisure. It is an angel in robes of Sistine blue that emerges from the clouds, spreading its wings; it is another angel that is a break in the clouds revealing a patch of noon sky from some long-forgotten childhood day. It's all true. The light is a halo and the light is the noonday sun; it dims and brightens, simultaneously. The light is a liquid seen through a liquid; a liquid through which he ascends and descends, simultaneously. Jim is both a particle and a wave. It is all light and water. He never knew he could breathe under water. How did he not know that? It's so...

* * *

"They got a gun!" Lee shrieks, pointing at the sky. "They shot the sheriff!"

Now everyone looks up to see a small plane, a sky-blue Yakovlev Yak, descending from the clouds. Something is sticking out from the plane's fuselage, aimed at the scene below, silhouetted by a searchlight that flashes through it. The searchlight sweeps across the scene, blinding the onlookers one by one and illuminating each of them in turn.

* * *

"I know what you did," Stevie had said. Gary had slowed down some when he heard that. That was unexpected. Stevie had had his head tilted to the ground but his eyes—canopied by his dripping brow like twin snipers behind a bulwark—were locked onto Gary. Stevie had walked straight into the storm. Hail balls had slammed into his face, shoulders and chest only to fall away, spent. Stevie was oblivious. Gary saw the bullet in Stevie's hand, offered—no, demanded—as evidence.

"What I did? I don't know what you're talking about. What I'd like to know is what the... fuck you're doing out here with–"

"You don't know what I'm talking about?" Stevie studied Gary's face. Gary stood there and let him do it. That was unexpected by either of them. Gary narrowed his eyes as if trying to communicate something.

"And I don't want to know." Gary would've liked to be doing something other than what he was doing, but he was not in control.

"I'll bet you I know someone who would like to know." Stevie was holding the bullet out toward Gary. Stevie pivoted, preparing to point the bullet at the chief, just as the chief fell forward from the slamming door. The noise caused him to squeeze the capsule, separating its halves and releasing the powder into the hail-ridden air.

Gary: "Wait–"

Poof.

Stevie: "Oh, shit."

Gary followed where Stevie was looking and saw the chief look up to heaven on his way to hitting the trona, which he did just like a seed bag full of concrete.

Poof.

"–got a gun!"

Now Gary turns, pulls his gun from its holster, and runs over to the chief. He attempts to locate the entry wound. The chief is heavy but Gary manages to get him onto his side. There doesn't appear to be any entry wound. He places his ear on the chief's chest and looks up at the sky. There is no heartbeat, no pulse, nothing. Not quite sure what else to do, he studies the airplane. He sees Stevie's friends wave at it. Now the searchlight finds Gary. It hits him square in the eyes, blinding him for a couple of seconds.

Gary immediately throws up his gun-hand to shield himself from the light. Now Raylene gets out of the car and runs over. She helps Gary get Jim onto his back. Gary administers CPR but Jim's dead.

Raylene stands up. She puts her hands on her hips. She stares, not at Jim but at a spot on the ground next to him. She remembers that she didn't bring a jacket tonight. Out of some idea of chivalry, Jim'd offered her his... just before seeing to it that she wouldn't be needing it. She looks up at the plane now. What someone thought was a gun is clearly a camera of some sort, infrared maybe, with something like an enormous telephoto lens attached to it. The two burnout kids are waving at the plane now. It appears that they know someone on board. She sees Candy and Stevie head in her direction. The hail pelts her back and shoulders. She had to go with the spaghetti straps. She looks at her car.

"Oh, for Christ's sake," she says (to Jim, mostly). She walks around to the passenger side of her car, reaches into the back seat, grabs the jacket, puts it on and walks back over to where Jim's body lies. She stands over the body; she puts herself directly in the path of the hail... herself, again, between Jim and the storm.

* * *

No one notices the go-kart. It is several hundred yards from the action now. Its broad orbital sweep takes it further and further out; it drifts like a distant planetoid about to break from its sun for once and for all. The hail has put out the fire. No one sees the go-kart's front tire hit the outcropping as it skirts the loneliest edge of the bay. The axle turns just enough to send the go-kart on an inward course. Unseen, a model of cosmic contraction is described on the trona as the spiral begins to collapse.

* * *

Gary sees Ray return wearing the chief's jacket. He looks past her. The Yak seems to be having trouble with the hail. It attempts a tight yaw to stay over the scene. Centrifugal force forces the tail into a slow spin, a spin that the pilot tries to correct by forcing the plane into a tortured roll. The wings seesaw wildly—at one point coming within inches of the ground—as the pilot struggles to regain control. The searchlight slices back and forth across the bay while the mounted camera flaps around in its moorings like a windsock. Eventually it straightens itself out and heads into the open lake to make an unsteady landing, Stevie's friends in hot pursuit. Gary stands up, wipes his hands on his pants and watches the plane.

24

"*Crisse de calisse de tabarnak de cave–*" Guy mutters to himself. He's almost got the batteries put back into the flashlight when the door opens. The hail has stopped. The peoples start to pick themselves up from the floor of the accumulator, rubbing various body parts; also muttering to themselves. Luckily, from what he can see there are no injuries beyond a couple of nasty red marks and several less-nasty pink ones. 'Ambrose Bierce?', on the other hand, has not fared so well. Guy steps up to the altar. All that remains on his stack of ceiling tiles are the jeans and shirt he only hours ago placed very carefully on the mummy, and tucked just so. Now they lay, twisted and curled; obvious forgeries. The mummy appears to have been pounded into the panels, leaving only a roughly human-shaped stain of a beautiful mahogany color. Water still drips from the sky-light as Guy knocks the clothes away and lifts the top tile from the stack. Everyone else has since rushed out of the building. Guy props the tile against the wall. It is heavy, as if it has absorbed something dense; but it is also strangely dry and rigid. This is a pleasant surprise to Guy. Now Guy listens to the dripping ceiling. He doesn't hear this dripping; rather, he hears another dripping sound outside. More like a banging. His first thought is that the hail is returning, but as the COA itself remains silent he determines that this must not be the case. He returns to the mummy-stained tile as Jeanne sticks her head in the door.

"You'd better get out here."

"One second."

"Make it quick, Guy."

Guy returns to the stack. The new top tile is almost fully dry and perfectly clean. He uses this to cover the other tile. He considers whether the 'release waiver' language he'd attached to the rental agreement—written to protect him from "unforeseen psychical reorganization due to orgone overload, or the like"—applies to physical reorganization as well. He looks around one more time, nods to himself, turns and walks out of the accumulator.

* * *

The Yak rolls to a stop. The hail stops as well, and just as suddenly as it started. The side door opens and Dena steps out of the plane. The plane taxis away, performs a one-point turn, and takes off in the direction from which it just landed. Wobbling, buzzing, it disappears back into the clouds. Dena looks around, letting her jaw hang at the scene, first in real astonishment, then for the benefit of Keith and Lee, who jog toward her. When they arrive she wrinkles her nose and puts her hair into a ponytail.

"What are you guys doing here?" she asks. The irony of the question leaves Keith almost speechless. He barely manages to say:

"What are we what–?" After a second Lee offers:

"Did you guys just shoot the Sheriff?" Now it's Dena's turn to be confused again.

"Did we what–?" They continue in silence, each of them trying to gather some thoughts. Finally Dena says:

"You guys, that was so weird–"

"Was?–"

"–so, I was talking to the girls at the plant yesterday, and I swear, all's I did was just barely mentioned the night before. Just about the writing, nothing else. So that was yesterday, right? So today I get done with my shift, and my supervisor calls me into his office, right? Says someone's there to see me. And this guy's sitting there in a suit. He wants to know about the lake."

Keith rattles his head in disbelief.

"Who was he?" he asks.

"That's the thing. He was super vague about it. A bio-engineer maybe, does that sound right? He said something about algae."

"Algae? What the fuck?"

"Yeah. He either said it presented an algae concern or he represented an algae concern."

"The fuck, Dena."

"I know, right? Then my supervisor leaves us alone and the guy hands me this." She takes an envelope from her purse. "A thousand bucks if I show him the spot. Cashola." Keith, dazed:

"Why? –"

"All he said was… said it sounded like… what'd he say again? Oh, yeah. Perfect conditions."

Lee asks:

"Is that a good thing or a bad thing?" Dena, taken by surprise by the question coming from Lee, hums the rising-then-falling three-note tune that means 'I don't know'.

"Let me check that out." Keith reaches for the envelope.

"Screw that!" Dena snaps, snatching her hand away. "I earned this. I've never been so freaking scared in my life! I had no idea where we were up there. We took off from China Lake, right? Everything was fine at first. Next thing you know we're bouncing around in these clouds like a bug or something. I think it was pure luck we popped out where we did."

A sound approaches them.

"Whoa!"

They scatter from the comet-path of the errant go-kart.

* * *

Candy examines the scene. The clouds are clearing a bit. The moon pops in and out of view like a dream-machine light bulb while strange shadows sweep across the lakebed. The outlines return as she watches; now the strange metallic luster she saw earlier. Candy walks over to the ATV, slides her camera from beneath it and turns it on. She follows the path of the go-kart while keeping the lens focused on the foreground. The camera slows as it reaches the Cadillac tableau. Gary's standing, facing outward like a sentinel and intermittently lit by the skittish moon. Raylene kneels over the body of Chief Hill. Ray's light comes from the other direction: the Cadillac's interior by way of the driver's side window. Ray's light is no-doubt due to the open passenger-side door, Candy tells herself. Candy does feel uncomfortable filming all this, she does feel like she's committing some offense. And why wouldn't she? But being here, now; to hold the camera and not film; would that be a lesser crime? She'll try to figure that out later. What the camera's telling her now is that Raylene could be a teenager in that jacket and dress. She's something from West Side Story, lit like a Caravaggio Madonna. She looks my age, Candy thinks. Wonder how long those two go back? Candy wonders. Sad. Sad and undeniably beautiful.

"Oh, for the love of…"

Candy sucks in her lips in frustration and disbelief, shaking her head slowly. She lowers the camera and looks with her own eyes. She thinks: it's all that not-grieving, isn't it? It is. The not-here, not-now all the time. It is. She bites down and tastes blood. She walks over to Raylene. She puts her arm over her boss's shoulders and leads her to the passenger-side door. Ray pauses at the door. Candy climbs in and motions for Ray to follow. Raylene follows and closes the door behind her.

25

The airplane's gone. The lakebed is a cratered moon-scape. The words are completely destroyed. Nothing but pockmarks where they used to be. Ray and Candy are sit-ting in the Cadillac. Fairytales is standing over the body of the chief, looking out at the lake. Keith, Lee and Dena are watching the go-kart. The chief is dead. Stevie climbs aboard the ATV. No one pays him any attention as he starts the machine. He puts it into gear. The rear tires spin in place. Stevie looks over his shoulder as the tires grab. The ATV lurches, jerks, and hits the ground rolling, just like one of those old Evel Knievel wind-up choppers. It pops a little wheelie and everything. Stevie hears a crunch. He smells the quick smell of shattering plastic and the more lingering aroma of heated nylon as he takes off. He turns around in his seat to see the source of all this. It's the recorder. The recorder makes a poor plow. A reel of mag-netic tape has become affixed to the undercarriage of the ATV. It unravels behind Stevie like a roll of toilet paper… no, it's like a Chinese ribbon… no, it's like a rope attached to a lifesaver…

It is like none of those things.

Stevie rolls up to Keith. Keith greets him warily.

"Don't say shit, Ludich."

"Sorry for calling you an idiot, man."

"Whatever."

"Look–" Dena looks at Stevie and interrupts:

"Wow. You called Keith an idiot? What'd you do that for?" Keith looks at Stevie. Dena looks at Keith. "What'd you do, Keith?" Stevie looks at Dena.

"Here it comes again!" Lee shouts. The go-kart drifts past, now several feet behind them.

"I didn't actually call him an idiot," Stevie explains. "I said he was being one." Aunt Jody's famous distinction.

Stevie turns and faces Keith. "Let me talk to you for a minute." Keith yanks at the cords of his hoodie and peels away from the others. His skeleton is glowing again. His eyes are narrowed differently than usual as he walks alongside Stevie on the ATV. Keith listens. Keith's listening strikes Stevie as a properly absurd and serious response to the absurd and serious situation with which they are both inextricably linked. Stevie suspects he would strike himself the same way. Eventually, Keith turns away from Stevie and starts walking back.

* * *

Gary watches Stevie head back toward Cartago. He lets his eyes rest on the thin black line of tape attached to the ATV. It looks like a contrail, the way it grows longer as Stevie grows smaller.

Dena shows Lee the money. Lee shows Dena his blister. Keith walks over to Gary as Lee interprets the events of the day to Dena. Gary leads Keith toward the Cadillac.

"You want to help me with this?"

Keith bends over the body of the chief.

"He wasn't shot, huh."

"Heart attack." Keith is silent for minute. He sighs quietly. Chief Hill has been giving him grief for as long as he can remember.

"What a trip."

"Yep." Officer Tales lifts the chief to a sitting position. He stands up, using his bent knees as a counterweight to the chief's torso. Feels like a waterbed. He nods to his sister.

* * *

Inside the Cadillac, Ray's eyes are glazed but dry. She closes them. Candy starts the car.

"I'll drive," she says.

26

Gary and Keith each take an arm and wrap it around their shoulders. They drag the chief to the squad car like a soldier. After they manage to get the body into the back seat, Keith asks Gary if they should ride back together.

"Huh?" Gary's watching the go-kart as it gradually makes its way to more or less where he stands. How the hell did those Indians do it?

Keith sees what Officer Tales is looking at. He points to the go-kart and looks at Lee.

"Lee!" Lee reads him right and gives him a thumb-up.

"God," Gary says, still looking out at the lake, "they just kill you. That's all they—"

"You all right, man?" Man?

"Oh yeah. I'm good." Gary nods at the chief. "Hop in."

"Sure." They climb into the cruiser. The clipboard is back in the passenger seat. Keith picks it up, sees the puzzle, and hands it to Officer Tales. Gary tosses it onto the dashboard and starts the car. He stares straight ahead. Keith tries to do the same but the vibe is too weird. Isolating. Too quiet for a cop car. The windows are up, the radio's off, and there's a dead body in the back seat. Keith clears his throat. He lets that sound die, takes a deep breath and says:

"So Stevie told me to tell you he quits. He said he'll tell you himself next time he sees you."

"Is that right... Stevie also tell you he's calling the shots now?"

"No. But he said I should ask you for his job."

"Yeah? What job is that? I'd say his work here is done."

"What about the one he was doing before?"

"You mean the... landscape maintenance? Window washing?" Gary takes a good long look at Keith. He smiles as he considers what kind of favor Ludich did for this kid. Well, Gary. You could be Chief soon if you want it. If you want someone you can shape... Shape? He looks in the rearview at the body of the chief. Still as all eternity, as the old man might say. Shape? What about those Indians, Gary? Gary doesn't know. And what the hell got into Stevie Ludich back there? Gary decides not to know. Whatever it was, he sure meant it. He wasn't backing down.

"You want that job?"

"I'll take any job you got."

What else don't you know, Gary? He looks again at Keith.

"You ever see yourself as a cop?" Keith shrugs.

"I could see that."

* * *

Stevie returns to the police station. He sees no one on the street or road. The tape stretches across the parking lot, crosses the 395, and cuts through some scrubby chaparral before ending in the lake. Must be a half-mile long. He walks up the steps, through the door, and straight to the back. Gallegos looks up from her reading and stares after him. Rude little snot, she thinks.

He opens the door to Chief Hill's office and scans the room for the tapes. The first ones he sees are the ones he filled earlier that afternoon. They're sitting on the desk underneath his notes to the chief. Stevie slides the boxes out and looks down at the paper. 'CARTAGO!' is circled once, while 'Jesus complex' is circled several times. He looks up from the desk and spots the other reels. They're stacked atop a filing cabinet, half-hidden by a folded scrap of canvas tarp that's on top of them. Stevie pulls down the stack of tapes and the canvas tarp. He unfolds the canvas and sees the familiar writing of David Edwards. The chief must've found it on the lakebed. Stevie goes back to the desk, finds a pen and piece of paper, and writes:

Candy,

Would you mind taking these tapes to UCLA with you? Feel free to listen to them if you want to. If you could make a copy for me that would be awesome. I might want to do something with them later. I'll be in San Francisco for a couple weeks at least, but you probably know that by now. First stop Atascadero (like you said I should, remember?)

I'll talk to you soon.

p.s. You don't even know how cool you are. I probably shouldn't tell you that, but you are.'

Stevie debates whether or not to write 'Love, Stevie', and in the end he decides to just go for it. It doesn't have to be a big deal. He doesn't mean it creepy so it's not creepy, so if she takes it creepy...

Stop it, Stevie. Now you're making it creepy.

Stevie looks around the office one last time. Why's he not that tripped out by the chief dying the way he did? For some reason it just seems... okay. He reaches down and removes the liner bag from the little trashcan at his feet. He doesn't bother emptying out the bag or anything; he just tapes his note to the top of the stack, grabs the piece of canvas and his notes and shoves the whole shebang inside. He turns off the light and head toward the front door.

"You forget your manners?" Stevie turns to face Gallegos. The first thing he thinks to do is to respond "Chief Hill is dead" and walk out of the building, leaving Gallegos agape in his wake. But instead he simply holds up the bag.

"Trash," he says. He walks out of the building. Stevie's had enough drama for one night.

"Mm hmm," Gallegos replies as the door closes behind him.

* * *

Candy and Ray step into the Golden Empire. They leave the lights off. Candy sits at the counter while Ray walks over and cuts them each a slice of pie.

"Ray?"

"Yeah?"

"You know your sister in Hollywood?"

Ray looks into Candy's dark blue eyes, takes a bite of pie and says:

"Yeah…"

Candy takes a bite of pie.

"I'm not sure this is the time to bring this up, but–"

"Spit it out, Candy."

"I'm leaving." Ray stops chewing and looks at Candy.

"Good."

"I got admitted to UCLA."

"Good."

"I just found out. I don't want to–"

Ray smiles.

"Candy honey, that's the best news I've heard in a long time." Now Ray begins to tear up. She stares at the ceiling and waits for it to pass.

"You tell your brother yet?"

"No. But after tonight? I'm not too worried about that."

* * *

Gary and Keith have attained the right-of-way. Gary finally turns on the radio. He tells Gallegos about the chief and instructs her to call for an ambulance. Gary figures it'll take at least a half-hour for the ambulance to show up in this weather. In the meantime he'll need to find some place safe and quiet; some place more dignified than the back of this squad car to keep the body.

27

Stevie reaches the concrete bunker. He stashes the bag in the corner and looks back to where Candy must've been standing when she took that shot of him. He turns around and looks in the other direction, toward the hidden bay. He listens. There's that sound again. It's the same sound that drew him out there in the first place. Is that–? That's too strange. Now it's coming from the direction of Valleroys'. Stevie steps out of the bunker and looks out at the silo. Strange. He sees the cruiser make its way up the transmission tower road. It seems to be headed toward the sound.

Stevie wanted to go home first. He wanted to talk to Aunt Jody in the morning, then head over to talk to the Beatnik band... to see if he can schlep gear—and that's just what he'll say, too: schlep gear—for them or whatever, whatever it takes to get a ride up to Frisco by way of Atascadero. He'd try to get Gary to give them their car back, tell Gary that'll make things square between the two of them. Even Steven.

Stevie climbs aboard the ATV. He'll change his plans. He'll go to Valleroys' now, he'll return this thing, he'll talk to everybody tonight, and he'll see what's making that noise. He'll bring the band over to meet Aunt Jody before he goes so she knows he's not just going to hitchhike. He knows what she thinks about hitchhiking.

28

When Guy walks out of the accumulator the scene that greets his eyes surprises even him. The first thing he notices is the 'peoples.' They are lingering in the driveway and chatting amongst themselves. And they're not chatting about lawyers. They seem to be enjoying themselves and, in the case of the married couple that arrived looking so tired and irritated, each other. Jeanne's busy passing out towels. The Dutch hikers are chewing milkweed and dancing something like a slow-motion Dervish whirl, all while singing a clearly improvised song about *overlijden-heropleving* vortexes. Cameras are everywhere. The owl lady, seeing an owl, hoots. The rock and roll band alternates between hopping around like children and looking damaged for the camera. The only person Guy doesn't see is the riding-boot man. Not the sociable type, him. The charcoal man has a camera too. His research assistant is posing in front of... Guy walks up to the thing. He gets right up close and listens to it. He examines its wiring. He sticks his hand in, pulls his hand away and grimaces; meanwhile he's precluding the professor from getting off his shot. Guy thinks: So that's what was making all the noise, eh? The power cords all run to a generator located in the back of the blue bus. The blue bus. The blue bus is back. When did that happen? Guy looks around for someone who maybe wasn't in the COA. He hears a familiar sound and turns to see the kid who borrowed his Polaris drive it around the bus and stop at the thing. Jeanne walks up to him now. She's holding an enormous trophy. She hands it to him and says:

"Someone left this outside the accumulator while you all were locked inside. Left all of this." She waves her hand around randomly. Guy looks puzzled.

"What do you mean locked inside?"

"I mean locked inside. I tried, but I couldn't budge the door, you know."

* * *

Stevie pulls up to the device. He also sticks his hand in and also quickly pulls it out with a wince. He also thinks: so this is what was making all the noise? An electrically powered… applause machine? Stevie looks up. He looks up just in time to see the flashing red and blue lights of a squad car. It's Gary Tales' squad car, coming in from the lake. The cruiser lets out a short siren blurp and introduces itself to the crowd like a drop of oil to a bowl of floating pepper. Hotel guests drift toward the perimeter as Gary pulls up next to the Orgone Hut.

* * *

Gary approaches Valleroys' from behind the motel, so he doesn't see the crowd until he's practically in the middle of it. It's not exactly the quiet, dignified place he had in mind. It's more like a carnival. Who are these people? he wonders. They're not… waiting for us, are they? He shakes his head.

"Huh," he says under his breath.

"Huh," Keith agrees.

It's too late now. Gary stops the car and gets out. Guy Valleroy rushes up to the car hoisting the giant trophy. He looks into the back seat and throws open the back door as if he's been trained for just this sort of thing. Keith gets out now as well. Upon seeing the body the crowd overcomes its initial repulsion and suddenly—with a euphoric communal 'what the hell'—swarms the car. Gasping, grasping; as a mass they lift the body of the chief into the air. Those who can't reach the body buttress those who can, while those with cameras snap and snap away. Valleroy wastes no time asking questions.

"In there!" he shouts, pointing at the COA with the trophy.

With the no-longer sullen siblings leading the way and the flashing red and blue lights adding to a sense of strange, ancient ritual, the procession files back into the accumulator. Stevie parks the Polaris and takes up the rear.

* * *

Lee and Dena are still out on the lake. By now the go-kart has almost reached the center of its spiral. They step out of the way and allow it to reach the point where the rear tires can no longer follow the front ones. Finally the tires kick out and the go-kart begins to rotate slowly in place. The way it gently nuzzles his leg as he climbs aboard reminds Lee of a horse. Of course that could be because of the man that's been watching them from the ridge. He's on a real horse. The man keeps pointing something at the lakebed. A camera, maybe. Lee doesn't mention the man to Dena. He's afraid that if he does the man will shoot. He holds out his hand. Dena takes it and climbs aboard.

* * *

The children peel back the rope and the assembly lowers the body onto the very same spot that moments earlier held 'Ambrose Bierce?'. The last of the moonlight trickles down from the broken skylight, turning the ebbing trickle of water into drops of crystal that in turn get absorbed by the chief. The first photos trickle onto the internet, courtesy of Kyle, the DeadBeats' bass player, who just manages to get a couple across before his cameraphone succumbs to the 'memory effect'. Guy leans over the body. He places the trophy on the stack at the head of the chief. He kisses his friend's forehead and whispers:

"You believe me now, you old hillbilly?"

* * *

Gary watches as Stevie walks up to the DeadBeats. Stevie's using his arms a lot, making lifting motions and pointing. The DeadBeats gather in close to listen. They seem to be asking questions, but Gary can't hear a word they're saying. Stevie gives the band a thumbs-up then uses the same upturned thumb to point to the silo door. The DeadBeats follow Stevie out of the building. Gary watches but doesn't follow. He's got no choice; he's got to wait for the ambulance. At least that's the justification he gives himself. He turns to Keith.

"Let's give these people five more minutes. Then we got to get them out of here." Keith nods. The remaining guests have given up trying to get their electronics to work and are now slowly circling the body. Keith is struck by the scene. It reminds him, if only for a fleeting second, of all the Whos in Whoville. The next five minutes are spent in solemn, silent communion. The only sound comes from the clapping machine. As Keith starts ushering the people to the door, and the wail of an ambulance siren can be felt but not yet heard, the machine also goes quiet.

29

The bus rattles away from Valleroys'. It gurgles and it purrs. Stevie is behind the wheel. Coincidentally it was just, what, yesterday... that Stevie first drove a stick. That was with the chief, in the Golden Empire parking lot and then to Valleroys' to borrow the ATV. Now he's driving from the Valleroys' to the Golden Empire in a bus full of musicians and equipment. Aunt Jody's tonight, Atascadero tomorrow and San Francisco after that. He's got a place to crash in the City for a couple of weeks. Maybe he'll try his hand at reciting poetry or something while he's there. He's gotten pretty good at reading into a microphone, even if it has been someone else's words, and he's only been reading to himself for the most part. His timing's gotten pretty good, if he says so himself. He considers his own notebook. He thinks of the words he transcribed on the first night. The words, picked up as they were from the part of the bay nearest to Cartago—the first words he saw and whatever else he could read from the spot where he stood, before he realized the breadth of the thing—came from near the end of the narrative. He recalls the line: '...*when I came out of my stupor, and they told me the things I'd done, smiling at my crimes...*' and the line directly below that: '...*when to speak to the man was like speaking into a mirror, only I was on the wrong side...*' and, below that line: '...*they had my name, my face, and a crucial piece of my past of which they had assumed utter possession, and which I…'.* There's more, but Stevie can't remember it. He'd been waiting to come across those lines again, or what would have been left of them, but, other than what Candy may have in her cameras, it's all gone now. Talk about bittersweet irony. It turns out that Dave Edwards couldn't escape becoming one of his 'retarded characters' after all. And he got so close, too. Stevie will try, but he doesn't expect to find David Edwards. He does, however, half-expect that someone will find Stevie Ludich. After all, it's not Fairytales he hid the tapes from.

Stevie considers the wisdom of retracing someone's steps in order to not do the things they done. David Edwards made a deal. Stevie wonders: would I do anything different? Would I do anything different now than I'd have done last week? He's doing something now. If he got anything from that sad, weird sea of words, it's the same thing Chief Hill told him as he released the clutch:

"Nothing to it but to do it, son." To which his aunt might add:

"Else someone else'll do it to you." Last week he'd still be waiting.

But, and most importantly, in the meantime he'll keep himself away from Candy until she leaves for L.A. If he doesn't go first he's afraid he might end up begging her to stay. She wouldn't—and she shouldn't—but she'd feel bad about it and so would he.

And then where would he be?

They left the clapping machine in Valleroys' parking lot. The DeadBeats wanted to bring it. Have audience, will travel, they said; or something like that. But Stevie talked them out of it. He'd just as soon it stay at the Orgone Hut. They've got the generator though, so the DeadBeats can practice by the side of the road if they want to. From the corner of his eye Stevie sees Candy walking away from the Golden Empire, holding the cameras. He pulls into the parking lot and honks the horn. Candy sees him and walks over, shrugging and smiling a half-smile. She looks exhausted. A couple of DeadBeats climb up front to see what's going on. They seem like pretty nice guys after all. Mellow stoner types, kind of dorky. The girl, on the other hand, is intense. She scares him a little.

"Hey Candy," Stevie says, smiling gently. "Want a ride?" Candy looks at the bus, at the band, then at Stevie.

"That's all right," she says. "I want to be alone for a few minutes. And I need to go talk to my brother."

"Ah." They stare at each other. "He's at Valleroys', last I saw."

"Oh." Candy stands still, looking at Stevie. She moves her lips to say something but Stevie cuts her off.

"You know that picture you took of me?"

Candy gives him a quizzical look while trying to anticipate where he might be going with this.

"Which one?"

"Not the one where I'm walking–"

"Okay. The one where you're–"

"Where I'm in silhouette? Writing? You know the, um, room I was in?"

"I think so."

"Well I left something in there. Would you mind getting it for me?" Candy suspects something close to the truth but asks anyway:

"Where are you going?"

"You'll see." Stevie sticks his hand out the window. Candy lifts her hand to meet his. They stay like that for a moment, holding hands.

"I'm going to come visit you in L.A., okay?"

"You better." They let go. Stevie grinds the bus into gear and checks the rearview mirror. Candy waves. Stevie smiles and turns on the radio.

"All right," he says to the DeadBeats, "let's hit the road!"

David Scott Ewers

PETRICHOR

CPSIA information can be obtained at www.ICGtesting.com
Printed in the USA
LVOW10s1648150913

352502LV00003B/196/P